The
KING'S BROAD
ARR⊙W

KATHRYN GOODWIN TONE

Copyright © 2019 by Kathryn Goodwin Tone

Published by Marron Press LLC

First paperback edition November 2019

*Cover illustration, book design, and interior illustrations
on pages 3, 23, 51, 85, 114, 137, 255, 311
by Crystal Cregge of Liona Design Co.*

*Interior illustrations on pages 11, 196, 289 by Shutterstock
Interior illustrations on pages 5, 62, 171, 225, 282 by Alamy*

Editor – Lynn Thompson of Living on Purpose Communications

ISBN (paperback) 978-1-7340028-0-5
ISBN (ebook) 978-1-7340028-1-2

INTRODUCTION

Originality is nothing but judicious imitation. The most original writers borrowed one from another. The instruction we find in books is like fire. We fetch it from our neighbor's, kindle it at home, communicate it to others, and it becomes the property of all.

- Voltaire

L ike many books, this one was born of others. Several years ago, inspired by *Little Big Minds* by Marietta McCarty, I designed and taught a course at my children's elementary school called Big Ideas — Introducing Philosophy to Children. We discussed many themes and the two that seemed to resonate the most with the students were courage and responsibility. Later, I decided to write a novel for young readers focusing on these two Big Ideas. After reading *Washington's Crossing* by David Hackett Fisher, I knew that the dramatic, fascinating events of the first years of the American Revolution would be the perfect setting. My goal was to create an exciting story that was as close to actual history as possible and to show how, in the face of a seemingly hopeless situation, the decisions and actions of individuals added up to change the odds for our struggling new nation. Sam and a few other characters are fictional — the rest are real. With profound respect and humility, I hope that I have honored them in this tale.

To me, Sam's story connects the reader to the past and the present. Two hundred and forty-three years later, the citizens of

America are still determined to live up to the promises of the Revolution, pushing forward with the stubborn optimism of our ancestors toward a just and humane society for everyone. All over the world, young people are experiencing a new Age of Enlightenment, empowered by its ideals — reason, science, humanism, and a challenge to traditional authority — as they imagine and work for a better world. Like the Enlightenment, this is a time of both tremendous criticism and passionate inspiration. And like Sam, each of us who envisions a better future for ourselves and our children can make a difference.

I hope you enjoy reading *The King's Broad Arrow* as much as I loved writing it.

Kathryn Goodwin Tone

TABLE OF CONTENTS

PART II

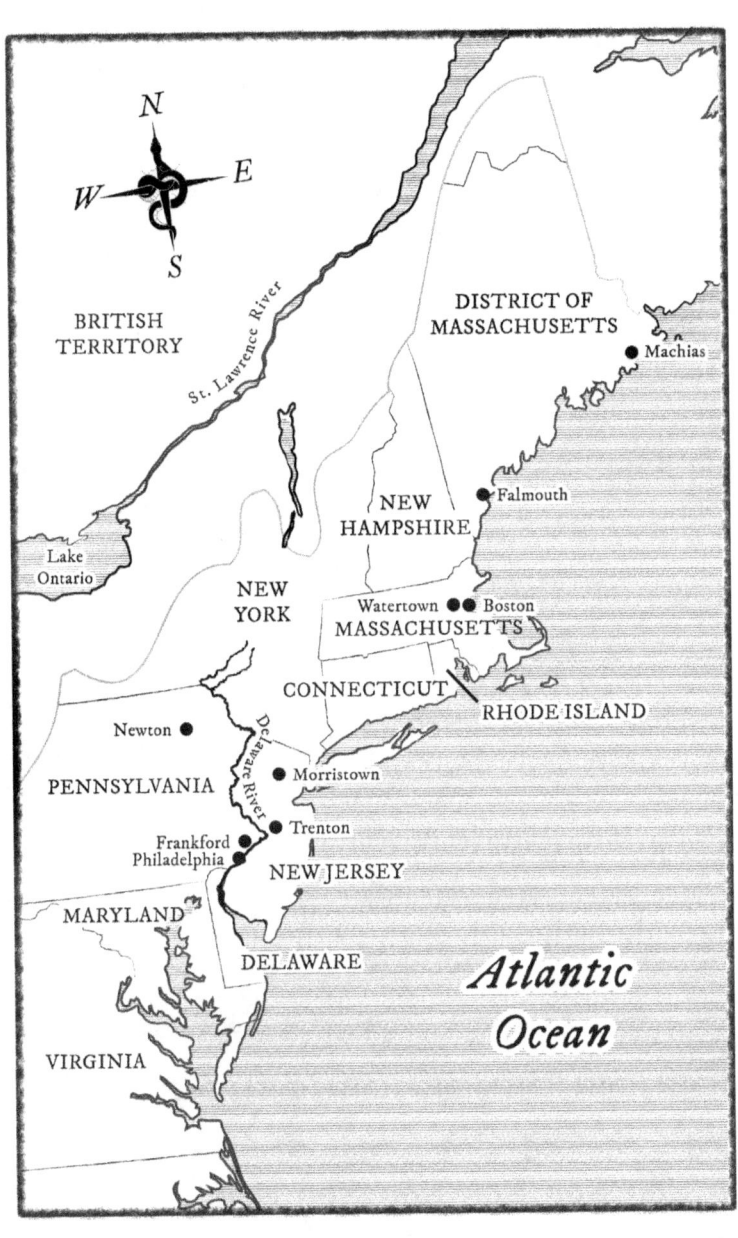

Deadly Disease

February 5, 1777
Morristown, New Jersey

Sam Nevens pulled the threadbare jacket tighter across his thin shoulders and studied the faces of the other soldiers sitting around the fire. At fifteen, he was one of the youngest, but most of the men's expressions mirrored his own — uncertain and nervous. Shifting his gaze to the fire, his eyes bore into the leaping flames as if they could reach through them far enough to thaw the cold dread he felt inside. Sam wasn't afraid of starving or freezing. He'd already cheated those slow deaths a few times this winter. He wasn't afraid of fighting either. Sam had been in several battles in the past few months and he had fought well. What Sam feared was what General Washington had just ordered them to do — what the entire Continental army must do — to defeat an enemy deadlier than the Redcoats.

Since the beginning of the war in 1775, more soldiers had perished from sickness than from English bullets. The worst of the diseases they faced was Variola, the smallpox virus. People sometimes called it "the speckled monster" for the scars it left on its victims. As hundreds of men fell ill, George Washington knew that if he didn't act now, this killer would run through their camp silent as a ghost — making short work of the already weak and exhausted men. Fear of smallpox was also scaring off new recruits. So today, General Washington had ordered that any soldier who had not already had smallpox, be inoculated. Inoculation. Variolation. Sam flinched at the words. It didn't matter what it was called — it was scary and dangerous. A doctor cuts into your skin and inserts pus from someone already suffering from the disease. That way you would get smallpox, but it wouldn't kill you. Or so the doctors thought.

Sam's village back in New England had been lucky. No one carrying the dreaded disease had come to Machias. In Boston and other parts of the colonies, though, lots of folks had gotten sick and died. Smallpox hit like a random storm — ravaging some, leaving others alone. Those who succumbed died in agony, their aching bodies racked with fever and swollen with lesions. Whole families perished. If you were lucky enough to live, you might be left blind or missing an ear.

General Washington wanted the inoculations to start tomorrow. He knew that each day of cold and hunger made the men less likely to survive the procedure. Adding to the danger was the risk that the British would learn of the plan. The effects of the vaccination lasted several weeks. During this time, the soldiers in the camp would be debilitated and vulnerable to attack. The plan must be conducted in complete secrecy.

Sam huddled near the fire, stretching his hands toward the flames to warm his aching fingers. Hank, a rifleman from Virginia, sat across from him. He'd been with the army since the first battles. Although he was a young man, almost two years of war had turned his hair completely white. His knotty hands gripped a tin cup. He blew on it, then slowly sipped. Next to him, a thin, lanky soldier, Jim, poked at the fire excitedly with a branch. Sparks leapt into the darkening air, mirroring his agitation. His voice shook with both fear and defiance. "I don't care what old George wants us to do. Nobody is going to stick me with a knife full of sickness. What if it don't work? What if we all git the smallpox? Then we're finished, the war's finished, and the Revolution is finished!"

Another soldier grumbled from the darkness beyond a cloud of gray smoke. "And it is against the law. There must be a reason why Congress declared a ban against it."

No one spoke for a minute or so.

Hank put down his cup. "Well, boys, I reckon the General wants to win this war as much as we do. He wouldn't risk it all if he didn't count on us coming through this variolation thing, ready to get back to fighting."

A few of the men shrugged in acceptance. Whether they agreed with Washington or not, they were soldiers and he was their commander. Later that night, as Sam lay shivering in his tent, he thought about Hank's words and his trust in General Washington. In a battle, getting hit was just bad luck. Once the cannons roared and the rifles cracked, there wasn't much you could do to protect yourself. Sam figured smallpox was kind of similar. But if Washington was right about the inoculation plan, you could defend yourself. You might get hit with the disease, but it wouldn't kill you. Hank was right. Washington had gotten them this far; he probably knew what he was doing.

The next morning Sam went to the village courthouse that had been turned into a hospital. It was already crowded with soldiers. Some were moaning quietly. Others were flushed with fever. Sam's stomach tightened as he walked through the rows.

Dr. Otto, the camp doctor, was in the back. He had treated Sam a few weeks ago for a slight leg wound.

Although the doctor looked tired, he smiled as Sam approached. "Sam. Good morning. How's the leg? You should be ready to travel now."

"Fine, sir. I'm here for the variolation." Sam managed a slight smile.

"Well then, I guess we'd better get started. Have a seat at that table while I get everything ready." Dr. Otto retrieved a small dish and a scalpel. The plate held a bead of pale white pus. "I need to wash your arm first, Sam. Roll up your sleeve."

Sam pulled back the frayed edge of his shirt and turned it up. Dr. Otto began to wash the skin on his right arm. Then he stopped and stared. Above Sam's elbow was a scar that was too precise to be accidental. There were three slashes in the shape of an arrow. The scar was old, but even time could not hide the brutal branding that had left these marks. Dr. Otto raised his eyes to Sam's face. "Who did this to you, son?"

Sam looked down at the angry red stripes on his arm and thought back to the week his life had changed forever.

PART I

CHAPTER I

Two Ships

May 31, 1775
Machias, District of Maine

C'mon, you yellow-bellied snakes. Come back and fight like men, you Tory pigs!"

Sam watched as his best friend, Eamon Collins, hurled insults and shook his fists at three boys running down a dirt road toward the harbor. Eamon had been arguing with them about the recent fighting in Lexington and Concord. The three boys' families were Tories — they were loyal to King George and thought the American colonies should continue being ruled by the British. Eamon's family was from Ireland — he didn't think Great Britain should rule *any* country. Most people in the small, coastal settlement where Sam and Eamon lived felt the same way. Only a week ago, the residents of Machias had voted to

11

put up a Liberty Pole, a tall tree stripped of all its branches and topped by a red cap, to show their defiance to England's ever-increasing taxes and oppression.

Eamon stood with arms folded across his chest as if his antagonists were running toward him and Sam, instead of away from them. The two friends wore coarse blouses, breeches, and vests, but the similarities ended there. Even though Eamon was smaller than Sam, he was full of so much energy and bravado that he seemed to fill a bigger space. Sam was tall and lean and usually moved with no particular hurry. His hair was light brown. His eyes as blue and serene as the sky on a warm summer day. Eamon did everything fast — he walked fast, talked fast and thought fast. His dark eyes and black hair practically flashed with sparks when he was worked up about something, like he was today. Eamon's mother said the boys were as different as night and day, but they had been friends for as long as either could remember.

Sam's gaze followed the boys running down the hill and then moved to the harbor where a schooner bobbed gently in the surf. He hungrily took in every detail — from the pointy jibboom all the way to the bright flag at the top. It was a small boat, the kind used to move quickly about the many inlets, bays, and islands that made up the rocky coast of New England. Sam wondered if it belonged to a great sailing ship, perhaps a massive man-of-war, anchored farther out in the ocean. How exciting it would be to sail on a ship like that — cutting across the foaming waves with the speed of the wind. Sam had never been on a huge ship, or even sailed farther than Machias Bay, so he thought life as a sailor would be a great adventure. *An adventure I'll never have. I'll be stuck in the sawmill, cutting shingles my whole life.* Sam frowned and turned back to Eamon. "Whose schooner is that?"

"I don't know — it's not the one we're waiting for." Eamon scowled. "Darn it! I'm tired of potatoes for supper!"

Sam and Eamon had come to the harbor to look for two ships, the *Polly* and the *Unity*. Every spring the ships brought much-needed provisions — flour, molasses, rum, sugar, cloth — and most important, gunpowder and bullets. The owner of the ships, Captain Ichabod Jones, had been trading with the settlers in Machias for ten years. His nephew owned the only store. Captain Jones traded the supplies for lumber, some of which came from Sam's father's mill. This year, the town was especially impatient for the ships to arrive. The winter of 1774-1775 had been severe. A drought the previous summer meant there were fewer crops to get them through the cold months. On top of that, in retaliation for the Boston Tea Party, the British had closed Boston Harbor, cutting off much of Machias' trade with other colonies. Few of the town's hundred or so residents had known a full stomach in months. Some families were down to only a few weeks' worth of food.

Eamon's brow tightened. He looked as if he was going to chase the other boys and continue fighting. Sam picked up a branch and swished it against the flowers growing alongside the road. The sun was shining and felt warm on their backs. Spring was finally emerging after the long New England winter. Sam didn't want to think about bullets and battles in some faraway town he would never even see. He didn't want to worry about what everyone called "the situation": the worsening relationship between England and the colonists.

"Let 'em go, Eamon," Sam said. "Why do you want to fight them? Who cares about some skirmish in Boston?" He started walking up the hill.

"Who cares? It's war, Sam! The Brits have pushed us too far." Eamon walked beside Sam; fists still clenched. "All these taxes and rules they force on us," he said angrily. "Why should some fat king three thousand miles away get to decide what we can and can't do?"

"We're still British subjects, even if we live here and never set foot in England again," Sam said.

"Sink me!" Eamon exclaimed. "I'm not British! I'm an Irishman, through and through, and an American, now. Besides, you're not British either. You were born right here in Machias, so that makes you American already."

"Well, what difference does it make?" Sam shrugged. "As long as we've got a house and food to eat, one country is pretty much like any other, as far as I can tell. Hey, want to go swimming before chore time?"

Eamon shot a scowl back toward the harbor, then shrugged and gave in to the beautiful spring day. "All right, let's take the Indian trail."

Sam and Eamon sprinted through the town. They ran past Burnham's Tavern and the meeting house. They slowed down when they saw Eamon's uncle, Morris O'Brien, farther up the road. From behind, they could hear him singing.

One morning early I went out
On the shore of Lough Leinn
The leafy trees of summertime,
And the warm rays of the sun,
As I wandered through the townlands,
And the luscious grassy plains,
Who should I meet but a beautiful maid,
At the dawning of the day.

"Hello, Uncle Morris!"

"Eamon. Sam." O'Brien smiled at their red faces. "And where are you two devils off to on this fine afternoon?"

"We're looking for the ships. No sign of them yet. So, we're going swimming." Eamon grinned.

"Swimming?! You're both braver men than I. It will be

mighty cold. Look how full the Machias is." He pointed to the wide river across the road. "Aye, she's a lovely river, almost as beautiful as the Liffey."

"Bye, Uncle Morris!" Eamon began running again.

Sam laughed as he followed Eamon. "Sometimes I think your uncle would rather be back in Dublin."

"Not as long as it's full of British clodhoppers!" Eamon darted down a narrow trail. "Race you to the fort!"

The boys ran around the O'Brien house and jumped over the small brook behind it. As they went deeper into the dense woods that surrounded Machias, the bright sunlight dimmed. They ran until they reached a large pond. Sam's legs were longer, but Eamon got there first. They stripped off their clothes and dove in. Gasp! The freezing water sent both boys straight up into the air and splashing back to shore. They threw their clothes back on and jumped up and down, trying to get warm again. The hot sun helped. They climbed up to the wide boulder that was the top of the fort.

The "fort" had been their meeting place since they were old enough to come to the pond by themselves. It was formed by three boulders leaning together at the edge of the water. Over the years, the three-sided cave had been many things — Ali Baba's den of treasure, a Viking lodge, an Indian teepee. The flat rock on top was sometimes the plank of a pirate ship, King Arthur's Round Table, or anything else two boys could imagine. Inside they had made a shelf with a shingle from Sam's father's mill. They stored whatever treasures the forest or pond revealed: a bear skull, a snakeskin, a bird's nest. Last summer, when the pond shrank from the drought, they found an old tomahawk embedded in the mud. It had been lost or discarded by one of Machias' original residents, a Passamaquoddy Indian. The ancient weapon now held a place of honor on the shelf. Sometimes the boys left notes for each other scratched on birch bark in the fort.

Eamon stretched out on the wide rock; his eyes closed against the bright sun. "Uncle Morris was right — swimming in May. Brrr!"

"Yeah," Sam agreed, "too soon, I guess. Hey, do you think Carl is out of the mud yet?"

Every spring when the pond thawed, Sam and Eamon searched for a huge catfish they had named Carl. It was the biggest freshwater fish either of them had ever seen. Two years ago, they had almost caught him, but he'd slipped from Eamon's grasp and dove back into the murky depth of the pond.

Eamon opened one eye and peered across the water, as if expecting to see Carl on the surface, waving a fin in defiance. He lay back on the rock and stared up at the massive trees that surrounded the water like the towers of a castle. "Sam, what do you reckon being in a battle is like? Scary or exciting?"

"I don't know. Probably both."

"Do you think they'd take me?" Eamon wondered.

"What do you mean? The militia?"

"Aye. Do you think they'd let me join up? I can't join here because everyone knows I'm only thirteen. Maybe somewhere else."

Sam put his hands behind his head. He tried to imagine Eamon running at a wall of Redcoats with a gun in his hands. At five feet, Eamon was only slightly taller than a flintlock musket. "They might," Sam said. "Why do you want to join up now? Can't you wait until you're old enough?"

Eamon sat up. "I can't wait. If we're going to fight the Brits, I want to do my share."

"You could get hurt really bad, or die. Aren't you scared?" Sam asked.

"Yeah, I'm more mad than scared, to be truthful. Damn those Brits and all their taxes and always telling us what to do. What about the Broad Arrow laws? How can they tell us we can't

16

cut down the trees on our own land? What about those surveyors walking around — marking our trees for the King?!" Eamon's anger flashed again.

Sam nodded. "My Pa sure gets mad about that law. Did you see the English surveyors who came to town last fall?"

"I saw them. Mean-looking fellows. One of them had a tattoo on his arm the size of an ax head. It was a serpent with a bloody knife in its mouth."

"Father was furious when he heard they were back in Machias. After they left, he felled a few marked trees near the north shore. He was able to haul in one this winter, and there are two left. If the surveyors find them, we're in for it. I reckon they'll fine Father. Do you think they would put him in jail?"

"They've got no right!" Eamon fumed. "The settlers are the ones who bear the burden of harvesting the trees. We fight the weather, the land, even the Indians sometimes! Why should some mast agent, who lives far from the danger, reap all the rewards for our trees?! We need to stand up to them."

"Who, the surveyors?" Sam frowned.

"The British, that's who. The surveyors, the mast agents all work for his Royal Arse — King George — and Parliament. First, they tax us; then they take our lumber, our livelihood. We need to stand up to King George and fight for our rights."

"What about your Ma? Will she let you go? You do a lot for the farm."

Eamon lived with his mother on a small farm. They moved to Machias from Ireland after Eamon's father died. Mrs. Collins' family, the O'Briens, had settled Machias in 1763. Their sawmill, the Dublin Mill, was the largest in the region.

"Ma will understand. It's my responsibility to go and fight. She can do without me for a few months. Besides," Eamon sat up a little straighter, "soldiering will make a man of me. Quicker than working in the mill, anyway."

"It won't make a man of you if you get killed." Sam shrugged. "Why is it your responsibility? You're just a kid. Wars are for grown-ups, Eamon."

"Wars don't wait, Sam. My Pa fought against the British in Ireland when he was a lad, same age as us. Besides, I can shoot like a man." Eamon pointed an imaginary gun across the pond. "Just give me a musket — I'll kill twenty Redcoats in a day. They'll be so scared they'll try to swim back to Mother England!"

The boys heard Mrs. Collins calling. Eamon jumped off the rock. "I've got to go. Ma will skin me if I'm late for my chores. See you tomorrow, Sam!"

Sam lay on the rock and stared at the sky. He knew he should get home too, but this part of the day was his favorite. The sun shone through the dense forest and lit up the birch trees, making their white, wrinkled trunks glow with the quiet warmth of the afternoon. Their pale green leaves rose and fell as if the breath of the universe was moving them. Towering above the birches were the emerald pine trees, swaying slightly at the very top with each shift in the breeze. Their branches stretched out wide and turned slightly upward at the ends — like arms extended in prayer. It seemed strange to Sam that something so peaceful could be a cause for war. Yet, in Machias, and other towns close to the ocean, the right to harvest their trees was a matter of life and death for the settlers. Apart from the lumber trade, there weren't many ways to make a living here.

The northeast part of the American colonies was full of three things — rocks, rivers, and trees. The rocks made farming the land a hard calling. The trees were tall and strong, and the rivers made it possible to bring them from deep in the forests all the way to the ocean, where the shipbuilders worked. The British had been building ships in the colonies for over one hundred years. Many were merchant vessels. They carried products from America such as fur, dried fish, tobacco, and rice to the coasts of

England and the rest of Europe. Many carried lumber and other naval supplies like pitch, turpentine, and tar. The ships returning from England brought things that could not easily be made in the New World, like fine china and cloth, fancy carriages, furniture, and books.

Along with merchant ships, the British built warships. The Royal Navy needed lots of wood to build their ships and one particular tree to sail them — the New England white pine. Sturdy, giant, resilient — the perfect tree for a ship mast. Without masts, England could not sail her ships. Without strong, fast ships, England could not rule the oceans, and the world, as she did now. Forever fighting the other sea powers of the world, England was determined to keep the supply of trees for her ship masts secure.

Long before Machias was settled, as far back as 1691, it was against the law in the New England colonies to cut down any white pine that was to be used for a Royal ship mast. The men who came to mark the mast trees were called surveyors. When they found the right trees, they cut into them with three hatchet slashes in the shape of an arrow — the King's Broad Arrow — a symbol hated by the colonists. The Broad Arrow mark was emblazoned on all property of the Royal Navy, including prisoners. To see it slashed onto the trees on their own property infuriated the New Englanders. They risked everything to settle the land, yet were not allowed to cut down its trees. If you wanted to cut down a white pine and sell it, you had to pay the King a fee. Every mast tree was very valuable and required dozens of men and oxen to harvest. It took weeks to move one tree from the forest to the ocean. The tree was more useful to the settlers as lumber that could be cut and sold quickly. England's grip on the supply was powerful. The surveyors could also check the local lumber mills for white pines. If they found any, the punishment was dear — sometimes it was a fine of one hundred pounds, sometimes it was a week in jail.

Sam had grown up hearing his father and other men in Machias rail against the Broad Arrow law. There were a few ways to keep the prized lumber out of British hands. One way was to partially burn the trees after they had been cut down. Burned wood was not suitable for use as a ship mast, but still valuable as lumber for a sawmill. Another trick was to cut down the marked trees, then mark some smaller trees nearby as substitutes. The settlers called these tricks "swamp law." They defied the Broad Arrow law because they believed that it was not fair. Sam knew that in Boston, people were angry about the Stamp Act, the Intolerable Acts, and the tea taxes. In this part of the colonies, though, the King's laws about the white pine were the cause of deep resentment.

Sam looked across the pond, his eyes squinting against the sun's bold reflection. He and Eamon had spent many long days here, but soon they would have to start working in the mills full-time. He sighed. He needed to get home for chores. As he climbed down from the boulder, Sam spied a mussel track in the shallow water. *I'll take some mussels back, and some crayfish. Maybe Mother won't scold me for being late.* He dug around the edge of the pond until he had two dozen shiny, black discs. *Now for the crayfish.* Digging up mussels was quick and easy — catching a crayfish took a lot of patience and a little nerve. Sam moved to the shallow stream that fed the pond. He squatted on a big rock and began carefully lifting smaller rocks, his eyes searching for the telltale dart of a crayfish.

While his hands moved slowly, pinching the crusty gray creatures out of the water, his mind was whirling with the idea of Eamon joining a militia. Machias, like every town or settlement, had one. You had to be sixteen to join. Sam was glad he was not old enough. Sure, it might be fun to practice drilling with muskets and parade around to the fife and drum. When it came to actual fighting, though, that was different. Sam didn't have the same fiery spirit that Eamon had. He wondered if some people were simply born braver than others. *Eamon doesn't seem scared at all. Will he really go off by himself to join a militia in some town where he doesn't know anybody? Why is he so determined to fight now? I guess it's because he hates the British so much. Or because of the Broad Arrow laws. He gets pretty worked up about that too.*

Eight crayfish later, Sam wrapped his catch in a few wet leaves and headed home. His house lay on the other side of a small hill, where the road turned toward the river. Like most houses in Machias, theirs had red-planked walls and a dark shingle roof. The front of the house faced the river and behind the house sat a small barn. Nearby stood the mill, the drying shed and the wood lot. Sam smelled the sharp, clean scent of pine before he could see the house and mill. He heard the massive water wheel turning in its infinite circles. The wheel caught the water through a trough and carried it up with thick wooden paddles, turning the axle inside to power the mill.

The strength of the river and the ability to harness that power had always fascinated Sam. When he was young, he would watch the wheel for hours. He didn't work with the actual saws yet; that was too dangerous for a young boy. However, there was plenty of other work to do: hauling the wood in, stacking the endless loads of barrel staves and shingles that the mill produced, and then tying them into bundles. Sam liked being around the mill — the sound of the enormous blades ripping through massive logs; the smell of freshly cut wood, the soft sawdust that crunched under his feet. What he didn't like was how hard the work was. His father worked every day, all day, except Sunday.

Mr. Nevens had been wounded in the French and Indian War. Although he'd lost three fingers on his left hand, he was able to work the mill and their small farm as well as a man with two good hands. He always seemed so cheerful about working from morning till night. Sam asked him about it once, at the end of a long day of hauling trees through the frozen forest. They were both cold and exhausted, thawing out in front of the roaring fire while Mrs. Nevens got dinner ready. "Pa, don't you ever get tired of working all the time? Wouldn't you rather go hunting, or fishing, or just plain sleep one day?" Sam asked.

Mr. Nevens stretched his red, cold hands toward the fireplace. He looked around their snug, warm house and nodded. "Well, yes. I am tired at the end of every day. It is a good tired."

"A good tired?"

"It is a good feeling to be tired from working hard for something you care about."

Sam was not convinced. "It is so much to worry about — the mill, the farm. Don't you want to forget about it sometimes?"

"I can't ever forget about it, Sam, and I don't want to. Our family, the mill and farm — it is all my responsibility. It doesn't feel like a burden; it is a privilege. It is a challenge to do your best; to be proud of yourself. Being responsible for the things you love is keeping a promise — to them, to yourself."

Sam sighed as he thought about his chores and tomorrow's work. Right now, his father had a hired man, Jim Lyons, to help him run the mill. But someday it would all be Sam's responsibility. Sam didn't think he cared enough about the mill to be "happily" tired working it the rest of his life.

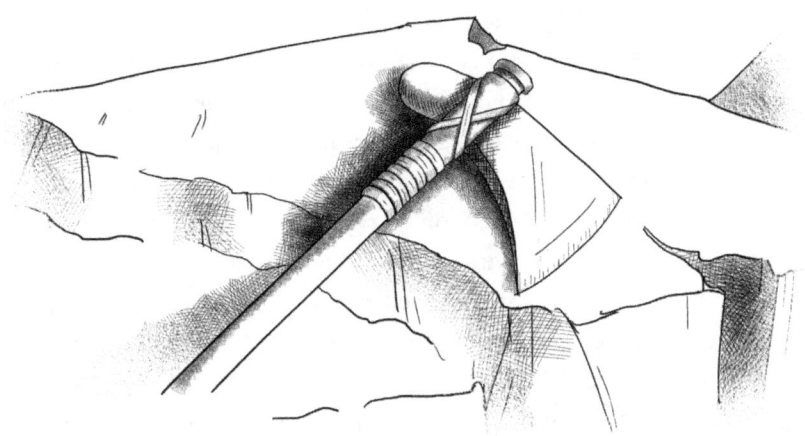

CHAPTER **2**

Three Ships

June 6, 1775
Machias

E amon, you're not going to believe this!" Sam burst into the
barn where Eamon was cleaning out the stalls.

"What? Did you see Carl?" Eamon kept pitching out old
hay with the pitchfork.

"The *Polly* and the *Unity* have docked!"

"All right, I'll come down later and pick up our supplies."

"You can't. Ichabod Jones refuses to unload the ships unless
everyone signs a paper promising we'll help load the lumber.
He's taking it to Boston to build barracks for the British."

"Wurra?! The Tory devil!"

"There's another ship — the *Margaretta*. She's a cutter with
four guns and twenty swivels!"

"A cutter?" Eamon's eyes narrowed. "Who's the captain?"

"He's British, with a crew of thirty-eight. Your cousin called a meeting. Come on. Let's get down there before we miss any more." Sam practically dragged Eamon out of the barn.

"All right, let me tell Ma." Eamon came out the door a minute later with Mrs. Collins right behind him, pulling on her bonnet. "Ma, can we go ahead?" Eamon asked eagerly.

"Go on, go on," she nodded sternly, "and don't cause any trouble. Tempers are already flaring. We don't need two excited boys lighting the fuse."

Eamon and Sam raced to the village center. Already a large crowd had gathered around the Liberty Pole. It looked like the whole town was there. Eamon's cousin, Jeremiah, stood in the center with his father and five brothers beside him. Although they were cousins, Eamon and Jeremiah looked nothing alike. Jeremiah was tall with sandy hair and blue eyes. He and Eamon both had the same spark, the same crackling energy. Jeremiah's deep voice boomed over the murmuring crowd, his face animated with excitement and indignation. "Neighbors, citizens of Machias, are we to stand passive in the face of this insult? This blackmail? Ichabod Jones has sold us provisions for ten years and traded for our lumber. They were fair trades among equal partners. Now he would refuse us because we do not wish to see our lumber go to the British troops who threaten our brothers and sisters in Boston. Are we to stand idly by and accept this ultimatum — to sign or to starve? Do we not have the right, as free men, to decide where our timber should go? This is yet another link in the chain the English will enslave us with, if we let her!"

The crowd shifted uneasily. Some faces bristled with anger. Others appeared to be resigned.

Morris O'Brien stepped forward. He raised his weathered hands and addressed the group with quiet strength. "Friends,

I came to this country to escape the bonds of British oppression in my homeland. I made a life for myself and my family with my sweat and blood, beholden to no one, something I could never do in Ireland. The power of the English crown still reaches across the ocean to take away my liberty, our liberty. Are we to suffer like beasts of burden, living and dying under the yoke of English masters? The King even dares to deny our very livelihood, the trees on our own land. We must not give an inch, or we stand to lose it all."

As Morris spoke, Ichabod Jones came out of his nephew's store. He was a small man with a thick neck and a protruding forehead. He stood some distance from the crowd, arms crossed and watching closely. His beady eyes narrowed into slivers as he scanned the uncertain faces before him.

Morris O'Brien continued. "Neighbors, I know your bellies are empty and your cellars almost bare. I ask you, though, to think long and hard about this. Surely, we can all pull together and scratch by until another sloop comes in. As for the O'Briens, we will not sign, nor will we run the mill to send any timber back to Boston." With that, he turned and walked away.

Ichabod Jones laughed with contempt and called out to him, "Starving your family is a hefty price to pay for your rebel politics, O'Brien!"

There were shouts in the crowd. Sam had worked his way up to the front. Eamon stayed in the back. As the others cheered and nodded, his face was still and thoughtful. He walked over to where his mother was standing and took her arm. Mrs. Collins looked at Eamon and then closed her eyes for a moment. Although they didn't speak, it was clear that an agreement passed between them. They left the crowd and began walking back in the direction of their house.

Sam wanted to run after them, but he was too curious about what would happen next. Was Jeremiah going to lead the whole crowd to the ships? How could they possibly fight against Moore's armed ship? Sam looked around for his parents. They were gone too. He stayed a bit longer until the crowd broke up, then he made his way home.

That night during supper, Sam's parents discussed the town meeting and Captain Jones' ultimatum. Even though his maimed hand kept George Nevens out of the militia now, he was as determined to defend Machias as anyone. "I'll be darned if I'm going to sign that blasted contract. What do you think, Eliza?"

"We can make it through another month or so," Mrs. Nevens said, "and I can spare some salt pork and flour to give to some of the larger families. I don't know how we will sell the lumber, though."

"There must be a way," Mr. Nevens said firmly. "There are two packets of shingles cut and drying in the shed, three loads of barrel staves too. But they are not going to do us much good here."

"What about the white pines near the river?"

"Yes, I wish we had them hauled in by now. Who knows when those surveyors will be back? I'll ask Zeblon Davis if I can borrow his oxen next week. We'll bring the pines in and cut them up." He finished his ale. "In the meantime, I'll find out when the *Packet* is expected. Perhaps Ned Avery will take the shingles and staves to Falmouth and trade for some supplies."

Mrs. Nevens began to clear the table. "Sam, you and I will plant the garden this week. We can at least get that done while we're waiting for news. We can plant everything except the corn. I was hoping for some corn seed from the *Polly*. Perhaps someone in town can spare some."

"Yes, ma'am." Sam helped his mother wash and dry the dishes. Then he went outside.

His father was sitting on a bench, smoking his pipe as he gazed at the darkening forest. The murmur of the river was a soft background to a chorus of crickets that seemed to be celebrating the first warm evening of the summer. A deep spicy smell of tobacco smoke mixed in the air with the fresh scent of a huge lilac bush that grew next to the house. War and starvation seemed far away on this peaceful night.

Sam was thinking about Eamon. He sat down on the bench. "Father, were you scared when you fought in the war?"

A puff of blue smoke drifted above Mr. Nevens as he let out a deep breath. "Yes. I tried not to think about it, though. If I worried too much, I think my nerve would have failed me."

"So, you were always brave?"

"Brave?" His father chuckled. "I don't know if it was bravery, son. I didn't want to be killed, so I fought the best I could."

"It seems like everyone in the militia is," Sam said quietly.

"Sometimes men find more courage when they are in a pack. But no man goes into battle without some fear in his heart. If you're not afraid, it means you don't care whether you live or die. And I've not met many men who don't care about that." He drew on the pipe and nodded in the direction of the river and mill. "It's a beautiful place, and a good life. This is why men fight, Sam. Not just because they don't want to die. They fight for the life they want to live."

Mrs. Nevens had been standing in the doorway, listening to her husband speak. "Aye, George, it is a beautiful place, and a beautiful night. Time for bed, Sam. We've got a lot to do tomorrow. The sooner we get that garden planted, the sooner we'll have more to eat."

Sam said goodnight and climbed to the small loft where his bed was. He fell asleep thinking about a winter with no corn. Visions of corncakes and spoonbread drifted through his mind. The next thing he saw was sunlight peeking through the curtains when his mother called him to breakfast.

The weather was perfect for planting — dry and sunny. The garden had been plowed in late March. Sam's job now was to till the soil — breaking up the large clumps and removing any rocks that remained, then laying out the rows. After the soil was soft and loose from tilling, he plowed it again — creating a checkerboard pattern. While he worked in the larger field, his mother tended to the herb garden. It was smaller than the vegetable garden, but also important. His mother grew dozens of herb plants — some were for cooking — most were grown to treat illness and injury.

Mr. Nevens had gone to town in the morning to see what had developed with the sloops. He came home at lunchtime, pensive and somber. "Well, it looks like most folks will sign, and help load Jones' ships with the lumber. He has them over a barrel, and he knows it." Mr. Nevens shook his head with disgust. "I knew Jones was a Tory. I would never have expected this from him, though."

"What about the O'Briens, Pa? Are they going to sign?" Sam asked.

"No, no. They'll not sign, and what's more, the boys are on fire because that young captain from the *Margaretta*, Captain Moore — he's demanding that the Liberty Pole be taken down. Says it's an insult to the Crown. I thought Jeremiah was going to chase him right back onto his ship."

"What about the *Packet?*" Mrs. Nevens inquired.

"Well, there's some good news. Mr. Burnham thinks she'll be in this week and can take a few loads back to Falmouth. Here," he said, tossing a small sack to Sam, "Mrs. Collins had some extra corn seed."

Mrs. Nevens smiled. "She is as generous as the day is long. Sam, when you're finished, please run over to Eamon's house with some of the venison in the smokehouse."

"I'm finished," Sam said, brushing the dirt off his pants. "I'll go now."

Eamon's house was about halfway between Sam's and town. From the road, Sam could see the bright new leaves of Mrs. Collins' rose garden. Even in this harsh climate, she managed to grow them. She said it was her little patch of Ireland in America. He knocked on the door and Mrs. Collins opened it. Sam could see that she had been crying. He'd never seen her cry before. He stood awkwardly on the step, unsure of what to say. She tried to smile. "Come in, Sam."

"Hello, ma'am. I brought you some venison. Thank you for the corn seed. Is Eamon home?"

"He's gone to town. He should be home any minute. Come and sit down. You can wait for him and keep me company." Mrs. Collins went back to her chair by the fireplace. She picked up a large piece of fabric she'd been working on.

Sam thought it was strange for her to be sewing at this time of day. Usually she was a flurry of activity right now. Sam looked around the tidy house and noticed a small pile of clothes and blankets stacked by the door. Suddenly he realized what was happening.

"Well, Sam, what do you think?" Mrs. Collins held up the white cloth — a large rectangle with a cross and tree sewn into the upper left corner. "Is this a flag my son can carry with pride?" She smiled, but as she spoke, her eyes filled with tears.

"Eamon is leaving?" Sam's throat went dry. A cold thud landed in his stomach.

"Yes, Sam. Eamon is going to fight. It's what he needs to do."

"What? Mrs. Collins, how can you let him go? Why don't you stop him?!"

"I couldn't stop him even if I wanted to, Sam. His mind is made up, and you know as well as I how stubborn Eamon is."

"Do you *want* him to fight?"

"No mother wants her son to go to war. Sometimes it needs

to be done."

Sam couldn't understand how she could be so calm. She was sending Eamon to war! "Aren't you afraid he'll be killed? Why can't he stay here and wait to see what happens?"

Mrs. Collins walked over to the mantle and picked up a small sketch. It was Eamon's father. "My husband, God rest his soul, worked himself to the bone in Ireland to save enough money to get us to America. He wanted his son to be his own man, and not spend his whole life slaving away for another man's prosperity. It was the Lord's will to take him away before he lived to see Eamon grow into that man. And if it's the Lord's will to take Eamon too, I'd rather he died free than live trodden upon." She put the sketch back and wiped the tears from her cheek. "If we don't stand up to the British here and now, America will become another Ireland. My husband would want his son to go." Mrs. Collins looked into Sam's confused and panicked face and put her hand on his cheek. "Sam, you're so young. Someday you will understand — some things are worth fighting for, worth dying for."

Eamon burst through the door, carrying a sack. Somehow, he looked older to Sam. "Hey, Sam. Hey, Ma. Sorry it took so long. Uncle Morris made me come in and pray on Granny's Bible. How's the flag coming?"

"Finished." Mrs. Collins showed Eamon the flag.

Eamon ran his fingers over the small pine tree she had stitched into the corner. He let out a low whistle. "Ma, sure it's grand, truly grand. This will show those blasted Redcoats not to mess with the boys from New England, or our pine trees!" Eamon turned to Sam. "I need to milk Bess. Come out to the barn with me."

Feeling dazed, Sam followed him to the barn. Eamon was so sure of himself, so fearless. He seemed like a man. Sam's chest grew tight. How could Eamon be casual about going off to war? Wasn't he scared? "So, when are you leaving?" Sam tried to sound relaxed as he picked up a bucket and filled Bess' water trough. He scratched the cow's forehead and stared into her gentle brown eyes. If only he could feel as calm.

"Whenever the *Packet* gets here. I'll take it back to Falmouth and then join up there. I heard there's a militia unit leaving for Boston soon."

"But you have to be sixteen to join a militia."

Eamon turned from milking Bess and gave his friend a mischievous look. "Sam, you know I can fib my way out of a hornet's nest. I'll fool them." Eamon cleared his throat and made his voice sound deep and scratchy. "Yes, sir. Born in 1759, just a wee short for my age."

Sam grinned. Eamon was a great fibber. Sam remembered when he and Eamon were ten and had snuck into the kitchen of Mrs. Lyons, the parson's wife. They ate an entire blueberry pie she had baked for a church dinner. Even though his mouth was stained blue, Eamon convinced Mrs. Lyons that a raccoon had dragged the pie out of the kitchen and into the woods.

"Sam." Eamon's face turned serious. "I need you to promise something."

"Sure. What?"

"I need you to promise that if I don't come back, you'll look after Ma."

"C'mon, Eamon. Don't talk like that. You'll come back."

"Well, I'm darn sure going to try. It would make me feel better about leaving if I knew you'd be here for Ma in case I don't."

"What do you mean? Do your chores and all?"

Eamon stood up and swished the milk pail around. "No, I'm not worried about that. Uncle Morris and the boys will take care of her. What I mean is, make sure she has a good laugh now and then. Make sure she keeps up her rose garden — that makes her happy."

31

Eamon stopped at the barn door and stood looking at his house, the rose garden, and the small field behind the house. The sun shone on his head and cast him in a glowing light. He looked peaceful and sad at the same time. It made Sam think of a picture he'd seen at church of the Angel Gabriel. Sam's heart twisted and he felt cold all over. As long as he'd known Eamon, their whole lives really, Eamon could fight, or run, or laugh his way out of any situation. But war was not a boy's prank or a quarrel between classmates. Sam felt a dark rush of fear for his friend.

"Sam!" Eamon punched him in the arm. "Why are you staring like a lost dog? Are you sick?"

Sam shook his head and returned the punch. "No, I'm feeling sorry for all those Lobsterbacks who don't know that an Irish hurricane is headed their way."

"Yes, sir!" Eamon threw back his head and laughed. "They won't know what hit them till it's too late." Heading toward the house, he turned back to Sam. "Hey, let me know if you hear anything about the *Packet* coming in!"

The next day, as he worked in the garden, Sam's head was still whirling with thoughts of Eamon's departure. *Eamon doesn't seem afraid at all. Doesn't he realize he could get killed?* Sam's fear for his friend was mixed with more than a little jealousy — something he'd never felt before. He envied Eamon's confidence and bravery. *Eamon is going to come back a hero with all kinds of battle stories and adventures, and I'll be exactly the same. Stuck in the mill. Maybe I should go with him. We could look out for each other.* He tried to picture himself running through a field with a heavy musket in his arms, smoke and bullets flying. But in his heart, Sam knew that he did not have that kind of courage and Eamon did. Frustration and shame rushed through him. He shoved and jerked the plow, taking twice the amount of time it should have to get through the field.

Sam was finishing the last row when his mother came out to the garden with a large basket. She pulled out a mug of ale and some bread and cheese. As Sam ate, she scanned the field and nodded approvingly. "Nice job, Sam. We can get the cornfield planted this afternoon. I need you to go to town and get some fish."

"Yes, Mother." He handed her the empty mug and grabbed the basket. There were a few coins in the bottom. Sam usually took the road to town — the quickest route, the one that went right past Eamon's house. Today he did not want to see anyone, though, most of all Eamon. He walked around the village center, avoiding Burnham's Tavern and went straight to a small wharf. He was in luck — Mr. Haskins, who ran a small fishing boat out into the bay each morning, was on the dock. Within a few minutes, Sam was on his way home with a basket full of menhaden. The small, oily fish were the perfect fertilizer for corn seeds.

The sun beat down on Sam's back as he carried the heavy basket through town. His blouse was drenched before he was even past the O'Brien house. *Maybe I'll take a quick swim. I'm going to be planting the corn all day — a swim would feel good before that.* He reached the pond in a few minutes, leaving the basket next to a large oak. He stripped off his clothes and dove in. Today, the water was perfect. He swam out to the middle of the pond and dove again — pushing farther into the silent, cool depths. Bobbing back up to the surface, he closed his eyes and floated. Water soothed Sam. He felt his whole body relax. Some crows squawked near the shore. Other than that, all was quiet.

Splash! Water sprayed against Sam's face. He sputtered and looked up.

Eamon was standing next to the fort and had thrown a mussel in Sam's direction. "Are you sleeping out there?" Eamon laughed.

Sam's peaceful mood disappeared. He swam to the shore and put on his clothes. "What are you doing here? I thought you'd be out looking for the *Packet*." Sam's voice carried an unfamiliar tone of resentment that Eamon did not seem to notice.

"I came to get the tomahawk."

"What do you mean?'

"I'm going to take it with me." Eamon's voice was muffled as he crawled into the fort.

Sam's chest and stomach tightened. So many feelings seemed to explode at once, everything that had been growing in his heart and mind for the past few days. His jealousy about Eamon's decision, his fear for his friend, his feelings of shame and cowardice; they all overwhelmed him. When Eamon came out of the fort, Sam stood with his arms crossed. His eyes blazed. "No."

Eamon straightened up. "What?"

"You can't have it, Eamon!"

Eamon stared at Sam. For a moment the only sound was the squawking crows. "Come on, Sam." Eamon laughed. "Quit messing around. I need it."

"No. You can't take it." Sam felt his voice rising a little, and he could feel tears prickling behind his eyes. He shook the water from his hair and stood up taller, trying to maintain his composure. "We said we'd keep it here."

"Sam, you are joking. That was before — I need this. I can't take the gun. Ma has to have one at home."

"I don't care. They'll give you a gun in the militia. If they even let you in!"

Eamon squinted in puzzlement. Sam's voice was so angry and spiteful. What was wrong with his friend? He frowned. "Don't be ridiculous. I'm taking the tomahawk."

"No, you're NOT!" Sam grabbed the tomahawk and flung it across the pond. It spun through the air and hit the water with a small splash.

"SAM!" Eamon's Irish temper took over. "You bloody fool! What did you do that for?!" He charged and pushed Sam down. The boys rolled across the sandy beach, punching and scratching at each other. They had wrestled a million times before, in play. This was the first time that white-hot anger fueled their actions. Sam's britches tore. Eamon's blouse was covered with mud and sand. Then they heard Eamon's mother calling him. He stood up and scowled at Sam. Both boys had scratches all over. Sam's lip was bleeding, and he could feel a knot rising on his forehead.

"I'm coming back for it, Sam. I'll find it, and you can't stop me, you mangy cur!" Eamon's voice cracked. His eyes were snapping with anger, but as he spoke, they filled with tears; the dark irises shone with hurt and confusion as he turned to go home.

Sam lay panting on the beach, trying to catch his breath and make sense of what just happened. He tried to justify his actions out loud. "Well, he had no right to take it. And I might need it too." His words sounded hollow, and his racing heart seemed to sink back down into his stomach, worse than before. He stood up slowly, wiping his lip and eyeing the rip in his britches with dismay. *Mother is going to be furious, and she's probably wondering where I am with the fish. So much for my peaceful swim. And why are those stupid crows still squawking?!* Sam looked over to where all the noise was coming from. He sucked in his breath as a terrible realization took hold. A dozen huge black crows were hopping around the overturned basket. He could see flashes of silver as the last fish was gobbled up. "NO!!" Sam sprinted toward the basket, scattering the brazen birds. The fish were gone. "Oh no no no! Ma is going to kill me! Stupid blasted birds!!"

Frustration consumed Sam. He kicked the ground. Nothing could possibly make this day worse. Exhausted, Sam picked up the empty basket and began to walk slowly home. His worry about facing his mother made his feet feel like lead. They had so little money, and now they'd have to buy more fish. "It's all Eamon's fault," Sam muttered to himself. His words rang false. Sam knew that everything — the fish, the fight — was his fault. Tired and sad, he reached home. He didn't see his mother in the garden. He walked toward the mill and found his father in the wood yard. "Where's Mother?" Sam asked wearily.

Mr. Nevens pulled a length of cord tightly around a stack of shingles. "Mrs. Earle is having her baby. Your mother went to help. She said for you to go ahead and start in the garden."

"Yes, Father." Sam did not mention the fish. He returned to the garden and stared at the freshly-tilled soil. His parents didn't have to know about the fish. He'd plant the corn without it. *How much difference could a few little fish make? If the corn isn't as tall as last year's crop, they'll probably think it was a bad growing season.* He moved hurriedly, planting the seeds and filling in each hole in record time. His pulse quickened with each completed row, as if wanting to push the guilt out of his heart by making it beat faster. He worked through the afternoon.

Sam planted the last seeds as his mother came up over the hill. Scanning the fresh mounds of dirt, her face showed surprise, then delight. "Sam! Have you finished?!"

"Yes, ma'am." He reached down for the empty basket, avoiding his mother's eyes. Sam had told fibs before, but this was the biggest lie he'd ever told. It seemed to sit right in his gut.

"My goodness! You must have worked fast," his mother exclaimed. "Did you have enough fish?"

"Yes. Um, I'm going to go wash up." He walked toward the well.

"What happened to your britches?"

"I, uh, I tore them on a branch on the way home." Another lie.

"Well, I can mend them tonight after supper."

"Yes, Mother."

Mrs. Nevens watched Sam walk away. He moved so slowly, hunched over like he had the weight of the world on his young shoulders. *Perhaps he's tired from working so hard in the garden,* she thought. She decided to make a quick batch of molasses cookies before supper. *That will be a nice surprise for him.*

But that night, Sam barely ate anything. He worked in the garden the next day, hardly speaking and again, eating very little. All he could think of was the fight with Eamon and lying to his parents. Watching him gloomily push his food around his plate during supper, his mother asked if he was sick. Sam said he was tired and only wanted to go to bed. He burrowed under his quilt and curled into a ball, feeling overwhelmed. The next morning, he woke to the loft bursting with sunlight. For one peaceful moment, before he was completely awake, he was happy and ready to start the day. Then everything he had done wrong came rushing back, and he was weighed down with guilt and sadness. Listlessly, he climbed down the ladder to the main room.

"Good morning, Sam! Wash up. Breakfast will be ready in a moment." Mrs. Nevens hummed at the stove as she fried salt pork and potatoes.

Sam splashed some water on his face and slumped down at the table, staring at the dark wood. He sighed. "Where's Pa?"

"Pa went to Jonesboro to borrow the oxen from Mr. Davis. He's going to pick up Jim on the way back. They should be back late tonight. They'll haul the pines up from the river tomorrow. Hopefully, we can have them cut by Tuesday. He'll need you to stack and tie the shingles. Maybe Eamon could come over and help. We must have that wood out and ready to go with the *Packet.* It's a good thing you got the cornfield planted the other day because ... Sam, what's wrong?!"

Sam sat perfectly still, with tears rolling down his face. He let out a sob and laid his arms and head down on the table. Mrs. Nevens came over and put her arms around her son. She waited until his shoulders stopped shaking, then she gently pushed a handkerchief toward him and sat down. Her blue-gray eyes were calmly questioning. "Now, tell me what's wrong."

Sam lifted his tear-stained face and looked his mother in the eye. Even her anger would be easier to cope with than the awful guilt. He told her everything — about the fish, the fight with Eamon, the cornfield. He dropped his head back on to his folded arms. It felt good to get it all off his chest. Whatever punishment came, he was ready. Silence. *She's furious.* Mrs. Nevens stood up. Sam held his breath, waiting for the angry rebuke. Instead, she placed her hands on his shoulders and gently kissed his head. She let out a deep sigh and walked to the stove, bringing the plate with Sam's breakfast back to the table.

"Aren't you mad? Aren't you going to punish me?" Sam said quietly.

"Mad?" She gazed at her son's anxious face for a moment. "Well, I am disappointed, Sam. You lied to Father and me, you behaved irresponsibly. You made a mistake. We expect you to fix it. However, I think you have punished yourself enough."

"How can I fix it?"

"You'll have to replant the corn after you get more fish. I won't give you money this time. You can work out some form of payment with Mr. Haskins. The soil is still dry, so it should be easy to replant the field." Mrs. Nevens sat down at the table. "As for Eamon, you'll figure out what to do. Now, eat your breakfast." She pushed the plate toward Sam and mussed his hair.

Suddenly Sam was ravenous. He cleared the plate in less than a minute. "Thanks, Ma. I'll be back with the fish!" Then he jumped up from the table and dashed out the door. He ran as fast as he could to the harbor and got to the wharf as Mr. Haskins' boat was pulling in. Breathless, Sam explained what had happened to the fish and asked if he could work to pay off another basket of fish.

Mr. Haskins chuckled. "Well, I guess those crows had a fine lunch! Aye, Sam, we'll sort it out. You go tend to your field. Come 'round on Monday and you can help me with the nets."

Sam was home so quickly the fish were still wet in the basket. He started working his way through the rows, carefully scooping out each mound of dirt, adding a fish then replacing the soil. When he got through the second row, Sam was surprised to see his mother coming out to the field, carrying a small basket. She filled it with fish and began working in the row next to Sam. "Mother, you don't have to do this. It's my responsibility."

"I have some time, and I was supposed to help you the first time."

They worked silently for a while. Each finished row of corn seeds made Sam feel a little better. *At least I can fix this. What about Eamon? Adults never make mistakes, or at least it seems that way. Maybe I just never notice when they do.* "Mother, when are you old enough to stop making mistakes?"

"Never."

"Never?"

"Never, son. Whether you are nine or ninety, you will still make mistakes. Maybe fewer when you're ninety, though." She smiled.

"You and Father don't."

Eliza sat back on her heels and laughed. "Of course, we do, dear. We make mistakes with the mill, with the farm, with you, and with each other. And hopefully, we learn from them. We do try to make the best of them."

"How can you make the best of something you did wrong? You can't take it back."

"You can't take it back, but whatever you do next is an opportunity to be a better person."

"I don't see how messing up makes me a better person," Sam said.

39

"It's not messing up that makes you better; it is what you do after. When you have made a mistake, whether accidentally or on purpose, three choices are facing you. One, you can ignore or deny it — which probably means you will repeat the mistake someday. Two, you can take responsibility for it and punish yourself, though you won't learn much from only that. Three, you can accept it and try to fix the damage as best you can."

"Like replanting the field," Sam said.

"Yes, and more important — telling the truth. Father and I might never have known about the fish. You would know, though, and living with a lie is a hard choice."

"I felt all sick inside."

"You're human, Sam. We're imperfect creatures, but we do have the power to choose."

They reached the end of the row. Both stood to stretch their legs and backs. Mrs. Nevens brushed the dirt off her skirt. She closed her eyes for a moment against the sun and let out a deep breath. She seemed very tired to Sam, not her usual energetic self. She opened her eyes and gazed across the field. "Perhaps we can get a few extra rows of potatoes planted. Your father cleared and plowed a patch on the slope above the herb garden a few years ago; we've just not planted there yet. We will need every bite of food we can grow to get through next winter." She turned to go and then noticed Sam's worried expression. Her face relaxed into a smile. Her small hand patted his face. "Don't worry — your father and I make mistakes, but so far, starving hasn't been one of them. And Sam, trying to fix your mistakes works with people, too."

Sam nodded. His mother knew he was thinking about Eamon. *Well, one thing at a time. First, I need to make this right. Is mother truly afraid we won't make it through the winter?* Under the hot June sun, next winter seemed far away, but his mother's worries about food made Sam shiver. He'd been in such a hurry to finish planting the other day to hide his mistake; he hadn't stopped to think about what this corn meant to his family. He would do an extra-careful job this time, and when he was done, he'd plow some new rows above the herb garden and set the potato plants before supper. *We won't starve if I have anything to do with it. But what about the bigger families in Machias? The Earles. The O'Briens. What will happen to them if there's no way to sell the timber? Ichabod Jones told Mr. O'Brien he would starve for his politics.*

Sam had always listened half-heartedly when people talked about England's tyranny. He didn't see how things like the tea tax and Intolerable Acts affected Machias too much, until now. For the first time, Sam saw how vulnerable their little town was. It wasn't right that from across the ocean, a king could decide to make a whole village lose their business and slowly starve. And while he didn't share Eamon's resolve to go fight the British, he could at least try to help his friend. *I can give him the tomahawk, and keep my promise to look after Mrs. Collins. I'll go to the pond when I finish the potato field. I remember where it hit the water. I'll take it to him and apologize.*

Finally! Sam pushed the plow through the last patch of bare ground. His back and shoulders ached. Blisters dotted the palms of his hand. He was thirsty and hadn't eaten since breakfast, but he'd finished! Six more rows for planting. He put the plow back in the barn. Coming out, he heard his mother's exclamation of surprise from the doorway of the house. "Sam! How wonderful! You did this and finished the cornfield?"

"Yes, ma'am." Her praise and happiness made him forget about his blisters and pains.

"My heavens. Your father will be so pleased. Thank you, son. Now, why don't you go wash up? I'll fix you something to eat. You must be starving."

"I could eat a bear." Sam grinned.

"Hmmm, I'm afraid you'll have to make do with bread and cheese. Oh, Mrs. Earle gave me some lovely apple butter. That should make a good sandwich for a hungry boy."

Two sandwiches later, Sam felt his energy return. He told his mother about his plan to go to the pond and retrieve the tomahawk. "I'll harrow and plant the potatoes first thing in the morning. Then I can help Father with whatever he needs."

Sam and his mother heard a loud bellow. They stepped outside and saw Mr. Nevens leading a black ox. Sam's father stopped and stared at the newly-plowed field. He turned to his wife with a questioning look.

"Sam did it." Mrs. Nevens placed her arm around Sam's shoulders. "He did it all by himself today." She gave his shoulder a light squeeze. Sam knew the missing fish would be their secret.

"Well, well." Mr. Nevens smiled. "Good work Sam. Have we got enough potatoes left to seed it?"

"Yes, sir. There are sixteen potatoes left. We should get about a hundred seedlings from them."

"You're home early." Mrs. Nevens glanced up the road. "Where's Jim? Is he bringing the other ox?"

"No. Zeblon could only spare one. This is Caesar." He patted the ox between its stubby horns. "Jim's coming tomorrow. He hurt his foot last week, wanted to give it one more day to heal. We'll have to cut the pines into smaller pieces with only one ox to haul with. I'll bring the first pieces up today."

"Can't it wait until tomorrow?" Mrs. Nevens asked. "You've already had a long trip from Jonesboro."

"I'll be fine. I won't rest until both trees are out of the forest and up here. Those surveyors could be back any day. With all that's happened in Boston, they'll be more determined than ever to get their mast trees." Mr. Nevens wiped his brow. "Jabez and Ned Simmons are already headed down there. I only stopped by to water Caesar and get a bite to eat."

"I'll water him, Father." Sam led the enormous animal to the trough. *Well, there goes my plan to get the tomahawk. Father will want me at the river to help.* "Do you need me to come with you, Pa?"

"No."

Whew — I can get to the pond after all!

"I need you here." His father continued. "All the stacks that are in the drying shed need to be put in the wagon. We can get a load to town tomorrow while we still have Caesar."

"Yes, sir." Sam sighed. *The pond will have to wait. Maybe I can run over in the morning.*

The rest of the afternoon, Sam stacked and tied endless bundles of shingles and loaded them into the wagon. His arms, already tired from plowing, now ached. His father and the Simmons brothers hauled up two twenty-five-foot sections of the first pine. Then they sawed those pieces in half so they would fit on the track that pulled the wood through the mill.

"That's enough for today, Caesar." Mr. Nevens handed the reins to Sam. "Take him to the barn, and then get your chores done."

Mrs. Nevens came out of the house and called toward the mill, "Supper will be ready in about an hour!" Then she turned to Sam. "You take care of Caesar, and I'll do your chores."

"But why?"

"I know you want to get the tomahawk for Eamon. If you hurry, you can be back here by supper. There won't be time tomorrow."

Sam's face brightened. "Thanks, Ma. I know exactly where it is!"

The cool water felt like heaven against his bare skin, but he couldn't dawdle. Sam swam quickly out to the spot where the tomahawk had sunk. It was too deep to see the bottom. *I hope it isn't stuck between some rocks.* Sam took a deep breath and dove down. Sunlight brightened the first few feet of water with a green-gold hue, then it became dark and murky. He scanned the bottom. Mostly flat, a rock here and there. *Dang! Where is it? I could have sworn this is where it landed!* He popped up to the surface and sucked in another deep breath. He plunged to the bottom again, swimming a little further toward the center of the pond. The water pressure against his ears felt like a giant was squeezing his head between two massive hands. His cheeks stretched out tight as he tried to hold his breath a few more seconds. *Nothing! I'm never going to find ... there it is!* Lungs ready to explode, Sam pushed down and grabbed the tomahawk. Kicking his legs furiously, he burst back up to the surface.

Sam dried himself off with his shirt, then dressed quickly. *I guess there is not enough time to run over to his house. I'll leave it in front of the fort with a note.* He jogged over to the nearest birch tree and tore off a piece of bark. Using a sharp rock, he scraped the soft bark.

Sorry about the fight. Leave this in a Lobsterback!

He propped the tomahawk against the larger boulder and stuck the bark underneath. He ran home and burst through the door. His mother was putting supper on the table. Her eyes met his with a question. Sam nodded enthusiastically.

"Good," she whispered, handing him a plate of food. Suddenly the whole day of work seemed to hit him. Barely able to stay awake long enough to eat his dinner, he was asleep before he could finish his prayers. For the first time in days, he slept with a peaceful heart.

Sam was in the yard chopping kindling the next day when his father returned from taking the first load of lumber to the harbor. Sam was surprised to see his father alone in the wagon.

"Where's Jim?" Sam asked as he took the reins.

Mrs. Nevens came out of the house and handed her husband a mug of ale.

"His foot is still too swollen to stand on," said Mr. Nevens, shaking his head as he sipped the cold drink. "It puts us in a bind. I need the Simmons brothers down at the river. But we've got to get this wood cut if we are going to get it out with the *Packet*."

"What about Sam?" Mrs. Nevens asked.

"He's never used the big saw. He's watched us, I know. Using it is a different story. It takes a lot of strength to keep the logs steady on the roller."

Sam looked at his parents' worried faces. "Father, I can do it. I'm strong enough. I know I am."

Mr. Nevens stroked his beard and contemplated Sam's words. "Well, son, I guess now is as good a time as any to find out. Let's get to work."

The Nevens' mill was an up-and-down sawmill. A strong frame held the carriage, the saw sash, and the wooden sash. The carriage held the logs in place. The saw sash held the sawblades at the top, the wooden sash held them at the bottom, as well as the pitman — an iron bar attached to a crank connected to the water wheel. The water moved the wheel, the wheel turned the crank, the pitman pushed the saws up and down. There were five blades attached with iron bolts to the saw sash. Sam's father readied the saw while Sam opened the trough.

The walls shuddered slightly as the water poured in and the mill churned into movement. Soon the tremendous noise of the blades vibrated through the mill. The sash thumped and clacked with each turn of the cogs. Sam and his father lifted the first log onto the rolling carriage where it inched toward the saw. Sam had seen this process a hundred times, but as he pushed the tree toward the sharp blades, he realized it was much harder than it looked. The tree shook with the contact. Sam struggled to keep the log in line with the blade.

His father watched closely. "Steady son, slow and steady. The minute you rush is when you have an accident." The sharp, clean smell of sawdust filled the room as the first boards fell with a clunk on the mill floor. "Nice work, Sam." His father smiled as he ran his hands over the smooth wood.

Sam felt a rush of pride. *Wait till Eamon hears about this. He's always wanted to use the big blade. Maybe Father will let him help us tomorrow. I wonder if he's been back to the pond? I hope he sees the tomahawk before he goes looking for it in the water.* After what seemed like hours, they had cut three of the logs. Sam's arms felt like jelly, and his eyes and nose smarted from sawdust. His thrill about working the saw disappeared. All he wanted to do was rest. How could his father keep working? Sam groaned inside. *Isn't he tired too? He's done twice as much lifting as me, but he's fine. He's even whistling! How can he be happy about working so hard? And we have to do the same thing all day tomorrow!* Irritated, Sam pushed a little too hard against the log on the carriage.

"Easy, Sam. You need to be ... look out!!" his father yelled.

SNAP! The outer blade cracked and sprung against the frame. His father pulled the lever to stop the sluice, and the mill groaned to a stop.

"Are you all right?" Mr. Nevens looked at Sam with concern.

"Yes. I'm fine." Sam warily eyed the sharp teeth of the snapped blade. "What happened?"

"Too much pressure on the blade." He inspected the saw sash. "The bolt is bent." He pried the bolt off the sash and gave it to Sam. "I think Mr. Foster will be able to fix it. You take this to town. I'll go down to the river and check on the Simmons."

"Father, I'm sorry. It's my fault."

"No one was hurt — that's the important thing. This is serious work, son. It isn't merely about strength. You can't lose focus for a single second." He looked at the wood still left to cut. "This will cost us some time. Let's hope Mr. Foster is not too busy today. Hurry back, Sam."

Sam thought about running over to Eamon's house on the way, but he knew he had to return home quickly. Town seemed quiet as he approached the blacksmith's shop. He knocked on the door. "Mr. Foster?"

It was strange to find the small shop closed. Sam sat on the front step for a few minutes. The shop faced the river and the harbor. The dark roll of the ocean flashed with sunlight as tufts of white foam twirled and bobbed like tiny dancers on the water. It looked so peaceful. Sam shook his head. Was it only a few days ago that all he'd worried about was the ships arriving? That problem seemed small compared to what was happening now. Sam noticed that the *Polly* and the *Unity* were in the same spots, but the *Margaretta* was now anchored closer to the shore. He saw another sloop anchored nearby. The *Packet!* It would be leaving soon. Was Eamon down there? There was no time to check — he had to find Mr. Foster.

He walked over to Burnham's Tavern. The main room was almost empty. Two men were sitting at a table next to the fireplace, hunched over mugs of ale. One of the men was small, with red hair and a face scattered with freckles. The other appeared to be much taller and had dark hair and pocked skin. Sam did not recognize them. *Are they from Moore's crew? But they are not dressed like sailors. And with the whole town angry at their captain, it seems strange that they would be sitting here so casually.* Sam walked into the kitchen. "Excuse me, Mr. Burnham, have you seen Mr. Foster? My Father needs something mended right away."

"He's over at the Dublin Mill," Mr. Burnham said, glancing at the two strangers. "He'll stop by on his way back. Should be here any minute. You're welcome to wait for him here, Sam."

"Thank you, sir." Sam sat down at a table near the two

men. They looked up briefly from their mugs but didn't seem to think a young boy warranted their attention for more than a glance. Mr. Burnham went back into the kitchen and returned with two plates of bread and cheese. He put them down in front of the men and nodded toward their empty mugs. "More ale, gentlemen?" The dark-haired man abruptly handed his mug to Mr. Burnham.

That's rude, thought Sam, wondering who these men were.

"Hey," the smaller man called after Mr. Burnham, "you got any rum?"

Mr. Burnham returned to the table with the refilled mugs. "I do have rum, sir. However, it is my policy not to serve it before five o'clock." He turned to Sam. "You look hungry. Would you like some cheese and bread too?"

Sam nodded.

"Arrgh, bloody Puritans! Who makes a man wait until five o'clock for a spot of rum?" The smaller man slammed his fist down, shaking the table. His mug turned over, and ale ran across the table and all over his sleeve. "Damn!" He jumped up to avoid the ale spilling on his trousers. He peeled off his wet jacket and hung it on the back of his chair. "We can't get out of this beetle-headed town fast enough for me!" As he leaned on the table to finish eating, Sam's eye was drawn to the man's right arm. There was a tattoo of a serpent with a knife in its mouth.

Sam gasped. *The surveyors! They're back! But where is their ship?*

"Aye, we'll be on our way soon, Nate." The dark-haired man looked around the tavern to make sure no one had come in. He lowered his voice to a whisper. Sam strained to hear what he was saying. "We need to be ready to leave soon. It will be safer to travel with the *Margaretta*, but I'm not waiting around forever. There are a few more pines that we marked last year, near the river. They were close to the shore. With the river as high as it is, we may be able to get them to the ship with no more than the crew. Once they're in the water, we'll move the ship into the cove and load her up." He took a long drink from his mug.

"I don't know, Robbie. Are you sure that cove is the best place to load them? It looks narrow. What if we have to leave in a hurry?" Nate said skeptically.

"Yeah, it will be fine." Robbie leaned back in his chair. "No one knows we're anchored in Petegrow Cove. That part of this God-forsaken pile of rocks is totally deserted. When we get to Boston, we can join up with the *Minerva* and sail back to England in the convoy. With this shipment of masts, we'll make a tidy sum and won't have to come back here for a long time."

"I'll drink to that!" Nate sat up and pounded the table with his fist again. "Barkeep! More ale!!"

Sam's heart raced — they were talking about his father's trees! *I've got to get home and tell Father. If they find those trees cut down, they'll fine him, or worse, take him back to England for stealing. We'll need to work extra fast now.* Sam tried to look casual as he got up to leave. He couldn't make the surveyors suspicious.

At that moment, Mr. Foster walked in the door. "Sam, what are you doing here in the middle of the day? Is everything fine?" He glanced cautiously at the surveyors.

"Sir, a bolt from the saw sash broke. Can you fix it?"

"I must speak with Mr. Burnham, and then we'll head over to the shop." He went into the kitchen for a few minutes. Coming back out, he handed Sam a chunk of bread with cheese. "Here you go, Sam. Mr. Burnham says it's on the house."

They walked out into the blinding sun. Mr. Foster was one of the tallest men in Machias. Sam had to practically run to keep up with his long strides. He opened the door to the shop, and a blast of heat hit Sam smack in the face — it felt like an oven inside. Mr. Foster didn't seem to notice the heat as he put on his leather apron. He took the bolt from Sam and inspected it. "Not too bad. I can straighten this out in no time." Mr. Foster whistled as he searched for a pair of tongs. The blacksmith's whistling was well-known in Machias — he whistled from morning till night. Some joked that he whistled in his sleep and that's why there was no Mrs. Foster. Small beads of sweat popped out on his bald head. His ruddy skin reflected the red glow of the fire while he held the bolt over the hot coals.

Sam leaned toward him and spoke anxiously. "Mr. Foster, those two men are surveyors! Their ship is anchored off the north shore, near Petegrow Cove. They're planning to take Father's pines tomorrow and leave. Should we try to stop them?"

"Don't worry, Sam. I don't think they will be leaving so soon," Mr. Foster answered coolly.

"What do you mean?"

Despite the fierce heat inside the shop, Mr. Foster motioned for Sam to close the door. He lowered his voice. "They'll want to go with Captain Moore. We're going to capture him and his crew at church. The O'Briens are going to run it. We'll hold them here for a while and get that lumber off the ships." He pulled the bolt from the fire and laid it against an anvil, tapping it back into the proper form with a hammer, then he dropped it into a bucket of water. Steam sizzled up.

"Done." Putting the bolt into a small sack, he handed it Sam. "It's still a bit hot. We can settle up later. Now get home and help your father finish that wood."

"Thank you, sir." Sam hurried out the door.

CHAPTER 3

Captured!

June 12, 1775
Machias

Capturing Captain Moore!! Wait till Eamon hears about this! Sam tore up the hill toward home. *Maybe he'll stay now instead of leaving for Falmouth. We can help with the capture. That's almost as exciting as shooting a Redcoat. I could run over to tell him right now. No, I've got to get home and tell Father and Mother about the surveyors.*

"Sam, where you have you been?" Mr. Nevens strode out of the mill. He was angry, and looked a little worried too.

Sam's mother came out of the house. Her face filled with relief. "Sam, what took you so long?"

"I'm … sorry." Sam could barely talk from running so hard.

"Did he fix it?"

"Yes, sir. Here it is." He handed his father the sack and bent over to stop his legs from shaking. "Father." Sam's chest heaved as he tried to catch his breath. "Father, I saw the surveyors at the tavern. They are looking for the trees. The ship is anchored in Petegrow. They're planning on loading the trees, then leaving on Monday."

Mr. Nevens frowned. "I was afraid of that. They are panicking. Lexington and Concord have changed everything and those surveyors know they'll have a harder time getting the trees out now." He stood quietly for a moment, turning the bolt over in his hands. "We're going to have to cut that load tomorrow. I know it is against the law to work on Sunday, but we've got no choice. I think the good Lord would rather see us miss a worship service than to starve this winter because we can't pay for food."

Sam's breath was steadier. "There's more. Mr. Foster told me that the O'Briens are going to seize Captain Moore and his crew tomorrow during church. They're going to stop Ichabod Jones from taking the lumber to Boston."

"That's perfect," Mrs. Nevens said. "With all that going on, no one will even notice that we're not in church and they'll be too distracted by whatever happens to ask about it. Jim will be here in the morning. He and Sam can do the sawing, while you and the Simmons brothers bring the other pine up. Sam, do you think the surveyors will start looking today?"

"No, they were getting well into their cups at the tavern. If Mr. Burnham serves them any rum this evening, I don't think they'll be up and searching too early tomorrow. They think no one knows where their ship is."

Sam's father rubbed his beard thoughtfully. "This will be a push, but we can get it done. It will be dark soon — too late to work anymore today. Sam, do your chores early and we'll all get a good night's sleep. Tomorrow will be a busy day."

It took Sam a little longer than usual to get his chores done. Earlier, his arms had felt like jelly from using the big blade. Tonight, his legs felt the same from running so hard. He sank gratefully into his chair at the table as his mother put a steaming bowl of stew in front of him. Sam's stomach let out a large growl of anticipation.

"Sam. Grace," his mother said.

"Yes, ma'am." Sam caught his father's glance as he lowered his head. His face was serious, but his eyes smiled at Sam. He remembered how hungry a thirteen-year-old boy could be.

"Our Father, who art in Heaven ..." Sam's mother quietly spoke, reciting the blessing Sam had heard every night of his life. He opened his eyes and looked around. The room glowed with a soft light from the lamps, and the warmth of the June evening filled the air. His parents' bowed heads and the wonderful smell of food on the table brought Sam a feeling of peace. Even though his whole body was sore, and tomorrow would be another long, hard day; even though he was worried about the surveyors and whether his family could get the pines in and cut in time, it felt good to have a plan and know that they were in control. Sam closed his eyes again. *Maybe this is what Father means by a "good tired."*

It seemed like he had barely gone to sleep when his mother called up the ladder, "Sam, time to get up. Breakfast is ready and Jim will be here any minute."

He rolled slowly out of bed and stretched his aching muscles. Still half-asleep, he dressed and climbed down the ladder. "Where's Father?" Sam asked, reaching for the jug of maple syrup. A stack of pancakes teetered on the plate as he poured a small stream of syrup over it.

"He's gone to get the Simmons. Do your chores quickly."

"Yes, ma'am." *But first, I will devour these.*

There was a knock at the door. Mrs. Nevens opened it and greeted their hired hand, "Good morning, Jim. How's your foot?"

Jim leaned his tall, wiry body against the door frame. "Mornin', Mrs. Nevens. I reckon I'll make it through the day. Mornin', Sam." Jim nodded.

"Have you had breakfast, Jim?" Sam's mother was already piling a plate with pancakes before he could answer.

"Yes, ma'am. But I'd be a fool to turn down a plate of your pancakes. They're the best in Machias, maybe the whole district."

Sam's mother smiled, handing Jim the plate. "Eat up, you two."

Jim poured syrup over his pancakes and closed his eyes. He let out a rapturous sigh. "Lord, thank you for these heavenly pancakes and the divine syrup that only the fine maple trees of Maine can produce. When I get to the pearly gates, I'll be sure to have a jug of this in each hand to share with the angels for breakfast. After they taste this syrup, they will sing sweeter than ever before." With that, he dug in and the plate was empty in less than two minutes.

Sam stared at Jim. *That is more than I've heard him say in an entire month. He must really like syrup.*

Later, above the noise of the mill, Sam told Jim about the O'Briens' plan to capture the *Margaretta* crew. "Don't you want to go help?" Sam asked.

Jim straightened the log on the carriage, then answered. "Well," he said slowly, "I reckon those O'Brien boys can handle it. They're a feisty lot. Your Pa needs me more today than they do."

Even in the early morning the heat was beginning to build. Halfway through the first tree Sam and Jim were dripping with sweat. "It's so hot already. This afternoon will be a scorcher," Sam said, wiping the sweat from his face.

"Nope." Jim did not even lift his head from the sawing. "Rain this afternoon."

Sam looked out the door at the clear blue sky. "Rain? There's not a cloud anywhere."

"Rain this afternoon." Jim continued to saw.

Maybe he has magical weather powers. As the temperature climbed and the ache returned to Sam's arms, he thought about the pond and how good a swim would feel. *Maybe Eamon and I can go swimming later. Eamon!* With all the excitement yesterday about the surveyors, Sam had forgotten about seeing the *Packet* in the harbor. *Is he truly going to go? What if he never comes back?* The thought of Machias without Eamon made Sam sick to his stomach. Tears filled his eyes. He shook himself. *Stop being such a baby. Eamon can take care of himself. He'll be home by October and we'll trap that old catfish like we always planned.*

Sam and Jim had worked through most of the stack when Mr. Nevens returned. He looked at the wood they had cut so far. "Good work, you two. Sam, I need you to go to town and tell Mr. Avery that we'll be ready to load the sloop tomorrow morning. Church will be over soon. Clean yourself up a bit and then head over. Jim and I will finish this."

"Father, what about the ships? Don't you want to see what's happening?"

"Getting this wood out with Mr. Avery tomorrow is more important. This may be our last order for a while. I'm counting on you to deliver that message and then I need your help here. Don't dawdle in town."

"Yes, sir." Sam went to the pump and washed his face, then walked toward the house. "Ma, can I have some bread to take with me?"

Sam's mother came out of the house carrying a small bundle wrapped in a square of blue cloth. "Here, I knew you'd be hungry by now. There's some bread and cheese and a few molasses cookies." She reached out and brushed some sawdust from Sam's hair. Then, much to Sam's surprise, she pulled him close and held him tightly for a long moment.

"Are you all right, Ma?" Sam wasn't used to hugs in the middle of the day from his mother.

"I'm fine, son. You're just growing so fast that soon I'll have to stretch my arms up to hug you. It's easier now, when you're still my size. Now get going and be careful." With that she gave him a gentle pat on his backside.

As he quickly got on his way, Sam wolfed down the food and stuffed the cloth into his pocket. He reached town in a few minutes. The streets were nearly empty; almost everyone was in church. Maybe he'd get a chance to tell Eamon about the surveyors after he found Mr. Avery. Sam decided to wait next to the tavern on a bench in the shade where he could see the door of the church. He leaned back and closed his eyes. The wind blew and flapped the of loose ends of wrapped ship sails nearby. Suddenly those sounds were drowned out by loud footsteps. He opened his eyes. A crowd of men was coming up from the harbor. Inside the church, Parson Lyons' voice got louder — whatever he was preaching about was getting him very worked up. Sam heard a shout, then another from inside the church. Sam saw a man climbing out of the church window. The man jumped down and took off toward the woods.

"There he goes! There he goes! After him!" The men from the harbor went running after the man. The church doors flew open, the congregation spilling out like an overturned beehive. More men ran into the woods.

Sam saw Mr. Avery following them. "Mr. Avery! Sir!" Sam caught up to him. "What is going on? Was that Captain Moore?"

"Yes, we need to stop him. Now where did he go?" Mr. Avery seemed glad to stop running. He was panting and bent over. "Sam, you know these woods. Go help look for him. We've got to catch him before he can get back to his ship."

"How can I stop him? I'm not as strong as a grown man!" Sam exclaimed.

"Give a loud shout if you find him, we'll come running. He can't get too far."

"Yes, sir!" Sam took off in the direction that Moore had gone. He had a feeling that Moore might run toward the river where it was a downhill slope to the shore and he'd be able to get to his boat quickly. *I forgot to tell Mr. Avery about the wood! Father will be so angry. I'll go back to town if I don't see Moore soon and find Mr. Avery. If I stop Moore, then I'll be a hero to the whole town. Surely that is as important as delivering a message!*

The shouts of the men grew fainter as Sam ran farther into the woods. He stopped to listen, hoping he'd hear Moore crashing through the forest. Nothing. Sam continued toward the river, running down a small slope that flattened out about a hundred feet before the shore. Suddenly he stopped in front of a huge felled tree. Even without looking closely, Sam knew what this was — the other marked pine. *Where is Father? And the Simmons? Why haven't they cut it yet? Maybe something has happened. What should I do?! If the surveyors find this tree we are in big trouble!* Sam paced around the tree. He had to do something. But he couldn't move this tree by himself and it would take hours to cover the whole thing with branches to hide it. Really, he only needed to cover the Broad Arrow mark. He thought of all the tricks he'd heard about when the lumbermen talked about "swamp law." Then it hit him. Fire! If the wood was even slightly burnt it was not useful as a ship mast. He could build a small fire around the lower end of the tree where the Broad Arrow mark was. Even if the surveyors found it, they wouldn't haul it to their ship. Sam scowled at the tree. He had no way to start a fire; no flint and steel. *Think, think!* The tavern! There was always a fire burning in the kitchen.

Gathering some twigs and the driest leaves he could find, Sam stacked them loosely around the edge of the tree. Then he made a small stack right over the hatchet marks. Sam picked up a branch and ran back in the direction of town. He saw a crowd of men at the Liberty Pole and heard lots of shouting. Perfect. No one would see him. Peeking in the back door of the tavern, Sam saw the kitchen was empty. He pushed the branch into the fire and waited. *Come on, come on! Why is this taking so long?! I should have grabbed a thinner branch.* Finally, the branch began to smoke and flames sputtered. He waited a full minute to make sure the branch was completely on fire, then he walked out of the tavern, hardly believing his luck that no one had come in. Keeping a close eye on the burning branch, he looked around to check if anyone had seen him. Strangely, town seemed completely empty now. No one was at the Liberty Pole, although he could still hear shouting coming from the harbor. He stood for a moment, scanning the harbor. *Why is everyone down at the harbor? Maybe they caught Moore. I'll go find out later. Wait till I tell Eamon about this! He'll think I'm pretty smart and Father will be proud of me for saving the tree for the mill!*

As he hurried through the woods, Sam watched the burning stick, careful not to go too fast and blow out the flame. It was still hot in the forest but the wind had suddenly picked up. It seemed kind of dark too, but the trees were so thick, he couldn't see the sky. Then Sam heard it, a gentle tapping. Rain! *No, not rain! Not yet! Darn it! Jim was right! I've got to get this fire started, a little burn will cover the mark and then it can rain all it wants to.*

Sam reached the pine as the first raindrops made their way through the dense canopy of leaves. He knelt down to where he'd laid the twigs and leaves. Starting with the small pile on top of the mark, he carefully held the stick against it. The flame was so small. *Please, please ... light light light.* Sam's heart pounded. Then a little flicker appeared — fire! He cupped his hands around the sparking twigs. Raindrops were plopping around him but so far it wasn't a downpour. The fire over the mark was taking. Sam moved the burning stick to the piles of twigs along the edge of the tree. The huge tree blocked the wind better there and the twigs soon began to sputter with flame. *I'll let it burn for a few minutes to be sure the mark is completely destroyed. Then I'll put it out with some dirt and the rain will take care of the rest.* For the first time in a while, Sam felt confident. He could be just as brave and daring as Eamon!

The rain was coming down harder. All he needed was a little more time! Sam crouched close to the tree, concentrating fully on keeping the fire alive.

"What the hell?!" There was a shout behind him and running footsteps. Sam turned his head to look and then everything went black.

"Blasted little rogue! He's trying to burn out the mark!"

Sam opened his eyes. His head felt like it was split in two. He was tied to a tree, with a shirt tied around his face, gagging his mouth. The two surveyors stood over the tree, stamping out embers with their feet. Sam struggled against the rope, he tried to yell. Nothing but a muffled groan came out.

Nate walked over to Sam and put his hand around Sam's throat. Sam stared at the serpent tattoo on his arm and an icy terror filled his whole body. "You're in trouble now, you bloody little rebel. Think you're so smart, eh?"

Robbie walked around the giant pine, surveying the damage from the fire. He kicked the tree. "Tarnation! We can't use this now! No mast agent will take it like this. Damn it! All right. No use in staying here any longer. Let's get back to the ship and go."

Nate turned away from Sam and stared at the smoking tree. The edges were still glowing where the fire had been the strongest. He pounded his fist on the tree and began cursing. He turned back to Sam and kicked him viciously in the ribs. The air in Sam's lungs exploded. He felt like he was going to choke on the shirt stuffed into his mouth.

"Let's go," Robbie grumbled. "I want to get out of that cove before the storm gets worse. Leave the kid. Someone will find him."

"I'm not leaving him," Nate snarled. "He's coming with us."

"What do you mean? What are you going to do with him?"

"Plenty of captains in London need boys this age to work on their ships. He'll make a fine powder monkey." Nate stood with crossed arms and clenched hands.

"C'mon, Nate." The tall man started walking away. "It's not worth the trouble."

Nate seized some of the scattered branches and pressed them against the embers on the tree. "He made us lose all that money from the tree. He's going to pay us back." Nate took a long narrow knife out of a sheath on his belt and pushed it into the fire. He stood for a full minute, staring at Sam with eyes full of pure venom. Then he pulled the knife from the flames. "But first, I'm going to teach him a lesson about messing with the King's trees." He walked back to Sam, holding the glowing knife, and pushed up the sleeve of Sam's shirt. Nate leaned into Sam's face and chuckled. "You shouldn't play with fire, boy." Sam's eyes widened in horror as the red-hot blade sizzled against his skin. Pain shot through him and the world went black again.

It was hot, unbearably hot. The hottest day he'd ever seen. He was on fire. Sam dove into the pond. The cool water wrapped around his burning skin. He turned around and around in the water then dove down to the bottom. There was a flash of a dark whisker and a gleaming broad tail. *Carl! Carl the catfish! I've got you now. Where's Eamon? We need to catch Carl together.* Sam pushed up and broke through the gold-flecked surface of the pond. "Eamon! Come here — you're not going to believe this!" Sam was rolling back and forth in the darkness, burning up again. Every inch of his body hurt. The sound of waves and shouting floated above. A door creaked open and angry voices

60

came toward him. He was lifted up and carried across the room, wrapped in a blanket that scratched and seared his feverish body. A blast of fresh air made Sam crack open his eyes. The white sails of a ship towered above him. Thud. He hit the floor. Darkness once more.

CHAPTER 4

The HMS Preston

July 2, 1775
Boston Harbor, Massachusetts

There you go, son. There you go. Lay still, now ..."

Sam opened his eyes. He was in a dark room, stretched out on a pile of straw with a ragged, dirty blanket on top of him. The room was slowly rocking back and forth. As his eyes adjusted to the darkness, Sam realized that an old man was sitting next to him and speaking softly. When Sam started to sit up, the old man gently pushed him down. "No, not yet. You'll faint right over if you try to sit up too soon. You've been feverish for almost ten days."

Sam lay back. His head ached and his throat burned. A dull pain throbbed in his right arm.

"Where am I?" he whispered. Before the old man could

answer, Sam fell back asleep.

The next morning, Sam woke up to the sound of seagulls fighting over their breakfast. He looked around the room. The walls were made of wood and curved outward from the ceiling to the floor. Dull sunlight pushed through a filthy, small window. A dozen or so men were scattered around the room, some huddled in the corners, others sleeping on grubby blankets atop piles of straw. Some of the men wore ragged uniforms of some kind; some wore the clothes of merchants or shopkeepers. Some had filthy bandages. The air, hot and foul, reeked of human misery. Sam felt a slight rocking motion. He was on a ship.

Nearby, the old man who had spoken to him the previous night lay sleeping. Sam looked at him closely. He seemed much older than most of the men in the room. His hair and beard were white with age, and deep wrinkles creased his forehead and framed his eyes. Like the other men in the room, the old man wore tattered clothes that were barely clinging to his small frame. Sam noticed a worn leather book lying next to him with a pair of glasses set on top. The old man shifted in his sleep and his hand reached over to the book as if to reassure himself that it was still there.

What is this horrible place? Where am I? Sam looked around and tried to clear his head. The last thing he remembered was Nate, the surveyor, burning his arm. As his memory returned, his arm seemed to remember too and throbbed with pain. A strip of blue cloth was tied clumsily around his arm. It was the napkin his mother had wrapped around the cookies. Sam gritted his teeth and slowly peeled back the fabric. His stomach lurched. Three angry welts marked his arm. The King's Broad Arrow. Sam felt sick as he realized "the lesson" Nate wanted to teach him about stealing from the Royal Navy. He'd said he was going to sell Sam to a ship captain in London. But this wasn't a regular ship. Why were they all locked in this room together? Was he in England?

The door burst open and two British soldiers entered. One carried an iron pot, the other a few loaves of bread. They put everything down and looked spitefully around the dank, silent room. "Get up, get up, you lazy rebel louts. Here's your grub." The other guard laughed as they left the room. "Don't fight over it!" He aimed a kick at a man sleeping near the door.

The old man had woken up. He went over to the pot and came back with a tin cup and a small piece of bread. Without saying a word, he handed both to Sam. Sam tried to sit up. His head began to swim. He closed his eyes and lay back down. He tried again, this time more slowly. He pushed himself up painfully on his good arm and reached for the cup — it was half-full of a brown, watery broth that smelled like week-old fish. He couldn't drink this. Sam felt the old man's eyes watching him so he took a small sip and gagged. It tasted worse than it smelled. He put the cup down, rolled over, and fell asleep again.

The next few days followed the same routine. Sam would wake up with the tin cup next to him. The old man was usually sitting close to the door, but Sam could tell he was watching him. Disgusting as the broth was, Sam drank a little each day. He was barely able to lift his head long enough to drink much. Then he would fall back into an exhausted slumber. One day when the soldiers brought the food in, they walked through the room kicking the sleeping prisoners. Laying on the filthy straw in a daze, Sam realized, with an unpleasant jolt, the soldiers' grim task. If after a few kicks a prisoner did not move, he was rolled up in a blanket and carried out of the room.

By the fifth day, Sam could sit up. He leaned weakly against the wall and for the first time in ages his head felt clear and awake.

The old man was sitting by the door, reading the book. Tucking it under his threadbare blanket, he turned to Sam and smiled. "Well, then. How are you feeling, young man?"

"Where am I?" Sam asked in a frightened voice.

"You are a guest of King George. Welcome to the *HMS Preston*."

The old man was clearly crazy. How could he possibly be smiling in a place like this?

"How long have I been here?" Sam asked.

"You were tossed down here about two weeks ago — sick with fever and barely alive. The man who brought you said something about a dying boy being worthless to him."

Nate! He must have taken me to their ship after I passed out. But how did I get here? "Who are all these men?" Sam looked around the desolate room.

"We are all prisoners of the British."

"A prison ship!" Sam gasped. "Why would I be on a prison ship — I didn't do anything!"

"You must have been delirious through the whole trip here. You have a brand on your arm that marks you as a criminal."

"But I'm not a criminal! I'm only thirteen! I was burned because I was trying to save my family's lumber!" Sam grabbed his arm as if to hide the burn. A flash of pain shot through his arm. His mind spun with shocked confusion. "Where are we? What port is this?"

"Boston. I'm not sure where your ship came from."

"I have to get home!" Sam's voice rose. "I have to get back to Machias, back to Maine!"

"What's your name?" The old man's eyes softened with gentle sympathy.

"Samuel Nevens. Sam."

"Sam, things look desperate right now, but you're still alive. You've still got hope."

"Hope?! What can I hope for here?" Sam turned back to the wall, unable to speak anymore. He let go of his arm. The burn

65

had started to heal and turn into a scar, but it still felt raw and agonizing. The pain in his arm was nothing compared to the terror he felt in his heart. He was a prisoner of the British army, trapped on a ship full of half-dead men. He would die here. He would die and his family would not know what happened to him. His parents would never know how Sam had tried to stop the surveyors from finding the pine tree and taking it to their ship. The last memory his father would have of him would be disappointment. Sam's eyes filled with tears. It wasn't fair. He'd tried to be brave and responsible, to stand up for his family, and he had ruined everything. And Eamon. He never got to apologize. Eamon would go to war angry with Sam.

Sam fell back on the straw. Fear, sadness, and anger seemed to choke him all at the same time. He could barely breathe. He closed his eyes, wishing it was all simply a terrible dream. If only he could go back to sleep, it would all go away and he'd wake up smelling his mother's spoonbread. But as he lay still, heart pounding and mind racing, Sam knew this was no dream. It was a nightmare, and it was real.

Time moved along in a dreary pattern of sleeping, waking, and drinking the foul broth. The guards also refilled a bucket near the door with water each day. The prisoners all drank from it using a bent, shallow ladle. Another bucket, in the back corner of the room, was for relieving themselves. Although the guards emptied it each night, the stench from that bucket filled the room like an oppressive poison. Sam could not guess the day or even month inside the dark, airless room.

One day the guards threw new straw into the room. Sam's heart leapt at the smell of salty, fresh air that clung to it. A desperate feeling seized him. When the old man handed him some broth that afternoon, Sam crossed his arms and turned away. "Why bother eating? I'm going to die here, anyway. If I starve it will be that much faster," Sam grumbled.

"That remains to be seen." The old man pushed the cup closer to Sam. "But until you are sure you want to die, you may as well try to get your strength back."

"What's that book you're always reading?" Sam asked, wanting to change the subject. The old man handed him the brown, weathered book. *Les Ecrivans de Epictetus, 70 AD*. Sam did not recognize the words, but he knew the language was French. Lots of French-Canadians came to Machias to trade furs. He handed the book back. "You're Canadian?"

"No, I'm French. My name is Gerard Sidos."

"You don't sound French," Sam said skeptically.

"I lived in England for many years," Gerard answered simply.

"Are you a criminal?"

"I'm a printer and a bookmaker. I came to America to learn about a new printing press in Philadelphia. And to visit my friend, Dr. Benjamin Franklin. A great man." Gerard pulled his beard thoughtfully.

"If you're not a criminal, why are you on this prison ship?" Sam asked warily.

"I was returning to France when our ship tried to intercept a British ship. We were overrun. A few of us survived. They decided to take us to an English prison. But the mast was damaged in the battle so they turned back to Boston for repairs. That's when you were brought here."

"Are all the other prisoners French as well?"

"Some. Although I believe a few are locals who have run afoul of the current occupiers of the city."

"Will they take us all to England?" Sam thought that if he was going to die on a ship, he'd rather it be in American waters than British.

"I don't know. It seems that the Americans are not cooperating with repairs for any British ships now that blood has been spilled in so many places."

Sam sat up. "You mean Lexington and Concord?"

"Lexington, Concord, and Bunker Hill. The British took quite a beating there, but they managed to capture the field. Charlestown was burned to the ground. Boston is still occupied and the Continental army has the city surrounded. Congress appointed a gentleman from Virginia, General George Washington, as the commander of the Patriot forces."

"How do you know all this?" Sam asked suspiciously. "Haven't you been on the ship for a long time?"

Gerard cocked his head toward the door he was always sitting beside. "The guards don't know I understand English. They talk very freely about what is happening."

Sam wondered if Eamon had talked his way into a militia and made it to Boston. Had he fought at Bunker Hill? Maybe he was nearby. Perhaps Sam could escape and make his way to find Eamon. He turned to Gerard. "Have you seen the rest of the ship? Is there any way to escape?"

Gerard shook his head. "The only prisoners who have gotten off the ship since I've been here are the dead ones. There are always two guards outside the door and at least a dozen manning the rest of the ship. Still, that doesn't mean an opportunity to escape will not present itself at some point."

The summer passed in sweltering monotony. Sam spent most of the time laying in the straw, wondering what was going on in Machias, how his parents were, and where Eamon was. His strength came back slowly and his arm healed but the vivid red slashes remained to silently mock him. Each time he rubbed the raised bumps of scarred flesh he relived the terror of his last day in Machias. How could he ever have felt ambivalent about the British and the King's Broad Arrow laws?

The weather changed and became bearable, then cold. At

night, Sam covered his blanket with straw and tied the blue cloth around his head for extra warmth. He figured it was autumn and that his birthday, October 19th, had passed. *Well, I guess fourteen is as old as I'm going to get. I'm going to die on this stinking ship sooner or later.* Sam was younger and healthier than anyone else in the room, yet to him it seemed inevitable that he would eventually succumb to sickness, starvation, or madness. Most of the other prisoners were too weak and ill to talk, although some had the energy to rave with insanity. Although Gerard was the oldest prisoner by far, he seemed to be the hardiest. He did a set of exercises every day and ate whatever the guards brought. Other than that, Sam could not figure out why Gerard seemed, well, not quite happy, but not hanging at death's door like the rest of the men.

One day, as Sam dozed in the corner, two men came into the cell. One was a British officer. He was tall with a sharp, lean face. His uniform was spotless. The other man was a civilian. He wore the clothing of a shopkeeper or merchant. He was dark-haired with a droopy mustache. As the officer surveyed the room, he sucked in a lungful of air as if hoping to get out before he had to inhale another breath of the foul air. Both men scanned the room quickly, then walked straight to Gerard, who stood up to meet them. He did not look nervous or intimidated by the men. In fact, as Sam watched, it was almost as if Gerard was not at all surprised by their visit.

The officer nodded and the dark-haired man began to speak to Gerard in French. They went back and forth. The officer would ask a question, and the civilian would translate. Sam was too far away to hear what the officer was saying. Gerard reached under his blanket. It looked like he was showing them his book, but the officer had moved slightly so Sam could not see. They continued to talk, Gerard pointing at the prisoners on the other side of the room, then at Sam. He seemed very adamant about something. Both visitors glanced at Sam for a moment, before turning back to Gerard. The officer glanced once more around the room and flinched slightly with disgust. He nodded to Gerard and strode out the door. The civilian spoke quickly to Gerard and followed the officer. Gerard slipped the book back under his blanket.

Sam sat up and rubbed the sleep from his eyes, wondering what had just happened.

Gerard sat down next to him, with a slight smile on his face.

"Who was that?" Sam asked.

"Lieutenant Drew, one of the ship's officers. He has recently been assigned to the *Preston*. They are going to move us into a different cell."

"Why?"

"Well, unlike most of these poor fellows, I am considered a potential bargaining chip, depending on the progress of the war," Gerard said quietly. Sam continued to look confused. Gerard went on. "It's complicated, Sam. It has to do with my family in France. At this point, the British want to keep me alive. They are going to separate me from the rest of the prisoners so I'll be less exposed to disease."

"But you said they are going to move *us*."

"Yes. That is the good news." Gerard's smile returned. "Have you noticed in the last two weeks that we have different guards bringing us food?"

"No." Sam shook his head. "I guess I wasn't really paying attention."

"Well, I took a chance that none of the new guards or officers would remember the circumstances of our capture. I told Lieutenant Drew that you are my grandson."

Sam stared at Gerard. "Why would you do that for me?"

"Why would I *not* help you?" Gerard said kindly. "I can't do much for the other prisoners, but I can try to help you stay alive long enough to get off this ship. And if not," his brown eyes twinkled, "starving or freezing to death would be sadder all alone in my own cell. Don't you agree?"

Sam smiled for the first time in months. "Well, I guess it couldn't be worse than here."

It wasn't much better. Their new cell was tiny. But it did have a small stove and plate-sized window that faced the harbor. Peering through the smudged glass, Sam saw the city of Boston for the first time. He had never imagined so many buildings in one place. He counted at least ten church spires. It was hard to make out much on the docks, but they seemed busy and crowded.

Although he still had little reason to believe there was a way off the ship, Sam began to pay closer attention to what was going on around him. They had climbed two decks to reach the new cell, so he figured they were almost at the top of the ship. On the wall opposite the round window there was a wooden shutter. Sam tried to open it but the hinges were tight with rust and age. From what he had seen coming to the new cell, it wasn't a window to the outside, but rather to another room. Both he and Gerard noticed a strange odor on that side, but could hear no sounds. Were there prisoners in there as well?

Sam also began to observe the guards more closely. There were two who watched their cell most of the time. The taller guard was Sergeant Hodgekins. He had thick blond hair and a round face. Hodgekins was huge. He had to duck under the doorway each time he entered and his broad shoulders barely fit through widthwise. Despite his intimidating size, his expression was open and relaxed, often with a wide, lopsided grin on his face. Hardly the stern demeanor of a soldier. He also had a habit of humming in a low, almost buzzing sound. The other guard, Sergeant Peale, seemed to be the complete opposite. Short, with a blunt jaw and jutting forehead, his face was always in a scowl.

One day, a boy who seemed a few years older than Sam was dragged into the room. He was unconscious and had a bloody strip of cloth wrapped around his leg, but otherwise seemed strong and healthy. He had red, wavy hair, and the faintest trace of whiskers on his freckled face. His clothes were simple — wheat-colored breeches, a long blouse, and a neck kerchief. After two days of fitful sleep, he woke up. Sam gave him a cup of broth and watched in amazement as the boy gulped it down like it was a savory beef stew.

"Thanks." The boy put down the cup and then carefully peeled back the bandage on his leg. A deep gash glared above his knee. He leaned against the wall and closed his eyes. "Bloody hell," he murmured.

"What happened?" Sam could barely look at the leg.

"Redcoat bayonet. He sliced me right as I was reloading. I still managed to shoot him, but then I got captured heading back to the woods."

"Where was the fight?"

"Over across the Neck. We've been harassing the Regulars early in the morning, soon as it's light enough to see, usually before they've had time to even get their precious tea brewed." The boy looked around the room, taking it all in very matter-of-factly. He didn't seem scared at all. Then he turned back to Sam. "I'm Josiah Woods."

"My name is Sam." Sam was so excited to talk to someone close to his own age, he forgot for a moment where he was. "Where are you from?"

"Boston. You?" Josiah asked.

"Machias, Maine Province."

"You been here long?"

"A couple of months. I was captured and brought here in the summer."

"Captured in battle?" Josiah's eyes flickered with a new interest.

"No, not a battle. I got caught burning a mast tree." Sam told him about the surveyors and showed him the three-pronged scar on his arm.

Josiah whistled. "Darn, that must have hurt." His voice contained an element of respect.

"A bit." Sam tried to sound casual.

"I'll bet you can't wait to kill some Redcoats now," Josiah added.

"I don't know." Sam traced his fingers through the dirt on the floor. "Honestly, I just want to get home."

"Home!" Josiah sat up straighter in disbelief. "Don't you want to fight the British? Look what they did to you!"

"Yeah, I know." Sam felt embarrassed by Josiah's indignation. "Anyway, it doesn't matter. Even if I wanted to fight, I'm stuck here on this ship. So are you," he said irritably. He almost wanted to puncture Josiah's doggedness.

Josiah was cheerfully oblivious to Sam's dig. He looked around the room and tilted his head toward Gerard, who was asleep. "Who's that?"

"His name is Gerard. He's French. Captured on his way home. He's a bookseller."

Josiah raised his eyebrows. "A bookseller? Why would the British keep him as a prisoner?"

"I don't know." Sam shrugged. "He doesn't say much about himself, except that he might be valuable to the British somehow, something about his family in France."

Josiah looked back at Gerard. "Can he be trusted?"

"Yes, he's a good man. I think he's pretty smart."

Josiah scanned the room again, his eyes soon focusing on the window. "Have you tried to escape yet?"

"Uh, no. The shutter is rusted shut. And there are always guards outside."

Josiah grimaced and pulled himself to his feet. He limped

over to the window. "There's got to be some way." He peered out the window and kept talking, seemingly more to himself than to Sam. "Hmmm, we're about two or three furlongs out. Maybe a ten-minute swim to shore. It will be too dangerous to go around the Neck. I can hide under Wentworth's wharf and wait for the tide to get me through to the Mill Pond to Aunt Susan's house." Next, he inspected the wooden shutter. He peered closely at the rusted hinges and lock, reaching under and tugging to see if it was at all loose. Again, speaking his thoughts out loud, he murmured, "Wonder what is in the room next door?" He returned to the blanket, his brow furrowed in deep thought. Then he reached for the empty cup. "Hey, is there any more of this crud?" Josiah grinned at Sam.

"I think so." Sam walked to the iron pot and scraped another half cup of broth from the bottom. He gave it to Josiah and watched in disbelief as he gulped it down — almost eagerly. "Do you like it?" Sam asked incredulously.

"Heck no! It's worse than the slop my pigs back home turn down. But it's food and it's the only way my leg will heal so I can get out of here." He spoke nonchalantly, as if it was only a slight inconvenience that he was wounded and trapped on a prison ship. Sam was intrigued. Their conversation woke Gerard up. After introducing himself and explaining his capture, Josiah asked Gerard what he knew about the ship.

Gerard shook his head. "Not much, I'm afraid. What I have learned from listening to the guards is that they have ship duty as a punishment for some trouble they got into while quartered in Boston. Hodgekins has a bit of a gambling problem and Peale committed some petty thievery." Gerard asked Josiah about how the war was progressing.

"Badly." Josiah ran his fingers through his hair and leaned against the wall. "The last I heard, General Arnold's expedition to Quebec was falling apart. Lots of men lost to smallpox and starvation. Nothing's really happened here since Bunker Hill. We've got the city surrounded, plenty of men and small arms, but no artillery. General Washington has sent Henry Knox to retrieve the guns captured at Ticonderoga." Josiah smiled at Gerard. "Mr. Knox is a bookseller, like you. General Washington has a lot of faith in him."

"And what about General Washington? What kind of man is he?" Gerard asked.

"What does he look like?" Sam said.

"Well," Josiah answered slowly, searching for the right words, "he's grand on a horse, and a head taller than most men, and he looks like ... like a General!"

Gerard chuckled. "I have heard he is very strong."

"Aye, he's strong all right," Josiah heartily agreed. "I saw him stop a brawl in Cambridge. A bunch of Virginia riflemen started it. They were messing with some of Glover's men from Marblehead. Guess they'd never seen a colored soldier before. After a few shouts, it turned into a huge riot — hundreds of men were fighting. They were biting and gouging each other — it was like a battle. I threw some punches. It was hard not to. Then I see General Washington ride straight into the thick of the fight. His slave, Billy Lee, was right behind him. Washington jumped from his saddle — quick as a deer. He threw his reins to Billy, then grabbed two men, each by the throat. He held the men apart and practically lifted them off the ground. Then he shook them and shouted like thunder. The fighting stopped and we all ran in every direction. Old George put a mighty fear into every man there." Josiah smiled at the memory, then his face turned serious. "So, he's a strong man and very brave, but ..."

"But what?" Sam asked.

"Well, after the fight, I started thinking about how different we all are."

"The soldiers?" Gerard said.

"Well, yes, except they aren't soldiers. They are farmers, plantation owners, fishermen, shopkeepers, hunters. The men from each colony have different ideas of what they are fighting for. Like there are thirteen separate wars going on. And militia men, no matter where they are from can be, well, ornery, and stubborn. They aren't used to taking orders like real soldiers. They like to do things their own way."

Gerard nodded in agreement. "England has manipulated the differences between the colonies for a long time. If they were arguing with each other, it weakened everyone. However, this will be a different kind of war and it will require a different kind of army. The militias and the men who have joined the Continental army are citizen soldiers. They will not be driven by fear or money — like a British soldier. They must be motivated by something deeper. General Washington has to find a way to unite them, not merely behind New England's troubles, but for a cause that is meaningful to all the colonies. That is the only way they can defeat the British."

Josiah sighed. "Like I said, the General is a strong man, but I don't know if anyone can make a real army out of what he's been handed."

Josiah's wound healed quickly. Each day he would stretch his leg and walk around the cell to speed up the recovery. His determination to escape had a powerful effect on Sam. Before Josiah's arrival, Sam had given in to the worst of his feelings — homesick, scared, feeling sorry for himself, and barely caring what happened. Josiah's presence — his energy and enthusiasm — made Sam turn from passive despair to shaky optimism. He began to believe in the possibility of getting off the ship and back to Machias.

After a few weeks of imagining every possible way to escape, they realized they would need to see more of the ship to come up with a plan. It was Gerard who offered a solution. "I've overheard our two guards talk about how much they despise emptying those waste buckets. If you offered to do the job for them at night, when the officer in charge probably goes ashore, you could get a good look at the entire ship."

After much discussion, they decided that Josiah should approach the guards. If he could make them think his injured leg had gone lame — they wouldn't worry about a crippled prisoner trying to escape.

That evening, Gerard sat quietly reading and Sam pretended to be asleep when Peale came in. He grumbled his way over to the waste bucket and Josiah approached him cautiously, walking with an exaggerated limp. "Nasty job that," he said, nodding toward the bucket.

Peale scowled at Josiah. "Of course it is, you stupid boy. It's the worst job on this ship."

"Well, I could do it for you. I'd be glad for the chance to breathe some fresh air."

Peale stared at Josiah with narrowed eyes. He looked at Josiah's bent leg for a moment. He seemed to be weighing the risks of getting caught against his own powerful laziness. A smug grin spread across his face. "Aye, I guess you'll not be going too far on that bum leg. Take this. Follow me."

Sam could hardly contain his excitement. It had worked! As Josiah slowly followed Peale out of the room, he dragged his leg awkwardly. Gerard winked at him, then lowered his gaze to his book again.

An anxious hour of waiting passed until Josiah came back. He looked a little green in the face, but happy.

"Well?!" Sam could barely wait for the door to close so they could speak freely.

"Aggggh! That was rough!" Josiah sat down on the floor and closed his eyes. "I thought cleaning out ship holds was foul work." Slowly the color came back into his face.

"Did you see the ship?" Sam asked impatiently.

"Some of it. Peale pointed to the side of the ship where I should dump the pails. I didn't look at much more so he wouldn't get wise. We've got to take our time with this, Sam. But guess what." Josiah continued. "There are two more rooms with prisoners. I'd guess close to seventy-five or so. That's probably why they put me in here with you — the other rooms are too crowded. Anyway, he had me take the pails from both rooms. Ugggh." His face went slightly green again at the memory.

From then on, every night Peale was on duty, he would have Josiah empty the buckets. The guards got used to seeing him limp across the deck. A few let him take over their turns with the noxious task as well. They began to ignore him and he was able to roam a little farther around the ship each time. Sometimes he found things that might be useful. A piece of oilcloth. A handful of nails. One night he found a pile of empty burlap sacks on deck. He also discovered that the room next to theirs was used for some kind of storage, and was unlocked. He had yet to look inside, but the strange smell, like garbage or rotting meat, continued to seep from that room.

After several weeks, Josiah had some ideas on how they could escape. He had Gerard and Sam look through the small window at the view of the city while he explained his plan. "Right off the stern a couple of boats are docked close enough to provide cover. We can lower ourselves part way down and ease into the water silently, hide by the boats, and then swim to the docks. The Mill Creek runs from there to a pond. My Aunt Susan and her husband, George Leonard, live on the other side of the dam. They own a flour mill. George is a Tory, but I know they will hide us until we can out of the city. We'll go to Watertown. The Whigs have been living there since the Brits took over Boston."

"How can we lower ourselves?" Sam said. "We need a rope or something."

They pulled out the sacks that Josiah had found. They were too thick to tie together and not long enough to make much of a rope. Then Sam got an idea. He grabbed his tin cup and pushed hard against the handle until it started to bend slightly. He pushed back and forth until eventually the metal began to feel warm in his hand and the handle broke off completely. The edges of the handle that had been attached to the cup were jagged and sharp. Holding a sack stretched out in one hand, Sam dragged the handle across it. He was able to cut the sack into smaller pieces. Sam tugged at a section of the cloth. It was fairly strong, but not strong enough to use as a rope. He frowned.

"We can tie them together and braid them," Josiah said, reading Sam's mind. "It will triple the strength. Should hold us long enough to get to the water. We still have to get out of this room, though." Josiah moved over to the shutter. He pulled and tugged to no avail, watching the two rusty hinges carefully. "There's some give here. The rust has eaten away at the wood. If we could dig around them a bit, I think they'd come right out. We can climb through here and sneak out through that door. We'd only need a moment to get across the deck and over the side." He picked up the tin cup handle and dug at the hinge. The handle edge was too wide. Josiah stepped back, hand on his chin, and stared at the shutter.

Gerard stood up and examined the hinges. Then he went back to where his small bag of belongings sat in the corner. He pulled out his glasses, held them in his fingers for a moment, then carefully twisted the metal frames until the glass popped out. He handed the metal frames to Josiah.

"Gerard — your glasses?!" Sam exclaimed. "How will you read?"

Gerard brushed away Sam's concern with a grin. "They have

79

served me well, but I think they have a higher calling right now."

Josiah grinned too. He bent the frames back and forth until the metal broke and he had a pointed, thin piece. He immediately began to dig around the edges of one hinge. Sam took the other half of the frames and worked on the second hinge. After an hour, they had worked the hinges out. They quietly lowered the shutter down. Instantly, a powerful, sickly-sweet odor assailed them. Sam reeled to the far side of the cell, covering his mouth and nose with his blouse. The smell seemed to land, cold and heavy, right in his throat. He approached the window warily and with Josiah, peered through into the connecting room. They both stared for a moment, then turned silently toward each other.

"Well?" Gerard had gone back to his blanket.

Josiah's grin was replaced with a somber expression. "Now we know why the door is not locked. And it's not garbage. There are a dozen corpses in there. Wrapped in sheets and stacked like firewood."

Gerard pondered this gruesome development for a moment. "The guards must have gotten tired of rowing the bodies to shore every day," he said quietly, "and now that the weather has cooled, I guess they can let them sit for a while."

Josiah put the shutter back, packing the holes around the screws with bits of straw to hold the hinges in place. Sam cleaned up the floor so there was no sign that anything had changed in the cell.

Each night when the guards were gone, Sam and Josiah worked on the rope. Gerard's hands were too stiff from age to do much tying. Sam noticed that before they began, Josiah would reach inside his shirt and pull out a small medallion attached to the chain around his neck, holding it a moment. Then they sat in the darkness, tying the strips of cloth together and quietly talking.

One night, Josiah told them about how he ended up as a soldier. "My parents came from England as indentured servants and my sister and I were born here. Pa worked for a whaling company from Boston. He had three years left on his service when he fell ill at sea and died. I took up to finish it. Spent over two years on that bloody ship — freezing, starving, and up to my knees in whale blubber half the time. Soon as the war started, my master sent me to fight in his stead. A few more years in the army and I'll be a free man, respectable and independent. Then I'll marry my girl, buy a farm, and raise a family. I'll never have to step foot on a ship again." As Josiah spoke these words, a look of grim determination settled in his face. He gently tugged the medallion on the chain around his neck.

"What's that?" Sam asked.

Josiah pulled the chain over his head and handed it to Sam. At the end of the chain, a silver disc gently twirled. Sam could see a tiny engraving of a house surrounded by seven stars. Josiah proudly said, "It's from my girl. Deborah. Seven stars for seven children. And our house. Her father made it."

Sam turned the medallion over and saw the initials *DLR*. Then he noticed in smaller letters *P. Revere*. Sam's eyes widened in awe. "Wait a minute — your girlfriend is Paul Revere's daughter?!" The story of the Boston silversmith's heroic ride before the battles of Lexington and Concord had even reached tiny Machias. And at Burnham's Tavern, a reproduction of Revere's famous print commemorating the Boston Massacre hung above the fireplace.

Josiah grinned. "My master ordered a set of buttons from Mr. Revere and he sent me to pick it up. Deborah was in the shop that day, the day my fate was sealed. The minute I saw her I knew there was no other girl for me. Like I said, soon as my enlistment is up, we're going to be married."

Gerard smiled. "A wife, a farm, and seven children. It sounds like a good life you have planned, Josiah. What about you, Sam? What will you do with your freedom once you are off this ship?"

Sam thought for a while. "I don't know. I always thought sailing on a ship would be exciting. I reckon what I should do is go back home and someday take over the sawmill for Father." Sam leaned back in the darkness and talked about Machias. He told Josiah and Gerard about his parents, the sawmill, and Eamon. He wondered aloud if Eamon had made it to join the militia and where he was now. Josiah had met some militia men from Falmouth in Cambridge, but he didn't remember anyone named Eamon.

"Some of the militias went back home after Bunker Hill," Josiah said. "Heck Sam, don't you want to join the war? You may not have a sawmill business to go back to if we don't defeat England. They'll tax us right down to our bread crumbs!"

Sam was uncomfortable talking about fighting. Josiah was so brave and sure of himself, like Eamon was; Sam felt ashamed for being afraid. He decided to change the subject. "How can we beat the whole British military with a couple hundred militia men and a ragtag army? It's like a mouse trying to fight a bear."

Before Josiah could answer, Gerard responded. "Actually, the British are not as formidable as you think. True, they have a powerful, well-trained army and navy, but they have to bring everything, from soldiers to bullets, three thousand miles across the ocean first. General Washington can retreat as far west as he needs to. The farther the British get from the ocean, the more vulnerable they are. And they've never fought a war like this. Look at what happened at Lexington and Concord. The strength of the Continental army and militias is their mobility. They can harass the Regulars and then slip back into the country and disappear. How long can the British fight an invisible enemy?"

"Hmmm." Sam thought England — the richest, strongest country in the world — could fight forever if it chose to.

Josiah sensed Sam's skepticism and argued. "It's about more than ships and men, Sam. We are standing up for our rights — to tell England once and for all that we are not going to let her trample us. British soldiers are fighting because someone is paying them. It's a job, nothing more. Sure, we're disorganized and green as spring corn compared to them, but we are fighting for a cause and our future. Believe me, marching in the rain day after day, hungry and crawling with vermin all the time; seeing your friends killed before your eyes — a bit of coin in your pocket isn't worth all that suffering. But a cause is. A cause is worth fighting for, worth dying for."

That's what Mrs. Collins said. Sam shook his head. "What good is fighting for a cause if you get killed doing it?"

"That is one way of looking at it," Gerard agreed. "Yet, as Josiah said, the rebels are fighting because they *want* to, not because they are being forced to. And their cause — it's bigger than one man's life. If America wins this war, it will change not only the future of the colonies, but the whole world."

"What do you mean?" Sam asked.

"It's a bold idea — men fighting for their own beliefs instead of going to war because the King or Queen demands it. Citizens choosing to govern themselves. For centuries in Europe, leaders have been chosen, not by their intelligence or their character, but because they were born into a royal family. And no matter how badly they may rule a country, the only way they will lose power is through death." Gerard scowled with disgust. "A monarchy is a ridiculous form of leadership. Think about it — a man can be feeble-minded or crazy or tyrannical or a combination of dangerous characteristics, but if he is a king, his power is absolute. That means he can tax his people until they slowly starve to death. He can start a war and send thousands of his countrymen into battle. Not one man in that army can choose whether it is a war *he* thinks is worth dying for," Gerard insisted.

Sam frowned. "The Brits have always crushed rebellions before. Look at what happened to the Scottish Highlanders, or the Irish. What makes this one different?"

Again, Gerard answered with total conviction. "What makes this rebellion different is our place in history, Sam. The ideas of the Enlightenment are changing the way people see themselves. If the thirteen separate colonies can come together and fight for their idea of what kind of country this should be, they will prevail. I know it may seem very far-fetched right now — self-government; the *idea* of a free country — but ideas are what change the world. Ideas matter. They are the dreams of humble souls that become reality and push the human race further."

Josiah leaned back and grinned. "Well, I'll leave it to the Continental Congress and George Washington to sort out the way to defeat England. All I'm sure of is that *my* idea of a place where I can build a life with Deborah, and be beholden to no one for our prosperity, is definitely worth having some Redcoats take a shot at me."

CHAPTER 5

Escape

November 20, 1775
Boston Harbor

Progress on the rope was slow. They needed another way to
add length to it. For several nights, Sam and Josiah wondered
aloud where they could find some other material to use. Once
again, Gerard offered the solution. He tilted his head toward the
shuttered window. "You know, boys, our companions in the next
room don't care how long their burial shrouds are."

Sam and Josiah looked at each other and quickly came to a
silent agreement. Cutting up dead men's sheets was a grim idea,
but no worse than ending up in one themselves if they waited
too long. They loosened the hinges and climbed through the
window into the dark room, carrying the tin cup handles. Again,
the pungent smell of dead bodies hit like a physical blow. Sam

held his breath and stared at the long, white rolls lined up near the door. There were seven. He shivered.

Josiah showed no hesitation. He squatted down next to the closest one to see what could be done. The cloths were rolled up, and tucked in at the ends. "All right, we'll unroll the sheets part way and cut a strip off each one. We won't unroll them all the way — it'd be disrespectful."

Sam let out a small sigh of relief. He had been more afraid of handling the dead bodies than showing them proper respect. He and Josiah pulled the first ghostly bundle from the stack. The clammy, stale smell reached into Sam's head. A deep shudder twisted from his neck to his feet. Sam held two corners of the sheet down while Josiah pushed the body a few feet. The roll lost its smooth edge as the bones of the corpse pushed through fewer layers of cloth. His hands shook slightly as he held the fabric taut while Josiah cut through it with the tin cup blade. They quickly got through the stack and climbed back into their cell.

After a few weeks, they had added several feet to the rope. Mornings were so chilly now; they could see their breath in the damp air. Even though he was hungry and cold most of the time, Sam's heart was lighter. Their plan was risky, but it felt good to be doing something besides wallowing in despair. Josiah's determination to escape was not the only thing that changed Sam's outlook — Josiah also had an intense curiosity. He asked Gerard questions about everything under the sun. It was a bit like being in school again, although Gerard knew more than any teacher Sam had ever met. Listening to Gerard talk about history, science, geography, philosophy, and books, the walls of the cramped dark cell seemed to recede and at times, Sam even forgot he was trapped on a prison ship.

One night, after hearing Josiah ask Gerard a dozen questions about the ancient Colosseum in Rome, Sam asked, "Josiah, do you think you are ever going to go to Italy?"

Josiah laughed. "Probably not."

"Then why so many questions?"

He shrugged. "Well, Ma used to say I was more curious than a bored cat. But it was Mr. Revere who taught me to keep my mind open to new things." Josiah tapped an imaginary pipe against his forehead and spoke with a deep voice. "Josiah, every person you meet in this life can teach you *something*. You just have to be willing to learn. And someday, that one thing they taught you will come in handy. It might even save your life."

Gerard smiled. "He sounds like an interesting man, your future father-in-law."

"Aye, he's a fine man, as fine a man as I've ever met — wicked smart, kind, generous, solid and true. If I can be half as good a husband and father as Mr. Revere, I shall be well pleased." Josiah reached for his medallion and turned the silver disc gently. "And," he continued, "without Paul Revere, the Revolution would probably never have started."

"Why?" Gerard asked.

"Well, Mr. Adams, Mr. Hancock, all those gentlemen — they're book smart. Full of ideas and words, not so much action. Mr. Revere can bring folks together and make things happen. His mind is always working on new ideas."

"He sounds like Johannes Gensfleisch," Gerard said, as he stretched out in the straw to sleep.

"Who's that?" Josiah asked.

Silence. They waited for the sound of Gerard's soft snoring. Then his voice, tinged with mystery, broke the quiet. "He's the man who changed the world."

The next morning, Gerard slept late. After he woke up and did his usual set of exercises, he stood at the tiny window. He stared at the harbor for a long time, seeming to have forgotten his dramatic words from the night before. Sam and Josiah, unable to contain their curiosity any longer, burst out at the same time. They sat together on Sam's blanket with expectant faces.

"Who was he?" Sam exclaimed.

"How did he change the world?" Josiah asked excitedly.

Gerard turned to them, eyes twinkling with promise. He returned to his blanket and pulled out his book. "Johannes Gensfleisch. Or, as the world knows him, Johannes Gutenberg." Gerard held up the book.

"He invented books?" Sam asked.

"He changed the way books were made, and who could own them. *That* is what changed the world." Gerard settled back against the wall. The sunlight streaming into the cell showed deep lines of age and illness on his face, yet his eyes were lit with excitement as he spoke. "Johannes was born in Mainz, probably around 1400. His family name was Gensfleisch, but in those days people often took the names of their homes. His was Gutenberg — the good mountain."

"Is Mainz in France?" Josiah asked.

Gerard shook his head. "It was part of the Holy Roman Empire, and a powerful trading city, because it sits on the Rhine River. It's a beautiful place, surrounded by rolling hills covered with vineyards. I went there about thirty years ago. Ahhh — the wine from Mainz." He sighed deeply at the memory.

"He was a bookmaker, like you?" Sam said.

Gerard shook himself out of his reverie. "Some people think he was originally a goldsmith. He was also an inventor, as many craftsmen were then, and now. Gutenberg's greatest invention was the printing press. Well, a new kind of printing press with moveable letters. He invented a different kind of ink as well."

"He does sound like Mr. Revere!" Josiah said, admiringly.

Gerard smiled. "Gutenberg did live in France for a while,

in Strasbourg. Perhaps he went to attend the university, or find work. While he was there, he was working on a secret invention, but ran out of money. He returned to Mainz and found an investor, a rich bookseller named Johann Fust. Gutenberg kept his work secret for several years, then in 1454 he showed up at the huge yearly book market in Frankfurt with several Bibles, printed by a machine."

"The secret invention was the printing press!" Sam's eyes were wide.

Gerard nodded. "Some people thought it was blasphemous — using a machine to reproduce the word of God. Of course, books had been printed before Gutenberg. One method was using a block-press, where the type is carved into a piece of wood. It was a very slow process and if you made a mistake in the carving, you were stuck with it in every copy that was printed. Before the block press, it took even longer! Most books were owned by churches and made by scribes — who copied religious texts one word at a time. It could take up to a year to complete one book. Gutenberg's moveable-type press meant new pages could be created and printed rapidly. From his work as a goldsmith, Gutenberg created a different kind of metal. The metal was heated and poured into a caster for each piece of type."

"Kind of like making bullets," Josiah said.

"Yes, but instead of one bullet mold, Gutenberg had to make almost three hundred different molds, one for each letter and symbol needed to print all the words on one page of a book."

"All that, for one page?"

"One page, that could be printed quickly. Gutenberg's press could print hundreds of pages in one day, compared to forty or fifty with woodblock printing."

"What about the ink?" Sam added.

"Ah, the ink. Well, compared to the rest of the book, the ink was fairly simple. Do you know what lampblack is?"

Josiah made a face. "Aye, it's the soot from inside a candle shade. That was one of my jobs on the ship — cleaning the candle shades in the officers' quarters. What a mess!"

"So, oil, linseed or walnut, and lampblack mixed together make ink," Gerard explained.

"Oil is so slimy. How could he print with it?" Sam wondered.

"Correction: cooked oil. Linseed or walnut oil was boiled for hours until it turned into varnish. It was very dangerous work — a boiling pot of oil could create a huge explosion. The work had to be done outside the city walls. The oil was cooked for a long time, but it was still a little greasy, so bread or perhaps an onion was added to soak up the extra grease. Once cooled, the varnish was ground together with lampblack until the ink was smooth. Gutenberg didn't invent ink, but he added something extra. Maybe tree sap. The ink he produced worked perfectly with the metal type he had created."

Sam shook his head in amazement. "All that work goes into printing a book. I never thought about it before."

"Did Gutenberg make his own paper too?" Josiah was impressed.

"Probably not. It's a long process with many people involved," Gerard said, fanning the pages of his book slowly. "I imagine Gutenberg would have bought paper that was ready to use. After the pages were printed, they were sewn together with thin cords between two pieces of wood. The wood was covered with leather and stamped. Very much like this one."

"May I see it?" Josiah reached for the book politely. Rubbing his thumb across the raised letters on the front, he stared thoughtfully, as if adding up all the time and people involved in creating it. Then he looked back at Gerard, more curious than ever. "Did he make a lot of money from his inventions?"

"At first, yes. He made calendars, grammar books, and Bibles."

"Bibles?" Sam repeated.

"Bibles." Gerard nodded.

"Calendars, grammar books, and Bibles changed the world?" Sam's expression was puzzled.

"Ah, I see your confusion." Gerard laughed. "No, it was not the actual books Gutenberg made that changed the world. It was the printing process. As much as he tried to protect the secrecy of his press in Mainz, other printing presses were soon popping up all over Europe. The ability to produce a book, any book — quickly and cheaply — was revolutionary. Before Gutenberg's invention, books were rare and expensive. Most people could not afford them. Even if they could, most books were written in Latin, which only scholars could read. After Gutenberg, books became available to more and more people, and in their own languages as well. Now the common people wanted to learn how to read. Knowledge and ideas spread across Europe, and the world, like never before. Information about every subject under the sun — politics, history, science, religion, medicine, philosophy, music, literature — was suddenly accessible to everyone. People who only a decade before had not known much about the world beyond their small villages and whatever the Church taught them, were reading books."

The boys absorbed Gerard's words, trying to imagine the before and after of such a change.

"It must've been pretty exciting," Josiah said eagerly. "Kind of like discovering a whole new world."

"Exciting is *exactly* what it was. However, not everyone was thrilled with this explosion of new ideas and information. Remember who made and owned most books before 1454?"

"Churches," Sam said quickly.

"Precisely. The Catholic Church soon realized that the changes brought by this new printing system were a dire threat to its influence. Religious leaders became particularly alarmed when scholars began to translate and mass produce the two-thousand-year-old writings from ancient Greece and Rome. The philosophers from those societies focused on man as an individual, and the value of his life on earth. It was a bold departure from the Church's doctrine, which prized the importance of eternal life."

"That probably made the Church leaders pretty angry," Sam said.

Gerard nodded. "The Church and monarchy controlled the wealth, the military, and the land for most of Europe at that time. People sharing ideas and starting to think for themselves was not a good omen for a king or a pope."

"Ideas matter," Josiah said softly.

"Ideas matter." Gerard smiled and continued. "Of course, as the demand for more information grew, so did the level of censorship against it. As the book trade in Europe flourished, the authorities were determined to control it. Some countries were stricter than others, and in those countries an illegal book trade developed. Anything that questioned or criticized the Church or the monarchy was considered threatening. In France, where I worked, a bookseller could be put in jail for selling banned books. They were called *marrons* — chestnuts."

"If you couldn't print them in France, where did they come from?" Josiah asked.

"Many came from Switzerland. We hired porters to carry shipments on their backs, sneaking into the country through the mountains to avoid customs inspections at the borders."

"What would happen if you got caught?"

"Well, a fine was the least punishment. Prison was the worst."

"Prison?!" Sam exclaimed. "For selling a book? Who would risk that?"

"I would. I did," Gerard said evenly.

"You're joking!" Sam exclaimed.

"I spent eighteen months in the worst prison in France, the Bastille."

Both Sam and Josiah stared at Gerard.

Sam shook his head in disbelief. "You went to prison *for a book?* That's crazy!" His eyes grew wider.

"Maybe to some people." Gerard shrugged slightly.

"How could you give up a year and a half of your life for a book? You could have died there!" Sam turned to Josiah for some reaction. "Don't you think that's crazy?"

Josiah was looking at Gerard, but seemed lost in a deeper thought. Finally, he answered Sam. "No, I don't think it is crazy. Not if it was a book that he believed in. It isn't any crazier than going to war for something you believe in." He turned to Gerard. "What book was it?"

"It was a simple book of essays. A few were written in defense of a young writer, Francois Arouet, who had criticized the government. I had recently received a shipment of the books from Switzerland, when someone tipped off the *Direction de la Librairie*, the 'book police' so to speak. Tried and sentenced in less than a day. I guess they wanted to make an example of me because rather than confine me to a local prison, I was delivered straight to the Bastille two days later. And that is when things got interesting."

The boys' faces mirrored their thoughts perfectly. Sam's still registered shock and disbelief. Josiah's eyes shone with admiration and respect.

Gerard chuckled and continued. "Whether it was deliberate or a wonderful, ironic coincidence, my cellmate in the Bastille was none other than Arouet himself. Of course, the world knows him now by the name Voltaire. Perhaps you have heard of him?"

Sam and Josiah shook their heads.

"Letters Concerning the English Nation? Candide?" Gerard seemed slightly disappointed when they both shook their heads again. "Ah, well, someday you must read his works. Of course, most of his work is banned in France, which makes it even

more in demand. Mr. Voltaire is an eloquent voice in the fight against injustice and intolerance. He can eviscerate his enemies in less than a paragraph." Gerard smiled. "So, despite being in a cell even worse than this one, with ten-foot-thick walls and no window, I actually look back at my time in the Bastille with some fond memories."

The rope was almost finished. Josiah began to work on other parts of the escape plan. He loosened a floorboard and, using the broken lens from Gerard's glasses, carved a simple map of Boston, showing the way to his aunt's house, and the way to Watertown. He wanted Sam and Gerard to know how to get to both places in case they were separated.

Early each morning, when it was light enough to see, Josiah would pull up the board so they could memorize the map. His finger traced the line of the narrow creek they would have to swim through. From the small window, he pointed to where they would be going. "The wharf with all the buildings on it is the Long Wharf. Four wharves over to the right is the Mill Creek. You can't see it from here, but there is a tunnel that runs under the streets to the pond. Aunt Susan's house is just past the dam. We'll rest a day or two, then take a boat from Hudson's Point, right there." Josiah tapped his finger on a small spot at the far northern part of the map. "If the water's frozen, we can walk across the back bay from Barton's Point. It's about fifteen miles to Watertown. We could do that in a night. The house the Reveres are living in has a copper rooster weathervane."

"What about the colonial troops surrounding the city? Won't they shoot at a boat coming from the city?" Gerard asked.

"Naw, they'll know me," Josiah reassured him. He pulled out his medallion. "And if not, I can show them this. Mr. Revere made medallions for the Sons of Liberty. If something happens to me, just get to the Charles River. There's an old Indian path that goes along the river all the way to Watertown. A trail tree marks the path about a half mile from the mouth, on the north side. The militia won't be watching the path. See, here it is." He tapped on the board with the glass bit.

"Forgive my ignorance," Gerard said. "What is a trail tree?"

Sam reached over and took the small piece of glass from Josiah. He made a few quick scratches on the board, then held it up for Gerard. "It's a tree that grew out sideways, then up. Indians made them by tying down a sapling for a year or two, to change the shape. They show safe travel routes or water sources." Sam studied the map for a moment, frowning. "We can get to your aunt's house, and Watertown, but we have to get off the ship first. Even if we are leaving at night, we should find a way to distract the guards."

"I've been thinking about that," Gerard said. "We know Hodgekins has a weak spot for gambling. If we could get a pair of dice to him that night, he'd probably get the other guards caught up in a few games."

"That might work." Josiah nodded eagerly. He dug around under his blanket, pulled out his knapsack and dumped it on the floor. A small sewing kit, several flints, and a wooden bowl fell out. He shook it again. Four musket balls rolled onto the blanket. "We can use these, but we need something heavy to shape them with."

"How about the shutter? And we can use one of the screws to make the pits," Sam added.

"Perfect." Gerard smiled at the boys. "I'm sure Mr. Revere will appreciate your ingenuity when you share this story with him."

That night they loosened the shutter and, as quietly as possible, pounded each musket ball into a square. Next, Sam held a screw in place while Josiah raised the shutter again to make the small dented numbers on each side.

"Wait! Let's mark them first. To be sure," Sam said.

"I'm sure I know how to make dice, Sam," Josiah said with slight impatience. "The opposite sides must add up to seven. So, six is opposite one; three to four and two to five. Now, hold that still."

Finally, the rope was ready. All they had to do was wait for a moonless night. Josiah watched the sky carefully each time he dumped the waste buckets. He guessed that in about five days the moon would be at its smallest and there would be the least chance of them being spotted. Then Gerard began coughing. During the day wasn't too bad, but at night when the damp air descended onto the water, he coughed continuously. After three days he was barely able to sit up. The night before their planned escape, as Gerard fitfully slept, Josiah and Sam listened to his wheezing, labored breath. The silent question hung in the air.

Josiah spoke first. "We can't go with him like this. He'll never make it down the rope, let alone survive the swim to shore."

Sam nodded. "We'll just have to wait for him to get better. We'll give him our food and build his strength up."

"Aye," Josiah agreed. "It may be a few weeks, by the next moon cycle, for sure."

The boys sat wordlessly in the dark, knowing in their hearts that no one ever "got better" on this ship.

"You'll do no such thing." Gerard's steady voice pierced the quiet. "You will escape tomorrow as planned. I'm an old man and the odds of me getting off this boat alive were slim to begin with."

"But, Gerard," Sam's voice caught, "you'll die here."

"Yes, I probably will. However, that is no reason for you to lose this chance to escape."

Sam turned in the dark toward Josiah, expecting him to protest.

Josiah did not respond at once. Then, in a voice heavy with

sadness and acceptance, he murmured, "Yes, sir."

Sam lay in the straw, Gerard's coughing and all the other sounds of the ship mixed with the whirl of thoughts in his head. It seemed so cruel to leave without Gerard, but he was right. It might be their only chance to escape. He was glad that Josiah was here. Sam wouldn't have risked escaping on his own. *This will be my last night in this hellish place. Maybe by this time tomorrow, I'll be sleeping in the Reveres' house, with a full belly and a real fire to warm me. Wait till I tell Eamon I met Paul Revere!*

The next night, as if Mother Nature had given her blessing to their escape scheme, a heavy fog settled across the harbor. It was impossible to see more than five feet. While dumping the buckets earlier in the evening, Josiah had left the dice out where Hodgekins could easily find them. Through the door, Gerard could hear the guards discussing when they could get a game going.

Darkness descended. It was time to go. They removed the shutter. Gerard would put it back in place after they were gone. Josiah's easy smile was replaced by a resolute nod of respect as he hugged Gerard good-bye, then climbed through the window, the rope under his arm. Sam's eyes welled with sudden tears as Gerard faced him. Pulling Sam into a shaky embrace, Gerard said softly but firmly, "You are braver than you think, Sam."

"Good-bye, Gerard. And," Sam whispered, "thank you."

Sam climbed through the window. He and Josiah stepped gingerly over the stack of rolled corpses. Josiah carefully opened the door, peered out, and then motioned for Sam to follow. They darted quickly across the deck. The shouts and jeers of the dice game could be heard from the room right below them. Josiah inched his way past the mizzen mast, pulling the rope off his shoulder. He tied it under the stern lantern. They had decided he would go first. When he reached the water, he would pull firmly on the rope twice and Sam could follow.

"Right then, it's now or never. Wait for my signal." Josiah's face was determined and alert as he climbed over the edge. Sam held his breath and felt the rope begin to tighten against the rail. He looked down, unable to see a thing. The mist, thick and unmoving, hid any glimpse of the water. The stern was the highest part of the ship. Had they made the rope long enough?

Where is he? Why is he taking this long? Sam's heart was beating so hard in his chest he thought surely the guards would hear it thumping away. Sam gripped the rope nervously and felt one sharp tug — then it went slack. *What's he doing? That wasn't the signal?!* Sam leaned further over the edge, then pulled up the rope. His heart froze. The rope was broken! More than half was missing! *What should I do? Should I try and climb down with what is left?! Where's Josiah? Why didn't he call out when he reached the water?* Sam was paralyzed with fear and indecision. If he tried using the rope and it broke again, he'd be dead. Yet, this might be his only chance to escape — was it worth risking death?

A shout flew across the deck. "Hurry up and piss, you sod. Let's have another game."

Footsteps were heading toward him. Sam quickly untied the rope and ducked behind a barrel. Hodgekins came out of the fog and stood at the railing. He urinated into the water and whistled. "There you go, little fishes. Swim around in that for a bit." Laughing, he returned to the dice game.

Sam sat behind the barrel, stunned and defeated. The rope would not hold him. He knew that. Still, maybe he should try. He couldn't. He was too afraid of hitting the water at full force, or bouncing off the side of the ship. A small voice in his churning head told him to move before the guards found him. But the thought of returning to the cell, back into that foul, dark room, was unbearable. He sat dully as the fog and cold rolled over him.

Finally, he made his way back, and pushed into the corpse room. The remaining rope, thrown sloppily on his back, dropped and tripped him. He fell across the stack of rolled-up covered bodies. A small cry of panic escaped his lips as he struggled to regain his balance.

Suddenly, Gerard's steadfast voice reached through the darkness like a beacon. He stood at the window. "Sam, get up. You are all right. Quickly, son. Take my hand."

Sam grasped Gerard's hand, climbed through the window, and fell to the floor.

Gerard pulled the rope in and put the shutter back. His startled glance took in the frayed rope and Sam's face all at once. "What about Josiah?"

Sam slumped against the wall. "I don't know. He didn't call up. I didn't hear anything. He must have swum away. He got away. He got away," Sam repeated numbly.

Gerard hid the rope back under the straw. He sighed deeply. "Sam, I'm sorry. You mustn't give up hope. We'll figure something else out."

Sam stared at Gerard like he was crazy. Then he lay down on his blanket and turned away, his face to the wall. He lay perfectly still, but his heart and mind were in a rage. *It's over. I'll never get out of here now. Why did Josiah get to go first?! It was my idea to cut the blankets! I should have gone first! Now he's free and I'll die here. It's not fair, it's not fair!*

Sam spent most of the next day staring at the floor. When Gerard brought him some bread and water, he didn't look up. Gerard was quiet — he knew nothing he could say would help.

Finally, Sam's anger burst out. "Why couldn't I go first? It's not fair. Josiah is free and probably eating breakfast right now. I'm the one that figured out how to cut the blankets. I should have gone first!"

Gerard answered evenly, "It's not Josiah's fault that the rope broke. You decided together who would go first."

"I don't care. Why does he get to be free and I'm still stuck here?" Sam slammed his hand against the wall in frustration.

"Are you sure he got away? Did you hear him in the water?"

"No, I couldn't hear anything except the waves sloshing against the boat."

Gerard watched Sam's distraught face. "Are you angry because Josiah got away, or because you didn't?"

Sam stared at his hands. "Both I guess. I'm mad at Josiah for getting away, but he wanted it so badly. He would have figured out a way without my help. I guess it's better that he escaped."

"Why are you angry with yourself?"

"Because I was too scared to try the rope after Josiah went. I was a coward."

"What do you think would have happened if you had tried it?"

Sam mumbled, "It probably would have broken again."

"And you would have been starting with half the length that Josiah did, so you would have fallen most of the way and been killed," Gerard said decisively. "Sometimes it is wiser to not take action. It took a lot of courage to come back here and start all over again."

"Or die here," Sam said glumly. "Josiah wasn't afraid. He is braver than I am."

Gerard shook his head. "Of course, he was afraid. Just because he did not say it out loud, doesn't mean he wasn't scared. Acting with bravery usually comes with a healthy dose of fear behind it."

Sam leaned against the wall and shrugged his shoulders. "That's what Father said, that even the best soldiers are a little afraid."

"It's true. I was a soldier for many years."

"Really?"

"Yes, I fought for the French army when I was young. The glory of battle never actually makes one indifferent to the idea of dying. In time, I learned to manage my fears — mostly from what I learned here." Gerard handed Sam his book.

Sam held the book and stared at the cover. "Who was Epicatus?"

"Epictetus. He was a philosopher, but before that he was a crippled slave in ancient Rome, about seventeen hundred years ago."

Sam peered skeptically at the book in the darkness. "What did a crippled dead guy teach you about war?"

Gerard leaned back and smiled. "Well, he didn't teach me about war so much as how to cope with whatever life might throw at me — like being a prisoner twice."

Sam was intrigued. "Is that why you are always so peaceful, because of the book?" He looked at the book as if it had mystical powers.

"Epictetus believed in a kind of philosophy called Stoicism. It means being able to contend with the circumstances of any life — no matter how difficult. The key is realizing that it is in your power to manage everything, that you can carry your burden. Epictetus said that every burden has two handles, one that you can carry it with and one that you can't," Gerard explained.

"What does that mean — 'carry your burden'?"

"It means that what happens to you in life, you can't control, but you can control how you respond to it. Your resolve is strong enough to take you beyond fear and to help you figure out the best way to cope with bad circumstances. Consider what you did last night, Sam. You knew that your best chance to stay alive was not to try the rope that had already broken once, and instead, to come back here and find another way to escape." Gerard spoke with certainty and respect.

"Yeah, I kind of knew that." Sam felt a flicker of pride in his chest. He had known it, deep down. He'd wanted to escape so badly he couldn't see beyond the utter desperation of the moment the rope broke. "What else does Epictetus say?" He opened the first page. He felt a surge of interest in the book, now that it had helped him see his actions in a new light.

"He says that the best way to go through life with calmness and courage is to know your strengths and weaknesses. That way, you know how to best handle any situation that you are in."

"You mean like how fast you are or how strong, things like that?"

"Those things don't matter as much as you might think," Gerard said. "Strength and weakness are more about what you are like on the inside, rather than the outside."

"So, Epictetus means you have to figure out how to carry your burden on the inside, in your head."

"Exactly, in your head or your heart. Many burdens we carry in our hearts forever." Gerard's expression changed. His ordinarily tranquil eyes reflected a pool of sadness, as if a painful memory had dislodged itself and released a fresh ripple of grief. "Every person you meet in life carries a burden, Sam. You will never know each one's story; even so, everyone has scars and pain that don't show on the outside," he glanced at Sam's right arm, "and everyone you meet has strengths and weaknesses that don't show right away."

Sam looked at Gerard as if seeing him for the first time. The painful look still held his thin, aged face. Sam felt a rush of affection and sadness for the person he'd spent so many months with, yet hardly knew at all. "Why do you keep the book if you know it by heart?" Sam said, carefully handing the book to Gerard.

"Oh, I can't imagine my life without this book," Gerard answered without hesitation. "It has helped me so many times. It's like a friend to me." He ran his finger along the spine of the book, then opened the book to the first page. "Although I had hoped, when I got back to France, to give it to my son. I went away when he was about your age."

"What's his name?"

Gerard's voice was so quiet; Sam could barely hear him. It seemed he was answering someone else's questions, not Sam's. "His name is Paul. I was forced to leave France in a hurry. I never got to explain to Elise, my wife. I sent a letter from England, but whether it ever got there or not ..." His voice trailed off. He was in an entirely different place. "When I finally got back to France, Elise had died. I don't know what happened to Paul." Gerard's fingers traced over an inscription on the page, but his eyes stared into the darkness.

"What does that say?" Sam asked quietly.

Gerard did not need to see the words. They were engraved in his heart. *"Veillez à laisser vos fils bien instruits plutôt que riche, pour les espoirs de l'instruction sont mieux que la richesse de l'ignorant.* Be careful to leave your sons well instructed rather than rich, for the hopes of the instructed are better than the wealth of the ignorant." Again, Gerard spoke as if someone else was in the room, searching for an explanation. "It means that knowledge is more valuable than money, or power. It is important to me that Paul gets the book, and that he sees the inscription. It may help him to understand some of the choices I made. Difficult choices."

"Like going to prison for printing a book you believed in?" Sam sensed that Gerard was struggling to apologize for something and let go of it at last. He could not bear the sorrow that engulfed his friend. He inched closer to Gerard and put his hand on his thin shoulder. "You'll find him. I know you will. I'll go with you, to France. We'll find him together and you can give him the book."

Gerard's smile returned, but it seemed a painful effort. "Perhaps, Sam. Perhaps. There are so many things I would like to explain." Unable to speak further, he lay down and closed his eyes. Alone in his memories and regrets.

That night, Sam was roughly awoken from his sleep by the push of Peale's boot against his leg. "Hey you, boy. Get up. You've got a new job," Peale snarled and pointed to the waste bucket by the door.

Sam followed him outside, carrying the bucket to the railing. He waited to see if Peale expected him to do any more, but Peale headed back toward Sam's cell. Did Peale realize Josiah was gone? Peale stopped at the door and a small glimmer at his neck caught Sam's eye. He squinted in the dim light. Then his stomach sank as he recognized the tiny silver disc. "Where did you get that?" Sam demanded, pointing at the medallion that hung from Peale's fat neck.

Peale shrugged. He chuckled as he twirled Josiah's medallion in his tobacco-stained fingers. "The cripple. He fell, or jumped, overboard. Must've hit the side of the boat. We found his body near the anchor line. Stupid boy — as if he could have made it to shore."

Sam felt a rage inside that almost choked him. He could barely speak. "You had no right to take that!" he growled.

"Oh, I don't, eh? A lot of good it would do him at the bottom of the bay. It'll fetch a pretty penny when I get my leave. I'm sure he would have wanted me to have it." Peale's face twisted into a mocking grin.

Blind with anger, Sam threw the bucket down and lunged toward Peale. He stumbled as he reached for the medallion and screamed, "You give that to me, you thieving, lousy pig!"

Peale stepped back and grabbed Sam by the arm. He twisted it behind Sam's back and shoved him up against the cell door, leaning in close. His rum-soaked breath made Sam's eyes water. Peale snarled, "Try that again, boy and you'll have a quick trip to join your dead friend. I'll throw you overboard and no one on this stinking ship will even notice you're gone, except maybe the old man." He pushed Sam into the cell and tossed the bucket in after him.

Gerard was asleep. Sam heard the thud of the lock closing. Grief, rage, and disbelief flooded every inch of his body. He wanted to scream, to tear through the walls of the ship, to smash his head against the floor to take away the pain he felt suffocating him. Josiah was dead. Dead. Sam had been furious and resentful, imagining Josiah laughing and reveling in his hard-won freedom, and the whole time ...! Clenching his fists to stop them from shaking, he drove his hands into his eye sockets to erase the image of Josiah's lifeless body floating in the black, unforgiving water. All Josiah's plans, his dreams — Deborah, the farm, seven children — gone. Suddenly his own anger and jealousy made him sick with guilt. If he had gone first, Sam would be the one floating in the water. A wave of nausea wrenched his stomach. He reached for the bucket and vomited, then lay on the floor, motionless. An unbearable sadness began to crush Sam like a cold fog — strangling him and taking every ounce of energy.

Although Sam's body was weak and tired, his heart and mind were strong. Stronger than he knew. He fought the despair that was threatening to pull him under and drown him. With a sharp mental gasp for rescue, he thought fiercely, *I will get that medallion and take it to Deborah Revere. I have to. I have to do it for Josiah. I need to stay alive. I need to stay strong. I need to take care of Gerard.* All those things seemed impossible, but somehow, he knew that he had to focus on something, or the cruelty of Josiah's death would be the end for him too. And without Sam, Gerard would surely succumb. Sam had to get through today. And the next day. If he could hang on a while longer, maybe another escape possibility would reveal itself. Suddenly he remembered what Gerard said the day when Sam had awakened from his delirious state and discovered that he was a prisoner on the ship. "You're still alive, you've still got hope." Sam repeated to himself like a prayer, *you're still alive, you've still got hope.* How far he had come from that day. He had resigned himself to dying on the ship until Josiah arrived. Josiah had saved his life. His determination to escape had given Sam a whole new perspective on their situation. Sam had gone from being almost paralyzed with hopelessness and self-pity, to being fueled with energy and purpose. *I must hold on to that. For Gerard. For Josiah. For me.*

The weather turned colder. Gerard was coughing less, but he was still becoming weaker every day. Without warmer clothes, he would die. Sam had to find a way to get some. Peale did not seem to possess a shred of kindness. Hodgekins was usually easygoing, almost friendly when he came to the cell. Lately though, he too had seemed angry, although not as mean as Peale. Perhaps there was a chance he would help Sam.

Instead of waiting for Peale to come get him, the next time Sam heard Hodgekins' voice on the deck, he called out, "Sir, the bucket in here is full. I'll dump it now." No response. He waited a minute, then called out again, a little louder. Soon he heard a shuffling and then the click of the lock as the door was pushed open from the other side.

Eyes half-closed, Hodgekins was leaning heavily against the door, reeking of rum. He had not shaved in several days and his uniform was wrinkled and spotted.

He's drunk. Sam thought about grabbing Hodgekins' gun and trying to overpower him, but quickly realized that it was too risky. He'd never get past the other soldiers, and he'd have to leave Gerard behind. Instead, Sam pretended not to notice Hodgekins' inebriated state. Casually picking up the bucket, he walked over to the other side of the ship. The cold air felt good — it cleared his head and sharpened his focus. Sam emptied the bucket over the side and scanned the harbor, taking in as much as he could see without drawing suspicion. Not much had changed, although there seemed to be more British ships. He walked back to Hodgekins to ask, "Should I empty the other buckets now, too?"

Hodgekins mumbled and nodded toward another cell. Pulling the keys from his pocket, he stumbled and nearly fell over a coiled rope. "Here." He shoved the keys toward Sam, then fell against the mast pole for support.

Sam was astonished that Hodgekins would hand a prisoner his set of keys. He kept his face neutral and opened the cell door. The stench was terrible. There were a dozen or so prisoners in this room, but they were so weak and dazed they barely noticed him. Sam quickly found the bucket, trying not to breathe the noxious air too deeply.

Up on deck, Hodgekins was slumped against the mast pole, mumbling to himself. "Bloody corpses. Bloody ghosts," Hodgekins muttered. It looked like he was about to start crying.

Something in Sam's gut told him this might be an opening to another way of escape. As he handed the keys back, Sam saw that Hodgekins' hands were shaking. Sam almost felt sorry for the disheveled soldier. *He's not much older than me. He probably wants to get home as much as I do.*

"Corpses, corpses. Bloody ghosts."

Sam took a chance. "Are you all right?"

"I hate 'em. Rolling them up and sending 'em to shore. It's not what I signed up to do," Hodgekins answered rapidly, almost as if he were confessing a crime.

"Why do you have to do it?"

"They sent more soldiers into Boston. Things are heating up. So now I have to get rid of the bodies. Gives me the bloody shivers." Hodgekins closed his eyes and winced.

A spark flashed in Sam's mind. This was the chance he'd been waiting for. He tried not to sound too eager. "That seems like a lot for one person, especially someone who has to guard all the prisoners. Maybe I could help you."

Hodgekins squinted, eyeing him skeptically. "Now why would you want to do that? Are you going to jump overboard like the cripple?"

Sam thought quickly, saying, "No. I'm not in a hurry to drown. I could use more food, and another blanket for the old man. If you can help me with those things, I'll help you with the bodies."

The weary sergeant continued to watch Sam, pondering his offer. He closed his eyes and nodded. "All right. But keep quiet about it. You can start tonight."

Sam could hardly believe his good luck. The thought of moving dead bodies didn't bother him half as much as it would have six months ago. Sam knew he had to do whatever it took to keep himself and Gerard alive.

That night, Sam heard a quiet tap on the door as the lock slowly turned. Hodgekins, carrying a stack of folded sheets, motioned with his head to the other room. Sam followed him, careful not to show his familiarity with what was in there. Three men had died that day. The bodies were lying near the doorway, already stiff from rigor mortis. Two were older men, about Sam's father's age. The third was a young man, maybe sixteen.

Hodgekins laid a sheet on the floor. He pulled the taller corpse onto the edge of the sheet and then rolled it up into a narrow bundle. He tucked the flaps under at each end, looking ill and miserable the whole time. His voice was almost pleading as he handed Sam a sheet. "Think you can do the next one?"

Sam nodded. He knelt down beside the second corpse and took a deep breath. Stretching the sheet alongside the body, he lifted and rolled it like Hodgekins had, tucking in the ends. He glanced at Hodgekins, who was sitting with his eyes closed. Sam moved over to the body of the younger man. He was so thin, he weighed almost nothing. Sam stared at his face before pulling the body onto the sheet. He looked so peaceful; like he had died in the middle of a good dream. *I wonder where he's from? His clothes are well made — he must be from a wealthy family. They'll never see him again. He was probably eager to go off and fight the British. Like Eamon.* Sam felt a little sick. Where was his friend now? *Is someone rolling Eamon up in a sheet, preparing to dump him in a nameless grave somewhere?*

"Best not to think about it too much." Hodgekins' voice broke into Sam's thoughts. "It will make you crazy faster."

"Yeah, you're probably right." Sam swallowed hard and rolled the body up into a tight bundle. They carried the bodies up to the deck and then put them into a small rowboat that was rigged to the side of the ship. Sam silently took in every detail. "Where do they go?" he asked casually.

"Rowed to shore in the morning. Buried nearby," Hodgekins mumbled.

Hodgekins was true to his word. As Sam went back into his own cell, Hodgekins handed him a sack with bread and dried meat inside.

The next few weeks fell into a pattern of sorts. Sam would dump the waste buckets each evening and every third night he would roll up corpses; then he and Hodgekins would move the bundles into boats. Hodgekins was so relieved to be free of the onerous task that he began to treat Sam with a certain amount of kindness. In addition to the extra food he brought Sam, he also found two thick blankets and a coat for Gerard. Gerard slept most of the day now, but he seemed more comfortable. Sam was grateful for Hodgekins' help. An odd friendship grew between them. Hodgekins returned to his cheerful self and began his strange humming again.

One night, Hodgekins was very talkative. He told Sam about his village in England and how he planned to return there once his service was complete. "Aye, three more years I owe to the Crown and then I'm done and good. I'll buy me a little farm, find a wife and settle down with all me bees."

"Your boys?" Sam asked. "How can you be sure you'll have sons?"

"Bees, not boys." Hodgekins laughed. "I'm going to raise bees. Maybe boys too, but first bees."

"Why bees?"

"Bees are amazing creatures. They're smart, they work hard, and they're right gentle, beautiful things."

"I never knew," Sam said, wondering if Hodgekins was about to start singing, or crying. He was so worked up about bees.

"Yes, sir. I'll be the best beekeeper in Dover — surrounded by flowers and honey. No more ships, no more marching, and no more stiffs." He finished with a shudder.

Sam's curiosity got the best of him. "Why do you hate rolling up the corpses so much?"

Hodgekins stared across the water as if expecting some of the bodies he'd dumped to come out of the black waves to seek revenge on their pitiless endings. "My Pa worked for the pastor in our village. Pa was a drunk and the pastor was the only one who would give the old man a job, digging graves in the church cemetery. But he never dug a single grave — I did. I dug them all — during the night so no one else would see. And if I didn't finish, Pa would lock me in the holding shed with the dead bodies. I sure learned to dig fast by the time I was about ten years old." His eyes darkened at the memory. "When Mum died, that was it. Hers was one grave I wasn't going to dig. I ran away. Lived on the streets a few years, till I was old enough to join the army —" A bitter laugh cut his sentence short. "And here I am."

Sam nodded slowly. "I don't blame you."

A relaxed silence settled between them, each immersed in their own thoughts. Sam winced at the image of a terrified little boy cowering alone next to a dead body. *Poor Hodgekins. I guess that's what Gerard means by scars on the inside.*

A few nights later, sounds of fireworks, muskets, and songs reached their cell. Hodgekins came quietly into the room long after the last rounds of the day. He carried a wooden bowl, steaming and full to the brim with stew. He pulled a spoon from his coat pocket and stood awkwardly. "Here," he said, handing the bowl and spoon to Sam.

"Thank you," said Sam, his eyes widening as he realized that the vaguely-familiar scent he was smelling was meat — it had been so long since he'd had any.

"Well, uh. Merry Christmas," Hodgekins said quietly.

"So that's what all the racket was about." Gerard smiled as he struggled to sit up. "Merry Christmas to you."

"Yeah, Merry Christmas, and I'm leaving. A new group of guards will be coming in." Hodgekins' voice dropped to a whisper. "Thought you'd want to know — word has come back from England. King George rejected the *Olive Branch Petition.* He issued a *Proclamation of Rebellion* — he called the colonists traitors. So, you may be in for a harder time of it." Hodgekins sighed heavily, looking nervously around the small room, as though he was struggling with what to do next. Then he reached back into his coat pocket and tossed something onto the blanket. It was Josiah's medallion.

Sam lifted the chain and watched the tiny orb spin. He turned to Hodgekins with an unspoken question in his eyes.

Hodgekins stared at the floor. "I won it off Peale in a dice game. Figure you should have it — the cripple seemed like a good kid."

"Thank you," Sam murmured again as he rubbed the medallion with his thumb.

"You are an honorable man, sir," Gerard said, nodding at Hodgekins.

Hodgekins lifted his head and stood up taller — as if a great weight had been taken from him. He looked Gerard in the eye and returned the nod. He walked back to the door and then turned around. "I hope you both make it through the war. If you ever come to Dover, ask for Hodgekins the Beekeeper."

The door closed. Sam handed the bowl to Gerard. "You first. Merry Christmas, Gerard."

Gerard held the bowl for a moment and breathed deeply. "And *Joyeux Noel* to you."

Between them, the bowl was empty within minutes, leaving them both with the strange sensation of a full stomach after months of near-starvation.

"Christmas." Sam said quietly, "This will be a sad one for my parents. They probably think I'm dead."

"You'll have many more Christmases with them, Sam. I feel certain of that."

"Not unless we can figure out another way to escape."

"You'll figure something out — I feel certain of that too." Gerard leaned back and closed his eyes. His breathing was labored, but a soft note crept into his voice. "Ahhh, *Noel*. My mother would spend two weeks preparing for that one meal. *Cannelés, pain d'épice, soupe de marron, paon rôti à la crème sure.*" Gerard smiled at Sam. "Fluted honey cakes, gingerbread, chestnut soup, roasted peacock with sour cream. And," he nodded seriously, "the star of the table was the *cassoulet*."

"What's *cassoulet?*"

"*Cassoulet* is a peasant dish that is fit for a king: duck, beans, sage, thyme, and a pork sausage you can only find in Toulouse. I've heard in Carcassonne they use mutton, but they don't know any better, poor fools. It's all cooked together slowly — you must break the crust seven times while it bakes. It takes a lot of patience and love to make a proper *cassoulet*." He took a deep breath, as if he was back in front of his mother's stove. "It's a torturously long day for a hungry boy. But when it's ready, the angels in Heaven would trade their wings for one bowl."

For the first time, Sam heard a whisper of Gerard's French accent. He smiled. "You sound like our hired man Jim, talking about maple syrup."

"Food is one of the greatest joys in life, Sam. Never take it for granted. What does your family eat for Christmas?"

Now it was Sam's turn to sigh dreamily. "Roasted venison or pork, potatoes, corn pudding, and Ma's spoonbread. I don't know what she puts in it that makes it so different from others I've tasted, but it's something special."

They spoke quietly for a few more minutes about Christmases past — feeling a sadness for what was lost and the dark uncertainty of what lay ahead. Sam stared at the ceiling and wondered what the new year would bring. Would he live through it? Could he and Gerard escape? And would he ever make it back to Machias and his family?

CHAPTER 6

Common Sense

February 15, 1776
Boston Harbor

The new year brought harsh changes. A blast of raw weather, and as Hodgekins had promised, a new group of guards. These men were much sterner and more hardened than Hodgekins and his fellow soldiers had been. Sam's "jobs" disappeared and with them his only opportunities to see what was happening on the rest of the ship and on the shore.

The cold weather turned the dank room into a teeth-chattering icebox. Sam was not sure if the small stove in their cell even worked. The extra blankets and coat that Hodgekins had found for Gerard were not enough. Gerard grew weaker and soon barely had the strength to sit up. Without his glasses, he could not read his book anymore, but he liked to hold it and brush his thumb against the worn cover — as if it were enough to reach the words inside. Sam wished he could read French; he knew that hearing the ancient words of Epictetus would comfort his friend.

After a week of bitter cold, a guard brought in a small bundle of wood and a burning stick. He opened the creaky iron door of the stove and pushed the branches inside. "There!" He slammed the stove door shut and grumbled, "We're not supposed to let you freeze to death."

As the small fire took hold and began to ease the frozen air, Sam gently helped Gerard to his feet, so he could lay by the weak heat that emanated from the stove. Once he was settled, Sam moved his own blanket closer. He wanted to ask Gerard what the guard had meant, but Gerard had fallen asleep again. Sam stared at the small flames flickering through the sooty grate of the stove door. *Why is Gerard so important to the British? He said it had something to do with his family in France. But he's a bookseller. He's not a general or anything. Maybe his son is in the French military?* Sam tried to keep the fire as small as possible, to make the stack of wood last longer. By the next day they were down to a few branches.

When the guard came in that night with their soup, Sam asked for more wood. Ignoring Sam, the guard simply slammed the door as he left. Sam decided it was time to burn the rope they had made. He cut it into smaller pieces and pushed a few into the stove. *Well, at least it turned out to be useful for something. I wouldn't have trusted its strength on another escape attempt. But once this runs out, we won't last more than a day or two in this cold.* When the door opened the next morning, Sam jumped up from his blanket, determined to get more wood.

Two guards entered, each carrying a large sack. They threw the sacks against the wall. "Here, burn this. It's complete rubbish," one snarled over his shoulder as he walked back out.

"Aye," the other said angrily, "he should be hung twice — once for treason and once for sedition!"

Sam reached into the sack and pulled out a handful of papers. They were pamphlets, hundreds of them, tied together in bundles. Sam had seen lots of pamphlets in Machias. Short in length, quick and inexpensive to print, they were the easiest way to spread news and political ideas. He read the cover out loud to Gerard.

COMMON SENSE;

ADDRESSED TO THE

INHABITANTS

OF

AMERICA

On the following interesting

SUBJECTS.

I. Of the Origin and Design of Government in general, with concise Remarks on the English Constitution.

II. Of Monarchy and Hereditary Succession.

III. Thoughts on the present State of American Affairs.

IV. Of the present Ability of America, with some miscellaneous Reflections.

Sam flipped through the pamphlet. "It's a long one — looks like about fifty pages. Well, they are a little damp, but should give us a few more days," Sam said, as he pushed a few stacks into the stove.

"Sam, let me see that," Gerard said, reaching over for one of the pamphlets. He held it as far from his eyes as possible, squinting, then giving it back. "No, it's impossible. You must be my eyes. Read this to me, please."

Sam unfolded the paper and began to read. "Perhaps the sentiments contained in the following pages, are not yet sufficiently fashionable to procure them general favor; a long habit of not thinking a thing wrong, gives it a superficial appearance of being right, and raises at first a formidable outcry in defense of custom. But the tumult soon subsides. Time makes more converts than reason. As a long and violent abuse of power is generally the Means of calling the right of it in question (and in matters too which might never have been thought of, had not the Sufferers been aggravated into the inquiry) and as the King of England hath undertaken in his own Right, to support the Parliament in what he call Theirs, and as the good people of this country are grievously oppressed by the combination, they have an undoubted privilege to inquire into the pretensions of both and equally to reject the usurpation of either." He stopped. "Should I keep reading?"

For a moment, with eyes closed, Gerard did not say a word. Then, though he lay still, his voice was alert and interested. "Yes, yes, please continue."

Sam read the entire pamphlet. He didn't understand many of the words, but the author railed against King George, Parliament, and the entire British monarchy. No name appeared on the cover except for *Written by an Englishman*. Sam looked at Gerard, incredulous at what he had read. "The author, the Englishman, he wants the American colonies to break completely from England and form a new country?"

Gerard's voice rang with excitement. "Yes! It's extraordinary!"

Sam fanned the pages. "Well, for an Englishman, he sure hates King George. Wherever Eamon is, I hope he can read this.

He would love this guy." Sam grinned.

Gerard struggled to sit up. He reached for the pamphlet and held it out, again laboring to read the cover. "Common sense, indeed! This is it, Sam!" Gerard exclaimed happily. "This is the voice that is needed — for all the people sitting on the fence, not sure about the way forward, yet definitely not wanting to go back to living under the old rules. Anyone whose will to fight is fading will be inspired. America doesn't need England to prosper. This pamphlet, these ideas — *Common Sense* will unite the colonies!"

"Do you honestly think a pamphlet can change the outcome of the war?" Sam was not convinced.

"I do. Absolutely. This writer, whoever he is, will change more than the course of the war, he will change the course of history!"

Sam frowned. "I don't know, Gerard. Defeating the British still seems impossible to me. How can an army of farmers and shopkeepers defeat the strongest nation in the world? It's not logical."

A new energy seemed to take hold of Gerard. "If human actions were based purely on logic," he said adamantly, "the future might seem truly dismal. But we have more than logic — we can imagine and hope. Isn't that what dreaming is, after all?"

"Well, sometimes I dream about my family, and my mother's spoonbread," Sam said wistfully.

"That is one kind of a dream," Gerard agreed, "our memories and desires mixed together in a state of semi-consciousness. However, dreaming when we are awake, dreaming about the *future*, is something only humans can do. We can dream, we can plan and we can work. Other species certainly plan and work — if you have ever seen a beaver dam, an ant hill, or a beehive — you know that. But their direction comes from a survival instinct that is inborn and unchangeable. Every person on this earth is capable of imagining a better life *and* moving toward it. We are not sustained by merely a desire to survive; we are sustained by the conviction of our dreams and the unspoken belief that our ideas *are* possible!" Gerard's voice, filled with passion and reverence, seemed to come from a different body. His bony frame was tense with excitement, then suddenly slipped back into exhaustion. He studied Sam's doubtful face. "*Common Sense* will give America both — hope and imagination. Read it again. You'll see." He closed his eyes, and smiling, fell into a peaceful sleep.

Sam moved to the window where the light was strongest and read the pamphlet two more times. For the rest of the day, the words from *Common Sense* circled in his head. He was determined to understand what the author was saying.

As soon as Gerard woke up, Sam was brimming with questions. "So, in part one, when he talks about society and government, it says 'Society in every state is a blessing, but government, even in its best state, is but a necessary evil.' I think what he means is that society, people living together and wanting to be safer, came from mankind's good intentions, and that the need for government comes from mankind's bad intentions." Sam looked up from the page. "Is that correct?"

"Yes, that is how I understood it. And what, according to our English friend, is government's purpose?"

Sam thought for a moment. "To protect people, and the laws and property. I guess he thinks that if a government isn't doing that, they are not doing their job. Well, what did King George send the British army here to protect us from? We wanted the same laws as the people in England have, nothing more. Sending soldiers has made it worse, not safer."

Gerard nodded and asked, "What about the second part that addresses the monarchy? Will you read that to me again?"

"Of Monarchy and Hereditary Succession…" Sam finished the section.

"Quite remarkable," Gerard said appreciatively.

"This is what you were telling Josiah and me about — how kings get to rule simply because they were born to a certain family, no matter if they are stupid or cruel, and that the people are the ones who suffer the consequences of a King's bad decisions. This part is good — 'One of the strongest natural proofs of the folly of hereditary right of kings is that nature disapproves it, otherwise she would not so frequently turn it into ridicule by giving mankind an ass for a lion.' Ha ha!" Sam chuckled.

"Interesting that he includes so many references to the Bible," Gerard said.

"So even though it is called the 'Divine Right of Kings,' the author doesn't believe that God or the Bible would approve of the monarchy, correct?"

"Exactly. It's very effective — the quotations from the Bible make it easier for the larger population of the colonies, most of whom are familiar with the Bible, to understand what he is saying. Have you read many political pamphlets?" Gerard asked.

Sam shrugged. "No. Usually they are full of Latin and stuff I don't understand."

"Most people feel the same way about the pamphlets written by Mr. Adams, Mr. Dickerson, and such. Their style of writing and references are often lost on the common man. This writer has a style that is entirely different. He is writing for farmers, not philosophers. Very interesting, very interesting. I wonder ..." He stared at the cover.

"You wonder what?" Sam pressed.

"I met a man in England. Mr. Franklin introduced us. Unfortunately, I have forgotten his name. He spoke about similar things, and with a fiery passion. Much like this author. Well, no matter. Let's look at the next section. 'The State of American Affairs.' Tell me what you think of that," Gerard prompted.

Sam lowered his voice slightly, as if he feared someone else was listening. "I've never heard anyone say such things about

King George before. He calls him a 'crowned ruffian'! Like I said, he and Eamon would get along well."

"They would indeed." Gerard laughed, then his face grew serious. "The author is helping the reader make the most important break."

"Breaking from England?"

"Breaking from King George. Have you noticed that the colonists who support the war are very resentful and angry toward Parliament, yet they still hold a certain loyalty toward the King?"

"Not Eamon," Sam murmured.

Gerard tilted his head in agreement. "Not Eamon, but many. It is a strong bond all Englishmen share — affection for the King and seeing him as a protective, kind father to his colonies. Our friend," he tapped the pamphlet, "has pointed out that in reality, that bond was shattered the minute British troops fired on the militia at Lexington."

Sam whistled softly. "I never thought about it like that, but you're right, he's right. The troops would not have come to America without the King's permission. And he did call us traitors."

Gerard stroked his beard thoughtfully. "Now, every colonist can abandon both King and country with a clean conscience. Not only that, he cleverly points out how much better off America would be — in trade, in military affairs, in foreign affairs — without the burden of England's 'protection.' What comes next?"

Sam read a few pages aloud, and then commented. "We make our own country. I mean, we start a new one. The author thinks we should govern ourselves, that each colony should be represented equally — if we're all in it together." Sam's face was a mix of wonder and uncertainty.

Gerard's showed no skepticism. "Yes. His suggestions are quite reasonable, I think. He's offering a glimpse of what is possible; what lies beyond the war."

"But we have to *win* the war," Sam let out a discouraged huff, "which still seems *not* possible!"

"I believe the last section addresses that, as well, does it not?"

The last few pages of the pamphlet had charts and mathematical equations on how much it would cost the colonies to build ships and a navy. The section talked about all the vast natural supplies available to the colonies — timber, iron, tar.

Sam nodded as he read aloud. "We ought to view the building of a fleet as an article of commerce ... it is the best money we can lay out." Looking up at Gerard intently, he said, "That does make sense. And if we defeat the British, other countries will respect us and want to trade with us. Then Britain cannot threaten or entangle us with her wars and foreign interventions anymore."

Gerard nodded. He reached into the sack and pulled out a handful of the pamphlets, flipping them absentmindedly. "Sam, can you help me up? I should like to see out the window before the sun goes down."

Sam jumped to his feet and held Gerard's arm, carefully pulling him up. Gerard steadied himself, then walked slowly to the small window. He stared at the dark outline of Boston; the pointy spires of the churches caught the last rays of sun. Then he held the pamphlet out again, trying in vain to read the cover. "What is the publication date on this?"

"January tenth," Sam answered.

Gerard's gaze returned to the city. "Astonishing, truly astonishing. I imagine these are all over the country by now. No name. Of course, the British will be eager to catch whoever wrote it. And to punish him. What courage!"

"It seems strange to think of writing a pamphlet as courageous."

"It took moral courage, which is different than what we usually think of as courageous," Gerard explained. "Physical courage is an instinctive, spontaneous reaction to something threatening. Moral courage, standing up for your beliefs, means you have more time to think about the consequences, yet you still choose to go forward. This man, speaking truth to the power of the British government — very bold. No wonder they want to destroy these."

"I won't burn any more," Sam vowed solemnly. "It's like burning something sacred."

Gerard leaned against the wall for support. While his strength was clearly fading, his voice was as resolute as ever. "Burn them. Knowledge is power, Sam. And as long as you keep the knowledge that this writing has brought you alive somehow — in your memory, in your actions — you will never lose that power. Once ideas are out, they can't be destroyed."

Sam said quietly, "I will remember it, and I do understand what he proposes. It doesn't make sense for us to be a colony. We need to fight and we need to win. But it all doesn't make a difference to you and me — stuck here, rotting away."

Gerard continued to contemplate the distant harbor as if seeking to hold fast to the vision before the impatient night transformed it to black. "It makes a difference to you, because you are going to escape."

"How?" Sam lifted his hands and shrugged. "We've burned the rope, which wouldn't have worked anyway. The only way we can leave this ship will be as corpses."

Gerard glanced out the window one last time. He sighed deeply, then turned away. "We are not escaping; you are." His eyes serenely focused on Sam.

Sam shook his head. "I'm not going without you."

"Sam, be realistic. I'm going to die soon. You must know that. And when I do, you need to be ready to leave too. You'll know what to do when the time comes."

"Don't talk like that, Gerard. I can't listen." Sam's voice faltered.

"I am not saying it will be easy, but you can do it. Whatever happens, it can't be worse than dying slowly here. You must face your fears and do what you have to do — get off this ship and on with your life."

"You're thinking about my life? I don't understand how you can be so calm. Gerard, aren't you afraid to die?"

Gerard slowly lowered himself back down to his blanket. He reached underneath and pulled out his book. He held it in his hand, as if the book would answer Sam's question instead. "I am a little sad. I would like to have seen my son again and explain some things. But Sam, my life has been happier than I ever had the right to expect — a joyful marriage, a healthy child, work that I loved and was proud of, the companionship and respect of true friends, including one who gave me a most precious farewell gift."

"Who is that?"

"You." Gerard's peaceful smile returned.

"What did I give you?" Sam looked around the barren room.

"Faith. I know you will get out of here. I know you will grow into a good man. I know you will make the most out of the kind of life you can have, once this revolution is won. And that makes it easier to say good-bye." Gerard brought the worn book to his lips, and whispered, "Promise me you'll take good care of the book. If you ever go to France, please take it to Paul." He lay back in the straw.

As darkness filled the room, Sam sat, legs pulled up, arms crossed and resting on his knees. His head felt heavy — full of questions and doubt — and at last dropped wearily on his arms. Then Gerard's steady voice broke into his thoughts. "And Sam, find him, and thank him."

Sam lifted his head. "Paul? Yes, of course. Thank him for what?"

"No, the Englishman. Whoever wrote this pamphlet. You must find him and thank him."

For the next three days, Gerard would not eat, insisting instead that Sam take his food. On the fourth day, he developed a fever and began talking in French. His frail body shivered and trembled. He kept repeating the same thing, *"Je suis désolé! Je suis désolé!"*

Sam tried to comfort him with quiet words. Finally, the delirium stopped and he was silent. Sam moved Gerard as close as possible to the stove and sat cross-legged next to him. He draped his blanket across his shoulders, trying to use it as a shield between the freezing air and Gerard. He balled his fists and silently pounded the floor in anguish. Although Sam could not see if Gerard's chest still rose and fell, he heard the soft push of his feeble breath, fighting against the cold air. Tears flowed down Sam's face and his breath hovered tightly in his chest. A sob escaped as he exhaled.

Gerard's hand searched along the floor until he found Sam's clenched hands. Gently pressing down on them, Gerard opened his eyes. "Sam, don't feel sorry for me. I'm not afraid. I'm ready. You're ready, too. Ready to live. Face your fears, know your strengths." Gerard's eyes closed again as he whispered, "Thank you, son, for your friendship."

The silence that followed Gerard's death reached in and gripped Sam's heart completely. He sat for several hours, holding Gerard's hand, now cold and still. Suddenly the world seemed dimmer, like one strong and steady light had been extinguished. He felt more alone and frightened than ever before in his life, more than when he had awakened to find himself a prisoner. Sam realized how much comfort Gerard's presence had given him during those first terrible days. He wanted to curl up in a ball and stop thinking. All the courage and exhilaration he'd felt while planning to escape with Josiah was replaced by a bleak, heavy fear that sat in his stomach like rotten meat.

Tears filled Sam's eyes again as he looked down on the

motionless body. Gerard's features, made gaunt from hunger and sickness, now looked peaceful. Gerard had not feared death; he only regretted the good-byes he could not say. Sam stared for a long time, then reached over to take the small brown book from Gerard's hand. The leather cover felt smooth and soft as Sam rubbed his fingers against it. He turned to the back page where Gerard had written his son's address:

Paul Michael Sidos
Rue d'Allemange, Rouen

Sam held the book. *I wonder if Paul is still in the same town, or even still alive. Well, that's a long way off — getting to France, finding Paul. First, I have to get off this ship.*

He had promised Gerard that he would escape the *Preston*. He had promised himself that he would return Josiah's medallion to Deborah. He had promised Eamon that he would look after Mrs. Collins. His father's words came back to Sam. "Responsibility is keeping promises. Promises you make to others and yourself." He had no choice. If nothing else, he would die knowing that he had tried. As soon as he made his decision, Sam felt his body relax, and a composed determination seemed to replace the sadness and fear that had overwhelmed him. It was time to go back to the world of the living.

Sam knew what Gerard wanted him to do, and that he probably would have enjoyed the performance that was about to take place. He stood up and took in a deep breath, glanced at his friend once more, and smiled. Then he began to scream at the top of his lungs. He howled and cursed and pounded his fists against the door. At first the guards ignored him, immersed in whatever card or dice game they were playing. But as his tirade continued, they finally sent one soldier down to end it. "What's all the bloody fuss about, you wretched boy?" the soldier growled as he walked into the cell.

Sam grabbed the soldier's arm, his eyes wide with terror. "He's dead! He's dead! You've got to get him out of here! I'm afraid of spirits!!"

The soldier threw Sam off his arm and peered at Gerard. He gave him a slight push with his foot.

Sam clutched the soldier's arm again — rolling his head and shaking. "You have to take him out. I can't stay in here with him!"

"Shut up, boy. He's dead. He's not going to hurt you!"

Sam continued to wail. "He's looking at me. I'm afraid. His ghost will come and steal my soul! Ahhhhh!" He fell to his knees.

The soldier was torn between impatience and fear of doing the wrong thing. He could care less about Sam being hysterical, but at this rate no one on the ship would get any sleep if the screams continued. "Be quiet, you fool! No one's taking your soul," the soldier snapped.

Sam began to rock back and forth — still wailing with all the energy he could muster. Disgusted, the guard shook his head and walked out. He returned a minute later carrying a burial sheet. He walked over to Gerard's body and rolled it up into the sheet, like Sam had done so many times before with other prisoners. Then he pulled the body over to the door.

"There!" The guard threw a withering glare at Sam. "He's not looking at you now. We'll get him tomorrow. Now shut up and go to sleep." He slammed the door behind him.

Sam waited until there were no sounds outside before carefully unrolling the sheet. He gently lifted Gerard's thin body and moved it over to his own straw pile. He removed the thick coat that Hodgekins had given him. Now for the shirt. Sam gasped and flinched away from the body. Gerard's chest, back, and right arm were hardened with the tight, shiny clench of old burn scars. Sam stared in horror and sadness. What could have caused such terrible injuries?

Sam took the ragged blue cloth that he wore around his head at night and wrapped it around Gerard's head. He kissed the cold skin. "I'll miss you, my friend. I hope they serve *cassoulet* in heaven."

He pulled his blanket over the body, almost covering the head, and turned it toward the wall. Gerard was smaller and thinner than Sam, but from the doorway the body under the blanket looked enough like Sam's that a guard probably would not give it a second glance. Moving quickly, Sam wrapped up the book as tightly as possible with the oilcloth and then cut a strip from the edge of the blanket. He held the book against his stomach and wrapped the blanket strip twice around his waist, covering that with his trousers. Next, he pulled up the floor board where Josiah had carved the map. Squinting in the darkness, he tried to memorize it one last time. Hudson's Point. Ann Street. The Mill Pond. After putting the board back, he searched under the straw pile for his tin cup knife and Josiah's sewing kit. He put the knife in his front pocket and then threaded one of the needles from the kit. Sam gave the medallion around his neck a quick tug to make sure it was secure, and then lay down on the burial sheet by the door and grasped the frayed edge with shaking fingers. He rolled himself up, leaving a small space for air near his mouth, and arm movement. Then, from inside, he pushed and pulled the needle to create a seam. It wasn't strong, but it would prevent the sheet from unrolling while being moved.

Now all he had to do was wait. The guards would come in the morning, put the bundle into the rowboat and take it to shore. After that, Sam didn't know what would happen. He wished he had asked Hodgekins more questions. Where did they take the bodies? Did they actually bury them, or just dump them into a hole? If he was buried, there wouldn't be much time to dig his way out. He lay still, his heart pounding against his chest like a trapped bird. Gerard's last words came back to him. "Face your fears, know your strengths." *Well, what am I afraid of? I'm afraid of being discovered. I'm afraid of laying in the corpse room for days. I'm afraid of suffocating before I dig myself out of the grave. I'm afraid I won't be able to find the Reveres' farm.* Sam had to laugh at himself. *No shortage of fears, that's for sure. But what are my strengths? Am I braver than when I came here? Probably. Am I more determined to live? Yes. Would I rather die than stay another day on this horrible ship? Yes. Even if I die trying, I will have been free for a few moments, and that is worth dying for.*

Sam began to think about being free again. After he'd brought the medallion to Deborah Revere, he'd have to figure out a way to get to Machias. Home — to his parents, to be safe and taken care of. The thought of seeing his parents again brought an ache to Sam's heart that felt like a punch. He closed his eyes and could picture it all perfectly — the river, the mill, his house, his bed. The images turned slowly in his mind and despite his nerves, the sheer exhaustion of the past few days took over and Sam drifted off to sleep.

"There he is. What should we do?"

Sam's eyes opened with a jolt. He recognized the voice of the guard who had rolled up Gerard's body. From inside the shroud, Sam could feel the ship being pounded by strong waves.

"Bloody hell — we were supposed to keep this one alive. All right, let's tie it up," another voice spoke with exasperation.

How could I have fallen asleep?! The bundle of sheet around him tightened at both ends.

The first guard spoke again. "I'm not rowing to shore in this storm. Let's get rid of it."

The sheet was lifted and pulled taut around Sam's head, blurring his eyes and pressing the rough cloth into his face. The stench of it made him almost gag. He held his breath and tried to stiffen his body — to seem more like a corpse. The shifting cloth rubbed against his ears, creating a muffled sound like the dulled roll of breaking surf.

"He's heavy for an old man," snarled the guard holding the far end of the bundle.

"Yeah. Still not much of a meal for the fish who will come to his funeral!" The other guard let out a harsh laugh.

What does that mean? Where are they taking me? Sam felt himself hoisted up the ladder and then suddenly they were outside. The wind was blowing hard. The urge to fill his lungs with fresh air, after months in the dank cell, was overwhelming. But he continued to be as still as possible. Thunder crashed and waves slammed against the side of the ship. Sam felt himself swaying slightly, then suddenly all movement stopped, and he was suspended, motionless. He clenched his hands. Hot, racing fear coursed through his veins. *What are they doing? Are they going to put me in the rowboat? Are they suspicious?* The next thing he heard made his blood turn cold.

"Make sure you throw him far enough. The last two crashed on the rocks over there and made a right mess."

"Yeah, yeah," the first guard grumbled impatiently. "Let's go. Au revoir, old man. One! Two! Three!"

Before Sam could even register their words, his wrapped body was swinging back and forth, then flying out into the air. Time seemed to stop as he felt himself arching up, then plummeting down. He let out a cry when he hit the water — too surprised by the impact and the ice-cold temperature to stifle it. When the sheet rested on the surface for a single moment, he took a deep breath. Rapidly, the tight bundle began to sink. Sam dug into his pocket and grasped the tin cup knife. Pulling the knife as hard as he could against the fabric, he prayed that he had not sewn a seam so tight that this would be *his* burial shroud. Like a white ghost, the sheet twisted in a sickening spiral as it continued to drop. Sam felt woozy. He could not hold his breath much longer. With one last tug, the sheet suddenly opened up and he was loose. He kicked his legs violently, turning his head up toward the surface, and gritting his teeth to keep from gasping. His lungs were on fire — demanding air as the freezing water seemed to burn him at the same time.

With one great push, he burst through to the surface, sucked in a huge breath, and dove under again. Lightning flashed across the night sky. Rain pelted his face when he came up for air. He began to swim away from the ship, but the heavy coat was pulling him down. He shrugged it off, knowing he would miss it dearly in the next few days. Checking to make sure Gerard's book had survived the impact, he continued. The water was choppy, and the wind pushed against it, making it difficult to spot someone in the waves, but also making it harder for Sam to see where he was going. He swam as quickly as he could, keeping his head under the water except to draw quick breaths and get a glimpse ahead. The adrenaline of the last few minutes seeped out of his body. His toes and fingers began to lose feeling as a bone-chilling exhaustion took over. Sam tried to remember how it felt to swim in the pond near his house in Machias, but even his brain seemed to be going numb. *Come on!* Sam berated himself. *You're almost there! This is NOT where you are supposed to die, Samuel Nevens!*

He could now see the Long Wharf to his left. *Josiah said the creek was how many wharves down? Three? Four? What else did he say?* Sam closed his eyes against the punishing waves, struggling to conjure up the map carved into the floorboard. *Four!* He blinked, eyes stinging with saltwater, and counted the wharves as he swam. He pushed harder, refusing to give in to the insistent grip of the ocean. Finally, he bumped against the slick wooden beams of the wharf. *There's the tunnel!* A few feet from him, a small boat bobbed wildly against the fierce waves. Sam pulled himself in, and then tugged with his numb hands at the rope holding the slender craft to the dock. He mumbled a silent prayer of thanks as the rope gave way easily. Crouching low in the boat, he pushed with one of the oars through the tunnel. Now, to cross the Mill Pond. The dam came into view. He rowed toward the shore and tumbled out onto land.

Teeth chattering and legs trembling, he dragged the boat out of the water. Sam leaned over with his hands on his knees. For a second, he allowed himself to feel the first breath of freedom he'd known in nine months. All that lay behind him and all that lay ahead receded from his mind as a powerful swell of confidence and pride took over. *I did it! I did it! It worked!! Gerard was right — I did have the courage to go through with it!* Relief and a giddy sensation bubbled up inside him. He dragged the boat a little farther up on shore, then clambered up the side of the dam. Josiah's aunt's house was so close, a few steps away, on the other side. *Almost there. Almost there.*

Rain continued to lash down on Sam. He wiped it from his eyes with shaky hands. The cold was taking over. He could barely think straight. He could see a mill, and a house, but the house was completely dark. Was it deserted? Sam's heart sank. Fear and desperation creeped in. He kept moving — thinking that at any kind of shelter would be a relief. He approached the house first, and knocked on the door. *Even if someone is home, I probably look like a spirit — standing here all skin and bones with my clothes barely clinging to me.* "Hello? Hello?" He tried the door. It was locked. He walked around toward the back. The garden was frozen and dead, but even seeing the empty cornstalks made Sam's stomach twist with hunger. He reached the back door — also locked. He saw a cellar door — most cellars had ladders going up into the main house. He could get in that way. The cellar door had a lock.

Sam sat down. He couldn't think anymore. Cold, exhaustion,

hunger, and dread were stifling the last of his energy. He wanted to lay down and sleep. He couldn't. If he fell asleep now, he would die. As he sat trying to figure out what to do, he felt something push against chest. It was Gerard's book. *Great, I saved the book, but it will rot away here next to my frozen corpse.* Yet, the feel of the book against his heart brought an instant picture of Gerard into his mind and made him think more clearly. This book had helped Gerard get through worse situations than this one. He stood up and began to pace back and forth — partly to keep warm and partly to help himself think. Then his eyes stopped on the mill. *The mill! Maybe there are some tools in there I can use to break the lock.* He examined the lock more closely to get an idea of what he would need. The lock was thick — pounding it open was not going to work. Then he noticed that the hinge that attached the lock to the door was slightly loose — perhaps it could be pried off? Sam ran down toward the mill, praying out loud that it would not be locked as well. He pushed at the door. Nothing. Frustration welled up inside him. He forced himself to stay calm. He had to keep moving. He circled the mill, the steel clamp of cold gripping his fingers and toes. Above the water wheel was a small window. Sam lurched toward the wheel. Sucking in his breath with trepidation, he stepped onto the first spoke. It held. Sam carefully climbed up the wheel. He balanced his legs on the top two spokes and pushed against the window. It opened! Summoning his last ounce of strength, Sam pulled himself up through the window and fell inside.

A pile of empty sacks lay in the corner and a thin layer of flour covered everything. Sam stumbled down the stairs to the main room. A flicker of hope pushed him along as he searched through all the tools. Ah ha! Sam found what he was looking for — an iron rod with a smooth flat end. He turned to go, then stopped at the door. *Is there anything else in here I can use?* Anxious as he was to get into the house, Sam paused to look around the mill. A box full of kindling — that would come in handy. He stuffed a bunch into his shirt. On a shelf near the door he found a tinderbox. Clutching everything tightly, he headed back toward the house. With numb fingers, he tried to slide the rod under the loosest part of the hinge, but it was no use. The cold metal felt like an icicle in his frozen grasp. Fists tight, he pushed with the palm of his hand and began tilting it back and forth — each time wedging it a little further under the hinge. Then, pop — the hinge came loose. Although the cellar door was heavy, he was able to lift it up far enough to slip inside. Sam could barely see the steps as he made his way down. He stood still for a moment — scarcely believing that he was really inside. He listened for any sounds that someone was in the house. Nothing. The house seemed empty. A year ago, standing in the cellar of an abandoned house might have made him nervous. Now, all he could think about was getting warm. Sam squinted in the darkness and made his way over to the ladder. He looked up, surprised to see that the trap door to the house was open. *How could that be? No one leaves a house with the cellar open. The cellar keeps a winter's worth of food from spoiling.* Barely able to grasp the ladder rungs, he slowly pulled himself up and emerged into a pantry.

The house was ice cold. The main fireplace was across the room. It was dirty, with ash scattered on the hearth. Sam's heart leapt at the sight of a huge pile of wood next to the fireplace. His body was almost motionless with cold. *Come on, Sam, come on, you're almost there. You can do this — it's a simple fire.* He fell to his knees, pulled the kindling out of his shirt, and dropped it onto the hearth. He tried to stack it into a small pile, but he could not grip the sticks. Using his hands like stumps, he pushed the sticks deeper into the fireplace. *Good enough. Now just get it lit.* He could not open the tinder box; the smooth tin was impossible to hold onto. Sam pressed down the panic he felt

134

rising in his chest. *Think, think.* His eyes fell on a blanket lying next to the wood box. He picked it up, then stood perfectly still with his hands inside for a minute or so while he tried to stay focused. It worked — his hands warmed slightly. Holding the tinder box carefully, he pulled out a flint and lay a small piece of char cloth on it. Sam's breathing stopped as he tapped the steel striker against the flint.

"Please please please." Sam's voice was a whisper, pleading for a spark that would ignite the cloth. Suddenly he remembered the last time he had coaxed sparks into a flame — the day he was captured by the surveyors. The memory took him completely by surprise. His pride and excitement at feeling like a hero for saving his father's pine tree had turned so quickly to terror. The surveyor Nate's face rose up in his mind. The searing blade of the knife burning three lashes into his arm. Smelling his own flesh burn. It all came back. He was going to faint. Snap! A small crackle pulled Sam back to the present. The cloth caught. Quickly he laid a small bit of frayed rope from the tinderbox around the tiny ember. All thoughts of the surveyors disappeared as he focused every ounce of his attention on keeping the fragile flame alive. He set the rope onto a small piece of kindling in the fireplace and began to cautiously stack more over it. The crackling sound grew stronger. It was like laughter to Sam. Relief flooded his entire body. He piled twice as much wood as necessary, and the effect was glorious. The fire pushed the crippling cold into the far corners of the house. Sam peeled off his sodden clothes and laid them across some chairs. He placed Gerard's book on the table, then stood as close to the fire as possible without singeing his skin. Slowly, slowly, the grip of cold left him. His hands and feet ached as they began to thaw and he could feel them again. Sam closed his eyes as the warmth and glow of the fire seemed to push the terror out of his heart as well.

It was hard to even think about what to do next. His mind

and body needed to rest. And eat. *Food. I need food. There must be something here. There are barrels in the cellar. And water.* He picked up the blanket again. It was a little dirty; more importantly, it was warm and dry. He draped it around himself and walked through the house looking for something to wear. In the back bedroom he found everything he needed — trousers, a shirt, socks. The clothes were too big, but they were clean and whole. Now time for food. He stopped to look at the bed. *A real bed with sheets and a fluffy quilt. I'm so tired. I need to eat. Well, maybe for a few minutes, I can rest. Then I'll find some candles and look in the cellar for some food and find a well and …*

CHAPTER 7

Freedom

February 20, 1776
Boston

S am opened his eyes to a howling wind and a freezing, dark
house. He lay perfectly still, trying to figure out where he
was. He was in a bed, in a house, on solid ground. There were
no sounds of a rocking ship. No smell of damp wood or dead
bodies. No scratchy straw beneath him. Slowly, his mind pieced
together the kaleidoscope of yesterday's events. Plunging into
the ocean. Clawing his way out of the sheet. Stumbling half-
dead over the dam, only to find a locked, empty house. Was this
real? The feather bed he lay in felt enormous, and soft. His skin
could barely remember that sensation.

With a groan, Sam sat up. His body ached from the impact
of hitting the water. His head throbbed from dehydration and

his stomach gnawed with hunger. Wrapping himself in the quilt, Sam hobbled into the main room of the house. It was day, but outside the sky was dark with a raging snowstorm. He took a pot that was hanging over the fire ashes and opened the door just wide enough to scoop some snow into the pot. He peered into the driving snow and sleet — everything around the house was deserted. *I guess I don't need to look for a well yet. Now for some food. If the Leonards left the cellar open, maybe there is food in here as well.* Moving to the pantry, Sam shivered violently as he pried the lid off a large barrel — salt pork! Ravenous, he reached in and grabbed a huge slice. The cold, greasy meat almost stuck in his throat; he ate it so quickly.

Weak and somewhat dizzy, he started another fire to warm the house, melted the snow in the pot, then heated more salt pork in a pan over the fire. It was even better cooked. Feeling a little stronger, he began to explore his surroundings. The house was not much bigger than his home in Machias. It had one large room with the fireplace and one bedroom, and a loft upstairs with a small bed. A spinning wheel stood in the corner. The pantry was well-stocked — flour, sugar, coffee, potatoes, dried corn, apples, and even some maple syrup. Strings of dried pumpkin and onions hung above the shelves that held a small collection of pewter plates, mugs, and some wooden bowls. He went down into the cellar. More barrels and dried vegetables hanging from the ceiling. *Strange. All this food, and firewood. The dirty fireplace. It seems like they left in a hurry. Did I see a smoke shed outside? Maybe there's some frozen meat.*

His clothes were stiff and dry in front of the fireplace. Staring at them, Sam realized how useless they were — frayed and worn thin. He thought about tearing them into pieces for the tinderbox, but even looking at them made him feel slightly sick. He threw them into the fire and watched with a grim satisfaction as they burned up. *That nightmare is over. I don't know what will happen next, but I will die before ever being taken as a prisoner again.*

Gerard's book was dry, too. Sam turned the pages carefully to make sure they were not torn. He found some grease in the kitchen and rubbed it into the leather cover. Somehow this gesture brought him comfort — he felt that he had kept one small promise. *I should have kept a copy of* Common Sense *too. That would have made Gerard happy. Well, I must know it by heart after reading it to him so many times.*

That night, taking advantage of a lull in the storm, Sam retrieved the boat. Even though no one lived along the shore, it still seemed wiser to bring it up and hide it in the mill.

For the next few days, Sam did nothing except eat and sleep. The storm continued, and until the firewood was used up, he saw no reason to go outside except to the outhouse. After months of living at the edge of starvation, always cold and sleeping on straw, his body began to heal and feel strong again. He knew he should make his way to Watertown, but the snowstorm was a perfect reason to stay in the Leonards' house a while longer. One day, when the skies briefly cleared, he looked out from the upstairs window to get his bearings on the city. It would not be safe to wander around without a pass, but he could see a lot from the house. The enormous hulk of a half-built ship was the closest thing he could see to the north. Beyond it, the burned-out ruins of Charlestown loomed across the water. Most of the bay was covered with a dusting of snow. *So, the bay is frozen. I wonder how thick? Could I walk across? It looks like the water between the North End and Charlestown is open. A boat could get across there.* To his far right, Sam saw rows and rows of gray, curved stones poking up out of the snow. *A cemetery.* To the west, across the bay was the Charles River. It looked frozen too. Sam decided to explore the mill again before the storm returned. Inside, he found a small axe that would come in handy.

Walking back toward the house he noticed a set of tracks in the snow. He stared at them. *What is that? A wolf? No, there can't be wolves in the city. And the tracks are too small...* Then Sam looked up. A black dog lay across the doorstep. Its shaggy coat was clotted with dirt and icicles. The dog stared at Sam. *Great. Now what do I do? Is it rabid? Maybe I can scare it away.* As if the dog had read his mind, it lifted its head and growled. Sam held up the axe and waved it around, yelling and stamping his feet. The dog growled again, but did not move. Sam stepped a little closer. "Go! Go! Get out of here, you mangy beast!" he shouted.

The dog began to get up. It wasn't very big, but Sam was sure the dog was going to lunge at him. As it tried to stand, the dog wobbled and stumbled. Sam could see it was in bad shape; a large gash on the left back leg, skinny with rib and hip bones showing through the wet fur. Suddenly all the fear left Sam. This dog was as scared as he was — it just didn't have an axe to wave, or the energy to bark. Sam bent down. The dog tottered warily, but stopped growling.

"You're a sorry sight, aren't you? I'll bet you're starving. Do you live here? Is this your house?" Sam felt a little silly, talking to a dog, but the change in his voice had an immediate effect. The dog sat down and looked into Sam's eyes with a cautious gaze. Sam continued to speak in a low, gentle voice as he stood up and walked bit by bit toward the dog. He stood still for several moments, still talking, then carefully offered his hand to the dog. Slowly, its tail moved back and forth. Sam smiled. "Come on in, dog. I'll take care of you. Wait till you see what's in the pantry! We're going to have a feast! Then I'll look at your leg." After days of being alone, it felt good to have someone to talk to.

The dog followed Sam into the house and went straight to the pantry. *So maybe it does live here. Why would the Leonards leave it behind? Poor thing. Out there in the snow and cold. I wonder how long it has been alone?* He filled a bowl with water, then fried some salt pork. Even though clearly starving, the dog could barely stand long enough to eat and drink. After eating a second piece of pork, the dog began sniffing around the wood box. Then it stared at Sam.

"What? Are you cold? Should I put more wood on the fire?" Sam waited.

The dog was having trouble walking, barely putting any weight on the wounded leg. It limped into the bedroom and returned, dragging the dirty blanket Sam had left there. Pushing with its nose until the blanket lay exactly how Sam had found it — right between the fireplace and the wood box — the dog turned around a few times, then lay down on the blanket, and let out a deep, tired sigh.

After falling asleep, the dog rolled onto its side. Sam could see the dog was female. *Hmmm, you can't tell me your name so I'll have to give you a new one. But let's take care of that leg first.* Without waking her, he examined the gash. The wound was not too deep, but looked red and inflamed. Infection had set in. Washing and wrapping it would hurt. He went to the pantry and found the soap barrel. After scooping some into a bowl, he then turned to the dried herbs. There were about a dozen glass jars filled with dried leaves and flowers. Some were labeled. Others he recognized by their shape or smell. He knew exactly what to look for because whenever he was sick or had hurt himself, his mother always explained which herb she was using to treat him. *Sage. Rosemary. Parsley. Lavender.* He searched for a familiar golden orange flower. *Here it is — marigold! I'll make a salve to fight the infection.* Sam crushed the dried flowers until he had a pile about the size of an onion, then mixed it with some bear grease. He heated some water over the fire, then added some to the soap. He tore a clean rag into strips and placed everything next to the dog.

Back to the herbs. *Hmmm, what was that stuff Mother gave*

me when I broke my arm? Was it chamomile? No, that was for stomach aches. He spotted a small jar holding brown, dried roots. *Valerian! That's it. Mother made some tea from it.* Sam opened the jar. The smell was horrible. He steeped some in a teapot for a few minutes. It still smelled awful, so he mixed in some sugar. *This should help ease her pain. What should I call her — maybe Eliza, after my Mother, no, that doesn't feel right. How about Mrs. Collins?* He looked at the dog. "Claire?" *No, that's not it either.* He started to put the herbs away and noticed a large jar of dried pink petals in the back. Taking off the lid, he sniffed the container. Roses. Sam was transported back to Mrs. Collins' rose garden. *That's it — I'll call you Rosie. It's a good name for a girl, even if you are kind of smelly right now.*

When Rosie woke up, Sam fed her again and put the valerian tea in a bowl for her to drink. She seemed completely relaxed — maybe it was the tea, maybe it was because she was home. Sam sat down and spoke to her, again in a quiet voice, explaining that he was going to wash and treat her leg. As he began cleaning the wound, she winced with pain and whined softly, but she let him finish. Then he covered it with the salve and wrapped it. Sam sat with her, rubbing her head and behind her ears till she fell back asleep. He ate some supper, then went back to sit with Rosie. She was still a mess — matted fur, skin and bones. Yet, even in her current state, she lay with her paws crossed gracefully.

"You're a beauty, Rosie, that's for sure. So why did your family abandon you here? Why did they leave in such a hurry? Are they coming back?"

It was nice — sitting by the fire with a full belly and watching the gentle rise and fall of Rosie's ribs as she slept. Sam felt safe and peaceful — for the first time since his last night at home. Home. Machias. Somehow, he had to get word to his parents that he was still alive, and on his way back. Maybe he could send a letter from Watertown. He stroked Rosie's paw. Should he bring her with him? What if the Leonards never came home? He needed to make sure her leg was stronger before doing anything — that meant at least a few more days here.

It took almost a week for Rosie's leg to heal. Sam spent most of the time sleeping and cooking. After a few days of only salt pork, he decided to experiment with what he found in the pantry and cellar. He tried making spoonbread, but without milk and eggs, it was nothing like his mother's. His pancakes were a little flat and runny, until he added some rye flour to the batter. Rosie ate whatever Sam made. Her favorite was salt pork cooked with dried apples and maple syrup. Sam was amazed at how quickly Rosie recovered.

When the gash on her leg closed up, he decided she needed a bath. He brought a tub up from the cellar and hung as many pots as he could over the fire to heat water, then got some soap from the pantry. When the tub was full of warm water, Sam called, "Rosie! Come here, girl. You're going to have a bath!" Rosie, who had accepted her new name readily, came over to the tub. She sniffed the water, then the soap, and looked at Sam. "Climb in, Rosie. It will feel good." Sam splashed some water at her. Rosie was not amused. She turned and walked back to her blanket. Sam swirled the hot water in the tub, unable to remember the last time *he* had bathed. "You know what Rosie? I bet I need this more than you do." Sam took off his clothes and climbed into the tub. He sat back and felt his whole body relax as the steaming water wrapped him in warmth. He couldn't remember ever enjoying a bath this much. Nor could he remember ever being quite this dirty. He sat until the water began to get cold, then he scrubbed himself all over and washed his hair. He felt like a new person.

Climbing out of the tub, Sam realized he had nothing to dry himself with. He ran to the bedroom and came back. Pulling a nightshirt over his head, Sam stopped and grinned. Rosie was sitting in the tub, waiting patiently for her turn. Rosie's bath took almost as long as Sam's. As he dried her off, he wondered again why the Leonards had left Rosie behind. She pushed against the cloth and nuzzled him. Sam rubbed his forehead against Rosie's, her damp fur tickling his nose as he breathed deeply. He knew whatever happened next, Rosie was coming with him. "What do you think, Rosie? Do you want to come with me and meet the famous Paul Revere? Or should we stay here until your family gets back?" Rosie's trusting gaze reassured him that he would make the right decision. To have the loyalty of such a beautiful, smart animal made Sam happy and proud at the same time. He scratched behind her ears. "Don't worry, girl. I'll take care of you."

The affection and sense of responsibility he felt for her surprised him. Sam had never been responsible for anyone besides himself. And truthfully, his parents had always taken care of him. He thought about what his father had said about responsibility. "When you care about something, responsibility doesn't feel like a burden. It feels like a privilege. It's an opportunity to do your best."

Sam added some wood to the fire and stretched out his legs to enjoy the warmth, with Rosie staying at his side. "I thought he was talking about the mill, but he meant everything — our family, our home, our livelihood." Rosie stared solemnly; she seemed to be pondering every word he said. "I wonder what's going on in Machias. Has Father been able to sell any lumber? I'll bet it was a tough winter. Did Eamon go home, or is he still off fighting somewhere? You'll like Eamon, Rosie. He's funny and smart and not afraid of anything. Machias is beautiful. And there's a big pond near our house. Ha! What would old Carl the Catfish think if he saw you swimming in the pond?!"

A wave of homesick sadness tugged at Sam. *How am I going to get back there? I've got no money. Maybe I can work for the Reveres for a while — earn enough to get a boat passage up to Falmouth.*

We can walk or hitch a wagon ride from there. First, I've got to get the medallion to Deborah.

It was time to leave Boston. He and Rosie were both strong enough to make the trip to Watertown. Sam stared at the fire, conjuring up Josiah's map in his head, and what he knew of the city so far. *Josiah said Watertown was about fifteen miles from Boston, once you were over the river. If we walk over the Mill Dam and cross at Barton's Point, it's the shortest distance. The ice is pretty thick along the shore, but what about the middle?* Sam shook his head. *Too risky.* The ice was probably broken between Hudson's Point and Charlestown. He could row the boat across there, to find the narrowest part to Lechmere's Point. The walk from there to Watertown would be a little longer, but Sam could think of no other way.

The boat. Sam had not checked it since he'd arrived at the Leonards'. He got dressed, set the fire screen in place, and ran to the mill. He took the boat out, carrying it down to the frozen shore. As he scanned the bottom of the boat, he noticed a crack about halfway up the side. *Maybe it won't leak.* With a stick, he smashed the ice until there was a hole big enough for the boat. Sam carefully climbed in. The boat settled in the water; he waited. *Hmmm, not too bad. But I'm not the only passenger.* "Rosie!"

Rosie trotted down the path and stood on the edge of the water. Sam reached over and lifted her into the boat. Water began to seep through the crack. "Dang it! Why didn't I check this sooner?" Sam shook his head with frustration. In the mill he found everything he needed to fix the boat. It took no time to seal the crack, but it would be at least two days before it would be dry and safe enough to use. That night, he tried to sketch Josiah's map on paper, to refresh his memory. The last thing he saw in his head before falling asleep was the ancient trail tree — silently showing him the way.

Sam awoke with a start. The stillness of sleep exploded as a barrage of thunder filled the night. He lay listening for a few minutes, then got out of bed and climbed up to the loft to see outside. There were flashes in the sky, yet no storm, no lightning — just booming crashes one after another, coming from the shore, in different places. The flashes were far away. Although there didn't seem to be any danger of the house getting hit, Sam still felt alarmed. *Those must be cannons. Are the British bombing the city? That doesn't make any sense. But the rebel army doesn't have that many cannons.*

The bombings continued for three full days. Sam was anxious to know what was happening. He thought about going out on the third night, but it seemed too risky without a British pass. He decided to wait it out. It was a good decision. That night a furious storm rolled in. Rain lashed against the roof and a loud wind shook the house. The boat was ready, but the weather was too bad for crossing the river.

By morning the weather had improved. Sam fried some potatoes and dried corn for breakfast. "Well, Rosie, if tomorrow is clear like today, we'll be on our way." As he ate, he looked around the house, thinking about what he would need for the trip and leaving the house. The wood box was almost empty. He knew he should stock it in case the Leonards did come back. It was the least he could do. After eating, he headed over to the main wood pile behind the mill. He whistled as he chopped a large stack of logs and then set to work making a good supply of kindling as well.

It was a cold day, but the sun was shining and the sky was clear and blue. Working his way through the pile of logs, Sam marveled at his situation. A few weeks earlier he'd stumbled up this hillside, barely alive. Now he felt strong, healthy, and optimistic. He'd go to Watertown, then home. It was a bittersweet journey, though. He did not look forward to telling Deborah that Josiah was dead. He didn't know what he should say. Sam turned to Rosie. "I guess I'll tell her everything. No, that's a bad idea. She won't want to know that he drowned. I'll say he died in his sleep, from sickness." Josiah's face, with all its enthusiasm, curiosity, and determination, rose up in Sam's mind. "No, that's not right either. He died trying to escape; to get back to her. She deserves the truth. Maybe in some way, that will comfort her."

Sam filled his arms with kindling and started back toward the house. Rosie ran ahead and began to bark. Coming from behind the mill, he turned the corner and Rosie darted in front of him. Kindling flew everywhere as Sam stumbled. He picked up the pieces while Rosie continued to bark. Suddenly a flash of red caught his eye.

"You there!"

Sam heard the shout at the exact moment his eyes registered two British soldiers standing on the doorstep of the house.

"You, there! Is this your house?"

Sam's stomach dropped. He stood perfectly still. Then he nodded.

"Come here, boy," a short, round-faced man barked at Sam. "Do you live here?"

Sam walked toward the soldiers and swallowed. "Yes, sir."

"What is your name?" The sun flashed against the brass buttons on the man's jacket. Sam looked at the insignia. He was a lieutenant. His face was pale and doughy. A layer of fat pushed up his soft chin, and two black, beady eyes glowered into Sam's. As his mouth pursed into a tight line, he looked exactly like a turtle.

"George. George Leonard, Junior," Sam replied, silently praying that Mr. Leonard had a son. The other soldier, a sergeant, was almost a foot taller than the lieutenant, with wide shoulders and long legs. His hair was the color of straw. His eyes were bright blue. He reminded Sam of Jeremiah O'Brien. The sergeant leaned over slightly and held his hand out to Rosie. She stopped barking and after inspecting his gloved hand, immediately allowed him to scratch under her chin.

"Are you alone?" the lieutenant asked curtly.

"Yes, sir." Sam hesitated.

"Where is your family?"

Sam glanced across the water. "They went to Charlestown."

"Charlestown?" His eyes narrowed with suspicion. "Charlestown is empty. It's burned to the ground."

Sam's mind raced, trying to concoct a believable story. "They went to visit my grandparents' graves, sir."

"Hmmm…" The lieutenant looked around the property, searching for a clue to support Sam's story.

Sam shivered, glad that the cold wind masked his shaking legs.

"Your family is loyal to his majesty, King George, correct?" the lieutenant demanded.

Sam nodded.

"And you will be evacuating the city with the rest of the Loyalists?"

"Umm, yes, sir." *Evacuating? The British were leaving Boston?!* Sam was completely confused.

"Fine. General Howe has issued an order to commandeer some small boats for loading the ships." The lieutenant turned toward the water.

"My parents took our boat. They should be home later." Sam hoped that he sounded sincere.

The lieutenant scanned the property, again with a skeptical gaze. Then he turned back to Sam. "I will have a look around anyway. Wait here, Sergeant Bennet."

Sam let out a breath of relief that the boat was hidden in the mill. Hopefully the lieutenant would not go inside. But he could not comprehend what the lieutenant was talking about.

The British were leaving Boston? He forced himself to sound relaxed and asked the sergeant, "So, when do the boats leave? I haven't been into town for the past few days."

Bennet continued to pet Rosie. "Don't know exactly. Supposed to go five days ago, then the storm came in. Now that the weather has cleared, we're loading up the ships."

"Where are we going?" Sam asked, too quickly. Now it was the sergeant's turn to looked at him oddly. Sam tried to cover his mistake. "I mean, which ship will the Loyalists be sailing on?"

"Don't know yet. There are about two thousand Loyalists who want to leave the city. We've got a hundred and twenty ships, but we've got to get nine thousand soldiers on them before we start taking civilians," Bennet answered.

Sam was still trying to make sense of this news. *If all the Loyalists were leaving Boston — where were they going? Was the war over?* He needed answers and could see that asking too many questions made him look suspicious. He decided to change tactics. "Boy, Rosie sure likes you!" Sam forced a laugh. Rosie was enjoying all the attention from the soldier and had rolled over onto her back for a complete belly rub. While Bennet was distracted, Sam casually asked, "Will it be a long trip?"

"To Halifax? Shouldn't take more than a week or so, depending on the weather."

Halifax. The British aren't returning to England. But why are they leaving? It has to have something to do with the bombardments of the past few days — who was bombing who?! The lieutenant was heading back toward the house. Sam threw out one last comment — desperately attempting to piece together what had happened — "I guess those cannons did the job then."

"Aye." Bennet chuckled. "That was quite a trick by the old fox."

"The old fox?"

"General Washington. Those cannon barrages. Kept them up for three nights to distract us while he moved a few thousand men and about thirty cannons to Dorchester Heights. Aimed them right over the harbor." Bennet shook his head slightly. "Our ships are easy marks. General Howe was fit to be tied. He said the rebels did more in one night than his whole army could have done in a month." Bennet stood up and brushed the fur off his hands. "How is it that you know nothing of the bombings and the evacuation?"

Sam felt his heart jump, but Bennet's tone was not distrustful. His eyes were kind as he studied Sam's face. "Well, I saw them from the house, but I, uh, thought it was best to stay close to the house and keep an eye on everything while my parents are gone," Sam answered awkwardly, fighting to gather his thoughts as the lieutenant returned.

"What did you say your name was?" the lieutenant snapped. Sam wondered if he was trying to catch him in a lie.

"George Leonard," Sam said evenly.

"George, we will expect you and your parents in the morning at the Long Wharf. With the boat. We will be assigning ships first thing, and moving passengers and supplies all day. If this blasted wind doesn't change again, the ships will depart the day after tomorrow."

Sam's racing thoughts finally focused. "Yes, sir. But I don't have a pass. Will that be a problem getting through town?" He spoke as respectfully as he could.

"Hmmm." The lieutenant stared doubtfully at Sam, then reached into his pocket and pulled out an engraved card. "Use this if you have any trouble." Even his fingers were pudgy. He also handed Sam a piece of paper with a Royal stamp on the top. "Give this to your mother. Sergeant Bennet, let's go."

Bennet leaned over to give Rosie one more scratch. "She's a beauty." He lowered his voice and his eyes met Sam's. "They won't take animals on the ships. She'll have to stay behind, *if* you are coming with us."

Sam nodded slightly — hopeful that the subtle gesture conveyed both understanding and thanks. Sam held his breath as the soldiers left the yard. He glanced down at the card inscribed with *Lieutenant James R. MacConnell.* Then he read the slip of paper — an order from General Howe.

AS Linnen and Woolen Goods are Articles much wanted by the Rebels, and would aid assist them in their Rebellion, the Commander in Chief expects that all good Subjects will use their utmost Endeavors to have all such Articles convey'd from this Place: Any who have not Opportunity to convey their Goods under their own Care, may deliver them on Board the Minerva at Hubbard's Wharf, to Crean Brush, Esq; mark'd with their Names, who will give a Certificate of the Delivery, and will oblige himself to return them to the Owners, all unavoidable Accidents accepted. If after this Notice any Person secretes or keeps in his Possession such Articles, he will be treated as a Favourer of Rebels.

Linens?! Sam groaned silently. That was the least of his problems! He and Rosie went into the house. Sam sat down and put his head in his hands. "Rosie, what are we going to do? It's too late to leave tonight. I'll never find those landmarks in the dark. And the only place to row across the river is at Hudson's Point. We'll surely be seen trying to cross."

He stood up and began to pace, turning over all the possibilities in his mind. Rosie lay down in front of the fireplace. Her chin rested on the floor, but her eyes followed Sam's nervous figure as he moved back and forth, muttering, "Should we walk across the ice? It's pretty thick — maybe it will hold us." He stopped and stared at Rosie — weighing her with his eyes. He paced again, imagining how horrible it would be if either of them were to fall into the river. The situation seemed hopeless.

Absentmindedly, Sam reached up and began to tug at Josiah's medallion — a habit he'd developed, which seemed to help him think. "Or maybe I should go to Halifax. It would be easy to get back to Machias from there — a week or so of walking, then a boat across the bay. I could pretend to be a Loyalist during the trip." The chain around his neck had twisted all the way up and pinched his skin. The small jolt of pain snapped him out of his reverie.

Sam stopped in front of Rosie again. This time he sat down on the floor and lowered his face to her eye level. He gently pushed back her ears with his thumbs and smiled as she licked his cheek. "Rosie, I'm sorry. How could I even think about leaving you behind? And I'm not going home without taking this medallion to Deborah. I'll figure out how to get us both across that river!"

Sam went outside to the mill and pulled out the boat. As darkness fell, he dragged it along the shore, stopping a few times to catch his breath and rest his arms, until he was close to Hudson's Point. The water was frozen, but the air felt warm. Perhaps it would break up enough tomorrow. He hid the boat under a low bush and returned to the house. After cooking them both some dinner, Sam busied himself with getting ready to leave. He tidied up and began to pack the few things he would take. He carefully wound a piece of oilcloth around Gerard's book, then put the tinder box, axe, and an extra shirt all into a cloth bag, along with some bread, dried apples, and salt pork. Before he went to bed, Sam opened the small writing desk in the bedroom and found a quill, ink, and paper. He wrote a short letter to the Leonards, explaining that he was Josiah's friend, and why he'd needed to stay there. He told them how he'd found Rosie, and promised to take good care of her. Sam didn't know if the Leonards would be coming back, but if they did, they would probably want to know their dog was safe. He laid the letter on the table, then gazed gratefully around the room one last time. If he hadn't found this place, the food, and even Rosie — he'd probably be dead. Instead he was alive, and heading home.

The morning dawned clear and fresh. Sam decided he would go to Hudson's Point first, without Rosie or the boat, to check the water. It had been too dark last night to see much. Although he had not ventured out beyond the Leonards' property since he arrived, from Josiah's descriptions he knew that he could take a quicker route to the ferry crossing point. He turned on Prince Street and cut across Copp's Hill — the cemetery he had seen from the window. The British had fired on Bunker Hill from batteries along two sides of the area. A few pieces of wood still stuck out from the packed mounds of dirt. Wide-eyed skulls — some with wings, some with crossbones — stared silently above the names of the occupants below the gray tombstones; the rounded tops glittered with a light dusting of frost. Sam shivered as he hurried through. His heart lifted as he approached the ferry point. The water was not frozen. A few boats were coming toward the city, although none headed toward Charlestown. That might be a problem. *Maybe we should go tonight, and hide out in Charlestown until morning. We can cross the ice at first light.*

Now that he had a plan, and Lieutenant MacConnell's card in his pocket, Sam felt a bit bolder. He decided to see what was happening at the Long Wharf, as well. He went along Lynn Street, which curved around the north end of the city. There were so many wharves and shipyards he could barely take it all in. He tried to get his bearings, but the street names kept changing. At the North Battery, it became Ship Street, then Fish Street, then Ann Street. Abruptly, Sam stopped. He was standing on the bridge over Mill Creek. He stared at the narrow tunnel where he had pushed the boat through the night he had escaped. Turning around slowly, Sam looked out across the harbor. There it was —

the *Preston*. It looked the same as all the other ships — not evil or menacing. He wondered about the prisoners still on board. What would happen to them if the British were fleeing Boston? He cringed a little at the thought.

As he got closer to the Long Wharf, Sam heard shouts, carts rolling over the cobblestones, and the rattle of drums. No one seemed to be in charge. The carts and carriages were full, lined up along King Street and the length of the dock — some held distraught-looking families and their baggage, others carried British soldiers and supplies. Wagons were piled high with furniture, paintings, clothing, dishes, linens. Sam saw a piano sitting near the water. A large man dressed in fine clothes stood between it and an open carriage where a mother and two young girls were seated. He was arguing with a British officer — alternating between pounding his right fist on the piano and shaking it in the major's face. The officer simply shook his head as they continued to argue. One of the little girls climbed out and stood next to the piano. Her pale face was a tight mask of fear and exhaustion. She stared briefly at the ships in the harbor, then turned and began to play. For a moment, all other sounds receded. The girl's face relaxed as sweet, clear notes floated above the noise and confusion.

At the edge of Butler's Wharf, British soldiers were lifting cannons — six pounders — from their carriages and rolling them into the water. Others were dumping wheelbarrows full of cannonballs and shot. A few larger cannons had been moved to the side. So many ships were already way out in the harbor. *What had Bennet said? One hundred and twenty ships?* Sam tried to count them all. *Thirty-five, thirty-six, thirty-seven ...*

"Young Mr. Leonard!"

Thirty-eight, thirty-nine.

"George Leonard!"

Sam jumped. Someone was yelling his name. His fake name.

Lieutenant MacConnell was walking toward him.

"Are your parents here?" MacConnell looked around behind Sam.

Sam shook his head. He was too surprised and devastated to even think straight.

MacConnell scowled. "Major Lowe has the passenger lists at the town dock. Bring your parents there. In the meantime, we'll need your boat. Where is it?"

Sam still could not answer.

Suddenly Bennet approached. He nodded to MacConnell and said with slight irritation, "We were about to get it, sir. The boy docked it too far up. I'll take him to the loading area."

"Very well, Sergeant," MacConnell said briskly. "I will see you at the town dock, George."

"Yes, sir."

Bennet turned and none-too-gently pulled Sam's arm. Sam stumbled along, not sure what was happening. Where was Bennet taking him? Should he try to break away and make a run for it? He doubted he could outrun this man. Something told Sam to trust Bennet, so he kept going, trying to keep pace with the soldier's long legs and rapid stride. He bumped into other soldiers and people pushing their way through the crowd. After a few minutes of walking, Sam said in a low voice, "Where are we going?"

Bennet turned sharply, heading back toward the water, then answered. "First, we are going to get you into a boat. If MacConnell sees you making a few trips back and forth, he'll forget about you."

"But I..." Sam stammered, not sure what do to next.

Bennet stopped and stared into Sam's ashen face. "Your name is not George. You are probably not a Loyalist, and I'm fairly certain you are not going to Halifax."

Sam spoke quietly. "My name is Sam."

The soldier's stern face softened and he grinned a little.

"Sam, you are a pretty bad liar. Lucky for you, MacConnell is very distracted today. I don't know where you are going. In fact, I don't want to know — it's better that way. But if you plan to get yourself and Rosie out of here, you'd better stay on your toes and be ready for anything."

Sam was so relieved he almost wanted to cry. That would not do! He shook himself into control. "Why are you helping me?"

Bennet shrugged his huge shoulders. "I've got a brother at home, about your age."

Sam waited for more of an explanation, but Bennet said nothing. He walked to the edge of the dock and called out to two soldiers who were coming in with an empty rowboat.

"Stay here." Bennet grabbed the rope tossed up on the dock. He leaned over and said something to the men. They handed the oars up, then climbed up the dock pilings. Bennet pointed in the direction of the soldiers who were busily dumping munitions. Bennet handed Sam the oars, and then lifted the small boat out of the water and raised it over his head. He carried it easily through the crowd, heading straight for the Long Wharf where the mountain of crates was being loaded. As soon as he spotted MacConnell, Bennet pushed his way to the water and lowered the boat near a ladder. After Sam climbed in, Bennet handed some crates down. Bennet's earlier quiet voice now boomed across the water, for everyone to hear. "Get going, boy. Take these to the *Minerva,* then come back here for the next load." He leaned over and pretended to shift the crates around. He whispered to Sam, "Make sure MacConnell sees you one or two more times. They'll do a final passenger check in the morning, so try to get out tonight."

Sam grabbed the oars and steadied the boat. He looked at Bennet, not sure of what to say. "Thank you."

"Take care of Rosie, Sam." Bennet winked and pushed the boat out into the foamy surf.

Sam rowed quickly out to the ship. He did two more trips, bringing more crates, then a boat full of saddles. On the third return, he searched the dock for MacConnell. He was standing at the end of the wharf, yelling at a red-faced man who had tipped an entire boat, full of boots, into the water. Sam rowed over and scooped the boots up into his boat. He took them out to the *Minerva*, then rowed the boat around the far side of the wharf. He tied it up and walked back to Butler's Wharf. The soldiers were still frantically dumping munitions of all sizes into the sea.

Sam looked at the sky. He had a few hours of light left. Perhaps he'd be able to help the rebels retrieve the valuable supplies once the Brits had gone. By now about a dozen cannons — the largest he'd seen — had been rolled down to the dock. Sam looked around quickly. MacConnell was nowhere in sight. He approached a soldier and told him, "I was sent over to help."

"You pigging out tomorrow with the rest of the Tories?" The soldier grinned.

"Aye, leave this stinking town to the Yankees. They can have it." Sam rolled his eyes.

"That's right. But they shan't have these. We're going to spike the ones we can't get in the water. Here, take this." He handed Sam a thin iron rod and a hammer. He pointed to a small hole at the wider end of the cannon. "Stick this rod in there. Pound it a bit. Done. Nobody can use this piece for a while."

Sam leaned in to start, then suddenly his breath caught.

"What's the matter?" the soldier asked.

Sam stared at the three slashes etched into the massive cannon. *The King's Broad Arrow!* Instinctively, he grabbed his scarred arm, thankful that it was hidden by his jacket. The soldier eyed him curiously.

"Ahhh, blasted bugs!" Sam pretended to scratch his arm. "I won't miss those. Spike them all?" he asked with exaggerated cheerfulness.

"Spike them all! And when you're done, throw a couple of these around. Some nice sharp crow's feet will slow down those rebel drubs." He handed Sam a small bag, chuckling as he walked away. The bag was full of caltrops, small spikes of iron that could cripple a man or horse unlucky enough to step on one. Sam stuck the bag in his pocket. Spiking the cannons was not hard. He finished quickly. Next, he went to help three soldiers roll the smaller cannons and shells into the water. They pushed the cannons in first, each one causing a huge splash as it hit the water. Once they were done with the cannons, the soldiers left, probably to join the looting of houses and shops. Alone with the pile of shells, Sam carefully marked where the cannons had gone into the water by pounding a caltrop into the dock with a piece of shot. Everything around Sam was so chaotic, no one noticed what he was doing.

The noise from the Long Wharf grew louder. The crowd of Loyalists was starting to panic — more fearful with each passing hour that they would not get on the ships heading for Halifax. When Boston fell back under American control, it would not be a safe place for anyone who had supported the British during their eight-month occupation of the city.

Throwing the heavy shells into the water was hard work. Despite the breeze, Sam was hot and sweaty. He took off his jacket and tossed it onto a piling. After he dropped the last shell in, Sam decided this was the perfect opportunity to get back to the house and wait out the rest of the day with Rosie. He threw his jacket over his shoulder and headed toward King Street. He could blend in with the crowd there and avoid the Town Dock, where MacConnell would be looking for him. Sam turned the corner and had walked a few yards when suddenly a hand clasped him roughly on the shoulder.

"George! There you are." MacConnell scowled impatiently

and motioned to another officer who was holding a stack of papers. "Young man," he barked, "where are your parents? We are loading the civilian ships in a few hours. Why haven't they signed in yet?" There were about twenty people crowding around MacConnell — some carrying bundles or children. They all looked frightened and tired.

Sam collected himself and looked MacConnell straight in the eye. "They are on their way, sir. My mother wanted to go back to our house for a few more items." Sam prayed that his fibbing skills were better than Bennet thought. "She's very upset," Sam said, trying to sound like a concerned son. "I'm supposed to meet them here."

"Very well. We must get you assigned to a ship. Sergeant Hunt, please find a place for the Leonard family." He turned back to Sam. "Do you have siblings?"

Sam thought about the Leonards' house. Had he seen any dresses upstairs? Any children's things? A cradle? Toys? "No, sir," Sam answered. "Just me."

MacConnell turned back to Hunt. "Three passengers. George Leonard, wife and son."

"George Leonard?" A man from the group of Loyalists stepped forward to look at Sam. "George Leonard left months ago. He fled when smallpox broke out in December," he eyed Sam suspiciously, "and to the best of my knowledge, George Leonard doesn't have a son."

Sam was speechless. He looked around desperately — maybe Bennet would step in and save him again. Sam turned to run, but MacConnell was quicker. He grabbed Sam's right arm. "Who are you?" he demanded. "Are you a spy for the rebels?"

Sam yanked his arm and turned to run. MacConnell caught his shirt. As Sam tried to pull away, the sleeve ripped off. MacConnell held fast to Sam's wrist. He stared at the three stripes on Sam's arm. "The King's Broad Arrow?! You're a criminal!"

he hissed.

"No!" Sam shouted, "I'm not! I'm just trying to get home!"

"I don't have time for this today! I'll deal with you in Halifax." MacConnell motioned to a soldier standing nearby. "Sergeant Baker, take him to the prison."

"Please, sir. My name is Samuel Nevens. I didn't commit any crime!"

"Your arm says otherwise! Sergeant, take him away."

Baker grabbed Sam's arm and marched him the length of King Street. He didn't say a word until they reached the prison on Queen Street. When they entered, Baker greeted another soldier who was sitting in a chair in the front room. Baker dragged Sam into the back area and pulled open the door to a small cell. The cell was empty except for a pile of straw in the corner. He shoved Sam roughly inside. Turning to the soldier, Baker said, "No time to get him on a ship today, we'll pick him up first thing in the morning." To Sam, he sneered, "Sleep tight, rebel!" and slammed the cell door shut.

Sam heard Baker laughing with the other soldier, then silence. He ran to the window and pulled against the iron bars until his hands bled. Then he shook the door. No way out. Sam thought about trying to bribe the guard, but what did he have to offer? All he owned in the world was at the Leonards' house with Rosie.

Rosie! Sam groaned inwardly. What would happen to Rosie? She was trapped. She would either freeze or starve to death in the house. Sam felt sick to his stomach at the thought of Rosie waiting patiently for him. He paced the cell, his chest tight with fear. What would they do to him? Would they put him back on another prison ship? The thought stopped him in his tracks. Sam knew he could not survive that again.

The cell grew dim as the afternoon sun disappeared. Sam stared out the small window. A bright half-moon popped out between pale clouds meandering across the sky, but Sam saw nothing. Hopelessness took over. He slumped to the floor, numb with sorrow. After all he had gone through, he was going to fail. He would never return the medallion; he would never get home. Rosie would die because of him. Soon, cold and sheer exhaustion overwhelmed him. He dug under the straw to conserve what little body heat he could. Turning to the wall, he fell into a fitful sleep. He dreamed he was back on the *Preston*, back in the same oppressive room — desperate and scared — with no Gerard to help him through it. He heard the guards talking and then Hodgekins' humming.

Sam opened his eyes. Hodgekins' humming? He was awake. Hodgekins was humming? Sam leapt to his feet and peered out the small window of the cell door. A British soldier was still sitting in the chair, but now he was humming! Sam looked to see if there were any other guards. A burst of hope electrified his entire body. "Hodgekins?" Sam whispered.

The guard turned around. Hodgekins' eyes widened with surprise. "Sam?"

"Hodgekins!"

"*You're* the prisoner?"

"Yes. Boy, am I glad to see you!" Sam grinned.

"You got off the ship?"

"Yes. It's a long story." Sam quickly told him everything — about Gerard, his escape, his plan to get to Watertown, and Rosie. "I've got to get out of here. Please, will you help me?" Sam gripped the bars of the cell door.

Hodgekins stared at Sam. Then he went to the door — checking the streets and the sky. "You have to hurry. It will be light soon." He strode to the cell door and unlocked it. "The ships are leaving today or tomorrow. You might be able to walk across the ice at Barton's Point. It was frozen solid two days ago."

Sam brushed the straw from his clothes. "I can't go across there. I have to get Rosie. She'll die if I don't go back. And besides Rosie, Gerard's book is there, too. I have a boat. I can row to Charlestown and walk over the ice at Lechmere's Point."

Hodgekins nodded. "All right. Try to cross tonight. Once the ships leave, I don't know what will happen. You'll be safer with the Reveres. Charlestown is empty, but we've left some dummy wooden soldiers around Bunker Hill to fool the militia." He grabbed some bread from the table and handed it to Sam. "How well do you know the city?"

Sam shoved the bread into his mouth. "Not well," he said, pausing to chew and swallow. "I saw a bit of the North End in the past two days."

"The last boats are loading from the Long Wharf, so don't go back that way. Go around the west side of the Mill Pond and cross the dam." Hodgekins wrapped the rest of the bread and some cheese in a cloth. Then he took off his scarlet uniform jacket and black wool hat and handed everything to Sam. "Put these on. No one will stop you if you are wearing these."

Sam stared at the scarlet jacket. "What about you? You'll be punished."

Hodgekins reached for his musket. He held it out to Sam. "Sam, you've got to hit me over the head with this."

"No!" Sam shook his head firmly as he pulled on the jacket.

"There is no other way. I'll say I was taking you to relieve yourself and you grabbed my gun. But it has to look real. Hit me."

"Hodgekins, I …" Sam stammered.

Hodgekins glanced at the door. Then he grinned and nodded. "If you are ever in Dover, remember — Hodgekins the Beekeeper." He turned the musket upside down, slammed the butt against his forehead and fell to the floor.

Sam stood over the gentle giant. Gerard's words came back to him. "You, sir, are an honorable man." Sam repeated them softly as he put on Hodgekins' hat. *Should I take the musket? Might come in handy. No. It's too heavy.* He stepped into the black night and glanced up and down Queen Street. To his right, the Long Wharf was lit with torches and rang with a hundred sounds. Sam turned left and hurried toward the pond. The dam was slippery with ice. He ran past the mill and burst into the house. Rosie, who lay on her blanket next to the wood box, barked a greeting, and jumped up, turning in happy circles. Sam grabbed the bag he'd packed the night before, made sure the fire was out, and took one last look around the house. "Thank you, Leonards! Let's go, girl." He opened the door and looked at Rosie. She sat down. "Come on, don't be stubborn. It's time to go. I know this is your home, but we've got to leave."

Rosie continued to sit.

"Rosie, I'm not kidding. Come on, girl."

With an exasperated huff, Rosie went to the wood box. She picked up her blanket and walked back to Sam, dropping it at his feet.

"Oh, I see. Yes, ma'am. We can bring this too." The blanket went into the bag. "Can we go now?"

Rosie lifted her head and walked past Sam, out the door, on her way.

Sam's nerves were on edge as they hurried along. As they passed through Copp's Hill, he heard British voices. He picked Rosie up and ducked behind a tombstone. Two soldiers were scouring the earthworks, perhaps searching for any weapons that may have been left behind. Sam held Rosie close and rubbed her head. It seemed to settle them both. The damp ground soaked through his pants. He pulled himself in tighter and stared at the gray tombstone in front of him. A scattering of bullet holes had punctured the smooth stone. One had gone into the right eye of the engraved skull. Nevertheless, the words were clear.

Here lies buried in a
Stone Grave 10 feet deep
Cap DANIEL MALCOM Merch
who departed this Life
October   23ᵈ   1769
Aged 44 Years
a true son of Liberty
a friend to the Publick
an Enemy to oppression
and one of the foremost
in opposing the Revenue Acts
on America

The voices drifted away. Sam peered around the tombstone and then stood up slowly, still holding Rosie close. All clear. He put her down and darted through the cemetery, climbing over the battery and dashing across the street to where the boat was hidden. Rosie stayed right behind him. He carried the boat to the water, lifted Rosie in, and pushed off. The oars barely broke the surface of the water as he skimmed across the dark water. Soon the shadowy outline of Charlestown appeared. It looked empty, but to be safe, Sam rowed far enough out so they would not be seen from shore. He went up the coast as far as possible until the river turned to ice. They left the boat under a low stand of bushes and began to walk, staying close to the water. The cold air bit into his lungs. He pulled the jacket closer to his chest, glad that he had not left it in the boat. It would take most of the night to reach Watertown; this coat would help. *I'll throw it in the river when I get to the Reveres'.*

Sam knew they had to follow the shoreline to a small strip of land that jutted out into the water. Directly across from there was Lechmere's Point, the narrowest part of the river and the safest, fastest place to cross. "It can't be far, Rosie. We'll be able to walk across the ice there." Sam tried to reassure them both. As they walked, he looked around for any signs of troops or Loyalists. Above them, gray wisps of clouds floated across the night sky, covering and uncovering the moon every few minutes. Suddenly the ground curved out into the water. This was it.

Sam stepped onto the ice carefully. The river groaned a little beneath his feet. The far side was a dark blur. "All right, Rosie, I'll go first. Stay." Sam walked as quickly as possible, with each step listening for the sound of ice cracking. He let out a huge breath as he stepped on the opposite riverbank. His legs trembled — from cold or fear, or both. Sam called for Rosie. She was barking at something. Sam could see three figures about two hundred yards away from her. "Rosie! They're fake. Wood dummies. Come on," Sam called a little louder, "come!" He tried again. Exasperated, Sam walked rapidly back across the ice. He scooped Rosie up, about to scold her. She was trembling too. Sam swallowed his frustration. "Shhh, girl. We're almost there." Sam walked back again, listening intently. *Halfway there, so far so good. The ice is holding.* The moon popped out and cast a bright glow over the river.

"Halt! Halt!"

Sam turned around. Three British soldiers, real soldiers, were shouting at them from the shore. And coming toward them. Sam started running.

"Halt! Deserter!"

They were almost to the other side. A few more steps. Sam put Rosie down. "Run, Rosie!"

Crack! Sam fell forward as a burning pain raced through his leg. He'd been shot! Sam groaned and crawled across the ice. Rosie scrambled up the bank and began barking. Sam pulled himself up next to her. Another shot rang out. The soldiers were running onto the ice. *I should have kept the musket. I'll never outrun them.* He stood up and leaned against a tree. Blood was running down his leg. Suddenly a splintering sound turned into a mighty roar across the river. One soldier dropped to his knees as the other two jumped backward. The ice had broken. Sam heard cursing and splashing as the two men pulled their comrade from the frozen river.

Sam hobbled a little farther, then collapsed. The pain in his left leg was excruciating. His sock was shredded at the top and soaked with blood already. *I need to stop the bleeding!* He dumped the contents of his bag. Rosie's blanket would work. He bit into it, ripping it into two pieces. "Sorry, girl," Sam whispered weakly, as he wound the fabric tightly around his leg. Rosie sat beside him. Sam stood up shakily. He could make it; he had to.

The rest of the night was a blur. Sam found the trail tree, grateful for the moonlight to see by. Even traveling on the Indian trail, he had to move slowly. The roads were full of Colonial militia. If he was seen in a British jacket, he'd probably get shot before having a chance to show the medallion. But if he took the jacket off, he would surely freeze to death. After what seemed like an eternity, they reached the crossing where the Charles River turned west. "Watertown is about seven miles from here," Sam said to Rosie, as he stopped to rest and get his bearings. Across the bay, he could see faint lights in Boston. He wondered if Hodgekins had been punished for letting him escape. He sat down against a tree and carefully felt around his leg. The cloth was soaked through, but the pressure of the bandage helped ease the pain.

Sam closed his eyes for a moment. "Ouch!" Sam grabbed his ear. Rosie had tugged at it with her teeth. His cheek was wet and slimy. Rosie barked at him and pulled his pants leg. "Yes, yes — I'm awake. You must have been trying to wake me up for a while." Sam pulled himself up to his feet, pain coursing through his leg. He reached down and gently rubbed Rosie's nose with his thumb. "Thank you, girl. You're right. We need to keep moving." He sighed.

They trudged along the river. Sam felt weaker with every mile. Surely, they would reach Watertown soon. Finally, he saw a house, then another. It was still dark, but all the houses were lit up like beacons. Sam squinted in the darkness until he saw it — the house with the rooster weathervane. Like the others, the Revere house was lit up inside and Sam could hear music. "That's the house, Rosie. They must be celebrating." Sam was so weak; his voice was barely a whisper. He looked down at his scarlet jacket. *I'd better take this off before knocking on their door.* Sam leaned against the side of the house, trying to undo the heavy buttons with his frozen fingers. A wave of darkness passed over him. He had lost so much blood. He tugged at the buttons, then felt something hard against the middle of his back.

"Stay where you are." A girl moved in front of Sam. She pointed a musket at his chest and pushed the door open with her foot. "Father!" she called inside. She had brown eyes, a small nose and a wide forehead. She was exactly how Josiah had described her.

"Deborah!" Sam whispered.

The girl's face darkened with fear. "Who are you? How do you know my name? Father!"

"Please, I'm a friend of …" Another wave of darkness. Sam stumbled into the house as a stout man rushed over to him. Sam crashed to the floor.

Paul Revere bent down and lifted him up by his jacket. "Who are you? What do you want?" Revere demanded.

Barely conscious, Sam reached into the collar of his shirt, pulled out the silver chain and mumbled, "Josiah. Josiah."

PART II

CHAPTER 8

Recovery

October 19, 1776
Boston

"Five o'clock and clear skies!"

The deep voice of the night watch rang out as Sam pushed open the door of the small barn behind the Reveres' house. The warm smell of animals, hay, and manure encircled him and took some of the dawn chill away.

"Good morning, Sherry," he called out to the back stall. At the sound of his voice, a stately horse approached the gate and began nuzzling Sam's arm — both answering his greeting and asking a question. "Yes, yes. Here you go." Sam pulled a carrot from his coat pocket and broke it into pieces. He fed them to the horse one by one and accepted her thanks — a gentle nudge with her velvet nose into his palm. Sam reached for one

171

of the brushes hanging near the stall and climbed in. He brushed the horse carefully, admiring her graceful strength. Although age was beginning to slow her down a bit, it was easy to see that Sherry had once been a powerful horse. Before the war had even started, she and Paul Revere had traveled many miles together — delivering messages and documents from the Whigs in Boston to the other colonies.

After feeding and watering Sherry, Sam sat down outside the barn to wait for Mr. Revere. They were going to the weekly market, where Mr. Revere would act as a clerk. A glittery frost covered the ground and the sharp bite of autumn added an extra crispness to the early morning air. Sam stretched out his left leg and rubbed the thick scar left from the bullet wound, still painful after seven months. The musket ball had splintered the bone, then the long walk to Watertown had almost shattered it completely. He had spent weeks in bed and then several months rebuilding the strength to walk again.

Although Sam's memories of the first few days with the Reveres were hazy, Deborah's cry when he told the family about Josiah and gave her the medallion, was a sound he would never forget. Her wrenching grief and the agony of his injury seemed to blend together in a painful, confusing fog in the weeks that followed. True to Josiah's word, the Reveres had taken him in like a family member. First, caring for his wounds, then bringing him with them when they returned to Boston following the British evacuation of the city. They even allowed Rosie to sleep in Sam's bed and seemed to understand that the gentle dog needed to be by his side to make sure he was getting better. Rosie was Sam's dog now. Like most of the Loyalists, the Leonards had not returned to Boston.

Although the British had departed on March seventeenth, their flotilla of ships — large and small — lingered in the distant harbor when General Washington and his troops entered Boston a few days later. Close behind were the families, tradesmen, and townspeople, all eager to reclaim their beloved city. The homecoming was marred by the destruction the British had wrought. Many soldiers had ignored General Howe's orders against looting as the army was leaving. Homes and warehouses were smashed and emptied. The trees were another casualty. Throughout the winter, the occupiers, cold and desperate for any kind of fuel, had cut down most of the trees. The Liberty Tree was felled in August, more out of spite by angry Loyalists than a need for firewood. For one hundred and twenty-nine years, the giant elm had graced Hanover Square and had been a gathering place for political meetings, celebrations, funerals. Even the churches were not spared. The Old South Church still stood, but its pews had been cleared out and burned. The empty building was filled with gravel and used for a riding ring by the Queen's Light Dragoons.

Fortunately, the Reveres' house at North Square had fared well during the occupation. The whole family, Paul, Rachel, seven children, and Paul's mother, had moved back in soon after the city was liberated. The girls had a room upstairs. Sam shared a small room with Paul Jr. behind the kitchen. For an only child, living with such a large family was a completely new experience for Sam. They were a happy, boisterous group, despite the uncertainty and hardships the war had brought.

The war. So much had changed since Sam had escaped the *Preston!*

The pamphlet *Common Sense* had spread like wildfire. Thousands of copies went out all over the country — first in the cities, where printers could barely keep up with orders. Next, pamphlets were carried by traveling book jobbers and Bible men to the farthest corners of the colonies; from fishermen in Massachusetts to farmers in South Carolina. A few copies, dog-eared and worn, might be passed around a whole village. The bold treatise was discussed in homes, churches, taverns, meeting posts, and stagecoaches rolling over cold, country roads. It was argued about over flip, claret, coffee, and ale. The pamphlet reached lonely stockades on the edges of Indian territory, tucked among the deep packs of fur traders, and was quickly translated into a dozen Indian tongues. Finally, *Common Sense* made its way across the ocean, and into a dozen more languages. England was enraged, France was delighted, and all over Europe the words of "an Englishman" were read with great curiosity.

As Gerard had predicted, *Common Sense* convinced many uncertain colonists that they could defeat England, *and* build a new nation. By May, assemblies from every part of the colonies were demanding that their delegates cast votes in favor of a complete severance from England. On July 18th, Sam went with the Reveres to the State House to hear the *Declaration of Independence* read from the balcony. The crowd was quiet as the solemn words rang out, and then broke into jubilant shouts. A few men climbed to the top of the building and tore off the two symbols of the British monarchy — the lion and the unicorn. The hated icons were thrown into a giant bonfire, burning rapidly as the crowd cheered. A similar event took place in New York City when a boisterous crowd pulled down a giant statue of King George astride a horse. As the statue fell, the King was decapitated. The lead from the statue — four thousand pounds — was sent to a forge in Connecticut to be quickly melted down and turned into over forty-two thousand Patriot musket balls.

The joyful celebrations of independence were short-lived however, and were followed by a string of disasters for General Washington and his fledgling army. Once Boston had been freed, the army moved to New York, where General Washington expected the enemy to strike next. Sure enough, early in the summer, even before the *Declaration*, British ships began arriving in New York Harbor — warships, frigates, transport vessels. Soon they had dispatched over thirty thousand professional soldiers, along with arms, supplies, horses — the largest expeditionary force ever launched by Britain. In addition to his own army, King George had hired eight thousand Hessians, dreaded mercenaries from Germany. The drastic difference between the well-trained, well-supplied British forces and the new American army soon became clear. In August, the Continentals were routed in the Battle of Long Island. For the first time, the untested rebel soldiers saw the ferocity of the invaders and learned to fear the long, shining blade of the British bayonet. Scottish Highlander and Hessian troops mercilessly slaughtered the Americans even as they tried to surrender. Over three hundred were killed and more than a thousand taken prisoner. The survivors barely escaped in a daring night crossing over the East River. The British now controlled all of New York City. General Washington had lost ninety percent of the army under his command.

Sam had listened to the war news with great curiosity, but the most interesting story for him was what had happened in Machias since the day of his capture. Mr. Revere had told him about it the day they went to retrieve the sunken British cannons at Butler's wharf. Sam, using crutches that Mr. Revere had made for him, was able to walk down to the docks and watch. According to Mr. Revere, on the day Sam was kidnapped, the rest of Machias had continued to search for Ichabod Jones and Captain Moore. Both had escaped — Moore back to the *Margaretta*, and Jones into the woods. Later, about twenty men from the village, led by Eamon's cousin, Jeremiah O'Brien, seized the *Unity* and outfitted her with planks and defensive breastworks. Ben Foster and another group joined them, sailing the *Falmouth Packet*. They chased down the *Margaretta*, armed with only muskets and pitchforks, and stormed the smaller boat. James Moore was fatally wounded by a musket ball to his chest. Later, Jeremiah outfitted the *Unity* with guns and swivels taken from the *Margaretta* and re-named the ship *Machias Liberty*.

Mr. Revere had laughed with delight when he told Sam the story. "O'Brien has been harassing the British ships bringing supplies to Boston. He's driving them mad. They call the waters near Machias the Hornet's Nest!" The British, however, did not find it funny that a group of unruly villagers had seized a Royal ship. In October, after several attempts to reach Machias, they sent a sixteen-gun sloop to Falmouth and bombarded the town and harbor until little was left.

Sam was amazed, and proud. He wondered if Eamon had still been there when the *Margaretta* was captured. Would he have already reached Falmouth and joined a militia? But with Falmouth destroyed, it would be much harder to return to Machias. He asked Mr. Revere about it.

Revere had glanced at Sam's bandaged leg, then patted his shoulder. "You are in no condition to make a trip like that now anyway, Sam. Write to your parents, although I am not certain that mail is even getting through yet. You are welcome to stay with us as long as you want."

Sam thought about that conversation now while waiting for Mr. Revere. A flurry of yellow and orange leaves floated down around him. The burning of Falmouth had been a year ago. Had they rebuilt the city by now? Could he find a ship to take him home? His leg was well enough to travel, but he had no money for a passage. He decided to look for work around Boston. Maybe Mr. Revere knew someone who would hire him. Sam smiled. If anyone could help him here, Mr. Revere could. Josiah had certainly been truthful with his praise and admiration for Deborah's father. Paul Revere was the most cheerful, energetic person Sam had ever met. His brown eyes sparkled with enthusiasm no matter what he was talking about. Each evening when he returned home from his workshop, he would call out as he walked through the door, "And how are my lambs today?!"

After supper, the family would sit around the hearth and he would share the news of the day. Or he would tell stories. Sam's favorite one, which every visitor to the house insisted on hearing, was about the night Paul Revere rode to sound the alarm that the British Regulars were marching on Lexington and Concord, and to warn Sam Adams and John Hancock that they were to be arrested. Sam heard it for the first time soon after he'd arrived in Watertown.

"The night was cold and the moon was as bright as day," Mr. Revere began. "Doctor Warren sent for me at ten o'clock and told me it was time to ride. Young Mr. Newman had hung the lanterns in the Christ Church and I made my way to the North Battery. The streets were full of Redcoats, all marching in full battle gear. They had moved the man-of-war *Somerset* to the mouth of the river — it almost completely blocked the way between Boston and Charlestown. Mr. Bentley and Mr. Richardson were waiting for me at the dock where a boat was hidden, and then we realized we had nothing to muffle the oars. Mr. Richardson had a lady friend who lived close by. He called up to her window and the next thing I knew, a petticoat came floating down, like a gift from heaven. And," Mr. Revere winked at Sam, "it was still warm. We wrapped the oars and made our way across, slipping right past the *Somerset*. When I got to Charlestown, John Larkin was waiting. He gave me his finest horse — ahh, she was a beauty, strong and sure-footed. From there, I rode to Medford and woke the captain of the militia. I warned every house till I got to Lexington. As I rode on, the sounds of church bells and drums filled the night. It was almost midnight when I arrived in Lexington and found Mr. Adams and Mr. Hancock staying at the Clarke home. It took a good hour to convince Mr. Hancock that he should not march out with the militia to meet the enemy." Mr. Revere shook his head at the memory.

"About halfway to Concord I was stopped by a mounted patrol of British officers. They didn't quite know what to do with me. They called me a damned rebel. One put a gun to my head and said, 'If you attempt to run, or we are insulted, we will blow your brains out.' Eventually they let me go, but they kept that beautiful horse. I made my way back to Lexington on foot and went to check on the situation there. Mr. Hancock was still insisting that he should join the battle which was sure to take place. He demanded his sword and gun. While the two of them argued about what to do next, Mr. Lowell, a clerk working for Mr. Hancock, begged me to help him retrieve a trunk from Buckman's Tavern, across the Common from the Clarkes' home. The trunk was full of important papers — information that could be used to convict every member of the Whig cause in Boston of treason. We found it in a chamber on the second floor as streaks of light appeared in the eastern sky. Through the window, I saw the British. Hundreds of soldiers, winding up Lexington Road like an enormous red serpent, their bayonets glinting in the gray light of dawn. We had no time to lose. Lowell and I wrestled the trunk down the staircase and out of the tavern. The militia was forming ranks on the Common, with Captain John Parker standing in front of the men. The British suddenly halted, but the militia stood solemn and strong." Mr. Revere paused, as if to honor the proud memory. Then he continued with the story.

"Lowell and I could not wait to see what would happen. We staggered right through the rows of men, making our way toward the woods to hide the trunk. As we passed through, I heard Captain Parker address the men, 'Stand your ground. Don't fire unless fired on. But if they mean to have a war, let it begin here!' All around us the bells continued to ring. Suddenly, a shot was fired, then another, with shouting from both sides. The British began chanting 'Huzza, huzza, huzza' amid a roar of muskets. Balls were flying thick around us. It was a miracle

Lowell and I made it to the woods unscathed. Well, you know how the rest of the day went. The militia scattered, a few lay dead on the damp ground. The Redcoats marched on to Concord, but the munitions they were searching for were well-hidden. As they rested, more militia arrived, from Bedford, Acton, Watertown. Our Minutemen chased the British Regulars all the way back to Boston with their scarlet tails between their legs!" Mr. Revere slapped his knee with delight, as if *he* were hearing the story for the first time.

Only once in the months he had been living with the Reveres did Sam see Mr. Revere in low spirits. It was the day Mr. Revere had gone to Bunker Hill to retrieve the body of his beloved friend, Doctor Joseph Warren, who had been thrown into a mass grave by the British after Bunker Hill. Ten months had passed since the June eighteenth battle and all the bodies were badly decomposed. But Mr. Revere, searching alongside Doctor Warren's brothers, knew exactly what to look for. Before the war began, he had used his skills as a dentist to fasten two artificial teeth for Doctor Warren, securing them with a silver wire. With a combination of heartbreak and relief, the three men finally found the one skull in the common grave with a silver wire still attached to the jaw. They carefully wrapped what remained of the corpse and carried their brother and friend home for a proper burial. That night Mr. Revere sat staring into the fire. He spoke softly to Mrs. Revere as she brushed aside the tears rolling down his face. "He was the finest of men, Rachel. Whatever shall we do without him? We need a leader like Joseph right now."

The insistent crowing of a nearby rooster interrupted Sam's thoughts just as Mr. Revere, with Rosie close behind, came out of the house. The market was near the town pump, directly across the square from the Revere home. Sam couldn't figure out why they called it North Square; it was actually a long triangle. The North Church, originally the tip of the triangle, had been destroyed, but houses and shops still lined the sides. From the waterfront, a block away, Sam could hear the cries of gulls as they woke up the city, and the groans of the huge ships nudging against the docks with the push and pull of the ocean. "Are we late?" He glanced up at the sky. He knew one of the duties of the clerk was to make sure no sales took place before the church bells rang to open the market. Most of the people coming from the countryside to sell their products had arrived hours earlier.

Mr. Revere chuckled. "Not if Abraham Hulton sleeps late, as he is wont to do on Saturdays. I've seen him ring the bells in his nightshirt."

"What else do you do as the clerk?" Sam asked.

"Oh, clerks generally keep the peace," Mr. Revere said. "I'll see that the stalls are set up correctly, and make sure no one gets cheated. Although most people won't risk their future customers on an underhanded short-term gain. It doesn't take long for that kind of black mark on someone's reputation to travel through this city." He patted Sam on the back. "I need you to run a few errands this morning, but you don't have stay for the whole market."

"Yes, sir," Sam said, his voice almost drowned out as they approached the market. Wagon wheels clattered against the cobblestones. Hammers rang out as the stalls were assembled. Sam followed Mr. Revere; Rosie followed Sam. He was glad she was small enough to be allowed to roam the city. In 1721, a law was passed forbidding large dogs from living within the town limits. The butchers of Boston, whose cows and sheep often lived right next to the shops, were frustrated with big dogs scaring their animals while they were still alive, and then jumping up to snatch at the fresh meat once it was hanging from the hooks.

Clang! Clang! Clang! The last traces of the night sky

disappeared with the ringing of the bell to open the market. Sam was still getting used to all the bells in Boston. Large and small, they rang constantly — from the deep, solemn toll of the church bells to the relaxed jingle of cow bells. The fire bell was fast and loud. The death bell slow and steady — sadly striking out details of the newly departed. Bells rang for school, for lunch at a tavern, for news, and most importantly, for church. Each church bell had a particular sound, like a dozen different mothers rousing sleeping children out of bed every Sunday morning. With the last clang of today's market bell, the noise level instantly tripled.

"Fresh haddock! Fresh mackerel!" The fish peddlers also piped tin horns to advertise the morning catch. Their stands, draped in cloth against the sun, shimmered with rows of slick, wet fish laid out neatly for inspection. "Oys! Fine Oys! Get yer oys!" The oystermen lumbered through the crowd, backs hunched over with wet sacks full of gray, bumpy discs. "Ha-penny for a Lob!" The lobster sellers kept their crusty wares in deep barrels. A flock of turkeys gobbled rebelliously as a young boy chased them into a pen. One particularly bold fellow took off before he could be corralled. He darted through the line of small carts moving slowly along. Sam stepped to the side to let the carts pass. One was full of vegetables — potatoes, carrots, pumpkins, onions. Another was stacked with bags of grain and cornmeal. Rosie sniffed curiously at a cart full of dead birds — pigeons, quail, ducks, and several fat geese.

Before things got too busy, Mr. Revere bought what he needed: a large leg of lamb, a firkin of butter, and two baskets of blueberries. He gave everything to Sam. "Here you go. Take this back to the house," he said with a quick wink. "Mrs. Revere needs the blueberries right away. Then you're a free man until suppertime."

"Yes, sir." Sam hurried home, proud to be helping one of the most important men in Boston.

The kitchen was crowded — Deborah, Rachel, and grandmother Revere, also named Deborah, were all busy cooking. A kettle hung over the fire and a delicious smell bubbled out of it. Sam knew they were making applesauce, yet it was strange to see the grandmother cooking. She usually sat near the stove and watched everything with a critical eye. Today though, she was mixing something in a large bowl. The younger Deborah was sitting at the table, with a mountain of apples in front of her.

Without turning around, her grandmother issued instructions. "Mind you put the sour ones at the bottom. They'll take longer to cook. And not too much molasses. Your father does not care for anything overly sweet." She huffed a little. "Now, where are those blueberries?!"

Deborah jumped up from her chair and took the berries from Sam before he could even put them on the table. She winked at Sam and seemed about to say something, when her mother shook her head slightly. Deborah grinned and handed the baskets to her grandmother.

"Mother!" an excited voice called out, followed by the sound of rushing feet down the stairs. "I've found the ribbon! It was in Fanny's sewing box!"

A small figure rushed through the doorway and crashed into Sam. She fell backward and let go of the bright pink ribbon she'd been waving. Her gap-toothed grin turned into a perfect "O" of surprise when she saw Sam.

"Is everything all right, Betsy?" He squatted down to help her and returned the ribbon to her hand.

Betsy, who was six, simply nodded. She pursed her lips closed, but her eyes were wide with excitement.

"Hey, do you want to walk over to Frog Lane later?" Sam asked.

Betsy loved listening to the endless croaking that gave the street near the South End its name. She nodded again, then she looked at her older sister and shook her head. Sam smiled at her. Usually Betsy talked non-stop. Today she seemed afraid to say anything.

Deborah spoke for her. "Betsy has a special job to do later."

"I want to play with Rosie." Betsy found her voice. "Can she stay here?"

Sam looked at all the faces in the room. A secret hovered in the air, but he did not stay to find out more. He left Rosie and walked toward the docks. A few loose hogs wandered ahead of him. He knew the city well by now and could navigate quickly through the maze of crooked streets and narrow alleys. His favorite time to explore was in the morning. The sun would flash first on the gray-green water, then slowly gleam against the dark hulks and rigging of the ships, finally lighting up the colorful signs swinging gently above the shop doors. For those who could not read, the signs showed what work was done inside. A pair of scissors marked a tailor shop; a gold lamb for a wool weaver; an ox skull for a butcher. Horses, lambs, and lions adorned different tavern doors.

As he walked toward the docks, a slight breeze brought the tangy bite of the saltwater to Sam's nose. Besides the ever-present smell of the ocean, Boston was a jumble of other scents. Not all were charming. The smell of dead whales and fish lurked in every corner. Barrels of burning tar made Sam's nose crinkle with a sharp sting. Most of the other smells were comforting, or at least interesting. The rich, deep aroma of coffee and chocolate that floated through the doors of coffee houses promised a hot drink and good conversation. Spice shops were a kaleidoscope of intriguing whiffs — like a colorful map of scents — nutmeg and mace from the Banda Islands; cinnamon from India; cloves from Zanzibar. Sam appreciated the smells from the taverns best. Roasted duck; crackling pig on a spit; and the sweet, tangy scent of flip — a warm concoction made of beer, molasses, rum, and cream or eggs.

The Long Wharf was always full of interesting sights. You might see a polar or brown bear chained to a post; or a pirate's head, pickled in a glass jar; or an Indian, selling the strong-scented Seneca oil that supposedly cured all ailments. Today, Sam walked directly to Hancock's wharf. On the way, he passed by a dozen different shops: Hiller's Waxworks, Smith's Apothecary, and Mr. Fletcher's Emporium with its mechanical planetarium and miniature model of an entire town. It was fun to watch all the tiny parts moving — ships, carriages, even a powder mill. But it cost four shillings and sixpence to go in. Sam had no money to spend on things like that. He passed Mr. Revere's shop and stopped at the one next to it. Over the door hung a black and white sign — Isaac Greenwood, Ivory Turner.

Sam opened the door. Mr. Greenwood was with a customer; Sam didn't mind waiting. As much as he liked to see all the beautiful things Mr. Revere made from silver — shining polished pots for coffee, tea, and chocolate; elaborate snuffboxes; shoe buckles, and buttons — Sam liked this shop even more. The shelves were filled with intricate objects, all carved from tusks, horns, bones, and wood. There were chess sets, hair combs, billiard balls, umbrella handles, walking sticks, even sets of teeth.

"Good day, sir." Mr. Greenwood opened the door for his customer's exit, then turned to Sam. "Hello, Sam. Are you looking for Johnny?"

"Good morning, Mr. Greenwood. Yes, I am. I also wanted to talk to you, sir. I was wondering if you might have some work for me. I need to earn enough to book a passage to Falmouth."

"Are the ships running there again?" Mr. Greenwood sat down and picked up a powder horn that was half-carved. Deep swirls covered the wide end, with long horns over them. He dug into the smooth tusk with a small chisel.

"Yes, sir."

184

"Going home?" He smiled at Sam.

"Yes." Sam pointed at the powder horn. "What is that going to be?"

"Ahh, the devil himself. A soldier from New York ordered it. Guess he thinks it will encourage him to shoot straight. Well, Sam, I wish I could help you. Unfortunately, things are a bit slow."

Sam nodded. "I understand. The war is hurting all the businesses."

"Aye, it's bound to change, but that won't help you right now. What about the Green Dragon? One of their helpers joined up last week. They could probably sort something out for you. No matter the state of things, a tavern will always be busy. People need to eat. And drink."

"Thank you. I'll go over there right now."

"Pick up Johnny on your way. He's at the town dock." Mr. Greenwood waved the powder horn at Sam. "Good luck!"

Sam went down Fish Street to avoid the market crowds. Along the way he passed several of the dozens of wharves that jutted out into the water like notches on a giant key. Halsey, Haywood, Gallop, Clark, Burrell. All old Boston families. The Hitchborn wharf had belonged to Mr. Revere's grandparents. Sam crossed over the Mill Creek, scanning the dock area, and saw a group of boys milling around behind Faneuil Hall. Nearby, Johnny was sitting on a barrel, surrounded by a small audience.

They had met in the summer, while the other boys in town were swimming off the docks every day. Sam was still recovering from his wound and Johnny was recovering from a horrific expedition to Canada under Benedict Arnold's command. Johnny was sixteen, about as tall as Sam, but pale and thin after nearly starving to death. Despite all he'd been through, Johnny was very cheerful. His eyes were brown and usually flashing with some mischief. His hair was brown too, and curly. He wore it tied in the back, but one long strand always managed to escape and bounce near his cheek like an added exclamation point to everything he said. His most prized possession was his fife. It had also survived the trip to Canada and back, although it now had a thin crack from the middle hole to the end. Johnny had filled it with pine tar, but the fife still made a slight wheezing, squeaky sound.

The other boys would tease him.

"It sounds like a mouse, dying an awful death."

"It sounds like a cat, killing the mouse and torturing it for fun."

"It sounds like you're trying to hide a fart during church."

Johnny didn't care. He played harder, louder — willing the fife by sheer breath to make music. He swore it was his good luck charm. Although he helped his father in the shop, he looked for every excuse to get out and roam the city, usually ending up with a pack of younger boys at his heels, like he had today. He loved to regale them with stories, sometimes playing the fife to add dramatic effect. One of his favorites was about the ghost of his friend, Samuel Maverick, who had been killed at the Boston Massacre in 1770. "You know," Johnny would declare proudly, "Samuel stood up to those soldiers. Everyone who was there remembered him, bold as brass, shouting — 'Fire away, you damned Lobsterbacks!' And they did. Shot him right in the belly. His poor mother. She already had the burden of being a widow. But we buried him in good faith. After his death, I used to go to bed in the dark on purpose to see his spirit, for I was so fond of him and he of me that I was sure it would not hurt me."

Today, Johnny was talking about fighting in Canada. Sam stood in the back where he could read the broadsides and newspapers posted on the building. He could see how entranced the boys were by Johnny's grisly details about the ill-fated mission to capture Quebec. Even though Sam had heard about it before, he still listened with amazement at all that the men had endured. They had left Cambridge in September, one thousand men strong, with their journey through the Maine wilderness plagued by leaky boats, impassable rivers, spoiled food, disease, and Indian attacks.

Johnny's usual grin disappeared when he talked about the worst parts. "Our boats were green. They started to leak right away. We had no maps. Started to starve by October. By the time we got to Quebec in November, we were down to less than five hundred men. Half had deserted and half died. General Montgomery had the great sense to order an attack in the middle of a raging blizzard. He was fatally rewarded for his wisdom with the very first blast of grapeshot. Colonel Arnold was hit early too. He tried to keep fighting, even after his leg was shattered. I don't remember much about the retreat except we ate candles and boiled moccasins. And the lice ate us. Men fell on the march and never got up. It was enough to make your heart burst." Johnny shivered a little bit.

A boy in the front, wide-eyed with curiosity, piped up. "Tell us about the Indians, Johnny."

Johnny hunched down a bit, his voice lowered to a whisper. His audience leaned in closer.

"The Indians fight like invisible devils. They'll follow you for days in the forest, never being seen or heard, slipping through the woods like shadows. But when they are ready, they attack with tremendous ferocity, at the same time making a most hideous noise. It's their war cry." He threw his head back and yelled, "Woo-woo-woo-whoop!"

A boy jumped backward from fright, tumbling to the ground. Sam felt the hairs on his arms prickle.

A few of the boys tried to imitate Johnny. "Woo-woo-woo-whoop!"

"That's right," he nodded, "except the last whoop is screamed and kept up so it's impossible to hear any commands from your officers. And when the fighting is over, the Indians strip the wounded and scalp the dead."

The faces around the circle were absorbed with fear and admiration. One of the youngest asked, "You going back, Johnny?"

Johnny shrugged nonchalantly and rolled his fife between his hands. "I reckon I am, Henry."

Henry let out a low whistle. "You sure are brave. Hey, play us a tune, Johnny."

"How 'bout I sing you one instead. I learned this in Albany," Johnny blew a single long note and began tapping his foot, "in honor of our esteemed trespassers."

By my faith but I think ye're all makers of bulls,
With your brains in your breeches, your bums in your skulls
Get home with your muskets and put up your swords,
And look in your books for the meaning of words.
You see, now, my honeys, how much you're mistaken,
For Concord by discord can never be taken.

How brave ye went out with your muskets all bright,
And thought to be-frighten the folks with the sight;
But when you got there how they powdered your pums,
And all the way home how they peppered your bums.
And is it not, honeys, a comical crack,
To be proud in the face, and be shot in the back?

He finished with a squeaky flourish from the fife, jumped off the barrel, and bowed. "That's it for today, fellas." Johnny walked toward Sam as his crowd of admirers dispersed. "Hey, Sam."

"Hey, Johnny. Have you been scaring these kids with murderous tales again?"

"Nothing that isn't the Lord's truth," Johnny promised,

putting his hand on his chest. "I swear."

"I'm going to the Green Dragon. Want to come?"

"Sure. Why are you going there?"

"Looking for work."

"Aye, I'll tag along. What about Mr. Revere? Can't you work for him?"

Sam shook his head. "No. I can't take money from him. It wouldn't be right. They've treated me like family. And besides, he's got seven mouths to feed."

For a few minutes they stood silently and read the broadsides. The wall was covered with public announcements — rewards for runaway slaves, horses for sale, dog fights, political cartoons, marriages, births and deaths. And news of the war, all bad. Sam looked for job and ship notices. Johnny looked for new ballads.

"What was that funny song?" Sam asked. "I've never heard it."

"The Irishman's Epistle. Hey," Johnny pointed to a large recruitment poster, "here's a job for you."

TO ALL BRAVE, HEALTHY, ABLE-BODIED AND WELL-DISPOSED YOUNG MEN

Sam read the poster. "Are you really going back?" he asked.

"Aye, I'll give it another go. Why don't you join up?" Johnny pointed to the smaller writing at the bottom of the poster. "Look at that — a twelve-dollar bounty and sixty dollars a year. You won't earn that at the Green Dragon in three years."

Sam crossed his arms and bounced on his feet to warm himself up. "Do you think the war will last much longer? The army sure has taken some beatings."

Johnny shrugged. "General George probably has a few more tricks up his sleeve."

"Starvation, disease, lice — sounds fun." Sam grimaced in

jest, but then became serious. "I want to go home. I can join a militia from there, if the war keeps going."

"How old are you?"

Sam smiled and pointed to the date on the Boston Gazette. "Fifteen. Actually, today is my birthday."

"Well, if the war does go on, you'll have to join up next year, anyway. It makes sense to see your folks while you can."

"Yeah." Sam put his hands in his pockets. "For all I know, they think I'm dead."

Johnny pulled out his fife, and playing idly, began to stroll. Sam gave a final glance to the newspaper. *Things do seem pretty grim for the rebels. And fighting will stop for the winter soon.* He turned away from the building and caught up to Johnny. *I doubt I could make much of a difference for the war. I need to get home and help run the mill.* Lost in his thoughts, Sam didn't realize they had reached the tavern — a two-story brick building with a square and compass symbol above the door to show that it was a Freemason lodge. A ferocious copper dragon, now green with age, stuck out from an iron bar.

Johnny smiled in admiration. "Ahh, the good old Dragon. The Sons of Liberty hatched many a revolutionary plot in this basement."

Inside, the smell of stew and cider made Sam's stomach growl. Johnny sat near the huge fireplace while Sam spoke to the owner, Benjamin Burdick.

Sam came back a few minutes later, looking much more cheerful. "He said I can start on Monday, if Mr. Revere agrees."

"Huzzah!" Johnny thumped the table.

"Let's go." Sam turned toward the door.

"We can't. I ordered some flip." Johnny shrugged.

"Flip? I don't have any money."

A tavern maid approached carrying a tray with two mugs of the steaming, frothy drink. She was very tall, with black hair and deep blue eyes. She put Johnny's mug down, then winked at him. As she gave Sam a mug, she leaned over and kissed his cheek. Johnny burst out laughing and leaned over to punch a red-faced Sam in the arm.

"It's on me! Happy birthday, Sam!" Johnny exclaimed delightedly.

Sam blushed again slightly a few minutes later when the tavern maid came back to settle up. Johnny pulled out a small coin purse, heavy and full.

"That's a lot of money," Sam said quietly.

"A hundred dollars in silver! I finally got paid from the round trip to Canadian hell and back." He jangled the purse.

"Are you sure you should be carrying it around?"

Johnny stood up. "I've got to go pay a big bill. It's something pretty special. Want to see?"

Sam nodded. They left the tavern and walked until they got to a tailor shop.

"Hello, Mr. Shaw!" Johnny greeted the man behind the counter. "Is it ready?"

Mr. Shaw nodded. "Do you want to try it on?"

"Try it on?" Johnny exclaimed, "I'm going to wear it home!"

He emerged from the back room a few minutes later wearing a blue suit lined with white fabric and laced with silver threads along the collar and sleeves. Beaming with delight, he stood in front of the mirror, turning from side to side. "Take a look at these!" He held up his hands. The buttons on the jacket were shiny brass, engraved with the image of a fox and the word *Tallio*. "Yes, sir, even George Washington himself would covet these. I'm a fine gentleman now!"

Sam suppressed a laugh. So, *this* was Johnny's big surprise. It certainly was special. His friend's face glowed with pride. Sam rubbed the sleeve of the jacket. The fabric felt rich and silky between his fingertips. "It's sharp, Johnny. Very sharp. I have to get back to the market. Thanks for the flip, and, uh, everything."

Johnny continued admiring his reflection and waved good-bye. "Many happy returns, Sam!"

Sam got to the market as it was closing. He was surprised to see Mr. Revere leading a horse home.

Mr. Revere saw Sam's puzzled expression and explained, "I borrowed her from Mr. Blake. I need to go out to the Canton mill today. Why don't you come with me? You can ride Sherry."

"Yes, sir. Should I make sure Mrs. Revere doesn't have any chores for me?"

"Oh, don't worry about that," Mr. Revere said casually. "I'll tell her. Go saddle up Sherry and we'll leave in a bit."

Again, Sam had a feeling that something was going on. And where was Rosie? Usually she would be waiting for him on the front step. *Well, it isn't my place to question Mr. Revere.* Sam led Sherry from the barn.

Colorful trees lined the road to the mill. The afternoon sun warmed their backs. Despite the beautiful day, Mr. Revere sounded discouraged while explaining to Sam the purpose of their trip. "This mill is one of only two working gunpowder mills in all the colonies. For decades, our gunpowder was shipped from England until King George outlawed it a few years ago because of our rebellious behavior. We've had to start from scratch with running new mills. The Canton mill has been up since January, but we have had reports that the powder produced there is of an unpredictable quality, not to mention how little we are able to make. I daresay our troops would have prevailed at Bunker Hill with more powder. Anyway, we'll see what's acting today. Major Crane is a talented man, and a true patriot. I feel certain he has made progress. If not, there is another mill outside of Philadelphia that may be able to help us resolve the problems here."

The mill was surrounded by a high post-and-rail fence. A guard, musket in hands, stepped in front of the gate. Once he recognized Mr. Revere, he nodded respectfully. Inside, Thomas Crane took Mr. Revere into his office, while another man showed Sam around the mill. The cogs and axles were similar to a sawmill, but instead of blades, they turned giant millstones around to crush the different components of gunpowder into a dusty mix. Mr. Revere and Sam stayed for an hour, leaving with a few samples of the newest batch of powder.

The sun was just beginning to set as they crossed from Roxbury to the Boston Neck. After they rode across the causeway separating Boston from the mainland, Mr. Revere stopped and climbed down from the borrowed horse. Handing Sam the reins, he said, "Please return her to Mr. Blake, with my deepest thanks. I'll take Sherry back."

Walking home, Sam stopped at the Long Wharf to check the ship schedules and prices. It would probably cost him seven dollars to get a passage to Falmouth. Mr. Burdick would pay him a dollar a week. *I wonder if I'll have to pay for Rosie too. I'd better plan on needing at least eight dollars for food and a coat for the walk from Falmouth to Machias. So, if I work for eight weeks and get a passage in the middle of December, I could get home by January.*

He swallowed hard at the thought. The pull of home was so strong. Maybe because it was his birthday. He never got a lot of presents, but his mother always made doughnuts — which made the day a little special. *She must be so sad today. If they had gotten my letters, surely, they would have written back by now.* Approaching the Revere house, Sam shook himself from his melancholy. He had a plan now. *And at least I'm not spending this birthday on a prison ship.*

He pushed open the front door with a small sigh.

"Surprise!"

Sam shuffled backward; eyes wide. The entire Revere family stood in the hallway, smiling at him. Mrs. Revere stepped forward and hugged Sam. "Happy birthday, Sam." She tousled his hair.

"Happy birthday, Sam! Look! Look at Rosie!" Betsy made her way toward him, holding Rosie proudly. Rosie, who looked like she had been bathed and brushed all day, also wore the bright pink ribbon he'd seen earlier. Rosie looked less than thrilled with her decoration and wiggled her way out of Betsy's arms.

"How did you know it was my birthday?" Sam said with astonishment.

Mr. Revere laughed and gently directed him toward the kitchen. "My wife must have asked you sometime in the past few months, and she never forgets a birthday. Now come sit down. I hope you are hungry. The ladies have prepared quite a supper to celebrate."

He *was* hungry, starving, actually. The meal was grand — roast lamb and potatoes, boiled corn, fresh applesauce, and for dessert, blueberry pie, baked by Grandmother Revere.

"This is the best blueberry pie I've ever tasted," Sam told her, as he finished off a second flaky slice. The blueberries reminded him of home, but something about this pie piqued his curiosity. "What is the special flavor?"

The old woman beamed uncharacteristically. "Lavender. *Un petite peu.* An old recipe from Paul's French grandmother, Serenne Rivoire."

"Lavender in pie. I'll have to tell my mother about this."

"Here Sam. These are for you." Deborah handed him a bundle wrapped in paper. Sam opened it to find a thick wool scarf and a vest of fine woven cloth.

"It was mine, but I outgrew it pretty fast," Paul Jr. spoke from the other end of the table, "and Father made a new set of buttons."

Sam looked closely. The pewter buttons were stamped with the image of a small tree, the same one as he had seen on the pine tree pennies Mr. Revere had made a few months earlier.

"Maybe soon we'll have enough copper to mint more coins. At least the penny mold is still good for something," Mr. Revere commented.

Sam looked around the table, almost unable to speak. "Thank you for everything. I didn't expect anyone to even know it was my birthday, and you did so much."

"You are part of our family now, Sam," said Mrs. Revere, smiling warmly at him.

"Aye." Mr. Revere raised his glass. "We know you are anxious to return to Machias. Just remember, as long as there are Reveres are living in Boston, you have a home here."

Sam raised his glass in thanks. The kindness and generosity of the Reveres overwhelmed him. He wondered if he could ever repay them for all they had done for him.

CHAPTER 9

Cowards and
Sunshine Soldiers

December 8, 1776
Boston

Eight sacks of coffee. Four sacks of sugar. One hogshead of molasses. Six barrels of salt pork. Two hogsheads of cider. Four barrels of rum. Got it?"

Sam checked the list in his hand and nodded. Once everything was rolled down to the basement, he counted out some coins and handed them to the young man helping him. "Here you are. Thanks, Caleb."

"See you next week, Sam." Caleb pushed his empty cart down the alley behind the Green Dragon.

Sam went inside and handed the coin purse and list

to Mr. Burdick.

"Well done, Sam. That should do it for today. How about a cider before you go?"

"Sure." Sam hung his apron in the kitchen and grabbed his coat. He sat at the counter.

The man next to him was reading the *Gazette*. He folded up the paper, scowling, and signaled for another drink.

"What's the news?" Mr. Burdick asked.

"Terrible, terrible," the man said. "Cornwallis is right on Washington's tail. He's chased him across the entire state of New Jersey. I don't see how the army can hold out much longer."

Mr. Burdick frowned. "Aye, the fall of Fort Washington was bad enough — two thousand men and all their equipment captured. And then to lose Fort Lee as well. It's a wonder there's anyone left to fight at all."

"If the Brits take Philadelphia, I'd say the war is finished."

Sam half-listened to the conversation. He was wondering if the new ship schedules were posted down at the docks. Behind him, the tavern door opened. Mr. Burdick's worried face broke into an amused grin. "Well, here's a beau-monde fellow!"

Johnny, wearing his blue suit, approached the counter. "Good day, Mr. Burdick."

"Good day, sir. What can I get for you?"

"Nothing, thank you." Johnny tilted his head toward Sam. "I was looking for him."

Sam pushed his empty mug across the counter.

"I'm headed to the Long Wharf. Want to come? Good-bye, Mr. Burdick."

Outside, Sam pulled his tricorn hat down against the damp air. He would definitely need a warmer coat for the voyage home. "Everything all right?"

"I came to say good-bye. I have to go join my unit." Johnny was as cheerful as ever.

"Where are you going? It sounds like the army is all over the place."

"New Jersey, Brunswick," Johnny said casually.

They reached the Long Wharf. Sam scanned the ship notices. "Look. This one is going to Falmouth on December twelfth. But it's eight dollars. I've only got six saved so far, seven when I get paid next week." He groaned in frustration.

Johnny looked at Sam for a moment, then pulled out his coin purse. "Here."

"What?!" Sam stared at the heavy coins Johnny had placed in his hand.

"Take it. I know how much you want to go home." Johnny nodded.

"Two dollars!" Sam gasped. "How will I be able to pay you back?"

Johnny reached out to shake Sam's other hand. "You can always find me here, when the war is over. Good luck, Sam."

Sam grabbed his friend and hugged him. "I will. I promise. Thank you, Johnny. And good luck to you too. Good-bye!"

Sam's thoughts were spinning as he hurried back to North Square. Home!! It was really going to happen. *The boat leaves on a Sunday; I'll probably have to stay one night in Falmouth. If there is another one going to Machias, I'll be home the next day. Otherwise, it will take at least two days to walk, depending on the weather. And I'll need food for Rosie and me.* He reached the house bursting with excitement. He couldn't wait to tell the Reveres the good news. Rosie rushed to greet him. He picked her up and squeezed her happily.

Suddenly, the sound of Rachel's angry voice carried from upstairs. "No! Absolutely not! Not this time!"

Sam stopped in the kitchen. He had never heard Rachel yell before. Still holding Rosie, he walked up to the second floor.

Deborah was standing in the doorway of her parents' bedroom. Paul was sitting on the edge of their canopy bed, with one boot on, his face was pale and sweaty. Rachel crossed her arms and stubbornly stood her ground between her husband and the door. "Paul, I insist. I have watched you head out of this house many times when you were exhausted. This time, you must stay. You are too ill to travel."

"Yes, yes. I know. But we need those mill plans! If we can't produce a better powder, the Revolution is finished!" Revere held his hands out helplessly.

"Well, you are of no use to the war if you are dead from fever. Someone else will have to go."

Mr. Revere knew he was defeated. He groaned and fell back on to the pillows.

Sam whispered to Deborah, "What's going on?"

"Father was supposed to go to the Frankford gunpowder mill, near Philadelphia," Deborah said quietly. "The powder coming from the Canton mill is not working properly. Father was going to bring back some sketches of the other mill, and some powder. But he's too ill."

Sam stood for a few moments, watching Rachel tend to her coughing, exhausted husband. He squeezed Rosie again, more gently, and whispered in her ear, "You're going to have to wait a little longer to see Machias."

The road to Philadelphia was smooth and well-traveled. Except for the cold weather, Sam enjoyed the eight-day journey. Sherry was easy to ride and each night they stayed with a different friend of Mr. Revere. He and Sherry had traveled this route countless times over the past few years. Every family Sam stayed with was eager to hear news of their old friend. Sam also carried a letter that read:

All persons along the road assist this Bearer with Horse or other things he may be in need of.
P. Revere

Even though Sam was a little nervous about making the trip alone, when he had offered to go, Mr. Revere's tired, flushed face relaxed. He did not hesitate or wonder if Sam could manage it. Sam felt proud that Mr. Revere had so much faith in him. Going to Philadelphia might mean a few more weeks' delay in returning to Machias, but it was worth it to Sam. He was glad to have found a way to help Paul Revere. Rosie would stay in Boston while he was away. Sam packed a small bag, with a spare shirt and socks, and Gerard's book. He carried the mill sketches and powder sample in a leather tube.

The Frankford mill was about six miles from the city and owned by Oswald Eve, a ship captain and merchant. Mr. Eve's letters to Mr. Revere concerning the visit had been less than enthusiastic. He reluctantly agreed to show Mr. Revere the mill only after he received a letter from two Continental Congressmen, writing to remind Mr. Eve that it was his public duty to help establish another source of gunpowder for the Patriot cause. Once he arrived in the city, Sam was to report to Robert Morris, also a member of the Continental Congress.

Before Sam left, Mr. Revere went over a map of the route to Philadelphia with him and expressed his frustration with Mr. Eve's secrecy regarding the mill. "Confound the man! He knows the situation is desperate. The troops are in dire need of powder! General Washington reports that the army is down to half a pound per man. Why in heaven's name would Eve not want to do something that will help our cause immensely?! It makes me question the gentleman's true loyalty." Mr. Revere also coached Sam on what to say, hopeful that Sam going in his place might yield more information from a wary Mr. Eve than

Mr. Revere would. "I know it is a bit dishonest, but it's best that you approach Mr. Eve under the guise of a traveler looking for work. Once you are in the mill, you must procure some powder, and memorize every detail of the works. Sketch it if possible. Mr. Morris will help you refine the sketches. He may also have some news on the saltpeter we are expecting from Barbados. Once you return, we can make the necessary adjustments and we'll have the Canton mill fixed in no time!"

It worked better than Sam could have hoped. He stayed one night with the Eves, telling them he was on his way to Philadelphia to return the horse to an uncle. The Eves were happy for an extra hand. Two of their mill workers had fled the previous day, fearing a British attack. Sam helped for a few hours in the mill, then left in the afternoon, anxious to get to the Morris house before dark.

As he rode toward the city, Sam marveled at how easy it had been to get everything he needed from the mill. He spoke cheerfully to Sherry. "Well, girl, I guess telling a small lie to the Eves is not a high price to pay for something as important as this." He patted her smooth, strong back. "Maybe I'm not cut out to be a soldier, but if I can help get another source of gunpowder for General Washington — that is a pretty good way to help the Revolution."

Sam figured he would spend two days in Philadelphia and let Sherry rest. If he left on the eleventh, got back to Boston on the twentieth … could he possibly be home by Christmas? It all depended on whether he could find a ship going to Falmouth, of course. Sam imagined surprising his parents for Christmas. He wondered again if they had received the letters he'd sent from Boston. Sam was so preoccupied with these thoughts that he did not notice that the road had become very crowded. Wagons piled high with belongings, and livestock tied to the back; young children seated in buggies and on smaller carts. The scene was eerily familiar. Suddenly Sam recognized it all — it was exactly like the evacuation of Boston. The only difference was that the people desperately fleeing Boston were Tories, and these people were Whigs. Their faces looked the same — frightened and panicky.

As he approached from the north to where the bridge crossed Frankford Creek, everything stopped. The crowd thinned on Sam's side of the bridge, but he could see that more and more people were leaving the city, coming down the road from the south toward the bridge. The narrow creek was frozen, so people on foot were able to cross. The bridge was blocked by a wagon that had turned too far to the right, wedging its left back wheel against the corner of the bridge. The owner of the wagon was visibly frustrated — it should have been a simple maneuver to loosen the wheel. But for some reason, the horse refused to move. Perhaps it was the glare of the icy creek. Perhaps it was the chaos of all the people crowding behind him. The horse was spooked. As the man grew angrier, the horse became more agitated. Sam climbed down and tied Sherry to the opposite side of the bridge. Sam and several men offered to help try to lift the wagon slightly and loosen it, but their efforts made no difference. It was up to the horse. The crowd waiting to cross the bridge grew longer, and Sam could see no solution. From Mr. Revere's directions and map, Sam knew the creek was too wide to cross at any other point for at least a mile east or west of where they were stopped.

The crowd's attention shifted to a man walking briskly down the road, coming from the north, as Sam had. Barely stopping as he approached the bridge, the man quickly evaluated the situation, his arms crossed, his intense gaze taking in every detail. He observed the position of the lodged wagon wheel, and then watched the horse for a few seconds, saying nothing. Standing nearby, Sam was able to study the man's face. Two thick, bushy brows arched above eyes the darkest shade of blue, almost black. A large, and slightly red nose. Weathered skin, creased with wrinkles around his eyes. Dark-brown hair streaked with gray. He looked about the same age as Sam's father. He also noticed the man's fingers — cracked and stained with ink. The faces of everyone else on the bridge reflected fear, frustration, even anger. Yet this man's face was completely different. Although clearly worn with fatigue, his face was lit up with determination. His eyes sparkled with confidence as he turned to the wagon owner and finally spoke. "Please, sir, give me your cloak." He spoke with a British accent. Instantly, the crowd grew suspicious.

"What?" the farmer protested.

"Your cloak, for a moment, sir," he repeated, impatient with the wagon owner's inability to see the solution as plainly as he did.

The cloak was handed over. The man approached the horse slowly and spoke in a quiet voice. The horse relaxed and seemed to be listening to his words. After a minute or so, the man carefully placed the cloak over the horse's head, and then pulled the end of it over the horse's eyes. Still speaking softly to the horse, the man gently tugged on the bridle. As if hypnotized, the horse moved steadily forward — pulling hard against the braces as the wheel slowly inched its way out of the wedge between the posts. The wagon rolled over the bridge, with its astonished owner scrambling to follow. "Many thanks, good sir!" he called out as he jumped up onto the wagon seat.

The dark-haired man waved easily in return. "It was only common sense!"

The crowd waiting to cross the bridge parted to let him continue down the road. Several people tipped their hats or bowed in silent gratitude. Sam, the only other traveler headed south, grabbed Sherry's reins and quickly followed him on foot.

The stranger slowed his pace to let Sam catch up. As they

walked together, with Sherry a few feet behind, the man eyed Sam with a curious expression. "Well, young man. Why are you not fleeing Philadelphia with the rest of this frantic mob? Aren't you afraid of the British?"

Sam was silent for a moment. This man was British. Could he be trusted? Sam decided to tell the same story he had given the Eves, and then concluded by saying, "So, after I return my uncle's horse, I'll make my way back to Boston."

"What is your name?"

"Samuel Nevens. Everyone calls me Sam."

"My name is Thomas. Sam," Thomas spoke rapidly, gesturing in the opposite direction, "do you know that thirty-five miles from here, General Washington is in desperate need of soldiers? In less than a month, hundreds of enlistments will be up, and the army will lose even more men."

"Yes, sir, I know the situation is pretty bad. With all due respect, though, I don't think I'd be much of a soldier."

Thomas frowned. "Why would you say that?"

Sam shook his head slightly. It was too complicated to explain his feelings, even though something about this man seemed so familiar and trustworthy. He decided to change the subject. "Do you really believe that they can defeat the British?" Sam asked doubtfully. "It seems that things are going badly for the army. I've heard they might not last the winter."

"Nonsense!" The frown on Thomas' face was replaced by an indignant scowl. "Do not be misled by the deplorable and melancholy condition of ill-informed people. They are afraid to speak, to think! Nothing in circulation except fear and falsehoods. Of course, the Continental army will last the winter, as long as those rascals in Congress give them the supplies they need." Thomas began to walk faster. "I've been with the Americans for almost a year. Their spirit and will are tremendous. And General Washington is a leader who comes once in a century. He will prevail. The Revolution will prevail. Can the British be defeated? Absolutely! Don't mistake the arrogant complacency that exudes from the lowliest officer all the way up to those intolerable Howe brothers for actual competence. The British are vulnerable in countless ways. First ..."

Thomas' words faded a bit as Sam stared at his face. Again, it occurred to him how familiar this man seemed. Sam felt he had heard these words before. And it was not merely his words. Although Thomas was obviously exhausted, as he spoke, he became so animated. His face flushed red with excitement and his eyes crackled with energy. Suddenly the recognition hit Sam like a thunderbolt. This man was exactly like Eamon — full of fire and spit. Sam chuckled as he made the connection. Then another realization struck. "Excuse me, sir. I don't mean to interrupt, you said you have been with the troops for a year. I wonder if you may have met a friend of mine from home. His name is Eamon Collins." Sam spoke eagerly. "He's Irish, about five feet tall. He would be with a militia from Falmouth or somewhere else in Massachusetts."

Thomas ceased his dissection of the weakness of the British military and thought for a moment. "Collins? Eamon Collins? No, I can't say I remember a lad by that name. Are you sure he is still with the army?"

Sam slouched with disappointment. "No, I don't know what happened to him after I left home."

Thomas watched Sam's face cloud over with worry. His own expression shifted quickly from indignation to sympathy. He placed his hand on Sam's shoulder. "I'm sure your friend is fine, son. There are over a thousand men in the camp. I didn't meet them all. Or perhaps he has made his way home already." By now, they had reached the outskirts of the city. Thomas glanced at the road ahead, and then turned to his young companion. "Are you sure you know where you're going, Sam?"

"Yes, sir. Mr. Rever — uh, I have a map." Sam caught himself in time. Although it was clear that Thomas was no British spy, Sam was still wary of revealing the true reason for his visit.

"Fine, then I shall make my way to Front Street," Thomas bowed slightly, "and if you find yourself staying for more than a few days, please visit me. I'll treat you to the finest oysters that can be found in this city. I wish you good luck, Sam."

"Thank you, Thomas. Good luck to you, too, sir."

They shook hands and parted.

Sam arrived at the Morris' home as the seven o'clock bells began to ring. He introduced himself to the servant who answered the door and then directed Sam to the barn. After Sherry was fed and brushed, he returned to the house. Deborah had said Robert Morris was the richest man in Philadelphia. His home was certainly the largest Sam had ever seen. It had three floors and a stable big enough for two buggies. The servant took Sam's coat and bag and told him to wait in the sitting room. Sam shifted nervously on the couch. He had never been in a home so grand before. Woven carpets covered the floors and real oil paintings hung on the walls. Sam heard the front door open and in the next second, a large man, his wide face flushed red with cold, burst into the room. He reached for Sam's hand and shook it vigorously. "Sam, Sam. Welcome. I apologize that no one from the family was here to greet you. Mrs. Morris and the children have gone to Baltimore, much safer for them there. How was your journey? Have you been to the mill? Please, come into the dining room. Dinner is ready."

The dining room glowed with flickering light from a large chandelier and a dozen more candles arranged on a long table. Gold-rimmed dishes and sterling silverware marked two places at the end, near the warmth of the fireplace. The servant began to bring in plates of food. Sam's mouth watered as their delicious aromas filled the air. Mr. Morris spoke rapidly. His round, soft chin bobbed up and down as he settled into his chair and began to serve the food. Sam's eyes opened wider with amazement when a huge steak was set on his plate by Mr. Morris.

Mr. Morris grinned. "Eat up! We slaughtered all the livestock at our country house. I'll forfeit whatever meat we can't eat, rather than let the British get it!"

Sam was ravenous. He told Mr. Morris about his trip, and visiting the mill. He wanted to ask Mr. Morris about the man he met on the road, although he felt foolish that he didn't even know Thomas' last name. In the end, Mr. Morris had so many questions about the state of things in Boston, Sam had no chance to ask any questions of his own.

After supper, he and Mr. Morris went into the study and sat down in front of a huge roll top desk. Mr. Morris read Sam's notes, Mr. Revere's notes, and reviewed the sketches Sam had been able to make. He sprinkled a small amount of gunpowder from each mill on to a sheet of paper and pinched each sample between his fingers. He took out some clean paper and began to write down his own notes. He asked Sam some questions as he worked. Sam, sitting close to the fire with a full belly, was soon overcome by intense drowsiness. He could barely stay awake. His head grew heavier, nodding precariously close to the edge of the desk several times.

Mr. Morris smiled at Sam's desperate, losing battle against sleep. He shook Sam's arm gently. "Go on then, get yourself to bed. I'll finish these up and we'll tend to any unanswered questions in the morning. Sam, you've done a fine job today. Good night."

Even from the second-floor bedroom, Sam could smell the wonderful aroma of bacon frying when he woke up the next morning. He inhaled gratefully, then quickly got out of bed and dressed. The servant from the night before was placing bowls and plates on the dining room table. He nodded to Sam. "Mr. Morris had an early appointment. He will return shortly to join you for breakfast."

"I'll go take care of Sherry first," Sam said, and breathing in another delicious, bacony whiff, he reached for his cloak and headed out the door for the barn.

When Sam returned to the dining room, Mr. Morris and another man were standing at a small table near the window, looking at a newspaper together. The other man was much older than Mr. Morris. He wore the uniform of a Continental officer. The buttons of his waistcoat seemed to be straining to hold his stout stomach in place. Creases of time and weather were etched in the corners of his deep, wide eyes.

"Good morning, Sam!" Mr. Morris' cheerful face was the complete opposite of his companion's serious countenance. "May I present General Israel Putnam."

General Putnam! "Old Put," as his soldiers called him. Josiah had talked about him with a mixture of admiration and fear. A soldier famous for his bold fighting as part of Roger's Rangers during the French and Indian War, Putnam had been scalped and almost burned alive at the stake. After the war, he had settled down as a farmer and tavern owner in Connecticut. When he learned of the fighting at Lexington and Concord, he left his plow right in the middle of a field and rode a hundred miles to Boston to volunteer for the Patriot cause.

Mr. Morris continued. "General Putnam is in charge of the city for the time being. Martial law has been declared, so he will write you a pass to get through any checkpoints you may encounter."

General Putnam stood up and bowed to Sam. He was barely taller than Sam's mother, but his face was as fierce as a bulldog. "It is indeed a great pleasure to meet someone who is so well regarded by my dear friend, Mr. Revere." He smiled, though his face was tired. "We are grateful for your assistance with Mr. Eve. You seem to have made great progress with that intractable gentleman where no one else could."

Mr. Morris interrupted him by gesturing toward the table covered with platters of food. "Yes, yes — for goodness' sake, Put. A man could starve, waiting for you to stop talking. Sit down, sit down. We can't win a revolution on empty stomachs!"

As with the night before, there was enough food on the table to feed twenty people. Pancakes, bacon, porridge, fruit. General Putnam filled his cup from an intricately-engraved silver coffeepot. Mr. Morris raised a small glass of claret. "To a short and honorable war!" he said eagerly.

General Putnam's face reflected another emotion. "Your optimism is admirable, Robert, but I expect nothing but a long war, and I would have it a moderate one, that we may hold out till the mother country becomes willing to cast us off forever." He turned to Sam. "Mr. Morris and I have been discussing the current news from General Washington. Unfortunately, the New Jersey militia has not turned out to support the Continentals as we had expected. The Howe brothers' offer of pardon has changed the minds of many from revolution to resignation."

"Ahhh, yes." Mr. Morris picked up the newspaper and began reading out loud, his voice tinged with sarcasm. "We are all invited to 'reap the benefit of his Majesty's paternal goodness, in the preservation of our property, the restoration of our commerce, and the security of our most valuable rights, under the just and moderate authority of the crown and parliament of Great Britain. Forgiveness and protection are promised to anyone who pledges to remain in peaceable obedience to his Majesty, and not take up arms, nor encourage others to take up arms, in opposition to His Authority.' Balderdash!" He smacked the paper against the table. "I am disgusted by how many of our brothers are lining up in Brunswick to concede defeat and swallow this rubbish! Did they not anticipate the hardships and calamities of war when they so boldly dared Britain to arms? Every man then was a brash patriot, felt himself equal to the contest, but now when we are fairly engaged, when death and ruin stare us in the face, many of those who were foremost in noise, shrink faint-hearted from the danger." Morris turned his frustration to a stack of pancakes, slicing them with ferocity.

General Putnam growled, "Cowards and sunshine soldiers. They discovered that actual war is harder than dancing around a Liberty pole or finding a convenient Tory to tar and feather. Nevertheless, we must return to the matter at hand. What of the gunpowder?"

"Clearly," Mr. Morris waved a piece of pancake on his fork, "from what Sam was able to find, our problem is either the mix of all three components, or the structure of one. I suspect it is the quality of saltpeter. We have never been able to master the production, and the inferior stuff we are using is throwing off the entire combination needed for a decent powder. We've got to find a way to produce the saltpeter we need here in the colonies and not have to worry about bringing it from Barbados, or some other unpredictable source."

A bell rang in the hallway. Morris' servant came in. "General, Major Burr is here for you."

General Putnam considered Morris' words as he pushed back from the table. "Saltpeter? Well, the one man I'd say can help us is Mr. Paine. He's familiar with the process developed in France. I recall that soon after he arrived here, one of his first articles for the *Pennsylvania Journal* was about saltpeter."

"Paine? Isn't he with General Greene in Newark?" Morris said.

Putnam nodded. "He has been. But I saw him last night at the London. I would seek him out myself, but I am already late for a meeting." He rose and walked to the small desk, returning with a note. He gave it to Sam, then shook his hand as he bowed good-bye. "Young man, I thank you again for your service to our glorious Cause. If you have any troubles, do not hesitate to contact me. Please give my warmest regards to Mr. Revere upon your return to Boston. Robert, a fine meal, as always. I will see you later, I'm sure. Good day, gentlemen."

As the door closed behind Putnam, Mr. Morris thumped the table and grinned. "Sam, your timing is excellent! Providence smiles upon us even on the bleakest days. Go find Mr. Paine and query him about the powder." He stood up. "I must get to the docks. A ship from the West Indies is due any moment with enough supplies to keep the army going a few more weeks. Take the notes and the powder samples. Keep your wits about you. The city is in chaos. The Whigs are panicking and the Tories are celebrating — two equally dangerous groups."

Sam, less sure of this plan than Mr. Morris was, asked, "How will I find Mr. Paine? I don't know what he looks like. And what if the British invade the city? Shouldn't I head back to Boston before the roads become too dangerous?"

"Don't worry. One thing the British army does *not* do is move quickly. You can easily leave from the south and make your way back through, if necessary. Now, go to the London Coffee House and ask for Mr. Paine. Everyone knows him. You may have to wait for a while, but he'll show up sooner or later. If all goes well, you'll be on your way tomorrow or the next day. And we can present General Washington with the timely gift of quality gunpowder for the new year!"

Still uneasy, Sam made his way to the London Coffee House on foot. Unlike Boston, with its crooked, rambling streets, Philadelphia was laid out in a perfect grid. The streets going north to south were numbered; the streets going east to west were named after trees — Walnut, Chestnut, Spruce. Most of the streets were eerily quiet, with shops boarded up and houses dark and empty. But it soon became clear that not everyone was fleeing the city. Sam passed a tavern where loud laughter and music burst from the door as a short, red-faced man stumbled out. He was dressed in fine clothing with a plumed hat atop a powdered wig. The wig had shifted so that one eye was covered. His dignified apparel was compromised by his weaving figure. With one hand, he gripped the stair railing and clumsily made his way down the steps. With his other hand, he pushed the hat down onto his head and covered up his other eye in the process. He tried to summon a pretense of decorum by standing up straight, but inebriation triumphed and he fell slowly backward into an awkward heap at the bottom of the stairs.

I guess he won't be the first in line to welcome the British. Sam continued down Front Street, still wondering if staying in Philadelphia much longer was a wise decision. *Well, Mr. Morris doesn't seem too worried. I guess I can get out quick enough with Sherry if I need to.* Sam reached the intersection of Front and Market streets and saw it — the London Coffee House. The smell of tobacco and coffee swept over him as he stepped inside. This was larger than any coffee house in Boston. Rows of tables filled the room and booths lined the walls. The crowded room hummed with men smoking pipes, drinking coffee or ale, and talking. Sam made his way to the back where the tavern keeper stood behind a wide counter, polishing a tall copper coffeepot. Two men sat at the counter, each holding a tankard.

Sam had to shout to be heard over the din.

"Mr. Paine?" The tavern keeper nodded. "Aye, he was here last night. I dare say he'll be back today, as well. Shall I take a message?"

"No, I can wait, thank you. Do you think he will be here soon?"

"Hard to say. Can I get you something while you wait,

young man?"

"A small cider, please."

The man seated next to Sam spoke. "I thought Paine was with the troops."

The tavern keeper handed Sam a small mug. "He was, but now he's here and in a right state, trying to find a printer. Most of the papers are closed up."

The other man at the counter spoke next. "Aye, he's working on another pamphlet. He's fired up about it, more than I've ever seen, to be truthful. Something for the troops, he told me. To get them through these black days."

"Well," the tavern keeper said adamantly, "if anyone can bring those men the inspiration they need, it's good ol' Common Sense!"

The man beside Sam nodded. "That's for certain. Half a million copies sold and he never took a shilling from that pamphlet — gave all the proceeds to the army, to buy mittens and such."

Sam nearly spit out his cider. *Common Sense?!* This Mr. Paine he was waiting for was the author of *Common Sense?!* Sam thought back to the sacks of the pamphlet the guards threw into their prison cell on the *Preston*. He could practically feel the damp, cold paper in his hands again. He remembered reading it to Gerard over and over, and Gerard's absolute conviction that this pamphlet would change the war, and the world. Gerard's words echoed in his memory. *Sam, you must find this man. You must find him and thank him.* Sam shook his head, smiling nonetheless. He didn't genuinely believe in ghosts or spirits returning after death, but somehow it felt like Gerard, wherever he was, had somehow orchestrated this meeting.

Sam thanked the tavern keeper and went to sit at a table by the door, although he realized he wouldn't recognize Mr. Paine whenever he did finally show up. Sam sipped his cider and wondered how long he should wait. A moment later, the door opened, ushering in a cold blast and a man draped in a cloak, who reached up with ink-stained fingers to pull back his hood.

"Thomas!"

"Sam! What a pleasant surprise! I didn't expect to see you again so soon."

"Well, I am here waiting to meet someone. Do you know Mister …"

"Ahh," the tavern keeper approached the table, "I see you've found Mr. Paine."

Sam's eyes widened. "*You* are Mr. Paine?!"

"Yes, yes." Thomas took off his cloak and spoke to the tavern keeper. "Please sir, a large coffee and a brandy." He sat down. "I apologize. Did I not introduce myself properly yesterday?"

Sam was speechless. Then, suddenly it all clicked into place. Everything Thomas said about the British yesterday had seemed familiar because Sam had *read* it all before — in *Common Sense!* He recovered quickly from his shock and began to tell Thomas about why he was there. Then he noticed how tired Thomas looked. Much worse than yesterday. Deep lines of fatigue furrowed around his eyes, which were red with exhaustion. Thomas put his elbows on the table and rested his head in his hands.

Sam's elation turned to concern. "Thomas … uh, Mr. Paine?"

"Please, call me Thomas," he said, raising his head from his hands.

"Thomas, are you alright?"

Thomas blinked a few times. "I am in dire need of sleep, yet I cannot rest until I have finished the essay and found a printer. The pamphlet must go out quickly. Time is of the utmost importance."

"Is there any way I can help you?"

A faint smile crossed his face as he focused on Sam. "What

a loyal and generous fellow you are. Thank you — I appreciate your offer, although I fear the only people who can help me now have fled. The papers have stopped publishing. I assume the printers are gone. I have not had time to check. Not to mention there is barely a ream of paper left in the city."

The tavern keeper brought Thomas' drinks.

Thomas closed his eyes as he gripped the coffee mug and inhaled the rich aroma. He sipped slowly, then let out a deep sigh. "Ahhh, there we are," Thomas said, lowering the mug to the table. "There are few problems in this world that are not best approached when one is buoyed by the power of a good, strong cup of coffee. Now then, Sam, what was it you needed to see me about?"

Sam was relieved to be able to tell Thomas everything — his real reason for coming to Philadelphia, his mission from Paul Revere, and his breakfast this morning with Mr. Morris and General Putnam. There were a dozen questions Sam wanted to ask Thomas, most importantly — did he know Gerard? But those could wait. He was here for information about gunpowder and Thomas' time was limited. "Can you help me, I mean, us? I have the notes I made and samples of powder from the Canton and Frankford mills."

Thomas gulped his brandy and stood up. Throwing on his cloak, he waved to the tavern keeper and called, "Put it on my tab, sir!" To Sam, he said quietly, "Come with me. Let's take a look at what you've brought. Not here, though. Too many unsavory individuals running around the city right now."

Sam grabbed his things and followed Thomas out the door. "Where are we going?"

"My lodgings, right there." Thomas pointed to a building across the street. The lower half of the building was painted green with black window frames. A wooden sign hanging in front of the door read Aitkens Bookshop. Thomas and Sam crossed the street and climbed up a creaky staircase behind the bookshop. Thomas opened the door to a small set of rooms. A bookcase covered most of one wall. A large table and one chair sat in the center of the big room, with a smaller table near the window. Both tables were covered with papers and books. A narrow bed with a side table could be seen in the back room. The rooms were bitterly cold — with not even an ember in the fireplace.

"Should I start a fire?" Sam asked.

"Yes, yes, good idea." Thomas cleared a place on the larger table, nearly toppling a brandy decanter that sat perilously on a stack of books. Sam got a small fire going with flint and steel. The room began to warm up. He pulled the notes and gunpowder from the leather tube. Thomas sat down in the chair and read through the notes. Then he compared the two powders, as Mr. Morris had done. "I see, I see," he mumbled to himself. He went to the bookshelf, bringing a leather folder back to the table. He pulled out some papers and continued muttering to himself, nodding.

Sam looked at some of the papers on the table near the window. He picked up a copy of the *Pennsylvania Journal,* dated March 1775. The paper was opened to an article entitled "African Slavery in America." The author was listed as *Justice and Humanity.* Sam glanced at the first paragraph.

That some desperate wretches should be willing to steal and enslave men by violence and murder for gain, is rather lamentable than strange. But that many civilized, nay, Christianized people should approve, and be concerned in the savage practice, is surprising.

"Are you 'Justice and Humanity'?" Sam asked.

Thomas merely nodded and continued writing, still talking to himself. "Yes, this should work. I think so." He looked up from the table. "Done. Come take a look."

Sam read what Thomas had written. "So, the saltpeter they have been using at the Canton mill is not ground fine enough?"

"Precisely. Without the proper consistency, the final composition will not adhere together and form a powder that can sustain the rigors of changing weather. Also, do you remember much about the drying shed at the Canton mill? What is the condition of the walls?"

"I think there were some cracks. The shed was built quickly, so maybe the wood was not seasoned enough."

"Yes, that will affect the final product as well. They'll need to shore up any gaps in the walls and make sure it is completely dry and free of drafts."

Sam grinned with satisfaction. "General Putnam was right, Thomas. You are the one person who could solve this problem. Won't General Washington be thrilled when the new powder reaches the troops!"

Thomas' face, momentarily brightened by helping Sam, shifted quickly back to a worried look. "I'm afraid he won't need any more gunpowder unless something changes drastically for the better. We are at our lowest ebb. The people of this area are choosing flight or capitulation. Who do they think should be fighting this war?" He poured some brandy, then slumped down in the chair, swirling the amber liquid slowly. "I met a tavern keeper in Amboy, a Mr. Crawford. He runs a tidy business, a tavern and gristmill. He stands as much to gain as anyone from a future unfettered by the bondage of English rule. Yet he is a Tory. We discussed the prospects and pitfalls of achieving independence. As we talked, his daughter played near the hearth, as healthy and happy a child as I've ever seen. And do you know what he said? 'Well, give me peace in my day.' Can you imagine, Sam?! Shirking his responsibility to the next generation! Why, a generous parent would have said, 'If there must be trouble, let it be in my day, that my child may have peace.' This single reflection is sufficient to awaken every man to duty!"

Thomas sat up and quickly shuffled through the pages in front of him. He scratched out a few lines at the margin of one. He finished the brandy and sighed. "The only glimmer of hope is that the men of Congress have finally realized that their intervention in attempting to manage the war is folly. They have voted to give General Washington full power of the direction of the war for the next six months, including extending enlistments. It is a positive step, sadly long overdue. The country must be strongly animated and the army must be rebuilt. That is why I have to finish this essay and get it printed and sent out."

Sam took the pages of notes from the table, blowing on them softly to speed up the drying of the ink. He carefully rolled them up and slipped them into the leather tube. "Thomas, you helped me. I would like to return the favor. You stay here and finish the essay, and perhaps get some rest. I will find a printer. Surely there must be someone. Give me the addresses of the newspapers. I can find my way around well enough."

Thomas' tired face lit up again, this time with surprise. "Of course! I'm afraid I was letting fatigue get the better of me. But there's no time for that, no time!" He began scribbling on the back of one of the papers on the desk. Suddenly he stopped. "What about your mission for Mr. Revere?"

Sam put on his coat. "Sherry needs one more day of rest. I can leave in two or three days instead of tomorrow. I probably won't get home by Christmas, but maybe by New Year's Day." He took the paper from Thomas, tucked it into his pocket and opened the door.

Sam was halfway down the stairs when Thomas called out to him, "Sam, you *are* a loyal and generous soul! I'm beginning to think that Fate put us together on that Frankford road for this purpose. Perhaps between the power of words and roar of gunpowder we can save this revolution!"

By late afternoon, Sam's optimism was dwindling fast. He had been to every address on the list and all were boarded up and empty. The last one he went to, the print shop for the *Pennsylvania Evening Post*, was closing as he arrived.

"Young man, have you lost your wits? The armies of Howe and Cornwallis are headed this way — twelve thousand strong!" The owner scoffed at Sam's plea that he stay open for one or two more days. He was stuffing papers into a trunk, while everyone else in the shop moved the printing presses to the back and carried boxes and furniture out to a wagon out front. "Haven't you heard? Congress is evacuating to Baltimore tomorrow morning. If they feel it is prudent to leave Philadelphia, then so do I!"

"But sir," Sam pleaded, "it's for Thomas Paine. He's writing a new pamphlet for General Washington and the army!"

"I'm sorry, son. General Washington needs more than words right now. He needs a miracle. The Cause is lost. Now be on your way. You'd be wise to get yourself out of the city, too." He firmly led Sam to the door.

The pungent smell of whale oil from the street lamps filled the evening air by the time Sam returned to Front Street. He had stopped at the Morris home to check on Sherry and drop off the notes and gunpowder samples. Sam knocked on the door of Thomas' rooms. No answer. The door was unlocked. Sam stepped inside and saw Thomas slumped across the table. The fire was almost out, only a few dull embers glowed in a deep pile of ash. A single candle, burned down to a stub, flickered weakly next to Thomas' arm. Sam tapped Thomas on the shoulder. "Thomas?"

Thomas lifted his head. He looked even more exhausted and disheveled. "Sam. What news?"

"It's not good. Everyone is fleeing the city. The *Packet* and the *Gazette* are both boarded up. Mr. Bradford has left to join the troops, so the *Pennsylvania Journal* is closed. When I got to the *Post* print shop, Mr. Towne was packing everything."

"What about the *Ledger*?" Thomas asked sleepily as he stood up. "Closed."

Thomas began to pace back and forth across the cold room. Sam added kindling to revive the fire and sank into the chair — glad to be out of the cold after a day spent running all over the city. Thomas continued to pace, then suddenly stopped in front of Sam. "My dear boy, have you eaten today?"

"Um, not since this morning," Sam said wearily. The massive breakfast he'd eaten that morning was a distant memory to his empty stomach.

Thomas blew out the candle and reached for his cloak. "Let's go, then."

Sam gave Thomas a dubious look. He had just sat down. "Where are we going?"

"The City Tavern! Didn't I promise you the finest oysters in Philadelphia?"

"Yes, but, what about your essay? The pamphlet?"

"The essay is finished!" Thomas was already heading down the stairs.

"How will we print it?"

"I don't know," Thomas called over his shoulder, "but we will find a way. A good meal will help clear our heads."

Sam broke up the newly-crackling fire and put the fire screen in front of the smoldering chunks. Then he picked up his bag to follow Thomas. For a man operating on little to no sleep, Thomas walked remarkably fast. Sam kept up as best he could and within a few minutes, they turned down Walnut Street and reached their destination. The City Tavern towered in front of them. Sam counted five stories. They found a table in the back near the kitchen where trays emerged covered with platters of food. Roasted hams and ducks, fried fish, heaping stacks of biscuits, steaming pepper pot soup. Everything looked and smelled delicious. The tavern was full and noisy, but Sam could hear his stomach growling over the din. "I'm surprised they are still open."

"Daniel Smith will cook for anyone who can pay." Thomas waved to a waiter, who swiftly approached their table.

"Good evening, gentlemen. Are you ready to order? May I recommend the braised venison? Or perhaps the Tavern Lobster Pie? It is very popular."

"Nonsense!" A booming voice behind him startled the waiter. A fat, cheerful man slapped Thomas on the back. "This man will have oysters. Raw oysters. Bring him two dozen!"

"Mr. Smith!" Thomas stood up and shook the man's hand. "Good evening, sir. May I present Samuel Nevens. I see that not everyone has abandoned our fair city."

"No, no. I'll not run like a rabbit. The Brits have to eat, too!" He waved to a different waiter and excused himself. Seconds later, two ales appeared. After a few minutes, the first waiter brought a large platter stacked with gray nubby shells — their smooth white interiors each held a liquid oval edged in black. Two thick lemon slices perched on the side of the plate. Sam stared at the slippery blobs.

"Have you never eaten raw oysters?" Thomas asked, watching Sam's anxious face.

"Never. Only cooked."

Thomas reached for a lemon slice. "May I?"

Sam nodded.

Thomas squeezed some juice over the stack. Then he picked up a knife and one oyster. He loosened the gooey center, then tipped the shell into his mouth, letting the oyster slide slowly down his throat. He grinned and let out a deep, satisfied sigh.

"You know, Sam, I was raised as a Quaker. Those good people believe that food is given by God for nourishment, not for pleasure. They will boil a piece of meat for so long you would never know whether the creature walked, flew, or swam during its natural life. Trust me. This is the way nature intended us to eat oysters."

Sam stared at Thomas' contented face, then reached for an oyster. The fresh, briny taste of the ocean filled his mouth. Thomas and Sam ate the whole platter in a matter of minutes. Thomas sat back with a look of profound happiness on his face. Sam felt his weariness retreat somewhat and he, too, smiled with satisfaction at the gray tower of empty shells.

"Now then, back to our dilemma." Thomas wiped his hands on a napkin and shook his head. "I can't believe the *Gazette* has closed as well! How could Mr. Hall and Mr. Sellers be so meek? Why, Ben Franklin would be appalled to learn that the men who took over his very first newspaper have fled the city faster than mice before a tomcat."

Ben Franklin? Sam remembered Gerard saying that when he had come to visit the famous Dr. Franklin, he had seen Franklin's printing press in his home. A small hope began to flicker in Sam's mind. "Thomas, do you know Mr. Franklin?"

"Do I know him?! Why, without Ben, I wouldn't be here. I wouldn't even be alive."

"He saved your life?"

"Yes, yes, he did — in more ways than one." Thomas took a sip of ale. "I came to America in 1774 at Ben's suggestion. We became friends during his stay in London. At the time my prospects in England were grim, to say the least. I had failed at everything I had tried — work, marriage, writing. I was a right mess when I met him. My clothes were falling apart, whiskers a week long on my face. Ben shook me out of my pathetic state with some stern, but kind words. He said, 'Clean yourself up.

Wash away the dirt, and the self-pity while you are at it. The world hasn't knocked you any harder than anyone else. In fact, you've got an advantage over most men — intelligence. Don't numb it with brandy and melancholy.' I sailed a week later on the *London Packet* with letters of introduction from Ben." Thomas shook his head softly. "While at sea, typhus swept through the ship. I was close to death with it when the ship docked in Philadelphia. Lucky for me, a Dr. John Kearsley heard that I bore letters from Ben Franklin, so he had me taken from the ship to his home. He nursed me back to health. So, you see, if not for Ben — I would either be penniless in England or dead from typhus in America." Thomas finished his ale with one long swallow. "Why do you ask? Ben has gone to France, to seek assistance for our cause. And he has been out of the printing business for nearly thirty years."

"I think he may still have a printing press, at his home." Sam sat up. "Perhaps we could use that."

Thomas held his empty tankard between his interlaced fingers and stared at Sam for a long moment. Then he slammed it down and leapt up from his seat. His eyes gleamed with the fire Sam had seen the day they met. "Of course! Oh, my addled mind! Why didn't I think of that?!" He grabbed his cloak and waved to Mr. Smith, calling out, "I'll settle up later! Come on, Sam, there is no time to waste!"

Thomas raced through the streets. Sam ran after him, nearly getting run over by a carriage along the route. "Wait here!" he told Sam when they reached his lodgings. "I'll be right back!" He ran up the stairs two at a time and was back on the street in a moment, clutching the papers he'd been working on. They walked briskly through the dark city. Thomas grew more and more excited and began to think out loud. "Yes, it will be the old one, so a smaller version, but surely serviceable. I doubt it has been used much since he stopped putting out *Poor Richard's*

Almanac. We shall have to scrounge up some paper. Ben probably does not keep much on hand. If we work all night, we can have the pamphlets finished by mid-morning."

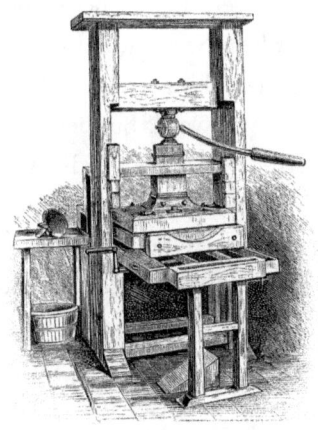

CHAPTER 10

Black December

December 20, 1776
Philadelphia, Pennsylvania

Ben Franklin's house looked like most of the others on Chestnut Street, except that there were several iron rods attached to the roof. Thin wires tied to the rods came down the side of the house and went directly into the ground. The house was dark. Thomas tried the front door. It was locked.

"Shouldn't we knock?" Sam whispered.

"No, no one is home. Mrs. Franklin passed away two years ago. And Ben left for France in October." Thomas began fiddling with the door.

"Are you sure about this?" Sam was a little nervous. Of course, he had broken into the Leonards' house, but that had been a matter of life and death.

"Hmmm, now if I were Ben, where would I hide a key?" Thomas either did not hear Sam's question, or simply chose not to answer it. He began looking around the door, then stood, chin in hand, scanning the yard. Suddenly he shouted, "Dost thou love life?" and strode toward a sundial set in the front yard.

"What?" Sam was cold, confused, and thinking about the huge feather bed at the Morris' house.

"Dost thou love life? Then do not squander time, for that is the stuff life is made of!" Thomas tipped the sundial slightly and bent down next to it. "Of course!" He stood up, holding a muddy key in his hand and declared, "That is one of Ben's favorite quotes — 'Do not squander time.' So, where better to hide a key than under a sundial, which would remind him of the passing of time! Here we are."

The door protested with a loud creak, then they both stood inside a dark hallway. Thomas walked straight to the back of the house. Beyond the kitchen was a long room that looked like it had been added after the house was originally built. Thomas lit three lamps and they were able to see the room clearly. At one end was a deep fireplace with two rocking chairs in front of it. Tall bookshelves lined the wall on both sides of the fireplace. A battered couch sagged against one wall. In the middle of the room, three tables held a variety of strange contraptions. Some had wheels and glass tubes, some had wires and rods. In the back of the room there was a large piece of furniture covered with a dusty sheet.

Sam did not recognize anything. He shivered.

Thomas did not seem to notice the cold. He strode to the covered object and pulled off the sheet with a sweep of his arm. "By George! It is still here! Sam, you are a genius, a genius!!" He brought a lamp over to inspect the press more closely. It was smaller than the ones Sam had seen earlier in the day — about seven feet high and four feet wide. The press was a large wood frame with a table in it. A strong beam between the two sides held a thick, vertical wooden screw. Below that were two smaller pieces of wood, one attached to the screw. A long lever, attached to a disc on the top board, turned the screw.

While Thomas wiped the dust off with a rag, he explained the different parts of the press. He tapped one side of the frame. "These are called the cheeks; the top bar is the head. This board connected to the screw is the platen. It presses down on the letters, or type, to transfer the ink to the paper." Thomas pointed to large tray with shallow sides under the platen. "This is the bed, it's where the type is placed. The carriage underneath rolls the bed back and forth with each printing." At the other end of the table, a large board covered with leather was attached by a hinge. Connected to that, also with hinges, was a wooden board with two rectangles cut out of it. Lifting up the top board, Thomas said, "This is called the frisket. It holds the paper in place on the lower board, which is the tympan. Now, let's see if the devil's tail works."

He reached for the lever and pulled. It did not budge. Turning to low shelves that lined the wall, full of jars and tins, he found a jar of grease. With a bit of cloth, he rubbed grease all around the disc where it attached to the platen. He pulled the lever again. Nothing.

Sam grasped the lever from the other side of the press. He pushed while Thomas pulled. At last the lever gave way and the platen was lowered down against the table.

Thomas was ecstatic. "It still works! Hmm, what do we have for supplies?" He moved through the room, first checking the shelves behind the press, then two tables on each side of the press. One had a shallow box on top that tilted up at an angle, full of smaller boxes, each holding small bits of metal. "Those are the letters. Yes, yes — it seems that the type is all here," he exclaimed, peering under the table. Thomas pulled out a stack of paper tied in a bundle. "Sam, we're in luck — there is about half a ream of paper here — maybe a hundred sheets. The essay shall run about eight pages. At two pages to a sheet, we should be able to print at least twenty-five copies."

Thomas turned to a square stand that held a thick, stone tablet — the ink stone. It was black and stained. He held up two leather pads with handles that were resting on the stand. "The ink pads are a bit worn, but they'll do. The galley is in good shape. Now, what about ink?" He searched the low shelves again — lifting jars and holding them up to the light, shaking others. Suddenly his enthusiasm turned to dismay. He groaned. "There's no ink. The bottles are all dried or empty! Egads — to be thwarted when we are so close!" Thomas began anxiously rifling through cupboards near the press.

"Well, maybe he kept the ink somewhere else. Let's keep looking. How much will we need?" Sam was frantically trying to think of a solution, and at the same time, keep Thomas from panicking. Sam looked at everything on the low shelves again. Thomas was right, most of the containers were empty. Sam picked up a tin that had no label. It felt heavy. He twisted off the lid — it was full of a black, fine powder. "Thomas, do you know what this is?" Sam asked excitedly.

Thomas came over and took the tin. "This is lampblack. It colors the ink. But we have nothing to mix it with. And even if we did, I know very little about the process of making ink. Every press I've worked at bought the ink from suppliers." He sank into the chair, wrecked with fatigue.

"Oil," Sam said briskly, "we need some oil." He started for the door to the house on the other side of the room, adding, "And a pot, and lots of firewood, and an onion!"

Thomas jumped out of the chair and followed Sam. "An onion?! What are you saying? Do you know how to make ink? I thought your father ran a sawmill. Who taught you how to make ink?"

"Gerard." Sam took a lamp into the kitchen.

"Who's Gerard?" Thomas was right behind him.

"It's a long story," Sam said as he went to the pantry and scanned the shelves. "We need about five gallons. Flour, sugar, herbs, spices. No oil. Hmmm, the fireplace in the kitchen is very large. Maybe it was too warm to store oil here. Is there a cellar?"

"Yes, of course. It's this way, bring the lamp."

They climbed down the ladder and surveyed the large cellar — full of barrels, jars, and boxes. They moved around the room, with Sam holding the lamp up close to read the labels. Thomas found a crock full of butter, but there didn't seem to be any oil.

Sam felt a stab of hopelessness. Handing Thomas the lamp, he climbed up a ladder that was propped against tall shelves to see what was on top. Then he let out a shout, "Thomas! Walnut oil! Two barrels — probably ten gallons each!"

They carried the barrels into the kitchen.

Sam tapped his fingers on the lids, thinking out loud. "The oil needs to boil continuously for several hours, at least twelve, I think. The boiling changes the oil into something like varnish. Then after it has cooled, we mix it with the lampblack. So, we'll need the firewood, and some longs sticks for stirring it and ..." Sam noticed Thomas was leaving the kitchen. "Where are you going?"

Thomas had gone back into the pantry. He emerged with a small coffee grinder and a sack of beans. "Twelve hours of boiling? We are going to need coffee! Here, you do this while I get some water from outside. I'll start bringing in some firewood as well."

Sam filled the small dome of the grinder and cranked the worn handle. This was a task he had learned at a young age. He would sit near the fire and grind beans for the morning coffee while his mother made breakfast. The tug of the handle, the smell and crunch of the beans as they filled the drawer under the blades — it was so familiar. Tears sprung into his eyes at the memory. Suddenly all he wanted was to be home. Home with his parents — safe and taken care of. Not running around a strange city that was about to be invaded by the British army. He wiped his eyes with the palm of his hand, glad that Thomas was outside. *Well, I must help Thomas get the pamphlet printed, and then I'll go back and get Rosie and be on a ship home in a few weeks. I can take copies of the pamphlet to Boston and Machias.*

Thomas was gone for several minutes, then he burst through the door balancing a full water bucket on an armful of wood. Sam took the bucket from him and Thomas dumped the wood on the floor. With a mischievous grin, Thomas reached into the pockets of his jacket and carefully pulled out several eggs. "From the hen house next door. I imagine Ben's neighbors won't miss them, considering they have fled the city with all the other dandy prats."

Sam kindled the fire. Soon the room was warm and smelled of coffee. Next, they hung the largest pot they could find over the fire and poured enough walnut oil in to fill three-quarters of the pot. "Once it begins to boil, we have to watch it constantly," Sam explained as they carried in more wood from outside. "If it gets too hot, it will explode. But it will turn to varnish faster if we can maintain a steady boil. It will smell pretty bad too, so it's best that we are boiling it in an empty house."

"Not quite empty!" Thomas laughed and pointed to a fat, brown mouse who was scurrying away from under one of the chairs by the fireplace. "Aren't you a clever fellow to find the perfect bed?" Thomas held up a ragged fur hat. "Ben wore this hat for a decade. Deborah threatened to divorce him if he didn't get a new one. I daresay he would be delighted that it has been given a second life."

Thomas stacked the wood and pulled the two chairs closer

to the fire. Handing Sam a pewter mug of steaming coffee, he sank gratefully into one of the chairs with a mug for himself. He let out a deep sigh and smiled. "Sam, you are a wonder. Who would have guessed that in my blackest hour of need I would meet a boy who can make ink? And now you must tell me who Gerard is."

They sat before the fire and took turns stirring the oil. Sam told Thomas everything, starting with the day the ships had anchored at Machias and all that followed. Trying to save his father's tree. The surveyors. His terror at waking up on the prison ship. Thomas grimaced when Sam showed him the scar from the surveyors, now three dark, shiny stripes. Sam told him about Gerard and Josiah and how Josiah's curiosity about everything had led to a lesson on Gutenberg and bookmaking. Talking about Josiah's death, Sam grew quiet.

Thomas poured more coffee. "Sam, you are very tired. Why don't you sleep for a bit? I'll watch the oil. You can finish telling me about Gerard tomorrow."

Sam shook his head. "I'm fine. It's just … I'm amazed I made it through all that. And that I'm here, and I can finally thank you.

"Thank me? Thank me for what?"

"*Common Sense*. Gerard wanted me to find you and thank you." Sam described how the guards had dumped the sacks of pamphlets into their cell and Gerard's excitement when Sam read *Common Sense* to him. Then he told Thomas about Gerard's death and his own escape. "I think the idea of me finding you someday made him happy, even though he knew he was going to die. He recognized your writing style. He thought he might know you. Do you remember meeting a French man in London about ten years ago?"

"What did he look like?"

"Well, I don't know what he might have looked like then.

On the ship his hair was long and he had a beard, all completely white. After he died, I saw that his right arm and most of his chest were covered with burn scars. He looked very old, except for his eyes. He had brown eyes that sparkled when he spoke about something he loved — like books, or food, or France."

"I think I do remember him. Ben introduced us. You say his eyes sparkled, but the man I am thinking of ... also had an air of sadness about him."

"Yes, he had that too. He didn't tell me much about himself. Only that he was a bookseller and had been imprisoned once before — in the Bastille. He met Voltaire there. I know he has a son named Paul. Right before he died, he was delirious and he kept saying, *je suis desolee.*"

"*Je suis desolee.* It means, I'm sorry," Thomas said softly.

Sam sighed. "I don't know what he was sorry for. Or how he was burned. And then he died. Now I'll never know. I have his book, though, and someday I will take it to his son." Sam got up and went to the workroom, returning with his bag. He pulled out the book and showed it to Thomas. The back of the book was beginning to crack, and some of the pages in the middle were loose.

"Ah, Epictetus." Thomas flipped through the book. He read the inscription out loud, "*Faites attention à laisser vos fils bien instruits plutôt que de riches, car les espoirs de l'instruction sont mieux que la richesse de l'ignorant.* Perhaps that is Gerard's message to his son."

Sam nodded. "Gerard did talk about that a little. He said that choosing knowledge over money had brought him happiness."

"This book may not make it to France. It's falling apart."

"I know. I think my jump into the ocean almost ruined it." Sam frowned.

"Perhaps we can fix it while we're here. I saw some book binding tools in the workshop. Gerard sounds like quite a man,

Sam. It would be an honor to repair something that meant so much to him."

Sam smiled sadly and murmured, "He was. You would have liked him, Thomas. Gerard said whoever wrote *Common Sense* would change the world. Like Gutenberg."

Thomas stared at the fire. His face reflected an unusual emotion — humility.

Sam continued. "He said you had moral courage. That if you were caught by the British you would probably be killed."

Thomas nodded. "That is true. If the British do take the city, I imagine I'll be the first hanged. Still, I don't know that I would call myself courageous."

"But you still wrote it, and everyone knows you are the author, and now you are writing another pamphlet. That is pretty daring."

"Daring?" Thomas chuckled. "Well, any one of the men under General Greene's command will tell you that during our skirmishes with the enemy, I have put myself as far from danger as possible. However, I am a good soldier in a different kind of battle, the fight for the minds of the people. The written word can be as powerful as the sword and cannons. That is how I can best contribute to the Revolution. Of course, there are risks. It's when something is important to you that courage reveals itself. I risk no more than anyone else in this fight. If Ben Franklin were captured on his way to France, the British would not spare a hair on his seventy-year-old head. The same with General Washington — he would be executed, in an exceedingly gruesome fashion, too."

Sam considered Thomas' words for a moment. "Do you think General Washington is brave?"

"His bravery is surpassed only by his judgment and integrity," Thomas said decisively.

"He hasn't won a single battle," Sam said with disbelief.

"He wasn't at Bunker Hill. Boston was evacuated without a shot being fired. And the rest of the war has been one long retreat. How do you know whether he is brave or not?"

Thomas drained his coffee cup before answering. "General Washington has understood from the very beginning that in a traditional, head-to-head battle, his forces do not stand a chance against the British and their Hessian guests. We don't have to overpower the British — we simply have to outlast them. True, we are weaker in men and supplies, but we have two weapons that cost us very little — time and space. As for time — whether it is their purse or their spirit that gives in first — England will tire of this folly eventually. And as for space — why, we have a whole continent behind us! We can retreat as far west in the Appalachian territory as we want. General Howe cannot go everywhere. General Washington must preserve the Continental army, for that is how this war will be won, by a united force, not merely with groups of militias."

"Well, even if that makes sense, I still don't see how it proves that General Washington is brave."

Thomas stood up and stirred the oil. "For a man like George Washington," he said firmly, "a strategy of waiting and retreating is a painful personal challenge. There is wisdom and honor in such a strategy, but not much glory. I know he would relish the chance to charge headlong into battle with the British. A great leader, however, does not put his own quest for glory before the goal of his army. Sometimes it takes more courage to wait and see what opportunities time and patience will deliver."

"That is what Gerard told me after Josiah died." Sam watched a log slowly break into a dozen chunks of bright orange. He let out a deep breath. "I don't see how we can defeat the British. The situation looks hopeless to me. You believe we can?"

"Yes, I do." Thomas answered with complete assurance. "I have been with the army for eight months — through the fall of New York, Fort Washington, Fort Lee, the retreat across New Jersey. The men have been challenged beyond comprehension — with never enough shelter, clothing, food, or munitions. They have endured every obstacle imaginable. True, things look dire at this moment. But there is a spirit to these men that is unlike anything I've ever seen. A tenacity, a grim optimism that will pull them through. It may take some time, but we will prevail."

"I don't understand. You're English — why would you fight against your own country?"

Thomas reached for the poker and shifted the flickering chunks of wood slightly. He turned around and focused his intense gaze on Sam. "I'm not fighting for a place or a people. Sam, this war is not about *one* country. It is not about taxes or territory. It is about one singular idea — that citizens of any birth, any station, are able and entitled to govern themselves. It is a psychological revolution — a complete rejection of the ridiculous concept that God would choose one family to rule over thousands of people. The divine right of kings is an abomination that has brought immeasurable evils to mankind."

"Do you believe in God?"

Thomas nodded. "With all my heart."

"But not religion?"

Thomas sat back down and stared at the fire. A bitter frown twisted his mouth. "When I was a child in England, there were over two hundred offenses punishable by death. Our cottage stood near a chalk ridge used for public hangings. Gallows Hill. From the window, I watched the condemned walk toward their fates. After being hung, the bodies were left on the gallows for one hour — to make sure they were dead, and to instill in children a gruesome lesson about the 'wages of sin.' I saw a girl of seven hanged for stealing a hair ribbon, a boy of ten for stealing a loaf of bread for his starving family. These brutal laws were based on tenets found in the Bible. Now I ask you, how can a religion that judges and punishes so severely, that would plant such terrors in the mind of a child, how can that be a force for good in the world? So, no, I do not believe in religion. God is in my heart; my church is in my mind."

Sam rocked in the glow of the fire. He was exhausted but wanted to stay awake. Being here with Thomas reminded him of the long nights on the ship, talking in the darkness with Gerard and Josiah. His mind felt lively, and his heart felt peaceful.

Thomas noticed Sam's pale, tired face. "You should get some sleep. I can manage here." He held up the book. "I have coffee and *Epictetus* to keep me awake. There is a couch in the workshop. I'm sure you can find a quilt upstairs somewhere. Now, by my guess, we have been boiling the oil for three hours. You said it would take about twelve to reach the consistency we need, correct?"

"Yes, about that."

"Here." Thomas unhooked a watchchain from his jacket. He handed Sam a small gold watch. "I'm terrible at keeping track of time. You mentioned needing an onion. What is that for?"

"Oh, that is to pull the impurities from the oil, so that it holds to the paper better. Sometimes they used bread."

"Hmmm." Thomas stared into the bubbling pot. "We have neither of those at the moment, but I have no doubt we will find a solution when the time comes. I'll check the cellar again. Now go get some sleep. I promise not to burn the house down."

Sam found a quilt in one of the bedrooms on the second floor. He was tempted to crawl straight into the bed and collapse, but he wanted to be where he could hear Thomas if something went wrong. He curled up on the couch in the workroom and fell asleep in an instant. He woke up to the sun coming in, lighting up all the glass jars, tubes, and instruments on the tables. It took a full minute to remember where he was. He could hear Thomas in the kitchen. He sniffed. The boiling oil smelled terrible, but his nose twitched with something else. A familiar smell. It reminded him of ... his birthday? Sam sat up and rubbed his eyes. *I must have been dreaming of home. I thought I smelled doughnuts.*

Thomas was wide awake, bustling at the stove. "Good morning Sam!" He put some fried eggs on a plate and handed it to Sam. "Perfect timing! Breakfast is ready — fresh eggs, coffee and ..."

"Doughnuts?" Sam stared at a tower of hot, golden doughnuts on the table.

Thomas beamed. "Without an onion or bread, I had to improvise. I found flour, salt, and sugar in the pantry, and butter in the cellar. I used the first two batches to pull out the impurities, like you said. But then the oil was clean, so I made some more. Here, try one." He handed Sam a hot doughnut from the top of the pile.

Sam bit in. "These are delicious," he said with his mouth full, "but hold on." He went into the pantry and looked over the small jars of spices lined up on a narrow shelf. *Here we are — cinnamon and nutmeg.* He mixed the two spices and some sugar in a small bowl. Then he sprinkled the mixture over the fresh doughnuts.

Thomas ate one in two bites. His face glowed with satisfaction. "Perfect! Is this a New England tradition?"

"I guess." Sam grinned and reached for another. "It's how my mother makes them. She always cooks them for my birthday. How's the oil coming?"

Thomas peered into the pot. "It may be ready. It's definitely thicker than last night. What do you think?"

Sam stirred the oil. "I don't know. Let's try a batch."

They poured a small amount of oil into a bowl and then added some lampblack. Using a mortar from the pantry, Sam ground the two substances together. Thomas brought a sheet of paper and a quill to the table. After dipping the quill into the mixture, he tapped it and scratched a few lines. "No, it's not sticking very well to the paper. We need to boil it longer."

"Definitely." Sam went back to stirring. "Why don't you sleep for a while, Thomas. You must be exhausted."

"I'm fine. No time for sleep! Now that we are close to finishing the ink, I will set the type for the press." He began to gather the materials needed for printing. Sam added several logs to build up the fire. An hour later, the oil was done. It had the right consistency, but needed to cool. While they waited, Sam helped Thomas get the press ready. The small metal letters were all sorted in a compartmented box. Thomas set the letters in the composing stick — a narrow box with sides — to form each line of the page. Next, he put the sticks into the galley, a shallow wooden tray. When the galley was full of type, Thomas tied it securely with a string and placed it in the bed of the press. The oil was still too hot, so they set as much type as they could before they ran out of empty composing sticks. Sam could not believe how long it took to make a single line of text — setting each word letter by letter, making sure the space between the words was correct. And it all had to be set backward because the printing would reverse the image they created!

Sam was impressed. "Mr. Gutenberg was a smart guy. I wonder how long it took him to figure this out."

"Well, the mechanism of the printing press is not too different than that of a wine press. Wine had been made in Mainz since the Romans arrived in the first century. So, a screw press would not have been new to him. The moveable type, though, that was quite a feat of genius. Is the oil cool enough yet?"

Sam stirred the shiny thick liquid again. "No. Are you sure you don't want to sleep? You look very tired."

Thomas shook his head. "Nonsense. I'm fine. Say — why don't I take a look at Gerard's book while we wait? Perhaps it is a simple matter to fix it."

"If you say so."

Thomas went to find the book binding tools.

Sam returned to the kitchen for another doughnut. While Thomas examined the book again, Sam wandered through the workshop, chewing on the doughnut. "I know Dr. Franklin invented the Franklin stove, and lightning rods. But what are all these things?" He held up two flat pieces of wood with leather straps attached.

"Those are paddles for swimming. Ben is an avid swimmer. In England, he swam in the Thames almost every day. He says the water energizes him and his mind works better horizontally than vertically. He swears that he gets his best ideas while in the water."

Me too. Sam remembered how floating in the pond at home always made him feel good. He stopped in front of a wooden structure that looked like a spinning wheel, except that instead of a spindle it held a large glass globe resting on a leather pad. A thin iron rod ran through a small wheel as well as the globe. A large wheel at the bottom was connected by a leather strap to the smaller wheel.

"That is an electrostatic machine." Thomas came over and began turning the larger wheel. The smaller wheel and the glass globe began to spin. Thomas handed Sam a piece of wire from the table and told him to press it against the globe. Zap! A jolt charged through the wire and halfway up Sam's arm. "Ow! What good is a machine that shocks people?" Sam shook his tingling arm.

"Imagine the potential if you can harness this power?!" Thomas' eyes were shining with admiration. He walked to the corner of the workroom and picked up a metal rod that was like the ones Sam had seen attached to the roof of the house. "Ben is a true genius, the greatest man alive, in my opinion! Look at this lightning rod. Hundreds of homes were burned from lightning strikes every year before Ben invented this."

Sam picked up a long wooden pole leaning against one of the bookcases. The pole ended in two points, one slightly shorter than the other. A thin cable ran from end to end. "What does this do?"

"This is a long arm." Thomas took the stick and lifted it toward the top shelf. He pulled the cable. The two ends closed around a book, which Thomas then lowered toward Sam. "Did you know that Ben established the first public library in the colonies?" Thomas asked as he sat back down, picking up Gerard's book again.

"Really?" Sam moved toward the other bookshelf.

"Yes, in 1731. He and other members of his philosophical meeting group, Junto, were frustrated when their discussions were stalled by a lack of references or information. None of them were wealthy enough to buy many books on their own, so they pooled their resources and devised a system of sharing books."

"What is this?" Sam held up a huge white object. It was heavy and had two smooth dents. "It looks like a tooth, but I've never seen one this big." Sam hoped that whatever creature this tooth came from was not one he might meet on his travels through Pennsylvania.

Thomas glanced up from the book. "It is a tooth. From some giant beast, close to an elephant, I suspect."

Sam put the tooth down carefully. "Dr. Franklin certainly loves science."

"Of course he does, as all thinking men do!" Thomas voice became tinged with contempt. "I will never understand the minds of those who fear science and knowledge. Or those who avow that curiosity and progress in the sciences are somehow a contradiction with believing in God. Does God intend for us to stumble through the ages blinded by ignorance and fear?

240

I think not! For goodness' sake, God gave us the ability to observe nature, to reason, to think logically, and to solve problems. Why would that be if not for the purpose of using science to help our fellow human beings?"

Sam sat down in the chair opposite Thomas. He looked at Gerard's book. "What do you think? Can it be fixed?"

Thomas nodded. "Yes. The leather is still intact, but the cords holding the pages together have come loose. If we can remove the cover, it will be easy to replace the cords." He pressed his thumb down against the back of the book. "It is odd the way the cover has been stitched together here, rather than in one piece. Look at this bulge in the spine."

"I don't know if Gerard made the book himself or not. It looks very old."

"Well, we'll mend it, nonetheless."

Using a small knife, Thomas carefully cut at the thread that made a seam at the spine of the book. At last, the cover began to give way. He cautiously pulled at the leather, peeling it back to reveal the cords that held the pages together. "Sam, look at this!" Thomas pointed to the book's exposed spine. Tied to the cords was a man's gold ring. He loosened the cords and pulled the ring completely out. The band was wide and thick. The top of the ring was the shape of a shield made from a red stone or jewel. The letter *N* was in the center, with a single stripe of gold behind it.

Sam's eyes grew wide.

Thomas turned the ring over, searching for an inscription or name. "That is a royal crest," he said quietly.

"You mean from a king?"

"No, I don't think so. Probably a duke or a count."

"Gerard was a count? Impossible! He hated the monarchy!" Sam stared at the ring.

"Perhaps there is more in the book." Thomas picked the book up again, turning it over slowly. "Wait, what is this?" He pulled back the lining fabric. Underneath, folded inside a thin, worn oilcloth, were two documents. The one on top was still sealed. The impression on the seal matched the ring. One word — *Paul* — was written in faded letters under the seal. The other document was a weathered, yellow piece of paper, folded into a square. Thomas spread the paper out. Although the writing was also faint, they could see this was a decree of sorts. At the bottom of the page on one side was a large stamp in black ink. Thomas gasped. "This is a *lettre de cachet!*"

"What does that mean?"

"It's an arrest warrant, signed by the King. I can't make out the name. *N, O, A*. It's too faded. Can you read it?"

Sam leaned over the letter. The only thing he could make out were dates.

"Wait." Thomas moved quickly through the workshop, bringing back a small magnifying glass. He read the document again. ***"Sa Majesté Louis XV, par la grâce de Dieu, roi de France et de Navarre croit que M. Noa est dangereuse a la sécurité de la mona, il ordonne que le dit M. est emprisonné à la Bas. Fait à Versailles, le 13em jou en l'an de grâce 1727.*** It is a *lettre de cachet*. It says, 'His Majesty King Louis XV believes that' whomever *N. O. A.* is, he is 'a threat to the royal court and hereby sentences him.' I think it is the Bastille."

"Gerard told me he was in the Bastille in 1717. That is when he met Voltaire. Why would he have a different arrest warrant?"

Thomas shook his head. "I don't know. I suppose he could have been condemned to prison a second time. Perhaps he fled to England to escape, but it doesn't explain the ring. The letter must be for his son."

Sam was lost in thought. "They need to keep me alive."

"What?"

"Gerard said the British needed to keep him alive. That's why they moved us away from the other prisoners and brought fuel for the stove in our cell. Do you think he could have been French royalty?"

"I'm positive this ring is from a noble family. Undoubtedly Gerard wanted to keep it safe. What do you want to do? Should we open the letter?"

Sam picked up the ring again. "Gerard had a reason to hide all this. If I ever get to deliver the book to Paul, I'll take everything out. Until then, they should stay with the book."

"Very well." Thomas found some string and restrung the pages of the book. He tied the ring back into place and tucked the letter under the lining. Before he reattached the cover, he placed a small piece of fabric to even out the spine. He sewed the cover back together again.

While Thomas was repairing the book, Sam checked the oil again. It was cool enough, and ready to mix. He scooped some into a bowl, then added some lampblack and mixed until the ink was dark and shiny. As he stirred the ebony liquid in circles, his thoughts spun as well. *Was Gerard a noble? Why would he hide it? He said his wife was dead, but what about his son? Would he know? Why would he have told us about only one imprisonment? And what was he arrested for? Where did the burns come from?*

"Sam!"

Sam looked up.

Thomas was loading the paper into the press. "Is it ready?"

"Yes."

"Bring some over here, please."

Sam carried the bowl of ink to the inkstand near the press. Thomas had already lined the paper up on the tympan. He took the ink from Sam and carefully poured enough to cover the stone. Next, he picked up the pads and rolled their tops across the wet surface, then against each other to distribute the ink. He dabbed the ink onto the type, flipped the tympan into place, and pushed the handle that moved the carriage. Once everything was in place under the platen, he pulled the lever. The platen pressed down on the chase. Thomas pulled the carriage back and lifted the paper off the tympan. He held it up for Sam to see.

The *American* CRISIS

Number I.

By the Author of COMMON SENSE

THESE are the times that try men's souls. The summer soldier and the sunshine patriot will, in this crisis, shrink from the service of their country; but he that stands it now, deserves the love and thanks of man and woman. Tyranny, like hell, is not easily conquered; yet we have this consolation with us, that the harder the conflict, the more glorious the triumph. What we obtain too cheap, we esteem too lightly: it is dearness only that gives everything its value.

Sam read through it twice. He smiled at Thomas. "Congratulations, Common Sense. You've done it again."

Thomas bowed his head. "Thank you. I only pray that my words are not too late to make a difference."

"What will you do with the pamphlets?"

"These I will take to General Washington. We only have enough paper for a few dozen, but it will be better than nothing. We can send one to be published in another city and distributed." As he spoke, Thomas printed more copies of the first page. Then he removed the type and reset the bed with the second page. Sam emptied the composing sticks used for the first page and began to pick out the type for the third page — slow work for him, until they switched jobs. The press was easy to use and Thomas was much faster at setting the type than Sam. Nevertheless, they both found that their fingers were equally ink-stained. Soon, page two was drying on the racks.

At mid-day, Sam scoured the cellar again, this time for food rather than oil. After a few minutes at the stove, he handed Thomas a plate of salt pork cooked with dried apples and maple syrup. The sweet, salty aroma reminded him of the long, snowy weeks hiding out at the Leonards' house.

Thomas devoured the hot food. He handed the plate back to Sam. "My compliments, sir. The City Tavern could not provide better."

Sam grinned. "Rosie liked it."

"It is quite remarkable, you know, what you have survived already. Kidnapping, a prison ship, being shot."

Sam shook his head. "Yeah, I can't believe I made it this far."

"I'm sure your friend Eamon will be impressed."

"He's probably got some good stories by now — after being a soldier. That's exciting."

"Exciting?" Thomas extracted some pieces of type from the composing stick. "I suppose you could describe it that way on the rare day. Most of soldiering is a tedious monotony of waiting, toiling, and bad food, with the occasional bullet whistling by your ear. Tell me, why did you not want to join a militia like Eamon?"

Sam frowned. "I was too scared. Eamon is much braver than me."

Thomas turned from the press and looked at Sam. "You are brave too, Sam. It certainly took courage to come to Philadelphia by yourself."

"Oh, well — I didn't think about it as frightening. I wanted to help the Reveres, after all they have done for me."

"You've done more than help the Reveres. You have helped the Revolution! Why, what would I have done without you?" Thomas picked up the remaining paper and fanned the pages.

"I do wish we could print more copies to send out with couriers."

"Maybe there is more paper somewhere in the house. Shall I go look?"

"Good idea. Try the library."

Sam had never seen so many books in his life. Every wall was filled with shelves from floor to ceiling. There were more strange contraptions. And a few shelves of animal bones, skulls, and teeth. He felt a little nervous going through Dr. Franklin's desk, but his efforts were soon rewarded. In the bottom drawer he found a mixed stack of paper. At first glance, he could see that they were already printed on, in another language. He took the whole stack downstairs and handed it to Thomas.

"*Die Philadephische Zeitung.* These are copies of Ben's old newspapers. He started the first German newspaper in the colonies. Well, well — look at this." Thomas held up a pamphlet. "It's *Common Sense* — also in German. He did mention getting copies printed for the Quaker community here."

Sam turned one of the pamphlets over. "They are only printed on one side. Could we print on the backs?"

Thomas unfolded the pamphlet. "The paper is thin. I don't know if it will hold up under the press. Perhaps a lighter layer of ink is needed. It's worth a try." The pages were a little hard to read, but it worked. It would be a strange pamphlet indeed — two different kinds of paper and languages.

As Thomas continued to print, Sam flipped through the whole stack of paper. At the bottom, he found a different document. Although this one was also in German, he recognized the *Declaration of Independence* immediately. "Hey, look at this last one." He handed Thomas the page. "You didn't write it, but I think a few of your ideas are in here."

Thomas chuckled, then his face grew solemn as he read the page. "*Wenn aber eine lange Reihe von Mißbräuchen und Anmaßungen, verfolgen immer das gleiche Objekt ein Design evinces*

246

sie unter absoluten Despotismus zu reduzieren, ist es ihr Recht ist, ist es ihre Pflicht, auf eine solche Regierung abzuwerfen und neue Garde für ihre künftige Sicherheit zu bieten."

Sam stood with a confused look on his face.

Thomas translated, "But when a long train of abuses and usurpations, pursuing invariably the same Object evinces a design to reduce them under absolute Despotism, it is their right, it is their duty, to throw off such Government, and to provide new Guards for their future security." He passed the page back to Sam and turned again to setting the type.

"I never quite understood that part."

"It means that if a people are being oppressed, those who have the *ability* to take action, have the *responsibility* to take action."

"That's kind of what Eamon said," Sam mused. "He was probably more afraid than I realized, but he still went, because he could."

"Every man who takes up a gun has fear, as does every man who challenges his fate. England and the Tories know we are fearful of what lies beyond the final battle of this war. Fear is the strongest weapon a despot can wield."

Sam stared at the document in his hands. "To me, it seems impossible — making up our own government and everything," he said glumly.

"It is intimidating, I agree," Thomas said. "Nevertheless, I am convinced we can succeed. For the same reasons I know we can defeat the British in the war. The spirit, the determination I see in the troops, is a characteristic not only of the men in this country. I believe it runs in the blood of the women and children as well. They will breathe life into this new nation. We are at a pivotal point in history where this great idea can become a reality." His voice was strong with conviction, but a trace of worry settled in the lines of his face.

"You seem to have doubts, though."

"I have no doubts that it can be done. However, I fear that one issue may pollute this prodigious opportunity."

"What is that?"

"Slavery." Thomas' whole body recoiled at the word. "The unnatural business of buying, selling, and owning human beings. The slave trade goes against every value the Revolution stands for — freedom, self-determination, dignity, respect. There is great hypocrisy in the cries of men who complain so loudly about being 'enslaved' by England, while they themselves hold thousands in actual bondage." He grimaced with frustration, clenching the half-filled composing stick in his hand. "If this issue is not addressed at this moment, it will continue to grow, as the nation grows. Slavery will embed itself like a toxic disease on the political, economic, and social foundation of America. And it will make her terribly sick, sooner or later."

Sam felt a pang of fear hearing Thomas' despondent voice. "Surely, the men who wrote the *Declaration of Independence* realize this, too. Why would they not just abolish slavery?" Sam asked anxiously.

Thomas let out a heavy sigh. "Unfortunately, for many, it is not that simple. Slavery is already woven into the fabric of this country. The southern states depend on it for their livelihood. To those men, slaves are considered property, therefore the ideals of the *Declaration of Independence* do not apply to them. It is viewed as an economic dilemma, not a moral one. And without the south, we will not be united against our enemy. But, Sam," the fire quickly returned to Thomas' eyes, "the creators of a document as ingenious and noble as the *Declaration* undoubtedly possess the imagination to solve this problem. Would that they had the courage to seize this glorious moment in time to rid their new nation of this odious sin! To do anything less is the height of hypocrisy. They must live up to the honorable words they have written."

"What would you suggest as a solution?" Sam had a feeling an explosion was coming.

"There are so many possibilities!" Thomas burst out. "After the war, a tax on the sale of western lands could buy the freedom of every slave in the colonies. Pay the tax now, save the stability of our fragile union and the honor of our cause. The freed slaves could be given land to farm. It would be an investment in the future." Thomas shrugged and turned back to the metal letters in front of him. "Will it be easy? Of course not. Neither will it be easy to create a new nation. Democracy is not made overnight. It is not won in a battle or decreed in a treaty. Democracy will be won by the courage and perseverance of its citizens. They must hold fast to the vision of what is possible, and see themselves as heroes for all mankind, not naïve rebels. What are they rebelling against? They betray nothing except a corrupt and oppressive system!"

Sam sighed. "You see it that way, Thomas, but I think, right now, most people are afraid — for their families, their property, the future."

Thomas sorted through the metal letters scattered across the table, momentarily lost in thought. He turned toward Sam; his eyes lit with emotion. "Naturally, people are afraid. But we must not give in to fear. Fear of failure. Fear of the unknown. Many of life's most rewarding experiences begin with a huge, terrifying question mark. A journey to a new land, marriage, the birth of a child, mastering a new skill or trade."

Thomas' face suddenly relaxed into a quick grin. He winked at Sam. "Why, even eating a raw oyster for the first time is frightening, yes? But without stepping past that fear, you will never know what lies beyond." His face grew serious again. "America should not fear the future. She must embrace it with joy and purpose. Surely, I am not the only person who sees that the citizens of these colonies hold the chance to shape their destiny like no other people in history. This country has the potential for greatness — far more than the wealth of its lands and waters. It can be a beacon to the whole world. A sanctuary for the oppressed and persecuted. A nation whose people can live with honor and forge their success purely on merit, not an arbitrary, hollow class system. It is our responsibility to create such a place, because we *can*. It is a responsibility we cannot run from or perceive as an obstacle, but must shoulder with self-respect and confidence. We should be grateful for this glorious task we have been given!" Thomas' voice rang with fervor. He held up the last composing stick like an offering to the Cause. Then he set it into the press, handed the ink pads to Sam, and bowed. "Sir, if you would do the honors."

Sam printed the last pages, while Thomas washed up. Sam was astonished that Thomas could still be awake. *He hasn't slept for at least thirty-six hours. Perhaps I can convince him to rest now that the pages are printed.* But as he hung up the wet pages to dry, Sam saw Thomas standing and pulling on his cloak, and asked, "Where are you going?"

"I've got to try to find more paper and see what news has come from General Washington. There is one last printer I will call on as well. And I will bring back some food."

"Thomas, you haven't slept for days. And the city is probably completely empty by now."

As Sam had noticed earlier, Thomas more or less ignored questions he did not want to answer. Instead, he walked through the drying racks, testing the pages with his fingers. "Hmm, these aren't quite ready. If you don't mind staying a bit longer — keep the fire going and clean up our great ink-making experiment. Ben would be very proud, by the way. I will send a message to Mr. Morris that he should expect you later tonight, or in the morning." Patting Sam on the shoulder, he walked toward the door. "You should try to get some sleep. You look exhausted."

Sam got a gust of wind and rain as the door closed behind Thomas. He shook his head. He'd never met anyone with so much energy and determination. He cleaned up the kitchen, happy to discover two last doughnuts, cold, but still tasty. Next, he sorted the type back into the small compartments of the box. He stacked the dry pages they had printed and folded them together. Work finished; Sam stretched out on the couch. He watched the flames jump and wave from the fireplace — as if challenging the bleak, wet night to dare come in and chill the workroom. He closed his eyes. The pages of the pamphlet danced before his heavy lids.

Not a place upon earth might be so happy as America. Her situation is remote from all the wrangling world, and she has nothing to do but to trade with them. A man can distinguish himself between temper and principle, and I am as confident, as I am that God governs the world, that America will never be happy till she gets clear of foreign dominion.

The words swirled in his thoughts, and at the same time, he heard voices. Thomas' — *This war is about one idea — that men can govern themselves.* Gerard's — *Ideas matter, Sam. They change the world.* The last echo before he fell asleep was Eamon's voice — *Wars don't wait, Sam. Wars don't wait.*

Coffee. Sam sat up. Thomas handed him a steaming mug, sinking into the other end of the couch with his own. His cloak lay in a heap on the floor. Thomas looked awful. His skin was gray with fatigue and his eyes gleamed feverishly. His hands shook slightly as he drank.

"What is the news? Did you find a printer? Did you speak to Mr. Morris?" Sam rubbed his face, trying to erase the fog of

251

sleep. "What time is it?"

"Three o'clock. General Lee has been captured by the British. It's a gift, if you ask me. The squeak-pig has been scheming behind General Washington's back for weeks. We are better off without him. Mr. Morris has arranged for the pamphlet to be sent out to several cities. So, you will be able to share your journey back to Boston with a courier."

"You found someone to print it?"

"I did. Mr. Steiner and Mr. Gist have agreed to print it. That is the good news. The bad news is that they need me to set the type; all their workers have fled. I'll go first thing in the morning. After it is printed, I shall rejoin the army. Oh, here." Thomas reached under his cloak and handed Sam something wrapped in brown paper.

Sam opened the small package — a large rectangle-shaped cookie with a raised imprint of an angel. Sam took a bite. "Molasses?"

"Gingerbread. From Ludwick's bakery. His last batch for a while, I dare say." Thomas broke off a piece and chewed it slowly. "A fine patriot, Christopher Ludwick. He's German, but has been in Philadelphia for over twenty years."

Sam was fully awake now. He took in Thomas' pale, drained face and trembling hands. "How long will it take you to reach the camps?"

"A day, I should think. It is about twenty-five miles. I made it here in one day."

"Will you travel along the Frankford road, or the one going to Newton?" Sam asked.

Thomas was so tired he did not notice the focus of Sam's questions. "The road to Newton will be full of people fleeing the city. As long as I keep my wits about me, I think the Frankford road will be safe enough. General Washington has commandeered every boat for fifty miles to the west side of the river, so British or Hessian patrols are less of a worry. Of course, you never know when you will run into skinners and ruffians." Thomas ran a hand through his disheveled hair. "I am more concerned with the Loyalist militia. They have been emboldened by events of the past few days. Philadelphia is fairly bursting with Tories. The cowardly poltroons. They are motivated only by servile, self-interested fear." He scowled with disgust, then said, "Our troops are scattered along the river. General Putnam sent word that I would be traveling and gave me the password."

"What is it?"

"Cato." Thomas smiled faintly. "It is the name of General Washington's favorite play."

"When will you leave?"

"Tomorrow. I think it will take a few hours to set the type, then I'll be on my way."

"But you haven't slept in four days. Can't you wait one day?" Sam asked, already knowing the answer.

Thomas shook his head. "Enlistments are up in ten days. On January first, General Washington will lose most of his forces unless something can persuade them to stay. If my words can change the minds of some of those men, I must make haste to deliver them." Much to Sam's surprise, Thomas stretched out on the couch and pulled his cloak over his body. "However, as nothing can be done until morning, I shall rest for a short while," he said firmly.

Sam thought Thomas was asleep, until he quietly said, "It would seem, Sam, that all is lost. Things are in a gloomy state indeed. Yet, I remain confident that we shall prevail. Why, look at what you and I have accomplished in a mere twenty-four hours. I do not know what will happen in the next few days, but my experience in life so far has taught me that these are the circumstances that reveal our true character. We rub on and drive in, beyond what could ever be expected, and instead of wondering why some things have not been done better, the greater wonder is that we have done so well."

Seconds later, Thomas was sound asleep.

Sam stood at the door and pulled on his hat. His small bag, with some clothes and Gerard's book, hung over his chest. He smiled at Thomas, who was snoring loudly on the couch. *Maybe I should wait until morning to leave. Then I could say good-bye. No, it's going to be a long day of travel. I need to go now. I'll write him a note instead.* He looked around the workshop and found the only piece of paper they had not printed on. "Sorry, Doctor Franklin." Using the ink that they had made, he turned over the copy of the *Declaration of Independence* printed in German, and began to write. He placed the paper on Thomas' hat. With one last fond look around the workshop, he opened the door and slipped quietly into the dark night.

CHAPTER **11**

The Game Is Nearly Up

December 22, 1776
Delaware River, Pennsylvania

A powdery snow dusted the road. It crunched softly under Sam's feet. That and the steady murmur of the river were the only sounds he heard, both muffled by the thick scarf and hat he wore. The first rays of daylight were slowly turning the black flow of the Delaware to a flat gray sheet. Ice had begun to crust along the banks. Sam guessed it was about seven o'clock. He'd left Dr. Franklin's house at four, which meant he was one-third of the way to his destination. He walked through the trees that lined the road. It would have been faster to go along the road itself, but he was wary of other travelers. He shifted the sack on his back slightly. The pamphlets were in the bottom, covered with a thick layer of flour. He went over in his mind what Thomas had said the night before about the camps of the Continentals. *General Cadwalader's troops are across the river from Burlington. I should see a sign for Dunk's Ferry in an hour or so. The road turns west there, toward Newton, so General Washington's headquarters will be somewhere between the river and Newton.*

Sam's stomach growled. He should have brought some food. He wondered if Thomas was awake and had found his note by now. Although he felt bad about not saying good-bye, Sam knew that if he had woken him, Thomas would have tried to stop him. *This way he can get more copies of* Crisis *printed and sent out, and not have to rush to get them to the troops, too. Maybe I'll see him in Philadelphia when I go back for Sherry. No, he'll probably go back with the army once the pamphlet is out. If only I could have left with Sherry! Then I could have made my way back to Boston without having to return to Philadelphia. But I couldn't take a chance with Sherry under these conditions.* Once he delivered the pamphlets to General Washington, Sam planned to look for Eamon among the troops. Surely they would all be gathered in the area by now. And if he did find him? Sam kicked at the dimpled slush of a frozen puddle. It reminded him of the pasty skins of freshly-plucked chickens. Chicken. His stomach growled again. Maybe some water would help. He pushed through a thick stand of bushes that hung over the water and chipped away at the ice until he was able to cup some water into his hands.

Voices. Thud. Sam heard the scrape of something being dragged on shore. He squinted in the dim morning light. About ten feet away, two men climbed out of a canoe. They were not dressed like soldiers. One was short, with thick eyebrows and a bushy mustache. The other man had a long black beard. Sam waited. *Maybe they're Colonial militia. Thomas said the river was controlled by the Pennsylvania Navy.* He was about to step out from the bushes and give the password when the bearded man spoke. "Zounds — that was close. I thought for sure that blasted galley had spotted us!"

"Aye." The other man scowled and held a musket close to his chest. "It was too close. I don't care how much we're getting paid; this is the last time we're crossing until those damned rebels give up once and for all."

"It won't be long now," the bearded man sneered. "Washington and his ragged Patriots are done for. The river will freeze in a few days and the Hessians will walk right across and finish them off. They don't even need to wait for Howe and Cornwallis to come back here."

"Consarn it! Where is the girl, Abe?"

"Relax, Joseph. She'll be here." Abe was undoubtedly in charge of the situation.

"How do you know she's one of us?" Joseph asked.

"Jacob Robertson. He's connected to all the Tories around here. She made contact with him two days ago. She'll have the password."

"What is it today?"

"Whiskey and women." Abe chuckled.

"Where is she going?" Joseph blew on his hands to warm them.

"Up to Princeton."

Joseph peered into the woods, then across the river. "Well, if she don't show up soon, we're leaving. I'm not taking any chances on getting caught here. It ain't worth a backside full of Yankee peas."

"For what she's paying us," Abe spoke firmly, "I'll swim her across on my back. Don't worry — if anybody finds us, we'll take them back as prisoners. Or shoot them."

Sam held his breath. They were going right back across the river. All he had to do was stay still. He stood up slowly, trying to move behind a thick tree where he would be better concealed. Only two steps to the left. He leaned out. Bam! Knocked from behind, Sam went sprawling onto the river bank, landing at the feet of the two men. Right next to him, a girl in a long gray cloak fell as well. She scrambled to her feet, pulling the hood of her cloak over her head. Instantly, Joseph's musket was leveled at Sam's head. "Who are you?!"

Abe grabbed Sam's collar.

"Uh, Sam. Samuel Nevens. I, uh. Mr. Robertson sent me." Sam's brain whirred. He tried not to panic. He looked at the road. Could he make a run for it?

"Robertson didn't tell us about you. It was just supposed to be a girl."

"I, I only met him yesterday. I need to get to Trenton."

Joseph turned to the girl. "Are you Maggie?"

"Yes."

"Maggie what?" Abe said.

"Just Maggie." Her voice was quiet, but steely.

"Well, *just* Maggie. What's the password?" Joseph demanded.

"Whiskey and women," Maggie and Sam said in unison.

Abe let out a breath. "Do you have the money?"

The girl handed him a small bag. Sam's mind raced. He had no money! He pretended to search the pockets of his jacket to stall for time. Then he felt a lump in his vest pocket. Thomas' watch! *I'm sorry, Thomas.*

"Will you take this?" He handed the watch to Abe.

"Aye." Abe examined it for a moment. "We'll take anything except that worthless Continental trash."

Joseph snickered. "The only thing that will be good for soon is wiping your arse."

Abe turned toward the boat. "Right. Let's go. Keep quiet till we get across."

Sam eyed the small canoe nervously. "Are you sure it will

hold all four of us? I can wait for a second trip." He knew the minute they were on the river he could run.

"No," Abe snapped. "We're not coming back — sun will be all the way up soon. We'll make it. Stay in the middle of the boat and keep still."

Sam and Maggie sat on the narrow seat that centered the small craft. Sam's heart sank as they pushed off and headed toward the New Jersey side. He was relieved not to have to speak. He needed to think. *What am I going to do now?! I'm going in the opposite direction of where I need to be. And if they find out I'm a rebel, I'll never get those pamphlets to General Washington.* Sam groaned silently. *I should have stayed in Philadelphia! Thomas will be so disappointed. I've ruined everything!*

He looked across the swirling river, wondering how on earth he would be able to re-cross. Then he shifted his eyes to look at the girl. Maggie. The cloak folded around her like a shield. She pulled the hood forward even further, making it impossible to see her face. *How old is she? She's not much bigger than me.*

In a few minutes, they reached the other side, pulling into an inlet. Joseph and Abe hid the canoe, while Sam waited beside Maggie.

"Where are you going?" Sam asked awkwardly.

"Princeton." Her answer was brusque, making it clear she did not want to talk.

They all walked through the woods briefly until they reached a horse and wagon. As they climbed in, the hood slipped back from Maggie's face. Sam caught a glimpse of red wavy hair and the greenest eyes he'd ever seen. Her cheeks were pink, either from the cold or nervousness. A small arc of tiny indentations across her right temple showed that she had survived smallpox. She was the most beautiful girl Sam had ever seen. He didn't know why, but his stomach felt like a bunch of tadpoles were swimming around in it.

259

Now that they were across the river, Joseph and Abe relaxed, guiding the horse with wagon and passengers through the woods. Joseph whistled and joked. Abe pulled out a pipe and began to fill it with tobacco. He turned around to face Sam. "So, what's your business in Trenton?"

"I … uh. Newspapers. I'm taking newspapers to the Hessians."

"Newspapers?!" Joseph scoffed. "Those German drumbles don't have time to read. They're exhausted."

Abe continued to watch Sam. "Let me see one."

Sam's chest tightened. He tried to keep his hands from shaking as he reached into his sack.

"Why are they covered with flour?" Abe asked.

"It was a decoy. In case I got stopped by the rebels." He pulled out a few copies of the pamphlet, making sure to hold up the *Common Sense* side. He held his breath. Did either of them read German?

Abe barely glanced at the paper before returning to his pipe. Sam moved to quickly stuff the pages back into the bag. As he did, he saw Maggie stare at the paper, then lift her gaze to his face. Her dark eyes narrowed with suspicion.

Sam covered the pages with flour again, then decided to change the course of the conversation. "Why are the Hessians so tired? There hasn't been much fighting for a while," Sam said.

"No big fights," Abe responded, "but their pickets and patrols are harassed by militia every time they go for a stick of firewood. The Germans are more nervous than a fox in a henhouse. Colonel Rall sent a hundred infantry and an artillery detachment just to deliver a letter to the British commander at Princeton. Even the river isn't a safe defense. That blasted General Ewing and his men keep coming across to shake them up. Rall has his men pulling patrol duty every waking hour and sleeping in their uniforms, cartridge boxes strapped on."

"Rall!" Joseph's voice rang with contempt. "All he cares about is his precious brass band! They parade in front of his quarters every day, pulling the cannon around like trained monkeys. The colonel has turned nary a spade of dirt to fortify the town."

Maggie suddenly spoke up. "He doesn't have the cannon set up against an attack? Sounds foolish to me." Then she casually asked, "How many troops does Rall have?"

"About fifteen hundred, I hear," Abe replied.

"If the Hessians are so worried, why doesn't General Howe send more soldiers to support them?" Sam said.

"General Howe?" Joseph laughed. "He's in New York — tucked in for the winter I'd say, with the rest of the troops. Besides, Rall and his men are in no danger — the rebels are done for. Sick, starved, no supplies. Whoever lives through the winter, Howe can finish off in the spring." Joseph drew his finger slowly across his neck and grinned.

Soon they reached the small village of Bordentown. Joseph and Abe insisted on stopping at a tavern before continuing. They settled in with two ales. Maggie sat near the door, still hooded and keeping to herself. Sam sat down at a table by the fire. The chill inched from his bones. The smell of roasting meat yanked his empty stomach. A plump, smiling tavern girl approached him. "Would you like to order anything?"

"No, thank you. I don't have any money. May I sit here?"

"No charge for that!" she answered cheerfully.

Other travelers came in and out of the tavern. Sam scanned their faces, their clothes. *Are they all Tories? Can I approach any of them? The tavern girl seems friendly. Maybe she can help me find a way back across the river.* A small boy was seated on the bench near him. He looked about five years old. He sat very close to his mother, who was talking quietly to another woman seated across the table. The boy stared at Sam.

Sam smiled at him. "Hello. What's your name?"

The boy's eyes grew wide with fear. Sam glanced at the mother. Had he done something to frighten him?

The boy's mother leaned in and said quietly, "Please excuse him. He hasn't spoken for a week. Some Hessians raided our home. They took everything — food, clothes, blankets, the featherbed. They killed our hog and cut it up right on the kitchen table." She lowered her voice to a whisper. "Thank goodness my husband is away with …" She looked cautiously around the room and then, apparently deciding Sam could be trusted, added, "with the Americans."

Sam nodded, then picked up his sack. "I can spare some flour, if you'd like it."

The young mother's face flushed with surprise. "How kind you are. Thank you."

He went to the kitchen to ask for a small sack. While he waited, he noticed the tavern girl standing out back. She wasn't smiling anymore. Her face was very serious. Sam took a step backward to see who she was talking to. It was Maggie. They stood close together, clearly not wanting to be overheard. Maggie's face was grave. As she was leaving, Maggie took the tavern girl's hand and cupped her own hands over it. She slipped out of sight.

Sam gave the flour to the young mother, then went outside. Maggie was sitting in the wagon. Joseph and Abe emerged from the tavern. Sam climbed back into the wagon and then felt a tap on his shoulder. The tavern girl stood beside the wagon. She handed him a piece of bread stuffed with salted beef and cheese. "Here," she said quietly, "you look hungry. If you come back through, you can pay up then." She held the sandwich for a long moment before letting go, waiting until Sam looked her straight in the eyes. "Be careful — the beef is a mite tough."

Sam was momentarily speechless. He took the sandwich.

"Thank you."

"Ho ho — looks like someone is a little sweet on you!" Abe said boorishly.

Sam blushed from his chest to the top of his head. Meanwhile, Maggie sat motionless and silent. The wagon rolled along and within a few minutes Sam's face resumed its normal color. Strange as the incident was, Sam was starving and very grateful for the sandwich. He bit into it and chewed carefully, as the girl had suggested. The beef wasn't unusually tough. Ow! Something sharp pushed against the roof of his mouth. Was it a bone? Sam reached into his mouth and pulled out the sharp object — a piece of paper folded into a small square. He turned slightly so the others could not see and opened it. It was some sort of message. Sam looked at the others. No one had noticed. He tucked the note into the sleeve of his shirt, more confused than before.

When they reached the crossroad between Trenton and Bordentown, Sam climbed out of the wagon and said good-bye. Maggie looked at him from under her hood and it seemed to Sam that she gave him a slight nod. *It's probably my imagination — I'll never see her again.* He sighed a little. *She may be a Tory, but she sure is a pretty one.*

As soon as the wagon was down the road, he pulled out the note. It was scribbled — obviously written in haste. He read,

Ewing will raid tonight. Midnight. Near the south dock. Password is ...

The last word was smeared with grease. He turned the note over. The paper looked like it had been torn from a drawing of a map. It had a strange compass. Arrows pointed in the four directions, and the north/south line had a snake intertwined around it. He read the message again. *Ewing? That was the man*

Joseph and Abe were talking about. He was coming across tonight? How did the tavern girl know that? And why would she want me to know? She had talked to Maggie, but Maggie is a Tory. Is she setting me up for a trap? Or trying to help me get back? I'll just hide near the dock tonight and see what happens.

Sam got to Trenton in the late afternoon. He had been through the small town on his way to Philadelphia, but since then, the Hessians had taken over, so Trenton was mostly abandoned. The main streets, Queen and King, formed a large oval. *I probably should avoid the town. I'll wait in the woods until dark, then sneak down to the dock.* Although the day was cold, at least it wasn't raining or snowing. He made a small fire near a stream and mixed some flour and water in a tin cup to make a firecake. He was sleepy. The events of the last twenty-four hours seemed to land on him all at once and a heavy fatigue took over. Sam shook himself. He couldn't fall asleep. He pulled out a copy of the pamphlet. *These are the times that try men's souls.* He read the whole thing again and found the sentence he was looking for. He read it softly, out loud. "A generous parent should have said, if there must be trouble, let it be in my day, that my child may have peace."

Sam stared at the glowing embers of red and gold that shimmered between the burnt sticks edged in pale ash, as the fire slowly died. The words echoed in his mind — … *that my child may have peace.* He found himself thinking about the terrified little boy at the tavern. He thought about the frightened, numb children he'd seen fleeing the two armies — in Boston and outside of Philadelphia. Sam had never actually thought about being a father. He'd never even thought about getting married. But he probably would one day. For some reason, Maggie's face suddenly appeared. He blushed for the second time that day. Someday he might be a father. What if *his* children had to flee or fight the British, or any other invaders for that matter? His father's words came back to him — *This is why men fight, Sam. They fight for the life they want to live.* Had it only been a year and a half ago that they sat together by the river on that beautiful June night? He could almost smell his father's pipe tobacco. What kind of life was Sam willing to fight for? For himself, for his family? Could he, at fifteen, truly make a difference for the future of his country?

Darkness was falling. It was time to head down to the dock. Sam picked up the sack. He almost dumped out the flour to make it lighter, then he thought about the hungry boy at the tavern. Someone else might want the rest. He headed back toward the river. He didn't have a plan, but figured this might be his only chance to re-cross. What if he told them who he was? Show them a copy of the pamphlet? If only he knew the password! The dock was across the road. He was about to dash over when he heard voices, speaking German. He ducked behind a stack of firewood. Two soldiers walked right past him. *Hessians! They must have an outpost nearby.* He peered into the darkness — intensely curious about the ferocious warriors he had heard so much about. They were very tall, maybe not as enormous as Johnny had described. They wore yellow trousers, green jackets, capes and tall boots. Both men had black moustaches, long black queues down their backs and pointed brass helmets. *Those helmets don't look very comfortable.* Both soldiers also wore long swords and cartridge boxes, and carried rifles. Sam noticed that their rifles were shorter than the ones used by the British. When the soldiers were out of sight, he darted across the road and hid behind an overturned boat.

Hours later, Sam was still huddled near the dock. The cold air had sunk into his bones like iron shackles. *I hope they come over soon. I may freeze to death waiting.* He tried to focus completely on the river, but the shimmery flow of the moon on the water was making him sleepy. Wait. He narrowed his eyes in the darkness. Was that a boat? He heard a faint splashing, but he still could not see anything. Suddenly, there was a soft crunch of wood against land. It *was* a boat! Then two more pulled up alongside the first. Sam watched as a dozen or so men climbed silently out of the boats. One man remained, while the rest of the men crept toward the town. Sam watched them disappear into the darkness, then he turned his attention to the boats. They looked about twenty feet long. He could probably fit into a hull and not be noticed right away. The man standing guard was good at his job, sneaking past him seemed impossible. Sam crouched near the edge of the water, wondering what to do. Wherever the men had gone, they would surely be coming back soon. He had to get into a boat. The smell of smoke drifted over to him. It seemed to be coming from the town. Now he could see scattered flames in the darkness. The raiders must have set some houses on fire. They'd be back any minute! Desperate, he grabbed a rock from the shore and threw it over the head of the man standing guard.

The guard moved toward the sound. "Who's there?"

Sam picked up the sack of pamphlets and scrambled to the closest boat. He climbed in and crawled back as far as he could go, pulling a coiled rope in front of him. He felt nervous but fairly certain he would not be discovered until they crossed back over the river. Hopefully the pamphlets would be enough proof of his loyalty. He wished he had a letter or something from Thomas. Thomas would want the pamphlets to go straight to Washington.

The smell of smoke was stronger now. Shouting from the landing grew louder. Footsteps crunched nearby. The boat rocked. He heard a man whisper, "Ha! We did it! Those Jaegers are as spooked as a goose on Christmas morning!"

"Yeah, but let's go, Robert. They'll be here any second."

"Ray, you know we have to wait for the others."

The first voice sounded anxious. "The river is making me nervous. It's getting choppy."

"The boat is solid. Why are you nervous?"

"'Cause I can't swim — that's why!" Ray said, in a tight voice.

Robert chuckled a little. "You can't swim? I thought you were a fisherman from Falmouth."

Ray grumbled, "I'm from Falmouth, but I'm a cooper, not a fisherman. I walked to Boston to join up. I hate boats."

Falmouth! Sam's heart jumped. *Maybe he is part of the militia Eamon joined. He must know him. Maybe Eamon is in their camp!* It was all he could do to stay curled up and quiet. Would he finally find Eamon? The boat moved again as a third person climbed in. Sam heard other voices, as all the raiders returned to the boats.

Robert's voice rose slightly. "Everyone here?"

"Aye."

"Aye!"

"We're all here."

"Push off, let's go!" With a small splash and a lurch, Sam felt the boat move into the water.

Loud voices could be heard from the shore. Some in German, some in English. "You yellow dogs. Black devils!"

Robert called out again. "Well done, boys! How many did we light up?"

Another voice answered. "About six. They don't know what hit them!"

The men cheered as the boats moved swiftly across the river. They began to speak at a normal volume, now that they were out of danger.

Sam heard Robert's voice once more. "Hey, did you two steal anything? The boat feels heavier."

Ray said, "No, there's probably some ice caked to the sides. I'll check."

Sam felt the boat shift strongly to the left.

"No, don't worry about it. We're almost there … Ray! Ray!"

Splash! The boat tipped further to one side, then rolled, with a jerk, back to the center.

Sam did not hesitate. Shoving the coil of rope out of his way, he jumped to his feet in the boat, and could see a man thrashing frantically in the water a few feet away.

"What the hell?!" Robert yelled. "Who are you?"

In one motion, Sam tore off his coat and dove into the river. His heart jerked in his chest from the cold shock. His whole body stiffened. The water ripped his breath away. The men in the boats were yelling and pointing at the water. Sam swam toward Ray, grabbing his collar just as he was about to sink. He pulled him through the water toward the shouting men. They pulled Ray into one of the boats and Sam into another. Out of the water, Sam could not speak, or even think. He shivered where he sat, hunched over, and stared at the floor of the boat. He tried to talk, but the words were slurred and thick. He began to feel sleepy.

Sam woke up in a canvas tent with muted sunlight, warmly wrapped in a rough blanket, wearing long johns, and a wool cap on his head. A man with dark hair and a long beard was sitting across from him, also wrapped in a blanket. Sam recognized him as the man he had saved from drowning.

When Ray saw Sam was awake, he left the tent and returned with a tin cup of steaming coffee. He handed it to Sam. "Wait." He reached for a flask near his blanket. "Rum." He poured some into the coffee. "It will get your blood flowing again."

Sam took the coffee and drank it slowly, letting the warm liquid slide down his throat. "Thanks," he said weakly.

Ray stared at Sam. He had brown, deeply-set eyes. "What's your name?"

"Sam, Sam Nevens."

"Check your feet. Are they white? Can you move them?"

Sam looked at his toes. They were red. He wiggled them.

"Hold on." Ray left the tent again. He returned with Sam's dry clothes.

Sam got dressed. He saw his small bag on the floor, but the pamphlet sack was missing. "Where are my other things?"

"Major Fisher has them." Ray blew on his coffee. "Sam Nevens ... well, thank you, Sam. You might be madder than a March hare, but thank you. What in tarnation made you jump in after me?"

"I don't know." Sam shrugged. "I heard you say you were from Falmouth, and that you couldn't swim. I didn't really think too much."

"You from Falmouth?" Ray squinted at Sam.

"No, I'm from Machias. But I'm looking for a friend who joined the militia in Falmouth in June of '75. His name is ..."

A soldier burst into the tent. He pointed his gun at Sam. "You — come with me!"

Sam was led to a larger tent. A major sat at a small table, reading papers. He glanced briefly at Sam, then back to the papers. Sam saw the flour sack in the corner. As he started toward it, the major said sharply, "Stay right there. Who are you and why were you hiding in the boat?"

Sam explained everything. But the major never looked up from the table. He seemed to be barely listening. Sam felt very uneasy about the situation. "Hmmm," Major Fisher mumbled, "yes, I see. And why were you in enemy territory?"

"I told you, sir. I was caught by the edge of the river. If I had revealed who I was, or tried to run, they would have shot me. I can show you the papers from Mr. Paine," Sam said, pointing to the sack. "They are right here."

"There are no boats on the New Jersey side," Major Fisher insisted.

Sam exhaled slowly. "With all due respect, sir. There are a few. I don't think they'll be making any more trips, though. And they mentioned the Hessians and Colonel Rall, if that is any help."

Ignoring what could be valuable information, the major was dismissive of Sam. "Hmmm, yes. Well, we'll hold you a few days until we can confirm your story."

"Major, I don't have a few days!" Sam was getting desperate. "I have to get these pamphlets to General Washington! Mr. Paine would have brought them himself, but he needed to get more printed!"

"Young man!" Major Fisher barked at Sam. "I do not have to listen to your ..." His next words were replaced by the slap of the tent opening brusquely. Major Fisher jumped to his feet and gasped. Blinded by the glare of the light coming in, Sam could see only a huge silhouette. A shadow that reached across the length of the tent. "Sir!" Major Fisher stammered, "I, I wasn't expecting you!"

He was one of the tallest men Sam had ever seen. As he stepped forward, Sam's gaze traveled from the sturdy black boots up to the man's stern face. He wore a long cape, a buff waistcoat and breeches, and a dark blue coat with yellow buttons. Even under the uniform and cape, his strong legs and broad shoulders showed a man of great physical strength. His light brown hair was powdered and pulled back in a queue. His face was slightly sunburned with a high forehead. A few smallpox scars dotted the side of his nose, which was broad and slightly flat. His entire presence was solemn and noble, reflecting an inner spirit of quiet dignity. Without a word spoken, Sam knew who this was. His pulse quickened even more, with nervousness. But then he looked at the man's eyes, and his heart calmed. George Washington's eyes were blue-gray — the same color as Sam's mother's.

"Are you the boy with papers from Mr. Paine?" Washington's voice had a slightly southern accent. His expression was both somber and open.

Sam swallowed. "Yes, sir. I'm sorry it took me this long. Thomas, I mean, Mr. Paine, he didn't know I took them. He was going to bring them himself, but ..."

"Your Excellency!" Major Fisher interrupted Sam. "We suspect this boy is a spy! The papers he is carrying are printed in German!"

Sam felt his frustration reaching a boiling point. He was exhausted and scared. But he couldn't let Thomas down. Not after all he, they, had gone through to print the pamphlet. "Mr. Paine's essay is printed on the other side! If you would let me open up the bag, I can show you!"

Major Fisher's impatience with Sam exploded. He seemed to forget that General Washington was standing there. His face grew red with anger, eyes narrowing as he leaned toward Sam. He lifted his hand as if to strike him.

"Major," General Washington spoke in a measured voice, "I will speak to the prisoner alone."

Major Fisher sputtered, "But sir, he might be dangerous."

Both Sam and General Washington stared at the major in disbelief.

"I believe I can manage," Washington said drily. "You are excused." He turned to Sam. "Now then. What is your name?"

Sam's heart began to pound again. "Samuel Nevens, sir. Sam."

"And you were sent by Mr. Paine?"

"Yes, sir, well, no, sir."

Washington's face was unreadable as he waited for Sam

to continue.

"Thomas doesn't know I'm here. Well, he must know by now because I left him a note. He had been up for four days." Sam briefly told Washington about the events of the past few days. When he described Maggie, and the strange note from the tavern girl tucked into the sandwich, General Washington watched him very carefully. He asked what Maggie looked like and if she had given a last name. Even while he was speaking, Sam wondered how believable his story sounded. "Sir," he said desperately, "please look at the pamphlets. I'm sure you will recognize Mr. Paine's work."

Washington sat down at the desk and reached into the flour sack. He unfolded one of the pamphlets and looked at the *Common Sense* side, then he flipped the pages over and began to read. After only a few pages, he closed the pamphlet and looked at Sam carefully. "You say you only met Mr. Paine a few days ago?" Washington asked.

Sam nodded. Washington's expression did not change. Sam held his breath; his stomach twisted into a hard knot.

"And you told him where to find the printing press?"

"Yes, sir, at dinner, when he mentioned Doctor Franklin. I have, I *had*, a friend who had seen the press."

Now a skeptical look crossed the General's implacable face. He seemed to be wondering how a boy Sam's age could have a friend old enough to know Ben Franklin.

Sam felt his fate was being sealed. Why should Washington believe him? If only he'd waited and let Thomas bring the pamphlets!

Washington studied Sam's face for one long, agonizing moment. "What did you have for dinner?"

"Sir?"

"With Mr. Paine. What did you have for dinner?"

"Oysters. Raw oysters."

Washington nodded, then stood up and swept his cloak around his tall body. He tucked the pamphlet inside. "Come with me." He headed out of the tent.

Sam swallowed hard. *This is it. I'm done. They are going to hang me as a spy!* He followed Washington out of the tent. Major Fisher, standing right outside with a furious look on his face, straightened to attention as Washington walked briskly past him to a huge horse that was tethered to a tree. The horse lifted its head as Washington approached. He patted the horse briefly and turned to the major. "I'm going to speak with General Ewing before I go. Please find a horse for this young man, and strap the bag he brought to Blueskin."

Major Fisher's mouth dropped open. "I beg your pardon?"

Washington let out a short puff of impatience. "I am leaving in fifteen minutes to return to my headquarters. Sam will be coming with me. Find a horse for him. Thank you, Major."

Sam and Major Fisher stood briefly, stunned into silence. The major glared resentfully at Sam, then stomped away. Sam remained standing still, more confused than ever. *I'm going with General Washington? Are they going to hang me somewhere else?* He walked over to Blueskin and pushed his hand against the horse's warm, smooth shoulder. His hide was a muted shade of gray; his mane was white with streaks of black and gray — the color of cold ashes. Blueskin turned slightly at Sam's touch and fixed his enormous black eyes on him. His gaze was deep and serene — it helped to quiet Sam a little. General Washington's face had revealed nothing as he'd listened to Sam's story, and yet, Sam thought, *His eyes were kind and he seemed to relax a little after I told him about the oysters.* Sam did not have time to dwell on it any further. Major Fisher and General Washington returned at the same time. Within two minutes, they were saddled up and ready to go.

Sam saw the pamphlet bag strapped behind Washington's

saddle, but where was his bag? "Sir," he said, turning to the general, "I don't have my bag."

"Your bag?"

"Yes, sir. My bag. It has my clothes and some other things. It's very important to me."

Washington nodded slightly. Sam climbed down from his horse. If they were going to hang him, he at least wanted to have the book with him. He bolted back to the tent where he had woken up. Ray looked up. Sam felt a cold pit form inside. Sam tried to sound brave, but his voice cracked as he grabbed his bag. "I have to go with General Washington. Do you think they'll hang me?"

Ray frowned. His brown eyes were twin pools of sympathy and acceptance. He reached under his blanket and handed Sam the flask. "Save it till you need it. Get heated, Sam. You won't feel the rope."

"Thanks. Well, good luck, Ray."

Ray nodded slowly — a wrinkle of sadness creased his already solemn face.

Sam ran back to the horse. After settling into the saddle, he looked inside the bag and saw Gerard's book with a breath of relief. They began to ride.

Sam had not seen any of the camp yet. He had been somewhat delirious after jumping into the river. Now as they rode out, he took in everything. White tents were scattered around, some with fires smoldering nearby. The soldiers he saw were barely clothed. Their faces were gaunt from hunger, their eyes blank with exhaustion. Thomas had said the army was on its last legs, but this was worse than Sam could have imagined. The pair on horseback moved along silently for a few minutes. The horses' feet clunked dully against the frozen ground. Puffs of white air pushed out from their velvety noses. Sam watched General Washington from the corner of his eye. He looked like a statue that had come to life. Sam remembered what Josiah had said: "Aye, he's grand on a horse." He *was* grand, and also intimidating. The general was unmistakably deep in thought, but after a few minutes Sam could not stand the suspense.

"Sir, may I ask a question?" Sam said anxiously.

Washington nodded.

"What is going to happen to me?"

"What do you mean?"

Sam let out his breath. "Will I be put in prison ... or hanged?"

"Hang you? Why would you think that?"

"Because you think I'm a spy!" Sam flushed as his voice rose. "Isn't that why you are taking me to your headquarters?"

Washington looked at Sam, almost as if seeing him for the first time. Then, much to Sam's surprise, a bemused smile appeared on his troubled face. He tipped his head slightly in Sam's direction. "Sam, I apologize. My mind is quite preoccupied." Washington's eyes softened with a kind light. "No, you are not going to be hanged. I'm taking you to my headquarters so you can deliver the pamphlets in person, as you had hoped to do."

Sam's body flooded with relief. He almost fell off the horse.

Washington continued. "Although I am curious about one thing. You only met Mr. Paine a few days ago, yet you took a huge risk in bringing these pamphlets to me. Why?"

Sam thought for a moment. "Well, it was partially to help Thomas, but I also felt that I should do it for Josiah, and Mr. Revere, and Gerard."

"Josiah? Gerard?"

"It's a long story, sir."

Washington turned to Sam with another half-smile. "It's a long way back to Newton, and any story would be a welcome distraction from all that has been pressing my mind of late."

Sam told him everything, almost everything. He showed Gerard's book to General Washington, though he did not tell the general about the hidden ring or letter.

Washington was silent for most of the story. He nodded approvingly when Sam talked about marking the sunken cannons, and chuckled when Sam told him about Hodgekins knocking himself out with his own musket. "Well, I imagine you are very anxious to return home after all that. Unfortunately, we cannot spare a horse to get you back to Boston."

"General Washington," Sam took a deep breath, "I am not going back yet. Whatever comes next, I want to help. To fight."

Washington looked at Sam, then turned his gaze back to the road. "How old are you, son?"

"Fifteen," Sam said, adding, "and two months."

"You said you wanted to find your friend. What is his name?"

"Eamon Collins."

"And if you don't find him, do you still want to fight?"

Sam nodded.

Washington was not convinced. "Are you sure, Sam? Of course, we are in a desperate state and need every man we can get. But you are a boy, untested in battle." Washington pulled his cape tighter around his shoulders. "And what about your family?"

"I'm sure, sir. I can write to my family and let them know. Mr. Morris can arrange for Sherry to be taken back to Boston, with the information about the gunpowder mill. The Reveres can keep Rosie for a while longer."

Washington still looked skeptical.

Sam shifted slightly in the saddle, sitting up as tall as possible. "Sir, I'm not battle-tested, but I have already been through a lot. I know my strengths. Well, some of them."

General Washington's face, imprinted with worry and fatigue, relaxed into thoughtful reflection. "Yes, know your strengths. The words of Epictetus." He smiled ironically and repeated, "Know your strengths. Well, our army is vulnerable at this moment. We don't have *much* going for us, however, one of *our* strengths might very well be our current dire straits. The British and Hessians hold us in contempt because we do not follow the traditions and strategy of European warfare. They refuse to imagine any other way to run an army and a war — and that will be their downfall. Just as we have the audacity to create a new nation, we have the willingness to try bold and unconventional tactics to win this war."

"Do you have something in mind, sir?" Sam asked.

"I do, Sam. I do. At the moment, that is all I am at liberty to share. Now, if you are going to stay, we will have to find a unit for you to join. Perhaps one from Massachusetts would be best."

Sam agreed. "Whatever you think is best, sir. Um, General? I don't know if this is important, but the two men who rowed me across the river said the Hessians are exhausted — from the raids and the skirmishes — and that there are about fifteen hundred soldiers at the Trenton post. And Colonel Rall has no redoubts set up. Instead he has them patrolling constantly and sleeping fully dressed."

Washington's brow furrowed even deeper in thought at this information.

Sam hesitated; afraid his next question was too bold. But he had to ask, he had to know. "General, are you ever afraid in battle?"

Washington shrugged slightly. "In battle? Fear, yes, of course. Although, there is something oddly charming about the sound of whistling bullets. In my experience, everything is happening so fast during a battle, fear is replaced by a stronger instinct. Actually, Sam, some of my hardest battles take place when I am alone."

"Sir?"

"It is when I am alone that fear visits me. Usually at the end of the day, when my mind and body are tired and less able to fight back. Fear comes and sits on my chest with a devilish smirk

— pressing down on my heart so that I can neither breathe calmly or think clearly. And his worst companions — doubt and imagination — linger in his dark shadow, waiting to help him. Those two can make even the smallest fear seem much more formidable."

Sam simply could not imagine this strong, giant man lying in the dark, being clutched by dread. "If you are not afraid of battle, what are you afraid of?"

Washington looked straight ahead, lost in thought. He spoke the next words so quietly, almost as a confession to himself. "My fear is that I am not up to the responsibility that has been entrusted to me. From every soldier in my care, to every battle, to the outcome of this war, and the future of our country."

Sam paused, unsure of what to say next. But Washington did not seem upset, so he continued. "How do you fight those fears? Alone, I mean?"

"Well, as in any battle, I use the weapons at hand. To conquer fear — faith, for one. I have faith in the justice of our cause, and in myself. My struggle is merely a smaller version of our country's. We must overcome our doubts and believe in what we can achieve. I also use the power of imagination."

"But you said imagination encouraged your fear."

"Only if I let it. The combination of dread and imagination can cripple and paralyze even the strongest person. However, if we harness imagination to hope instead, it is capable of pulling one through the most wretched times. Even at this dark, seemingly hopeless time, my belief in America's future greatness endures."

A memory echoed in Sam's mind. *Imagination and hope —* Common Sense *will give America both. Perhaps* American Crisis *will do the same.* "Sir, I'm sorry about the delay in delivering the pamphlets. I hope I didn't bring them too late."

General Washington stared between the gray triangles

of Blueskin's ears. "It is late," he said quietly, "but perhaps it is not *too* late."

They rode silently the rest of the way.

Sam was assigned to a unit that was cobbled together from several Massachusetts militias. He was told to find a space in a tent. He approached a group of soldiers sitting around a fire. Like all the men he had seen so far that day, they wore tattered clothes; some were merely wrapped in blankets. They eyed Sam curiously — his clothes were whole and he looked well-fed. Sam introduced himself.

One of the men questioned him. "You seem pretty young to be a soldier, boy. Can you carry a musket?"

A man with a bloodied bandage around his head tapped his pipe on the ground, barely glancing at Sam. "You sure you want to fight? You might be climbing onto a sinking ship."

"Aye," another soldier murmured as he stared hollow-eyed at the twisting gray smoke of the fire. A long, red scar marked his jaw. "Seems like the game is pretty much up for us."

"Yes, I'm sure. And yes, I can carry and fire a musket." Sam hoped he sounded casual and confident, but his mouth went dry and his voice sounded a note higher. He asked if there was anyone from Falmouth.

"Falmouth?" The white-haired soldier took a long pull from his pipe. "I think John Trott is from Falmouth. Conrad Heyer, too. They're over there, at the last tent."

Sam practically ran to the tent. Both men were chopping wood. He quickly introduced himself, then asked if either of them knew Eamon.

Conrad spoke with the flat, drawn-out accent Sam knew well. "Eamon Collins? Ayuh, I think so. Hey, John, you remember that crazy kid with the tomahawk?"

John looked up from his work. "Oh, yeah, the Irish kid."

Sam's heart jumped! "Is he here?!"

John frowned. "No, he took a musket ball during the fighting in New York. Busted up his leg pretty bad. Not sure if he made it to a hospital or not, or maybe he went home."

Conrad chuckled. "He was wicked feisty, full o' sand that one. Always waving that tomahawk like a devil."

Sam smiled, but his heart twisted in a strange, bittersweet way. Eamon had gotten the tomahawk! That means he'd found Sam's note too. Eamon knew that Sam regretted their fight. And now Sam was here and Eamon was not. Well, he had not come only to find Eamon. He'd come to bring the pamphlets. And to fight.

Sam found room in a tent with two soldiers from the Fourteenth Mass Continentals. This group of fishermen and sailors from Marblehead were led by Colonel John Glover. One of the only regiments with Indians and Africans, they were already known for heroic work in the war, having rescued most of the Continental forces in August when the Americans had been hemmed in on Brooklyn Heights. In one night, Glover and his men had rowed silently back and forth across the East River — moving more than nine thousand men, horses, baggage, cannons, and provisions.

One of the soldiers was stretched out on a blanket in the tent. Through the flap, Sam could see a head of thick blond hair and the clothes of a fisherman — tarred, loose britches, a blue coat with leather buttons, and a bright red kerchief. The other soldier was a black man, much older than Sam. Although seated, he looked quite tall. His arms were lean and roped with long muscles. His hair was cropped very close to his head, with a dusting of gray at the temples. As he offered Sam a stick of dried beef, Sam noticed that his eyes, though deep brown, had tiny flecks of gold in the center.

"I'm Cyrus Reed." He nodded toward the tent. "That's Christopher Masters."

"Sam Nevens," Sam said between bites of the chewy meat. He noticed that Cyrus wore a blouse and breeches, like his own. "Are you from Marblehead?"

"New Jersey, near Monmouth. Just got thrown in with this bunch yesterday," Cyrus said.

A voice called out from the tent. "It was your lucky day. Marblehead men will go down as the saviors of the Revolution!"

A half-smile creased Cyrus' face. "And they are a humble lot as well," he said with a friendly roll of the eyes. "What about you?"

Sam explained how he'd ended up in the camp. As he was talking, Christopher emerged from the tent and squatted in front of the fire. "Sounds like yesterday was your lucky day too. Let's hope both your luck holds," Christopher said with a grin.

"Have you seen much fighting?" Sam asked them.

"A bit." Cyrus stretched his legs out. His feet were wrapped in ragged strips of cloth. "Mostly in New York. We were lucky to get out. The Hessians and Regulars were out for blood," he added gravely.

"Time for revenge!" Christopher declared; his face less cheerful than before. "Although there is one soldier on the other side that Cyrus will *not* shoot."

Sam tilted his head in an unspoken question. Cyrus reached for his knapsack and pulled out a piece of paper, folded over and well-creased. Sam could see it was a newspaper clipping.

Sam's eyes widened as he read the runaway slave notice. "Is this you?"

Cyrus shook his head. "My younger brother, Titus. Although I think he goes by Tye now. We were both owned by Quakers, but my master freed me when I turned twenty-one, like most of the Quakers do. But Titus' master, John Corlis, never abided by the same rules. He never taught his slaves to read or write. He whipped them often. I'm not surprised my brother escaped when he got the chance. I know he was headed for Virginia."

Sam stared at the clipping again. "This is dated November eighth of last year. The day after Dunmore's Proclamation."

"Aye, did his Lordship ruffle some southern feathers with that?!" Christopher said heartily. "Dunmore turned a lot of folks into rebels by promising freedom to any of their slaves who would fight on the British side." He turned to Cyrus. "Titus probably joined up with the Dunmore's Ethiopian Regiment."

Sam handed the paper to Cyrus, who carefully put it back in his bag.

"I heard they disbanded in August," Cyrus said. "Anyway, first I have to find him."

"What will you do, if you find him? You are fighting against each other," Sam asked.

"I will try to convince him to join the Americans," Cyrus answered calmly. "The way I see it, Titus and I are fighting for the same thing. We both want freedom, real freedom. Not just to live as free blacks, who are subject to the same laws and curfews as slaves." Cyrus shrugged his broad shoulders. "Titus thinks the British will bring true liberty and equality. I disagree. They are determined to crush the white colonists' rights; why would they treat anyone else here differently? As the *Declaration* says, we are all endowed by our Creator with certain rights. If by right of birth these things belong to all men, who has the power to give or take them away?"

"Life, liberty, and the pursuit of happiness!" Christopher added.

"Yes," Cyrus agreed. "I'll take my chances that the men who wrote those words will stand by them. Hopefully Titus will too."

Sam thought back to his conversation with Thomas about slavery. *It is viewed as an economic dilemma, not a moral one.* "I hope they do, Cyrus."

After being issued a musket and a blanket, Sam walked around, taking in his new surroundings. This camp was exactly like the one he'd seen yesterday — row upon row of small, triangular tents and groups of men half-dressed and half-starved, sitting around fires. Some were playing cards or dice — all were attempting to stay warm. Voices spoke in a dozen different accents — Irish, Scottish, Dutch, German. Suddenly, from one of the tents near him, he heard a strange sound. A squeaky, wheezy, familiar sound. He stopped at the tent and opened the flap. "Johnny?"

"Sam!" Johnny popped out of the tent. "What are you doing here? You're supposed to be home!"

Sam grinned, happy to see his friend again so soon. He told him everything that had happened.

"Where did they put you?" Johnny asked.

"With some militia from Massachusetts, but I'm not sure if I'm staying there."

"Well, you've got a musket. That's a good start. Say, when's the last time you fired one?"

Sam thought for a moment. "Not since I left home. Eighteen months."

Johnny's normally carefree face grew serious. "Maybe you should practice a bit. Things are pretty fast and furious once a battle starts. You don't want to be figuring it out then."

Sam nodded. "Are we going into battle?"

"Something's up. They even issued muskets to the drummers and fifers this morning," Johnny said quietly. "Come on, let's go fire off a few rounds."

They practiced until Johnny had to leave to play his fife for evening muster. *Johnny was right*, Sam thought later as he lay in the tent. *No matter how many times I've done it before, it'll be different firing a musket during a battle.* There were twelve steps to go through to load a musket. And even after the gun was ready, so much could go wrong. Using too much powder could cause an explosion that would hurt both gun and shooter. Not enough powder would cause the gun to fire weakly. Now he felt a little more prepared for whatever lay ahead.

In the morning, Sam took part in his first formation. Exhausted, cold, and starving, the men stood in rows, stomping their feet to keep warm. They assumed this was another drill. An officer rode up. Sam immediately recognized the paper in his hand. *American Crisis.* He felt a surge of pride when the officer held up the pamphlet — still dusted in a few places with flour — and said in a loud, strong voice, "Men, we received this last night. Sent by Common Sense himself."

Some of the men murmured in approval. Even though he knew what was coming, Sam still listened with awe as Thomas' powerful words rang out in the bitter December air.

"Let it be told to the future world, that in the depth of winter, when nothing but hope and virtue could survive, that the city and the country, alarmed at one common danger, came forth to meet and repulse it."

The men around Sam shifted. They looked up from the ground. Some stared intensely at the officer, as if trying to memorize every word he spoke. Some looked at each other, seeking affirmation that they were worthy of the honor of these words. Their faces changed; their posture changed. Standing taller and stronger, a new energy and determination rippled through the ranks. Each man seemed to take Thomas' words for his own.

Later that day, Sam was called to Washington's headquarters — a two-story house surrounded by giant oak trees. A captain seated at a desk near the entrance pointed to the set of double doors down the hallway and told Sam to wait there. One of the doors was open a few inches. Sam did not intend to eavesdrop, but he was standing close enough to hear the conversation inside. He recognized General Washington's voice right away. The other voice was very deep, with a Boston accent, speaking with great enthusiasm and confidence. "We will send two groups ahead of the main force. They'll be responsible for blocking the roads, and taking anyone prisoner who could jeopardize the attack."

We are going into battle! Sam moved a little closer to the door.

"Excellent. I know this mission is in good hands with you, Colonel Knox. Now, what is the artillery tally?"

Colonel Knox! The bookseller Josiah had talked about. He'd brought the captured artillery from Fort Ticonderoga to Massachusetts. Those were the guns that had chased the British out of Boston.

"General, I've got seven batteries from five states. Eighteen guns total," Knox responded.

"Are we going to be able to move them fast enough?" Washington asked.

Sam heard papers being shuffled.

"Yes, sir. We're using some of the new carriages I designed. They are lighter, easier to maneuver. This is the most current map we have. The critical battery position is here — if we control these two streets, we control the village."

General Washington said with firmness, "I cannot stress enough how important an initial overwhelming artillery strike will be in this operation. Our army is vastly inexperienced compared to the soldiers we are facing. Using tremendous firepower at the beginning will boost their confidence."

Knox answered eagerly. "Absolutely, sir. We are ready. Our enemies are accustomed to dealing with two or three guns for a thousand infantry. They won't be expecting the barrage we will bring. We'll use the cannons as shock weapons, in addition to supporting the infantry. I am confident we can take advantage of the chaos and perhaps seize their cannons as well."

Washington spoke again. "Major Lee, what about the horses? The river is running high. They will be more skittish than usual, making a crossing."

Sam leaned closer, straining to hear every word. *We must be crossing the Delaware. But where? Who are we attacking? There are Hessian garrisons all along the river, and the troops in Princeton as well.*

The next voice twanged with a strong Massachusetts accent. "I've delegated three men per horse, sir. That should be enough to keep them steady."

"And what of Captain Hamilton?" Washington said.

Henry Knox answered quickly. "He's recovering, sir. He's at a farmhouse, nearby."

Washington sounded doubtful. "Will he be able to lead

his company?"

"He says he will be there, although they are down to thirty-six men. Sir, I'd like to include a small detachment to the artillery. They will carry drag ropes, spikes, and hammers. Either we'll seize the cannons or spike them."

Washington's voice seemed slightly more animated now. "Excellent, gentlemen. We must be prepared for any possibilities. Go ahead with that detachment, Colonel Knox. And I have another addition to Captain Hamilton's company. The lad who brought the pamphlet to us. He's young, but he's had some experience with spiking cannons." Washington called to his aide in the hallway, "Captain Gibbs!"

The captain at the desk nodded to Sam, and he stepped into a room that was flickering with candlelight. A few tables lined the sides of the room, with two more standing in the center. The largest table was covered with papers, some torn into small scraps. The three men, all officers, were looking at a map spread on the larger table. General Washington stood in the middle. The man on Washington's left wore the uniform of a Marblehead regiment. Sam assumed the man on the right was Henry Knox. He was even taller than Washington! His uniform, like General Putnam's, struggled to contain his huge girth. As Sam approached them, Knox turned the map over. Sam noticed that his left hand was missing two fingers.

Washington turned to Sam. "Sam, have you been taken care of?"

"Yes, sir."

"Good." Washington's tight expression released to a brief smile. "Colonel Knox, Major Lee, this is Mr. Paine's newest courier. Samuel Nevens. Sam, we are moving you to Captain Hamilton's artillery company." Washington reached for a piece of paper and quickly wrote something down, then handed it to Sam. "The captain is ill, but go find Ben Thomsen. He'll see to your instructions."

When Washington reached across the table, a few of the scraps of paper fluttered to the floor and fell at Sam's feet. Sam picked them up and put them back on the table. He saw that each paper had the same thing written on it — *Victory or Death.*

CHAPTER **12**

Victory or Death

December 25, 1776
Newton, Pennsylvania

Christmas morning dawned bleak and gray. The damp, smoky air lay heavy on the rows of tents. Breakfast was a cold firecake washed down with colder water. Most of the day was spent standing in lines. Robert Morris' wagons from Philadelphia had arrived the day before with supplies. Blankets, clothing, muskets, pistols, lead, and — most important — gunpowder, were handed out. Sam was given a cartridge box, flints, and sixty rounds of ammunition. In the last line, he got a packet wrapped in rough cloth. More firecake, and some salt pork.

"Three days' rations," the man behind him said knowingly. Sam wondered what that meant.

The rest of the day the soldiers waited near their tents. A few speculated quietly about where they were headed. Sam said nothing about what he had heard yesterday at Washington's headquarters. Despite the uncertainty, most of the soldiers seemed relieved, almost happy to be doing *something*. An undercurrent of excitement and anticipation rippled through camp. After months of humiliating retreats and losses, these ragged men still possessed a grim optimism. Sam began to understand what Thomas had described to him at Ben Franklin's house.

Sam spent part of the morning with some soldiers from the artillery battery where he'd been assigned. The team had been together since March, when their captain, Alexander Hamilton, had raised the company in New York City. They were all older than Sam. James, the company's second lieutenant, had been a student at King's College when the war started. He had a soft, pudgy face and reddish blond hair. Noah was a wheelwright. He was tall, with narrow features and a deep cleft in his chin. Robbie, a blacksmith, was stocky with a square face. His hair was jet black, except for a wide streak of complete white that went from his forehead all the way back.

The team's task that morning was to weather-proof the cannons. They plugged the muzzles and vents, then covered them with pieces of oilcloth to keep them dry. Sam asked about Captain Hamilton, who had been very sick for days. It was clear from the conversation that Hamilton's team all worshiped their young captain.

"He's fearless!" James said with admiration. "Maybe because he's an orphan, he feels like he's got to prove himself. He'll do whatever it takes to win a fight."

"Aye, we've seen plenty of action. If you want to be in the thick of the fight, this is the battery to be in," Noah said.

"For sure," Robbie added, slapping the cannon they were working on. "The army would never have gotten out of New

Jersey if not for our battery. We blasted the Redcoats across the Raritan for hours. Kept Cornwallis on his toes that day!"

Noah nodded to Sam. "We may be the smallest, but we're the best, thanks to Captain Hamilton."

"Why is that?" Sam said.

Noah leaned against the cannon carriage and pulled out a small bag of tobacco. He scooped some into his mouth, then answered. "He's young, but the captain knows what he's doing. He's smart, and careful. He sees the situation in a battle and knows how to use the battery. And he's an honest man. He speaks his mind, no matter the consequences."

Late in the afternoon, drums sharply rattled out the order to muster. As the troops lined up, Sam watched carefully, wondering how this mass of men would fall into place. Two small groups, forty men each, left ahead of the main group. *Roadblocks and prisoners.* Sam recognized the next line by the long pale hunting shirts and buckskin trousers — a Virginia regiment. They were seasoned veterans of the frontier wars. *Washington probably wants them to go first because he trusts them.* The rest of the infantry formed columns, eight men across. Henry Knox's prized cannons went first — four for each column. Sam joined his artillery team behind their two cannons. They all exchanged nervous looks. Their commander had still not arrived. Was he too sick to fight? Suddenly a chestnut horse pulled up alongside them. The rider was a slim, pale young man. He nodded at the crew, who all grinned back. *So that is Captain Hamilton!* He looked exhausted, but his blue eyes gleamed with a determined light. In his hat there was a white piece of paper, to show that he was an officer. He leaned in toward his team and said in a low, hoarse voice, "Did you think I was going to miss this?" The crew grinned even more. Then, in a louder, sterner voice, Hamilton said, "Men, you are to remain completely silent. Any man who quits the

291

ranks shall face immediate punishment."

Under a darkening sky, the columns began to march. They moved slowly through the shadowy forest, like a giant beast emerging from deep hibernation. A full moon rose — cold and indifferent to the fate of the hundreds of men trudging below. Soon, thin clouds interrupted the moon's glow, then the full darkness of a storm filled the sky. An icy drizzle fell. Sam's clothes and bag were quickly soaked. As he settled into a steady pace, he thought about what he learned yesterday and what his job was today. Even though Sam would only be carrying ammunition and water, he needed to know all the positions and firing sequence for working the cannon.

Ben Thomsen, part of Hamilton's crew since the beginning of the war, had shown Sam what to do. Ben was short, with a flat, wide forehead and the shaggiest eyebrows Sam had ever seen. They moved up and down as he spoke, like two lazy caterpillars working their way across a thick branch. He had chewed on a clay pipe as he walked Sam around the cannon, showing him each crew member's position and duties. He stood on the left side of the gun carriage. "Of course, Captain Hamilton is the gun commander. Usually, he only gives the commands and makes sure everyone is squared. But we lost Rob Dalton, our firer, to smallpox last week, so the Captain is doing that, too. He stands here."

Ben pointed with the pipe to the other side of the carriage. "There are five commands — 'Sponge,' 'Ram,' 'In Battery,' 'Point,' and 'Give Fire.' The vent tender, that's James, stands here. He primes the vent and keeps the air out during the worming, sponging and loading. Right here," Ben waved the pipe toward the opposite wheel, "that's Robbie. He worms the barrel — takes out the old cartridge, makes sure there's naught left, then he sponges it with the swab. That's 'Sponge.' After it's clean, Noah," the pipe pointed at the left side of the cannon, "puts in a new cartridge, and then Robbie charges the piece. That's 'Ram.' And in the back, that's me. I handle the powder. I keep it away from the gun and man the tiller."

Ben moved to the powder box behind the cannon. He pulled out a small canvas bag. It was full of gunpowder and sewn closed at the top. "After the powder is rammed, the shot goes in. We'll be using grapeshot and canisters." He held up another bag, bulging with round lumps, about the size of plums. "This has thirty-five one-inch lead balls." He handed the grapeshot sack to Sam. "Once she's loaded, we prick the powder bag inside, then pour powder into the touchhole to light the charge. When Captain Hamilton says 'In Battery,' we put the piece into firing position. 'Point' is for the final adjustments. When you hear 'Give Fire' step back from the piece and cover your ears. The firer will light the powder and that's that. Now, Nevens, your job," the clay pipe bobbed in Sam's face, "is to make sure Robbie has got the pieces he needs, and water in the bucket. Sponging and ramming are the most dangerous positions. We lost a few men in New York from carelessness. Keep your wits about you and pay attention to Robbie, nothing else, and you'll do fine. You got all that?" He stared intently at Sam, his two eyebrows nearly meeting in the middle, like a hairy hedgerow.

Sam nodded enthusiastically.

"Good. Now, tell it back to me."

Sam swallowed and stared at everything in front of him. He picked up the long wooden pole with a spiral coil on one end and a sheepskin tuft on the other. "This is the worm ..."

Ben had been satisfied with Sam's answers, yet now, a day later, Sam hoped he could remember it all as well in the thick of fighting. Soon Sam was too distracted by the cold to think of anything else. Snow and sleet cut into his face like a hundred tiny knives. The wind rose and fell in a high screeching pitch. The men pushed forward, heads lowered, shoulders hunched.

Although they were silent, it seemed to Sam that there was a cacophony of noise. Thousands of feet thumped dully against the frozen ground. Hundreds of muskets clacked against bent backs. The artillery carriages and wagons clattered as they rolled obstinately over the rough terrain. The horses puffed and snorted. Sam began to wonder how long they would have to march, when the column slowly came to a halt. He looked up through the driving snow and saw the rolling dark outline of the Delaware River.

Boats of all shapes and sizes lined the shore. The biggest were Durham boats — large, flat-bottom craft painted black with yellow trim. They reminded Sam of the fat bumblebees who hovered around the lilac bush at home. The frightened horses were being led onto a ferry. Sam's eyes searched the darkness, looking for Blueskin. Surely General Washington's horse would be one of the first across. A second ferry rocked slowly as the cannons were loaded. Men from the Marblehead regiment were maneuvering all the boats, and above it all, Henry Knox's booming voice shouted out instructions to everyone.

As they moved toward the boats, the darkness, blinding snow, and mass of men made it almost impossible to see one foot ahead. Someone nudged Sam from behind. He stumbled slightly, stopped from falling only by the tight pack of bodies. His row stepped onto the boat, then filed to the far end in a jostling, clumsy forward motion. As many men as could fit were squeezed in. They all remained standing as the crew pushed off from the shore with oars and poles. Pressed on all sides with the breathing of other soldiers close against his face, Sam stared at the spinning current, almost hypnotized as jagged chunks of ice the size of small boulders twisted and bobbed past. It seemed like the first enemy that they would have to contend with this night was Mother Nature herself — angry that a ragged collection of mere mortals dared to challenge her power. Hailstones slammed against the curved hull and bounced back into the dark water. Rain, snow, wind, sleet — every element seemed to be in play. Sam half-expected a sheet of fire to rise up from the river in a complete attempt to oppose them.

The boat hit the shore with a rough jolt. Wind whipping against his face, Sam climbed out with the others and trudged along in a crammed huddle up a short bank. They were told to move farther down the road and wait. Sam could see General Washington sitting slightly off to the side of a group of officers. He was wrapped in his cloak, sitting on a box that had stored a beehive in warmer weather. He pulled out his timepiece, wiped the snow from the glass, and stared at the heavy gold watch, his countenance unreadable.

While they waited, a few soldiers hastily built fires from nearby fences. Sam worked his way toward one — the wind and flames cut through the fence rails quickly so the fires did little good. He turned to look back at the river. At this spot, the Delaware was only nine hundred feet wide, normally an easy crossing. But tonight, each boat brought over was a herculean effort by Glover and his men. At last, everyone was across the river. The men were lined up again. The New Jersey militia had been waiting and now served as guides. They moved away from the river, into the woods, the road sloping upward. Incredibly, the storm grew worse as the chain of drenched soldiers pushed straight into it. Sam felt a hard chill settle between his shoulder blades. The rain pelted his face and dripped into his eyes, making it almost impossible to see anything in the dark forest except the legs of the men in front of him. They filed past a snug building surrounded by a white picket fence. A sign nearby read — Bear Tavern. After about a mile they came to a crossroads, shifting their direction south.

Sam knew exactly where they were. *We're heading toward Trenton. It's the Hessian garrison!* A knot of fear tightened in his stomach. Was he ready? How would he fight? Could he kill someone? He wished he knew what to expect. He wished Eamon was here. Eamon would be strong and confident. He thought about his parents. *Did they get his letters? What if they think I'm on my way home?* He should have written another letter yesterday! What if he was killed today? He saw their faces exactly as they had looked on his last night at home — heads bowed at the supper table. *Why am I doing this? Fighting for a lost cause? We are all going to die or be taken prisoner!* His heart clutched. Tears pinched his eyes. He squeezed them shut and gritted his teeth. This was no way to behave going into battle. What had General Washington said about overpowering fear? Suddenly he thought of a page from *American Crisis*. The words jumped into his terrified mind like rope to a drowning man — *Panics in some cases have their uses. They produce as much good as hurt. Their duration is short; the mind soon grows through them and acquires a firmer habit than before.*

A firm mind! He needed to be firm. He looked left and right at the men walking beside him. They didn't look afraid. Sam could see Cyrus was a few rows up, staring straight ahead — face as stern as a preacher. Sam took a deep breath and focused on marching. A flash of scarlet in the snow caught his eye. A bird feather? Then another. They were not feathers, they were bloody footprints from the barefoot soldiers in front of him. After the columns changed direction, the storm was not blowing in their faces. The pace became slightly faster, but it was short-lived. A deep ravine lay before them. Jacob's Creek. Even in daylight the rocky slope was difficult to navigate; tonight, in the snow, sleet, and darkness, it was almost impossible.

The horses were unharnessed from the wagons. Long ropes were attached to trees and the guns were lowered slowly to the bottom, then hauled up to the other side. Despite the cold, the teams of men moving the cannons were red with exertion as they grasped the heavy ropes and fought to keep their balance. At the same time, the columns of soldiers inched their way down, then plodded slowly up. Legs shaking with cold, Sam struggled to stay upright on the slick path. He reached the top and looked across. General Washington was riding Blueskin down the ravine, urging the men on. Suddenly the horse's back feet slipped. Together, the horse and Washington began to slide down the icy slope. Washington's face braced, but showed no alarm. He dug his hand into Blueskin's mane and pulled his head up forcefully. At the same time, he shifted backward slightly. Every muscle in the powerful animal's legs pulled taut as he fought against the combined danger of ice and gravity. Blueskin regained his footing and reached the bottom safely. Sam had never seen anyone display such skill and strength with a horse.

After crossing the ravine, they marched to an open stretch of road. The terrain was flat, but out of the woods the army was exposed again to the full brunt of the furious storm. Many of the soldiers began to weave and stumble with exhaustion. Sam's feet and hands were numb. The wind dug into his face with one icy blast after another. Even over the wind he could hear Washington's unmistakable voice, deep and steady. "Keep with your officers, men. For God's sake, keep with your officers."

Captain Hamilton had gotten off his horse at Jacob's Creek. Now he walked alongside a cannon. Sam saw him occasionally reach over to affectionately pat the gun — as if it were an animal needing encouragement. Some cannons had torches affixed to their carriages. The bright flames fought with wind and elements — bravely casting dancing circles of light against the relentless night. The dark trees along the road stood silent and firm like sentries.

The march slowed and ground to a halt. Sam looked up to see a pale streak of light in the eastern sky. *Almost dawn.* Washington and his officers gathered in a tight circle. Washington remained astride his horse. After a brief discussion, all the men pulled out their timepieces and adjusted them. Then the entire force split into two columns. Washington and General Greene led one, including Sam's unit — along Pennington Road. *We must be attacking from the north side of town. The other column will be going in from the south.* They marched another mile; visibility in the storm was murky. Although exhausted, a ripple of energy seemed to course through the ranks as they drew closer to the target. General Washington's face could have been cut from stone — it was resolute and unyielding. Yet he knew, better than any man here, that if this surprise assault failed, the game was up. The Continental army would collapse, the militias would return home, and he, if unlucky enough to be captured rather than killed, would be hanged for treason.

Now marching in daylight, Washington continued to encourage the men with shouts of, "Press on, press on boys!" The column met up with the advance parties. A sudden call from the front put them on alert. Washington spurred Blueskin toward a group of thirty or so men. This was not one of the advance parties. Was it an enemy patrol? As he trudged past the group and the General, Sam was close enough to hear their conversation. They were a part of a Virginia regiment, led by General Adam Stephens. The previous day, without informing Washington, Stephens had sent a raiding party across the river to attack a Hessian outpost in revenge for killing one of Stephens' men. The raiders had shot a sentinel and then quickly retreated after the whole Hessian garrison responded to the attack.

Sam watched in amazement and alarm as General Washington's expression veered from self-control to barely-contained rage. All of the frustrations of the night seemed to coalesce in this one moment. Washington's voice was a lash of white-hot fury. "Is this true?" he thundered at General Stephens. "How dare you authorize such a mission without my permission!

You, sir, may have ruined all my plans by having them put on their guard!"

For a split second, Sam thought Washington would strike Stephens, but quickly composing himself, the General turned away and spoke in an even voice to Stephens' men, inviting his fellow Virginians to join his column. It was now almost seven-thirty in the morning, well past the target of a surprise dawn attack. But the raging storm had concealed both the sight and sound of the Americans as they approached the outskirts of Trenton.

A messenger rode up to Washington. "Sir, General Sullivan says the powder is wet down the lines."

Washington did not hesitate in his response. "Fix bayonets. I am resolved to take Trenton."

The column stopped behind a screen of trees. Washington pulled out his watch. Through the flurry of snow Sam could see a small hut — a Hessian outpost. In spite of the hundreds of men standing around him, the only sound Sam could hear was the thud of his heart against his chest. Everything seemed to move in slow motion.

General Washington raised his arm and then brought it down. "Advance and charge!"

The mass of men moved forward at a quick pace. The door of the outpost opened, and a Hessian soldier stepped out. Sam saw the red burst of a muzzle, then three more full volleys. Flashes of blue, red, and yellow spilled out of the hut as Hessians emerged, tugging on their uniforms and loading their weapons. They formed rank and fired a volley back. As hundreds of rebel soldiers streamed past, the Hessians realized that this was not a mere skirmish. From the south, Sam heard a roar of cannons, punctuating the dawn stillness like a dam breaking. The multiple attacks had been perfectly timed. In an instant, a hundred sounds filled the air. From the river came the boom of artillery. From the center of the village, the pounding of German kettle drums. Their need for silence finished, the Americans charged toward Trenton, shoulder to shoulder, screaming through the driving snow, **"These are the times that try men's souls!!"**

Now everything seemed to move at triple speed. As the soldiers ran forward, a new spirit animated them. Their voices rose as one single cry of attack. Sam's legs and hands were shaking. His mouth went dry. He swallowed and a bolt of the frozen air stopped in his throat. But in the next moment he felt as if a wave had picked him up and lifted his heavy feet from the frozen ground. He was screaming, too. His heart rushed with adrenaline as he raced behind the jolting wheels of the cannon carriage. The guns were unlimbered from the horses, then pushed the last few hundred yards to the junction of King and Queen streets, the highest part of the town. *If we control these streets, we control the town.* A tremendous crash rattled Sam's entire skull as the earth shuddered. Smoke billowed around them. Captain Forrest's team had gotten there a few minutes earlier and had already fired off one round, sending a barrage of shot down Queen Street.

Hamilton leapt off his horse and began shouting orders to the team. The two guns were set up, pointing down King Street. While Hamilton fixed the positions, the ammunition boxes were lifted from the sides of the carriage and placed a hundred feet or so behind the pieces. A small cart, with water and tools, was rolled up. Sam ran over to pull a barrel of water out. He pried out the cork and filled a bucket. Sharp acrid smoke filled the air, burning his eyes and nose. Everyone took their positions. James stepped forward and placed his thumb, wrapped in a thick piece of leather, over the vent. The slightest draft during loading could ignite the cannon too soon.

Sam heard Hamilton shout. "Sponge!"

Robbie, pulling on a pair of heavy gloves, pointed with

the wormer to a spot next to him and nodded. Sam placed the bucket down and ran to bring a round of grapeshot. The bulky canvas bag weighed about as much as a new-born pig and felt just as slippery in his numb hands. Sam gave it to Ben, then stepped back. Robbie wormed and swabbed the barrel. Ben passed the grapeshot to Noah, who held it while Ben placed a powder charge in the barrel and rammed it down. "Ram!"

Noah loaded the shot and pushed it to the end of the piece. Ben stepped forward with a thin metal pick and stuck it in the vent hole to rip open the powder cartridge inside. Next, he poured priming powder in with the quill, a bird feather cut and filled with powder.

"In Battery!" Hamilton squinted down the barrel of the first cannon, nodded, then checked the second one. He waved his hand upward. Ben grabbed a wedge from the cart and pushed it under the end of the cannon, lifting it slightly, lowering the muzzle.

"Point!" Hamilton lifted the rope that would spark the powder. "Give Fire!"

Everyone stepped away from the gun, bent sideways and covered their ears. Hamilton released the rope. Sam put his hands over his ears just in time. BOOM! The earth shook again and the cannon leapt backward. A blast of white smoke billowed into the air. A spray of iron tore down the street. CRACK! Forrest's crew fired again. Sam could see a stream of Hessians scrambling out of their barracks down below. The enemy had been taken completely by surprise and they now rushed about struggling to gain control. They began to form ranks and the regimental flags came out. As they moved toward the center of town, a torrent of artillery fire slammed their left flank, sending them into total confusion.

The rebel cannons continued their relentless barrage. Sam raced back and forth between the water bucket and ammunition wagon. Snow and smoke mixed together in a stinging blur. The men hunched over the touchholes and powder, fighting to keep them dry. General Washington galloped toward them and pulled Blueskin to a stop. From here, he could see the entire battle as it unfolded. Although Sam was not as high up as Washington, his view was almost the same. The Americans were moving in, firing from three sides. Sam could see the German officers wheeling their horses and shouting, frantically trying to bring order to their chaotic troops as they desperately tried to fight back. The artillery men brought out their horses, already harnessed and ready to move, but spooked by the noise and fury. They strained to hitch the horses to the two cannons and move them into position. Despite the mayhem, they managed to fire a few rounds at the high batteries. A cannonball whizzed toward them and took out the front horse of one of Captain Forrest's guns. The horse's scream pierced the din and it seemed to fall in slow motion. It kicked for a moment, then lay still. A scarlet pool of blood seeped onto the frozen ground beneath it.

BLAM! A surge of firepower tore down through the raging fight below. Sam watched a howitzer shell, low and murderous, bounce down the street. It exploded in the midst of the Hessian gunners. Five lay dead near their silent cannons. Two remained standing, but quickly abandoned their guns and fled. With their gunners gone, the soldiers behind them were unprotected. They soon began to follow their comrades in a disorderly scramble, but they were being shot at with both cannon and musket fire from all sides. The clamor of a thousand sounds pummeled Sam's ears as he gaped momentarily at the kaleidoscope of carnage in the streets below.

"Nevens!"
"Nevens!"
"SAM!"

Sam whirled around. Hamilton was shouting at him. Legs shaking, Sam ran over to him.

Hamilton motioned to another crew member. "Eli, take over for Nevens!" He turned to Sam and pointed toward the center of town. "Saint Clair's men need cartridges. Take as many boxes as you can carry. Stay behind the houses. They are in that church. Take your musket."

Sam slung his musket over his back, then grabbed two of the boxes. Each held sixty cartridges. He tucked them under his arms and ran, darting through backyards, gardens, and fruit trees. The noise grew louder as he got closer to the center of town. He could hear the Germans shouting. *"Der Feind! Der Feind! Heraus!"*

Sam rushed into the church and headed toward the closest officer. He put down the boxes. A dozen men were positioned at the windows. Others were loading their guns, faces already streaked black by powder.

"Are you loaded?" the officer asked him. Sam shook his head. "Do it." The officer turned back toward the soldiers and commanded, "Take cover now and fire low. Bring down your pieces. Fire at their legs. One man wounded in the leg is better than a dead one, for it takes two more to carry him off. Leg them, damn 'em, I say, leg them!"

Sam flipped open his own cartridge case. They were all soaked. He refilled the case from the box he'd delivered, then pulled out one cartridge. Leveling his musket, he opened the flash pan cover. Then he bit the top half of the cartridge open. The sharp taste of metal buzzed against his tongue as he poured some powder into the flash pan, then closed it. Next, he turned the musket upright and poured powder into the gun's barrel, followed by the rest of the cartridge that held the musket ball. With two quick strokes, he pushed the little paper and ball wad completely down with the iron ramrod. The gun was ready to fire.

He went back out to Queen Street, glancing toward the river. The American artillery from that direction had smashed the ice along the waterfront. A musket ball flew past his ear, then another. He ducked and rolled under a wagon covered with oilcloth. As he stood up, his knee pressed against something soft. It was a child's shoe, crushed into the dirt. Sam lifted the oilcloth. The wagon was full — a jumble of clothes, blankets, dishes, silver, rugs. He saw the other shoe. *Hessian plunder!!* The terrified face of the boy from the tavern rose in his mind and a rage charged through him. Instead of returning to the battery the way he had come, he turned and ran toward the thick of fighting.

Hessians were dropping left and right as the Americans continued to overpower them. Glancing across the street, Sam saw Cyrus sprinting between a small barn and a stone house. Suddenly, from behind the barn, a huge Hessian jumped out, his face twisted in a murderous rage. Bayonet held high, he charged at Cyrus' back. Sam raised his musket and focused on the barrel. He pulled back the flintlock, then let go. The hammer sprang forward. Crack! The butt of the gun pounded against his shoulder. Smoke and fire spewed into his face. The Hessian shouted, dropped his weapon, and crumpled to the ground. *I hit him! Is he dead?* The Hessian didn't move. *Did I kill him?* Sam's breath exploded. He had been holding it the whole time. He stared at the man's face, now peaceful and still, blue eyes open to the sky. A dark circle was slowly spreading across his broad chest.

Cyrus must have heard the Hessian's cry because he spun around and stared briefly at his would-be killer. He looked over at Sam, whose gun was still pointed at the fallen giant. Cyrus nodded to Sam, and then continued running. Sam's stomach lurched; his mouth went dry. He had taken a life. And saved another. *No time to think about it.* He reloaded his weapon, then moved behind a fence to get his bearings. The Americans were firing from inside the houses and buildings. Their powder and muskets, protected now from the weather, poured down on the enemy who struggled to fire their wet weapons in the heavy snow. Civilians were running into houses and cellars to escape the fighting, but a few were joining in. Across the street, a window on the second floor of a house opened. Sam saw a flash of flowing red hair. There was something very familiar about it. The dark line of a musket stretched out through the window. Sam watched the woman carefully take aim at a Hessian captain — who fell dead on the spot one second later.

Hessian officers on horses rode toward the center of the village. Sam was sure the one in the middle was Colonel Rall. He rode into the thick of his men, which seemed to rally them. He called out to them to follow him, determined to recapture their guns. His bright sword flashed through the air as he cried, *"Alle meine Grenadiere sind vorwärts!!"*

Drums rattled as the men marched back toward King Street. Sam heard fifers and even horns. *That must be Rall's precious brass band.* But they headed straight into a fiery deluge. The Germans briefly recovered their guns and began returning fire. One American gun fell silent — its carriage shattered. In a moment, Colonel Knox rode up to the crew and called out in his thunderous voice, "My brave lads, go up and take those two held pieces, sword in hand! There is a party going and you must join them!"

The gunners rushed forward and attacked with a ferocity the Hessians had not yet seen. It was too much. They scattered through the cataclysm of smoke and noise. Each blast of artillery was followed by the clatter of exploding wood, glass, and iron. The clang of swords and crack of muskets rang out over the groans of the wounded men and animals. Sam started up King Street. He had to get back to the artillery battery. He pressed up against the side of a small building. He could tell by the grain and tracks on the ground that it was a henhouse, probably with a feed loft above. He peered through the smoke, trying to see the best way to get back. Suddenly a shell slammed above him, sending a mass of hay and corn into the air. Sam flew backward. A burning corncob smashed into his face. He stood up shakily, hand pressed over his seared skin, then stumbled over to the porch of a house and leaned against the door. It opened behind him. A wiry figure with a shock of white hair stepped out and tossed him a kerchief. Then he stepped past Sam. Moving with slow and steady patience, the man aimed his rifle carefully and shot. One hundred yards away, Colonel Rall arched backward, then fell forward onto his horse's neck. His officers pulled him from his horse and carried him into a church. The battle shifted. The loss of their commander broke the Hessians. They fled into buildings, cellars, and barns. As the enemies' ranks fell apart, General Washington galloped past Sam. He rode alone toward the spot where the last of the Germans continued to fight and cried, "March on my brave fellows, after me!"

The Americans surrounded the remaining Hessians. Soldiers from the Haussegger battalion, made of mostly German immigrants, shouted at them in German and English to surrender. The disoriented Hessians lowered their flags and began to stack their weapons. Sam stood up shakily. He tied the kerchief around his head, wiping his bloodied hands before picking up his weapon.

Both Hamilton and Forrest were running toward Washington, their teams close behind them. Captain Forrest called out, "Sir, they have struck!" to General Washington, who had turned to ride in pursuit of the soldiers fleeing toward the creek.

Washington wheeled his horse around. "Struck?"

"Yes, their colors are down, sir."

"So, they have." General Washington seemed momentarily

stunned. The entire battle had lasted about ninety minutes. The smoke lifted, revealing the wrecked remains of the bloody fight. The streets of Trenton were strewn with fallen Hessians, their bright blue jackets ripped and splattered with dark ribbons of blood; bodies and faces contorted by pain into gruesome shapes. General Sullivan's aide rode up to tell Washington that all the enemy had completely surrendered.

Sam went to join his battery. The men were jubilant. Hamilton's face, still pale from illness, radiated a gritty, satisfied glow. He greeted Sam with an enthusiastic handshake. "You did well today, young man! Is it Samuel or Sam?" Hamilton asked.

"Sam, sir." He looked at the other soldiers — laughing and slapping each other on their backs — then kicked at the ground, eyes lowered. "I shot a Hessian. I killed him," Sam said quietly.

Hamilton turned to face him. He said nothing at first, then reached over to grip Sam's shoulder. "War is a nasty business. A nasty business." A sad expression flickered in his blue eyes as he looked at the young, confused face before him. "Sam, get that eye looked at. Wounded are being tended in the dock house."

Sam walked toward the dock, his mind spinning as he attempted to process everything that had just happened. The destruction around him assailed each of his senses — his eyes took in all the wreckage — bodies, buildings, animals, weapons; his ears rang with cries of agony and shouts of victory; the acrid smell and taste of powder lingered in his nose and throat; his legs and hands felt slightly numb as the adrenaline of battle seeped away. He reached the dock house and sat down on a bench. His tent mate, Christopher, was taking care of the casualties among the Americans. Miraculously, there were only a few. When Sam got there, Christopher was bandaging the shoulder of a young lieutenant from Virginia, who looked pale and shaken.

"What's your name?" Christopher asked cheerfully.

"James. James Monroe."

"James, you're going to be fine. A few weeks' rest and you'll be back in the fight!"

Monroe closed his eyes and leaned back in silence.

Christopher turned to Sam. "Sam! What happened to you?!"

"I picked the wrong henhouse." Sam's face was caught between a smile and a grimace as Christopher gently pulled away the kerchief and examined the wound. He reached over for a nearby flask. "Here."

Sam took a deep swig. The sharp bite of rum filled his mouth. He looked at Christopher, who nodded. Sam took another drink. A warm feeling traveled down his throat and into his stomach.

"Better?"

Sam nodded.

Christopher carefully pulled bits of charred corn from Sam's skin. "You are lucky. Two inches to the left and you would have lost your eye." He leaned back and grinned playfully. "Geez, there are easier ways to get a meal."

Head bandaged and feeling slightly tipsy, Sam went down toward the river. He was not the only one who was tipsy. Soon after the battle ended, forty hogsheads of rum were discovered in an empty tavern. Many of the American soldiers, astonished by their improbable victory, were celebrating with glee, and rum. Wearing the tall brass caps of their vanquished foes, they danced around near the docks where the dazed Hessians were lining up. The dancers, some wearing only shirts and blankets, strutted around with their elbows out, doing a comical jig. Johnny was there too, adding to the merriment with a squeaky song.

Sam walked over to his friend.

"Are you all right?" Johnny stopped playing.

Sam laughed. "Aye, I'll make it. Looks like your fife is still lucky."

"It is. It is," Johnny said, "and look at this!" He held up a long sword, with a brass handle and tassels. "I took it from one of the dead ones." He pointed the sword toward the Hessians.

"They sure look scared," Sam said, watching them file toward the boats. He almost felt sorry for them.

"That's because they think we're going to eat them." George Keeport, one of Haussegger's men was standing behind them. "They were told that the Americans are a race of cannibals who would tomahawk a poor Hessian, use his skin for a drum, and barbeque him like a pig."

Two of the defeated Germans standing near them were more furious than scared. They were arguing back and forth about something. One was red-faced with anger. Sam heard the name Rall and Donop.

"What are they talking about?" Johnny asked.

"Whose fault it is that they lost." George tilted his head toward the Hessian on the left. "He says its Rall's fault for not putting up any defenses. The other one blames Colonel von Donop, who was tarrying in Mount Holly at the home of a beautiful widow."

At the mention of Colonel von Donop, the red-faced one grew even more irate. He spat on the ground. *"Von Donop sollte aus Scham sterben. Er ist nichts als ein Sitzpinkler!"*

George burst out laughing.

"What did he say?"

"He called him a 'sitzpinkler' — a man who sits down to pee. It's not a compliment!"

Whoever's fault it was, the Hessians' defeat was nothing short of a miracle for the Continental army. The Hessians had twenty-two soldiers killed, eighty-three wounded and eight hundred and ninety-six taken prisoner. The Americans had two officers and several soldiers wounded, and no fatalities. The Americans seized enough weapons and munitions to supply several brigades. The grandest prize was six German cannons. After the shock of victory subsided, the first order General Washington gave was that all the prisoners be treated humanely, not only the officers. While the prisoners and guns were moved into boats, Washington and his officers gathered to discuss what to do next. Should they strike again and attack another post, or go back across the river to the safer territory of Pennsylvania? They quickly realized that the men were too exhausted to pursue the enemy deeper into New Jersey. And the British, who had considered the rebellion crushed, would be bent on revenge. Probably the angriest of the King's officers would be Lord Cornwallis. He had been planning to sail back to England on December twenty-seventh, to visit his family and inform King George that the pesky colonial skirmish was finished.

News of the heroic river crossing and battle began to spread even as the exhausted troops made their way back across the Delaware. Washington and his men had found the strength, audacity, and courage to change their fate — at least temporarily.

CHAPTER 13

The Speckled Monster

February 6, 1777
Morristown, New Jersey

The smudged courthouse window framed an iron sky and black leafless trees outside. Sam lay stretched out on a rough blanket; a makeshift mattress stuffed with straw beneath him. Forty or so soldiers were scattered in one big room all the way to the door, mostly lying and sitting down. Sam moved to sit up against the wall, hoping to get more comfortable, but the wall was as hard and cold as the thin mattress. He knew he couldn't complain — at least he had a roof over his head. Many of the men in camp were housed in tents or barns — neither offered much shelter from the unforgiving cold of a New Jersey

311

winter. Sam twisted his arm to get a better look at the cut where Dr. Otto had inserted the pus. It looked huge and ominous to Sam. All around him, the room murmured with subdued conversations, and a sense of waiting, similar to what it felt like before a battle. They had all been inoculated together that morning, and much like a battle, Dr. Otto had tried to prepare them for the enemy they were about to meet — smallpox.

"You won't be contagious right away. The disease starts with a slight fever, then you may feel perfectly fine for a few days. The fever will return; sweating and shivering is normal, along with possible headaches or back pain. Next, sores will appear in your mouth, throat, and nose. By the fourth and fifth day the rash will move to the surface of your skin."

At this point, Dr. Otto had paused briefly and gazed at his captive audience. He deliberated about how much information to share with them, before deciding that preparing them for the worst was a better choice. After all, every one of them had faced death many times over the past few months. "Now men, this is a dangerous stage in the virus' progression. If the rash turns inward, internal bleeding will take over. It is … unpleasant. And fatal."

Sam heard a soft groan next to him. Young Jim's face went ashen and his knuckles turned white as he gripped his pipe to quell the shaking in his hands.

Dr. Otto continued. "The rash usually begins on the face, emerging in reddish-purple patches. This may fade slightly but will be followed by blisters — on your face, neck, hands, and soles of your feet."

"The pox!" Jim said, sucking in his breath.

"Yes, the pox," Dr. Otto echoed grimly. "The blisters will darken from purple to black. This stage is also quite dangerous. If the blisters break, large pieces of skin may come off and the risk of infection is great. However painful it is, you must

312

try not to scratch or move too much. It should all be over in a few weeks."

Sam stared out the window. *A few weeks. I have a little time to make a decision — and whatever I choose, at least I won't have to worry about dying from smallpox.* Laughter from across the room caught his attention. Someone from the Connecticut militia was telling jokes, probably trying to relieve the tension after Dr. Otto's gloomy speech. Sam looked around the courthouse. He knew most of the men here. He thought about his first day in camp, how scared he had been. How much he had hoped to find Eamon among the troops. He had not found Eamon, but he had made new friends; the men from Hamilton's battery, from the Marblehead regiment, Cyrus, and others. His closest friend was Ray. Maybe it was because Sam had saved his life? For whatever reason, Ray felt like an old friend to Sam from the moment they met.

Ray did not speak much. When he did, his voice was so quiet and low, you almost wondered if he realized he was speaking out loud. His words were spare and chosen carefully — as if they came from a finite supply that he didn't want to squander. Ray sang more than he talked, but to Sam, it was an entirely different kind of singing. When Sam's mother sang, usually when she was cooking or working in the garden, it sounded like she was happy and singing was the best way to savor it. Then there was church singing. Those songs were solemn and musty — it felt like work to sing them. When Ray sang, there was a shadow of sadness tucked behind each word. His songs were like the chapters of an ancient, mysterious book he had inherited and had to read, but would never really finish. Even when he sang funny songs, like "Fish and Tea," there was an air of sorrow to them. Truthfully, he seemed to prefer playing the fiddle to both talking and singing. Sam had never heard anyone play the fiddle the way Ray did. In his hands, the simple instrument of wood and horsehair became a powerful, living thing — with a soul and mind of its own. When he played fast songs, the fiddle almost buzzed. Ray's hands barely moved, yet the bow dipped and swayed, like a bee rapidly working its way through a flower patch. When he played slow songs, the long, clear notes seemed to reach straight into Sam's chest — pushing the corners of his heart to remember the saddest and happiest he'd ever felt. The music of the fiddle made him feel old too, or at least what he thought being old felt like.

The courthouse had grown quiet again. Looking for anything to relieve his boredom, Sam picked up his bag. A wooden bowl. Flints. Gerard's book. He still had Josiah's sewing kit, too. Sam dug around to find what he was really looking for. There it was! The powder horn — his souvenir from Trenton. After the battle, many soldiers had helped themselves to the belongings of the defeated Hessians — both dead and alive. Sam had found the powder horn in one of the Durham boats, after the prisoners had been rowed back across the Delaware. He turned it over and rubbed his thumb across the rim. It was pearl gray with a silver band around the top and a raised engraving of a wild boar. The color reminded him of the oysters he and Thomas had shared.

Sam wished Thomas were here now, but he had stayed in Philadelphia, producing another *Crisis* pamphlet. He planned to write thirteen in all — one for each colony. Sam frowned. *Thomas could help me decide what to do. And maybe he's heard from the Reveres. I wonder how Rosie is doing. And if there are any letters for me. I guess I should write to mother and father, so they know I'm still alive.* He rolled the powder horn back and forth in his hands, wondering how he could possibly explain in a letter all that had happened — the battle at Trenton and then, the week after that remarkable victory, how close the Americans had come to being annihilated, how the Continental army had almost dissolved. Sam's memories flooded in ...

While the troops were still recovering from the first battle,

Washington and his staff decided to cross the river once again, seizing the momentum and staging a second offensive strike. Although his troops were far outnumbered by the enemy's, Washington knew that the Hessians had abandoned their other posts at Burlington and Bordentown. Another surprise attack would fuel the panic that Trenton had caused. It would also prove to the rest of the world that the Continental army and the Cause it fought for were doggedly surviving. It was a huge risk, but Washington's confidence was buoyed by the magnificent feat of his gamble at Trenton.

Crossing on Christmas night had been horrendous. The second time was worse. Sam was still part of Hamilton's battery. They struggled to move the cannons onto the boats, slick with sleet and snow. The Delaware had frozen by then, but the ice was not thick enough to support the weight of the men, horses, and equipment. It took two full days to get everyone across. By then, Washington was losing precious time — his vision of another quick shock to the enemy was vanishing in the cold winter air. But the General's problems were more serious than the weather. By the time they had all crossed, the date was December thirty-first, the day enlistments for most of the soldiers were due to expire.

December thirty-first. Sam closed his eyes, thinking back to that day. If he lived to be a hundred, he would never forget it. The snow came up to their ankles, the air so cold that breathing too deeply caused a sharp tug in Sam's lungs. The drums began a sharp rattling call for them to form ranks. The men, lined up around him, were starving, ill, and wearied. Some shivered with only blankets clutched across their hollow chests. Most, he knew, were leaving. They were worn to exhaustion, wanting nothing more than to have the strength to get home. Twelve months of hunger, disease, hardship, and death had defeated the giddy talk of freedom and patriotism that had brought them here. Even the ten-dollar bounty offered to anyone who would stay for six weeks more did not seem to be enough.

General Washington rode Blueskin to the front of the troops and reined in to a stop. Bright puffs of smoke pushed out from the horse's smooth nose. Washington cleared his throat. Sam guessed that Washington did not enjoy this. He preferred to lead by example. But he would rise to the role of orator now. He scanned the pathetic group assembled before him. Surely Washington's mind was reeling with all that he, the usually reticent general, kept guarded: his devotion to his soldiers, his fear for them, and his steely determination to fight until all possibilities had been exhausted. Finally, he spoke. "Men, you are the soldiers that Thomas Paine has immortalized. You have carried the Revolution on your shoulders while others chose the safety and comfort of home. If you can remain but a few more weeks, you can do more." Washington rode off to the side. Sam stood still, weighing the words in his mind.

The regimental commanders called out, "Every man who will accept the bounty, step forward." The drums rolled again, then a perfect silence hung over them, colder than the air itself. Not a man moved.

Sam watched Washington. As always, his face remained composed, yet his eyes revealed everything. He saw the end of it all: the war, the army, his reputation, and probably his life. Yet with everything at stake, perhaps the most desperate moment of the war, he did not react in anger or disappointment. Turning Blueskin around, he rode again before the men. Rather than threaten or berate them, Washington's voice rang with respect and affection. "My brave fellows, you have done all I asked you to do, and more than could be reasonably expected; but your country is at stake, your wives, your houses, and all that you hold dear. You have worn yourselves out with fatigue and hardships, but we know not how to spare you. If you will consent to stay one month longer, you will render that service to the cause of liberty, and to your country, which you probably never can do under any other circumstance. What we are facing today is the crisis which is to decide our destiny."

Another terrible silence. Then glances among the men. A few had stepped forward, then more. Sam had stepped forward, too. He couldn't leave in such a desperate moment. So many men had already left. Johnny had gone back to Boston. Somehow, he managed to find a horse, the boniest, skinniest one Sam had ever seen. Johnny still had his Hessian sword, but his fancy blue suit had disappeared in the chaos of Trenton. He'd waved cheerfully good-bye to Sam and promised to check on Rosie for him. *Rosie. Boston. The Reveres. Home.* Sam missed them all.

Now, the extra month Washington had asked for was up. Sam could go back home if he wanted, after the inoculation. The Americans were desperate for soldiers, he knew that. But what about his parents? He should be home, helping to run the mill. He dropped the powder horn and flopped back with a growl of frustration. He wished someone would just *tell* him what to do.

"Hey, Sam." One of Glover's men approached. "Doc Otto says we have one more day before we're all stuck inside. We're going to see Queen Elizabeth. Want to come along?"

Queen Elizabeth was the nickname for one of the sutlers — traders who sold tobacco, coffee, and other goods to the soldiers. Sam shook his head. He decided to go see Captain Hamilton. Although chosen by General Washington to be an aide, Hamilton still looked after the men on his artillery team. Sam felt like he could go to him for advice. He might have some spare paper as well. Sam walked across the muddy street to the tavern that General Washington had taken as his headquarters. It was one of the few places in Morristown that was large enough to house Washington and his aides. The tavern was yellow with red shutters and a wide front porch. It looked cheerful and snug even on the grayest winter days. Sam had heard that Mrs. Washington would be coming to the camp soon. He went through the kitchen, where Isaac, the cook, winked at him as Sam scrambled up the backstairs. The aides all worked and slept in one cramped room. The door was open, but Sam knocked to be polite. James McHenry smiled at him and called out, "Hammie!"

Sam grinned. Even though Hamilton was now on the Commander's staff and would soon be promoted, the other aides still called him Hammie. Sam stepped into the small room. Four cots were pushed up against the walls. Three large tables made a u-shape in the center. Hamilton was deeply engrossed in writing something, papers stacked in seemingly endless piles around him. He saw Sam and waved him over. "Sam! Come in. Sit down, if you can find a seat. How are you?"

Sam pulled a nearby chair up to the desk. "I'm fine, so far, I mean. I got the inoculation today." He held up his arm.

Hamilton nodded sympathetically. "Ahhh, so now quarantine awaits."

"Yes. I'm bored already."

"Well, let's hope the least of your suffering is boredom."

Sam's eyes widened a bit.

"It's fine." Hamilton assured him with a quick smile. "Perfectly safe. My experience was quite mild. And you know, Mrs. Washington was recently inoculated, without any problems." His face grew serious. "It is safe and absolutely necessary. Despite the resistance General Washington has had from Congress on this, it is our only choice."

Sam shrugged. "I suppose. Sir, I was wondering if you have any paper to spare. I'd like to write to my parents. And, um, can I talk to you about something?"

"Of course," Hamilton continued writing, "but I have to give this report to the General in a minute. You can come wait for me." Hamilton blew on the ink. "Then we can talk."

Sam followed him downstairs and stood outside the door. The sitting room of the house had been turned into an office. General Washington stood by the window. Henry Knox was there as well, sitting next to the fire, in a chair barely big enough to hold him. Washington saw Sam and nodded slightly. "Sam, you are welcome to come in. There's a terrible draft in that hallway. Does your report contain anything confidential, Captain Hamilton?" Washington asked.

"Not this one, sir," Hamilton replied.

Sam sat down in front of the wide desk, slightly nervous, as always, in Washington's presence.

"Shall I begin?" Hamilton spoke with ease.

"By all means," Washington said.

Hamilton cleared his throat. "As you know, the New Jersey militia has been turning out in greater numbers in the past few weeks. Recent intelligence puts their number at twelve thousand. They are enraged by relentless plundering and looting by both the British and Hessian armies. Our victories at Trenton and Princeton have infused their motivation to fight. But, as you are also aware, the militia are not regular army."

Washington shook his head and scowled. "I should say not. A more undisciplined, stubborn group of men cannot be found. They come and go as they please — like a maiden turning down unappealing partners at a country dance."

"Yes, sir," Hamilton agreed. "But when they choose to fight, as they are doing now, they are a highly effective force. And the time is right to utilize their value — they are highly mobile and familiar with the territory. In addition to the scarcity of food, the British are having tremendous difficulty finding forage for their horses. They never anticipated having to remain here beyond a summer campaign, and their supply route has been hampered by privateers and bad weather."

Washington stared out the window silently for a moment, then he turned back to the group with a calculating spark in his eyes. "If their horses grow weak in the winter, they cannot attack in full force in the spring."

Henry Knox chimed in decisively. "They can't do anything without feed for their horses. Artillery, supply wagons, cavalry. They cannot move or fight without horses."

"Exactly!" Hamilton said. "General Howe has sent forage parties deep into the countryside, searching for hay. The militia have taken it upon themselves to attack these parties — quickly and lethally. Last week, twenty militia captured a British convoy and all their baggage — clothing, blankets, tents, flour, and salt pork. The British have grown more afraid and keep sending larger and larger parties out. Some are as large as five hundred men. It is also affecting their morale, sir. They have pulled back and are now overcrowded in the few places they feel safe in New Jersey. Fresh food is scarce and disease is rampant."

"Meanwhile in New York," Washington said scornfully, "General Howe continues to behave as if the war were merely a continuation of London's social season."

Again, Hamilton spoke with total confidence. "Sir, I recommend we offer some Continental troops to assist in their efforts."

Washington's tone was now resolute. "Yes, gentlemen, we must take advantage of this situation. The troops who are fit for battle will be assigned to support the local militia."

Hamilton nodded. "Do you wish to delegate our officers to supervise the militia units?"

"No, I don't think that is necessary," Washington answered. "As you said, when they choose to fight, the militia are very effective, and while my frustration with them is sometimes keenly felt, if they are succeeding on their own, I shall not interfere. My orders are that they sustain high levels of harassment against the enemy. Excellent, gentlemen. Colonel Hamilton. Is there anything else?"

"Yes, sir. It concerns an intelligence report. From Princeton, sir."

Washington's gaze was directed to Sam. "If you will excuse us."

As Sam left the room, Hamilton whispered, "Wait in my office."

Sam went back upstairs. Hamilton returned a minute later, holding a rolled-up document in one hand and tapping it rapidly against the palm of the other hand. His face was lit with excitement. "Outstanding!" He beamed at Sam. "Oh, yes, paper. Let me look. There must be something here." He laid the document on the end of the table.

Sam stared at the mass of papers — reports, maps charts, books. He felt overwhelmed by the sight. "Is this all your work?"

Hamilton continued sifting through stacks. "We share the load, the other aides and I. Although I will admit it can be daunting at times. Despite the lull in fighting, the war goes on. Recruiting, supplies, munitions, promotions, prisoners, and dealing with Congress' incessant demands."

He moved a stack of paper and the rolled-up document fell to the floor and opened. Sam reached down to retrieve it and recognized a map of New Jersey. Then something caught his eye. It was a compass, with a snake on it. A faint memory jogged his brain. Where had he seen that symbol before? When he leaned over to look more closely, Hamilton took the map and rolled it back up, without a word, and placed it on the table. His face held its friendly expression as he handed Sam a few sheets of blank paper. Almost blank. Sam looked down and saw that on one page a letter had begun.

My dear Miss Livingston, ...

He held the page up with a questioning look.

"Oh, here." Hamilton took the page back and swiftly crossed out the writing. "I'm afraid that is all I can spare, Sam. Now, what was it you wanted to talk about?"

"Hamilton," Lieutenant Tilghman leaned into the room, "the General needs to see you again. And bring the Basking Ridge map."

"Coming!" Hamilton grabbed the rolled-up map, and smiled reassuringly at Sam. "I apologize. Perhaps we can talk later. Don't worry, Sam. I'll come check on you in a few days."

By the time Sam returned to the courthouse, it was too dark to write. The limited supply of candles at camp had to be saved for use in the headquarters. Ray came in and played his fiddle for a while. He had survived smallpox as a young man, so being around the newly-infected soldiers was no danger to him.

Sam lay in the dark, listening to the unhurried pull of the music. His mind went back to the snake symbol on the map. Where had he seen it? Suddenly he remembered. The message from the tavern girl at Bordentown. The map on the back had the same symbol! *So maybe the tavern girl was a Whig. How else would she know about the raid that night? But how did she guess that I needed to get back across the river?* Sam let out an irritated sigh. He should have asked Hamilton about it. He tossed in his sleep with the image of the twisted snake in his dreams.

The next morning, he woke up drenched with sweat. Yet he was shivering and felt cold and clammy. Ray brought him a cup of broth, but looking at it made Sam's stomach turn. He dozed fitfully most of the day, wondering if this was what the rest of the quarantine would be like. The next day he felt perfectly fine. Sam decided to write the letter to his parents while he was feeling up to it. He found an empty desk upstairs and sat down. Dipping the quill into the inkstand, he stared at the blank pages, then began to write.

Dear Mother and Father,

I am writing to you from New Jersey. I hope that you got the first letter I sent, the one from Watertown. Things did not go as I planned, and I ended up fighting with the army in December. To be truthful, my first battle, Trenton, was a bit of a blur. I was so scared and everything happened very quickly. But the next battles, at Trenton and Princeton, I remember quite well.

On January second, we were in a very dangerous situation, having staked out a defensive position on the eastern side of Trenton. In front of us was Assunpink Creek and the Delaware was to our left. Cornwallis was marching toward us from Princeton with eight thousand men. It's only twelve miles between Princeton and Trenton, but Mother Nature smiled upon us — the weather was warm and all the roads thawed. All those men and equipment turned the road into a huge sloppy mess. The soldiers were sinking halfway to their knees in the mud. It choked the spokes and axles of their wagons and cannons. If the mud didn't slow them down enough, our pickets did a fine job too. They were from the Pennsylvania Rifle Regiment. No guns can match theirs at long range. The Brits and Hessians are terrified of them! Our pickets harassed the British lines every step of the way. They popped out from behind trees and fences. The British would form a battle line to strike back, only to see our riflemen disappear into the woods. Thanks to them, Cornwallis did not reach us until late in the day, with only half his troops. In spite of all that, he still held the advantage. Cornwallis could have sealed us off from the east right then and there, and attacked in the morning at full strength, but I guess he was impatient to avenge the humiliation of our taking Trenton the week before. The Hessians were bent on revenge as well. Their commander, Colonel von Donop, told his soldiers that any man who captured, rather than killed, a rebel would be punished with fifty lashes.

By the time they reached us, there was only about an hour of daylight left. Our guns were set up all along the creek at crossing points. The water was running high and strong. In the center was a stone bridge, strong, but narrow. As our pickets retreated across it, General Washington rode up and sat upon his horse, inspiring the men with his quiet courage. He stayed until the last man crossed safely. We drew up in lines for battle. Cornwallis did too. It was a terrible thing to see how trapped and outnumbered we were. Our chances of survival seemed hopeless. Like I said, Cornwallis should have waited to attack. But he didn't. First, he sent German grenadiers to storm the bridge. Our guns were ready. We kept them back. They tried again and again. The bridge was red with blood and covered with dead and wounded soldiers. When darkness fell, Cornwallis had no choice but to retreat and prepare to attack the next day. He was so sure he would finish us off that he bragged about it. "We've got the Old Fox safe now. We'll go over and bag him in the morning."

Well, there is a reason they call George Washington "the Old Fox." Cornwallis must have forgotten how clever foxes are! General Washington ordered us to build fires and make a lot of noise, like we were setting up camp. But really, we wrapped the wheels of the cannons and wagons with cloth to muffle the sounds, and retreated. We all thought there was no way out, then a civilian sent Washington a secret map. It showed an old back road to Princeton. We marched all night. The weather changed again — a hard freeze firmed up all the roads so we were able to move quickly. I would have liked to see Cornwallis' face in the morning when he woke up — expecting to see cannons and soldiers on the other side of the creek and instead saw only smoking campfires!

We attacked Princeton in the morning. The British were taken completely by surprise and surrendered. It was a short, but bloody battle. I think they lost about four hundred and fifty soldiers.

It felt strange, writing about that terrifying morning. He recalled every second vividly. It was so frightening to watch the British advance toward Assunpink Creek. The cheerful military music filled him with hollow dread as the tall black hats and glinting bayonets bobbed above the rows and rows of men. Each soldier was perfectly outfitted in a bright, whole uniform and kit. It was an awesome, terrifying thing to see. Sam's heart inched up his throat as the thousands of marching men came closer. He looked around at the disheveled, peculiar American line and gasped a little. Hamilton, standing nearby, moved over to the cannon Sam stood behind. Hamilton stared straight ahead, but asked Sam, "Are you all right?"

Sam closed his eyes and tried to nod.

"You're afraid," Hamilton said quietly.

Again, Sam attempted to nod.

"It's natural," Hamilton assured him. "Every man here is afraid. There is no weakness in it. Courage comes after you admit that you're afraid. Remember your training. You'll be fine." Hamilton crossed his arms and scanned the scarlet ranks that filled the road. He chuckled softly. "Look at them. Pompous idiots. Cornwallis is an arrogant, impatient fool. He has no respect for us, and that will cost him. He isn't even bringing up the guns, because he thinks all they have to do is charge and we'll scatter like a flock of hens." Hamilton leaned over and stared down the barrel of the cannon. "Wait till he tries to take that bridge. We'll see how cocky he is then."

Sam put the quill down as more images from that day filled his mind. Should he tell them about the battle later at Princeton? Clouds of thick smoke and flames shooting from the cannons like white demons. Bodies of the dead and wounded scattered about the orchard where he had fought. General Mercer bayoneted to death by British troops who screamed, "Call for quarter, you damned rebel!!" And later, after the British had surrendered, watching the prisoners being led away, covered with blood, soot, and grime. Civilians were rounded up as well. Sam had seen a slight young woman in a gray cloak walking with the prisoners. He was sure it was Maggie, the woman from the boat. She was a Loyalist, and he knew she lived in Princeton. He asked Hamilton later what would happen to the Tories. Hamilton's answer made Sam's heart chill. "I can't say for sure, but we have heard that rather than protecting them as promised, the British and Hessians are abandoning the Loyalists to the furious revenge of their Whig neighbors."

Sam shuddered at the memories. No, he would not tell his parents all that. He blew on the ink and folded up the letter. He would finish it later. His head was beginning to pound. A small mirror near the desk reflected his face, flushed with dark red patches. Sam's stomach turned and a rush of heat made him dizzy. He made his way slowly downstairs and back to his mattress. Closing his eyes, the sounds of the room washed over him. Some men were chattering easily; others were mumbling or softly groaning. The virus was setting in.

It was worse the next morning. His body felt sore and weak. He tried to drink water, but his mouth was swollen. The clatter of horses outside the window caught his ear. He saw a carriage stop in front of the headquarters. A slim foot stepped down, followed by a gray cloak. *Is that Mrs. Washington?* Hamilton came out of the building to greet the new arrival. She moved toward the door and a gust of wind blew her hood back. Dark red hair, high cheekbones. Sam gasped. *Maggie?! What is she doing here?! She's a Tory! I saw her being taken prisoner at Princeton. Why would she be visiting the headquarters?*

Sam knew he had to warn Hamilton, but he couldn't leave the courthouse now. He'd have to send a note. Clutching the last blank sheet of paper, Sam stumbled back upstairs to the desk. As he scribbled a short note, he noticed that sores had broken out on his hands and arms. He felt his face — there were a few. Sam folded up the note. Now, how to get it to Hamilton?

"Nevens! You've got a visitor!" someone called from downstairs. Sam stood up and felt another dizzying wave of heat. Sweat popped out across his forehead and it felt as if his face were on fire. He leaned against the wall for support and shakily descended the stairs.

"Sam!"

"Thomas!" Sam was so glad to see the craggy face of Thomas

Paine. "What are you doing here?" Sam asked in a weak voice.

"I came with Mr. Ludwick from the capital. He's going to help with translating with some of the Hessian prisoners." Thomas took Sam by the arm. "How are you? You look feverish. Which mattress is yours?"

"Do I?" Sam's head felt stuffy and thick. He swayed slightly and pointed to his spot near the window.

"When did you have the inoculation?" Thomas asked, as he carefully led Sam to his mattress and sat down next to it.

"I'm glad to see you, Thomas," Sam said quietly.

"And I, you, my friend."

Sam closed his eyes and smiled. Thomas' voice weaved in and out. "Stuck in Philadelphia ... and came here to thank you."

"Thank me? For what?" Sam asked.

"For bringing the pamphlets. It was very brave of you, Sam. It sounds like quite an adventure — whisked across the river by smugglers and being taken in as a spy."

A spy! Sam's eyes popped open. He sat up abruptly. Pain shot across his forehead. He whispered in an urgent voice, "Thomas, there's a spy in the headquarters! It's a woman. A Tory! Her name is Maggie. She was with me in the boat. She was captured at Princeton, but she must have escaped because I saw her here. She's beautiful, but she's a Tory. Take this." He handed the folded paper to Thomas. "You must give this to Captain Hamilton."

The room was so bright. Everything seemed to shift back and forth. Sam squinted, trying to focus. Thomas was nodding, then his face stretched to a narrow, shiny point and his ears dropped. Fur sprang out. It wasn't Thomas. It was Rosie! Rosie was here. Sam reached out to pat her. "That's a good girl."

Thomas wiped the sweat from Sam's head. "Can you hear me? Listen to me, Sam, it's best not to fight the visions. Think about positive things if you can. Look, I've brought you some gingerbread from Mr. Ludwick's bakery. It will be here when you wake up. You're going to be fine, Sam."

Sam opened his eyes again. Thomas was back. He was putting something into Sam's bag. The gingerbread. Sam stared at the round face of the angel imprinted on it. As she was tucked into the bag, she winked at Sam. He shook his head. "Thomas, don't forget. The note. Hamilton."

Thomas smiled and patted Sam's arm. "Yes, of course. Don't worry. Try to rest."

The next morning, a thick, smoldering weight pressed down on Sam. It seemed as if everyone in the room was talking very loudly. He was shivering, but his body felt like he was lying in a bed of embers. Dr. Otto was walking through the room, checking on each patient. He stopped at Sam's mattress, a kind smile on his round face. His lips were moving, but no words came out. He checked Sam's pulse and looked in his throat. He tried to get Sam to drink some water. Sam's throat burned inside too. Pain pulsed through him with each breath. It was agony. He tried to control his thoughts, but there was so much noise in his head. His mother was singing. Hodgekins was humming. The Hessians were shouting. The surveyors were laughing as they pushed the burning knife into his skin again and again.

Sam looked down at his hands. The blisters had darkened. They were almost black with a ring of red around them, like hot coals. As he stared at his left hand, the blisters began to move around. They stretched out longer and thinner into three lines, then joined together at the top. Sam recoiled in horror. *The King's Broad Arrow! No!* That scar was higher on his arm. The blisters shifted — now they rearranged themselves into a cross. A cross, then the vertical line split into two. The second line began to twist itself around the first, like a snake. It was the compass. The secret symbol on the maps. *The symbol. The maps. Maggie. I have to tell Hamilton. No, Thomas will do that. He promised. What else had he said? "Don't fight the visions. Think positive thoughts."* Sam's mind spun. *Positive thoughts? What makes me happy? Home. Mother and father. The pond. The fort. Eamon.* He closed his eyes and saw the pond. It was still, cool and silent. Eamon wasn't there yet. They would play in the fort later. Sam stretched out his arms to float. A green circle of trees danced above him. They moved gracefully, swaying to the music of a fiddle. Sam opened his eyes halfway.

He was back in the courthouse. A huge, brown bear was sitting in a chair, playing the fiddle. The bear was enormous, but Sam wasn't afraid. The bear nodded at him, its brown eyes shining with a gentle light. The bear's shaggy paws held the fiddle easily, pulling the bow gently. Sam's breathing eased. Suddenly, the fiddle leapt away from the bear. It sprouted arms, legs and a narrow face. It grinned playfully, then grabbed the bow and began to play itself. The fiddle laughed and began to dance a jig. Next, Sam saw something move from his bag. The angel on the gingerbread had jumped off the cookie and grew until she was two feet tall. She danced with the fiddle. Sam smiled despite the raging storm in his head. All the while, the bear sat with its paws crossed over his chest and his head tipped to one side in amusement. His thick claws tapped on the floor as he waited for the fiddle to finish its performance.

The fiddle took a bow and the gingerbread angel curtsied. Then she sat on the edge of Sam's blanket, while the bear took up the fiddle again. Sam watched her small feet swinging back and forth as she hummed. Her face was flushed from dancing. Two green eyes sparkled above her nose, like shining emeralds. Sam sighed, strangely happy as the fiddle eased him back to sleep. Just as he drifted off, the angel reached over to pat his head. Her hand cooled his fiery skin. "Well, I have been waiting days for you to wake up," the angel said softly.

Thomas was right. It was better not to fight the visions. Sam sleepily opened his eyes. Then he sat up in complete shock.

"Maggie?!"

Maggie was sitting on a footstool, holding a basin of water and a cloth.

"What?" Sam's head swam. "How did you get in here?" He fell back on the blanket.

Before she could answer, Sam heard the cheerful voice of Hamilton coming toward them. "Sam! You're awake. How are you?" Hamilton sat down at Sam's other side, opposite Maggie.

Sam stared at Hamilton, then at Maggie, certain that he was still dreaming. "I'm alright, I guess."

Maggie smiled. "Sam is no doubt surprised to find me here."

"Oh, yes, of course. Sam, may I introduce Miss Margaret Denton."

"Sam and I have met." Her eyes were kind.

Sam stammered in confusion. "You're not a Tory?"

Maggie shook her head.

"And you are not a spy?"

Maggie said nothing. Hamilton spoke again, this time in a low voice. "Miss Denton has been providing us with information about the local territory, and the movements of the British. Her map was the key to our retreat at Assunpink Creek and march to Princeton."

"The snake symbol! It was on the note from the tavern girl. You wrote the note?" Sam asked.

"Yes. When I saw the copies of *Common Sense* in your bag, I guessed you were not really taking newspapers to the Hessians. And you looked completely terrified when we were crossing the river," Maggie added.

Sam blushed, hoping his current appearance, blisters and all, covered his embarrassment. "I would never have gotten back across the river if it weren't for you. Thank you." He shook his head in amazement and murmured, "The secret map, at Princeton — you saved the battle."

Hamilton whispered eagerly again, "I should say so! Not only did she bring General Washington crucial intelligence, she fed the British false information! She told them our troop size was triple what we really had. Cornwallis would never have committed so many soldiers to the attack at Assunpink Creek if he had known the truth. And Princeton would have been much better defended. Brilliant, Miss Denton, absolutely brilliant!"

Now it was Maggie's turn to blush. "I suppose it did not occur to them that a woman could be a spy." She shrugged.

"Hey, look who's finally awake!" Ray approached them, smiling at Sam.

Sam smiled weakly back. "Were you playing your fiddle at all?"

Maggie answered. "He played it every night for the past week, Sam."

Ray said quietly, "Miss Denton noticed it seemed to calm you down quite a bit."

Sam looked at his bag, relieved to see the gingerbread tucked in and not moving at all. "I guess I was hallucinating for a while."

Hamilton stood up and stretched. "And Miss Denton spent many hours watching over you, too. She's helped us tremendously during the most difficult stage of the variolation process. You had a more severe case than many of the other soldiers. I daresay we are through the worst of it." Hamilton fixed a stern gaze on Sam's pale face. "Now you need to concentrate on recovering completely. I'm counting on your help to kick the British back across the Atlantic when our spring campaign begins."

Ray sat down in Hamilton's empty seat. He leaned forward, arms on his knees with his hands clenched together. Uncomfortable nervousness replaced his usual placid demeanor. He glanced at Sam, then at Maggie, almost like he was looking for help. He let out a deep breath, then spoke. "Sam, I have some bad news. Well, maybe its good news. A friend of mine, Will Darlington, got here a few days ago. He escaped from a British prison in New York. He mentioned an Irish kid, from Machias."

"Eamon!" Sam sat up.

"I think so," Ray said, "but his leg is in mighty bad shape. He may lose it."

Sam's voice had an edge of desperation in it. "But he's alive. That is good news!"

Ray and Maggie exchanged hesitant looks, as if attempting to agree on how much to tell Sam. "Mr. Darlington's stories from the prison are terrible," Maggie said angrily. "Men are dying like flies. The British are not following the usual rules of conduct for prisoner treatment because they don't consider the Americans true soldiers."

"They're all starving, and racked with disease. Worse than here. Much worse. I'm sorry, Sam." Ray's voice was heavy with sadness.

Sam felt a wave of sickness engulf him, then relief, then fear. *Eamon is alive! I have to find him!*

Maggie watched his face and seemed to read his mind. "You can't do anything for Eamon right now. You have to regain your strength. Are you hungry?"

Sam fell back on the mattress, eyes closed. "No." He opened his eyes. "Thanks, Ray."

After a few days of rest, Sam was allowed to leave the courthouse. Maggie offered to walk with him. The sky was flat and gray. They moved very slowly along the ice-packed path. Sam's legs were shaky. He still felt weak but it was good to get out of the stuffy courthouse. He took deep breaths of the cold, crisp air. "Thank you for taking care of me," Sam said hoarsely. Even his voice was unsteady.

Maggie nodded. "I'm glad I was able to help. General Washington's inoculation order was a good decision, but the past few weeks have been very perilous."

"When did you have smallpox?"

"My father had us all inoculated a few years ago." She smiled wryly. "He holds more faith in science than divine providence."

They walked a bit farther in easy silence. Sam tried to piece everything together. His thoughts were fuzzy, but he still had a few questions to ask. He didn't know where to start. "That day we crossed the Delaware," he said, "I would never have gotten back across the river if it weren't for you. I'm very grateful."

Maggie chuckled. "Well, you probably would have found a way. I felt terrible for running into you and getting you captured. Thank goodness you didn't eat that note in the sandwich!" She grinned. Sam did as well. He hardly recognized the intense, mysterious girl from the boat. She was even prettier when she was smiling.

Sam continued. "But then I saw you after the fighting at Princeton. You were with a bunch of prisoners."

"Those were Whigs. My father was one of them. He'd been held for several weeks. I was trying to find a way to help him escape. I sold eggs and milk to the British quartermaster to get a closer look. Then I reached out to contacts in the area with what I found and we sent it to General Washington." She rolled her eyes. "Those British officers, so arrogant, so stupid. Serves them right that they got trounced at Princeton."

"How did you get the information to Washington?"

Maggie's face shifted slightly back into the serious countenance Sam did recognize. She shrugged. "That part I'm not going to share yet. No offense."

"No offense. Hey, were you shooting at the Hessians at Trenton?"

Her grin returned. "You saw me?!"

Sam whistled softly with respect. "I'm glad you are on our side, Miss Denton."

"Sam, you can call me Maggie."

"Is it scary? Being a spy?"

"Sometimes. I was afraid, crossing the Delaware that day," Maggie admitted. "You can't let it show."

"What was that strange symbol on the map?"

Maggie's eyes twinkled a little. "Oh, the snake? It's something I made up. The snake is considered a symbol of knowledge by some, and maps guide us and bring knowledge."

Sam shook his head in amazement. "Your information — you saved the battle, the whole army."

"Well, we can't all be soldiers, but one person can make a big difference. Look at what Mr. Paine has done, and you — bringing the *Crisis* pamphlets, and staying to fight."

Maggie's praise left Sam momentarily speechless. His gaze dropped to his feet and he kicked a chunk of ice on the path. "It seemed more important than going home," he said quietly.

"What will you do now?"

Sam kicked the ice again, hands in his pockets. "I don't know. I feel that I should go home to help my parents. We have a sawmill. But Washington needs everyone he can get. And, well, Eamon in prison — maybe I could find him if I stay in the army."

"If you join up, you can send your pay home. That would help your parents a lot." Maggie pulled her cloak tighter around herself and blew out a puff of cold air. "It's hard sometimes to know what the right thing to do is, but it seems to me that you have made good decisions so far. Like I said, one person can make a big difference." She leaned over to place a gentle kiss on Sam's cheek. "I've got to get back to Princeton. Good luck, Sam. I hope our paths cross again."

"Me too. Good-bye, Maggie."

As they walked silently back toward the courthouse, Sam heard his name being called. His smile was equal parts surprise and delight as Thomas Paine approached them. He looked as

335

disheveled as ever, his eyes still sparkling with energy. He bowed to Maggie. "Good afternoon, Miss Denton."

"Mr. Paine." Maggie smiled at both of them as she continued down the path.

Thomas grasped Sam by the shoulders and eyed him from head to toe. "So, you remain in one piece after your adventure with that nasty smallpox beast?!" He looked closely at Sam's face. "And no scars! You're a fortunate lad!" Thomas patted Sam's back enthusiastically. "I only have a minute. Late for a meeting with the General. I have something for you. Mr. Morris sent this, but I didn't want to give it to you until you were well enough to read it."

Thomas reached under his cloak and pulled out a letter. Sam's heart jumped as he recognized his mother's handwriting. "Sam," Thomas added, "I am returning to Philadelphia tomorrow. You are welcome to join me. Mr. Morris can arrange passage for you back to Boston. If you are leaving." His dark eyes locked with Sam's in a searching gaze before he turned to walk away.

Sam read the letter with shaking hands. It was dated October 5, 1776.

Dear Sam,

We received your letter last week with great joy. To know that you are alive brought peace to our hearts for the first time since the day you disappeared. All we knew from Mr. Avery was that you had gone into the woods after Captain Moore. When we learned that the mast agents had left Machias quickly, we feared the worst. Thank God you are safe.

I'm sure you have heard by now about the capture of the Margaretta. *Poor Mr. Avery was killed in the battle. Some of the men from Machias have gone off to join the Continentals. It has been difficult, especially after the British burned Falmouth, but we are managing. Jim is staying with us now and helping with the mill full time.*

We have some happy news for you. You have a sister! I was only a few months with child when you were captured. Eleanor was born the following November. She is a healthy child, sweet-natured with occasional bouts of impishness. We call her Elly.

Sam, it pains me so to write this. Eamon is missing and feared dead. He was wounded somewhere in New York, but then disappeared. Mrs. Collins is holding up as well as can be expected. We shouldered the pain together of both sons gone. The news that you are alive has given her renewed hope that Eamon is as well.

We pray for your safe return home, son.

All our love, Mother and Father

A brave winter sun broke through the next morning and bathed everything in a bright, hopeful glow. Sam sat on the steps of the courthouse, his face lifted toward the sky, feeling like a normal human for the first time in weeks. Gerard's book, with the letter from his mother tucked inside, was on the step beside him. He'd read the letter ten times since yesterday. Sam picked up the book — holding it gave him a feeling of peace. He needed it right now — his mind was spinning. The news about Eamon gnawed at his heart like a worm. And the news from home gave him a strange feeling of intense happiness and sadness at the same time. Eleanor! Elly. He had a sister. Jim was helping with the mill. And Eamon. They didn't know that Eamon was in prison. *And they never will, if I can help it.* Sam rubbed his thumb against the spine of the book, thinking about the ring and letter hidden inside. He looked at the last page, where Gerard had written his son's address. *Someday, Paul will have this book. But right now, Eamon needs me more.*

"Nevens!" One of Washington's aides was calling him from across the street. "The General wishes to speak with you."

Sam hurried across and up the steps of the house, following the aide to the sitting room. Sam knocked softly on the door. "Sir, you wanted to see me?"

Washington looked up from the mountains of papers stacked on his desk. "Sam, come in, sit down. How are you? Through the worst of variolation, I see."

Sam lowered himself into a chair and laid the book on the edge of the desk. "Yes, sir. It wasn't too bad. I'm glad it's over."

"As am I," Washington said. He looked better than the first time Sam had seen him. He looked rested and confident. He shuffled through some envelopes, then handed Sam a small cloth bag. It had the initials *PR* stitched in black thread. "Mr. Paine forgot to give this to you. It came with the packet sent by Mr. Morris. I'm afraid there is no letter. It may have gotten lost along the way."

PR? It must be from Mr. Revere. Sam opened the bag and pulled out a fine silver chain, with a small medallion attached. Had they sent him Josiah's medallion? No, this was not Josiah's. Engraved on one side were the words **Know Your Strengths.** Sam turned it over and flinched slightly. The other side had an engraving of the King's Broad Arrow! He clenched his fist around it. "I don't understand." Sam's voice was faint with confusion and hurt. "Why would Mr. Revere give me something that brings back an awful memory?"

Washington leaned forward. "May I?" He took the chain from Sam and lifted it to eye level. The shiny orb turned a slow half-circle. "Look closer."

Sam squinted at the medallion. There was more than the symbol. Each stripe had a word etched on it. ***Courage. Loyalty. Responsibility.***

Washington watched the confusion still clouding Sam's face. He lowered the chain back into Sam's palm, then put his hand on his shoulder. "I think Mr. Revere seeks not to remind you of a terrible event, but rather that you were tested by a great adversity, and prevailed. It took the worst experience to reveal the best in you. Courage, loyalty, and responsibility — all honorable qualities you have demonstrated in very challenging circumstances."

Sam continued to stare at the medallion. Did Mr. Revere truly think he possessed such traits? Did General Washington? He looked up at the imposing figure in front of him. "Me? Courageous? Responsible?"

"Yes, Sam, you most certainly are." Washington paused. "Look at the choices you have made since you left that prison ship. You could have gone home from Boston. Instead you chose to go to the gunpowder mill in Mr. Revere's place. You found a printing press for Mr. Paine, and brought the pamphlets to me. And you chose to stay and fight with the army in its darkest hour."

Washington picked up Gerard's book. He slowly fanned the pages with his thumb, briefly lost in thought. "You even chose to save your friend's book." He handed the book to Sam. "Epictetus was a wise man. There is much to admire about his virtues — discipline, patience, self-control. He was able to bear great hardship with calm dignity."

"Carry your burden," Sam said, nodding.

"Indeed." Washington sat back in his chair, his crossed hands resting on the desk. "Yet, I would challenge his philosophy in one respect. Epictetus chose to tolerate the things he saw as beyond his control. He did not contest his fate. It is a position we cannot afford in times like these. The world is changing, whether we like it or not, and we must rise to defy, not simply accept, that our fate is determined. These times call for men and women who embrace the challenge and the responsibility to fight for a better world. It does require courage to endure hardship, but it takes more courage to change the state of affairs that forms the hardship."

Washington leaned forward again. His blue-gray eyes softened with affection. "You have already played an important part in our great struggle, and your country is grateful. I am grateful. The question is — are you finished?"

Sam knew the answer. It felt like he had known it for a long time. "No, sir. I'm not. I want to enlist. As long as it takes, I will fight for the Revolution."

Washington's eyebrows raised slightly. "But you were doubtful about the war, about fighting, what changed your mind?"

Sam answered slowly, as if putting the last pieces into a puzzle. "Well, everything — meeting Thomas and helping print the pamphlets, seeing the camps and soldiers, fighting at Trenton and Princeton. I never felt like I had enough courage to be a good soldier, like Eamon and Josiah, and you. Now I realize it doesn't matter as much as I thought. Whether I'm ready or not, fighting in this war is my responsibility, for my future and so my children can live in peace. I guess a person *has* to be brave and responsible to protect something they care about. You don't really get to choose."

Washington nodded. "Sam, I believe that it's the price you pay to live a life you can be proud of. That does not mean it is a burden. Taking responsibility for your life is also an opportunity to rise beyond your own expectations, to reveal your true measure."

Sam smiled slightly. "That's what Thomas said about the

war, that America should be thankful and inspired that we have the chance to create a whole new country."

"No doubt Mr. Paine put it much more eloquently than I can, but he is right. Our cause is worth whatever we must endure to achieve it," Washington said.

An aide knocked on the door frame. "Sir, Mr. Paine is here."

"Perfect timing," Washington said with an amused smile.

Sam stood up as Thomas entered the office.

"So, are you coming with me?" Thomas was dressed for travel. "I have two horses saddled outside."

Sam glanced at Washington, then turned to Thomas. "No. Will you take a letter and send it to my parents? I need to tell them I'm not coming home, yet."

Thomas' ruddy face broke into a wide grin. He put his arm around Sam's shoulders and beamed at George Washington.

"Gentlemen, we shall make the world anew."

THE END

ACKNOWLEDGMENTS

When I stood before my husband and children several years ago and declared, "I want to try to write a book," no one batted an eye. Since that day, they have never wavered in their support, excitement, love, and faith in me reaching that goal. They know more about Thomas Paine, smallpox, ink-making, and myriad other 18th century facts than they ever could have imagined. Chris, Jack, and Alex — a thousand Gutenberg presses could not express my love for you, and gratitude that you believed in me. My extended family, especially my sisters — Andrea Wheatley and Carolyn Andrukonis — have all been wonderfully supportive about this endeavor.

Living in many different places has given me the privilege of making friends all over the world. Near and far, my friends have always been tremendous sources of strength and joy in my life. To name them all would add another page to the book, yet I am particularly thankful for a few girlfriends who have cheered the long journey of *The King's Broad Arrow* with constant enthusiasm and encouragement. Jan Workman, Valerie Laragy, Jameelah Arcila, Stasia Bryant, Maggie Gifaldi, Jo Ann Kessler, Simone White, Lisa Rowell, Jansy Robinson, Valerie Plame, Gaby Jack, Kirstin Hegner, Alex Buchwieser — you all inspire and amaze me. There is one person, without whose friendship, expertise, and dogged confidence in me, this book would never have made it to the finish line. Patti Exstein — thank you for holding my literary hand, and with gentle tenacity, pulling me through many moments of doubt.

The decision to self-publish my first book was as daunting as climbing a mountain without a map. Fortunately, some kind of artistic karma kicked in and I found two women whose fantastic talents made the journey to publication joyful, exciting, and not at all scary. Lynn Thompson's calm wisdom and laser focus turned the precarious work of editing the manuscript into a delightful experience. I am grateful for her expert workmanship, dedication to perfection, and extraordinary positivity. Crystal Cregge's remarkable array of skills — design, illustration, and formatting — carried the book to completion. Her incredible attention to detail and fabulous imagination brought many parts of the story I love the most to beautiful, visual life. Many thanks to Kim Eley, of KWE Publishing, for connecting me with such great collaborators.

I would also like to thank other artists whose work inspired this story, and who have kindly given me help and encouragement — Marietta McCarty, James Rumford, and Odds Bodkin.

ABOUT THE AUTHOR

Kathryn Goodwin Tone is a former teacher, amateur philosopher, and avid traveler. She is an American who has lived in Russia, Armenia, and currently lives in Germany. *The King's Broad Arrow* is her first book. You can visit Kathryn's website at:

www.revolutionrings.org

Sam's adventure continues in

The Forage War

September, 1777
Philadelphia

"Can you see them?" Sam gasped as Cooper pulled him out of the water and up onto the riverbank.

Cooper shook his head. "Did Caleb get hit too?" he whispered.

"In the chest," Sam answered, panting. "I think it killed him."

"What about Colonel Hamilton? What should we do?" Cooper sounded panicked.

They lay breathless on the rocky ground, listening for more shots from the road. Sam tried to slow his racing heart, while his eyes and ears searched the darkness for any sign of Hamilton or Caleb. After a few moments of silence, Sam spoke. "We need to figure out where we are." He warily stood up, and immediately felt a gush of warm blood running down his leg. "This wound is deeper than I thought. We've got to tie it." As Cooper stood up, Sam held his arm out. "Tear my sleeve off."

Cooper grabbed Sam's shirt at the shoulder seam and yanked it. He knelt down and carefully pushed around the wound, while Sam tried to stifle a groan of pain. Cooper wrapped the sleeve around Sam's leg and tied it. "I didn't feel a ball. Maybe it's not too bad. Can you walk?"

"Yes," Sam said, but after two steps he leaned shakily against a tree.

Cooper was calmer now. "Stay here. I'll take a look around."

After a few minutes, Cooper returned. "There is a wagon

trail not far from here. I think it will take us back to camp. It's not too far. At least we are on the right side of the river."

They made their way through the woods. Although Sam's leg ached with pain, he was too distracted by the deaths of Caleb and Hamilton to even notice. Sam had only met Caleb a few days ago and knew little about him, except that he resented the Quakers. But Hamilton! It wasn't possible! Hamilton had survived countless brushes with death already — he seemed invincible, a life force all his own. And he had been so good to Sam, looking after him like a brother. Sam stumbled in the black night as Hamilton's determined face rose in his mind. Besides his own choking grief, Sam could not imagine how others would react. Lafayette, who had become very close to Hamilton in the short time he had been with the American army, would be devastated. And Washington! The General had come to depend on his young, energetic aide so much, and he seemed to be personally attached as well. It was a terrible blow to the army, to the Revolution.

Sam and Cooper reached camp about two hours later. Sam went straight to the headquarters for news. The stone house was full of people, frantically packing everything to move to a safer location. Sam met Tench Tilghman outside of Washington's office. Tilghman's face flooded with relief. "Sam! You're alive! What happened?"

Sam began to speak, then stumbled. Weak from the loss of blood, he leaned against the wall for support. Tench opened the door and led Sam into the office where Washington and a dozen officers were gathered. Someone gave Sam a blanket and a dose of brandy. Washington stood next to the fireplace, a letter in his hands. "Sam, I'm glad you are safe. We just received word from Captain Lee that Colonel Hamilton has been killed. Is it true?"

Shaking with cold and shock, Sam relayed the details of

the raid. He bit his lip as his eyes tightened and tears welled. "He dove into the river, sir. The last thing I saw was Colonel Hamilton going under."

The room fell silent. Washington stared into the fire. He crumpled the letter, then threw it into the flames. One hand clenched into a tight fist which he pressed against his mouth. That and the slightest forward shift of his massive shoulders were the only signs of Washington's reaction. The small movements spoke volumes. It was as if he had taken a physical blow. Tears rolled down Sam's face as he struggled to maintain his composure, but as he looked around the room, he saw tears on many faces. They were all stunned at the loss of their vibrant friend and comrade — who accomplished so much every waking minute of his short life. Sam felt the familiar numb weight of grief settle over his heart. A draining fatigue seemed to take over.

Suddenly, the door burst open.